Sally Martin has moved from one small American town to another for the past three years, running from a nightmare that occurred during Argentina's 'dirty war'. Very pregnant and newly widowed after her Argentinian husband's murder, Sally had been thrown into the Carmesi – a hellish torture prison. Her baby was born in her filthy cell, and Sally was told it was dead – though she could swear she'd heard it cry. Sally was freed soon after, but the baby's wail has haunted her ever since . . .

Now, in a small Maine town, she has found a man who loves her. But she cannot return his love until she has squarely faced the past, until she can find out the truth about her child.

SURVIVORS AND CASUALTIES. HEROES AND VILLAINS. THE PEOPLE OF *HEARTSEARCH* ARE ALL THESE AND MORE . . .

Also by Patricia Wright

I AM ENGLAND
THAT NEAR AND DISTANT PLACE

and published by Corgi Books

HEARTSEARCH

Patricia Wright

writing as Mary Napier

CORGI BOOKS

HEARTSEARCH

A CORGI BOOK 0 552 13520 8

Originally published in Great Britain by
Severn House Publishers Ltd.

PRINTING HISTORY
Severn House edition published 1988
Corgi edition published 1990

This book is set in 10/12pt Times by
County Typesetters, Margate, Kent

Corgi Books are published by Transworld Publishers Ltd.,
61–63 Uxbridge Road, Ealing, London W5 5SA, in Australia by
Transworld Publishers (Australia) Pty. Ltd., 15–23 Helles
Avenue, Moorebank, NSW 2170, and in New Zealand by
Transworld Publishers (N.Z.) Ltd., Cnr. Moselle and
Waipareira Avenues, Henderson, Auckland.

Printed and bound in Great Britain by
BPCC Hazell Books
Aylesbury, Bucks, England
Member of BPCC Ltd.

1

I knew I would never go back.

And yet, nearly every night for three years I dreamed about the Estancia Santa Maria. Haunted, boisterous dreams about galloping with Roberto over pampa that looked like a glassy sea, and thinking: If there is a heaven on earth, it is this, it is this! Or Roberto might be tilting his chair in the shade of the estancia courtyard, laughing when I exclaimed that one day he would break his neck on the flagstones. The terrible times came when I lay awake. I can't explain why it was that once I slept – if I could sleep – I lived with delight again.

Which left each waking as a time to be endured, a fierce intensity of effort while I forced myself to face life again. I had come a long way from the Estancia Santa Maria, Argentina, trying to live again. After I left the hospital, there was that first year spent in my hometown of Shuckatee Falls, Montana, until my family and neighbors agreed that what I needed was psychiatric attention. Then six months in the Greer Clinic near Philadelphia before I ran out on them, unable to endure another day of smothering reasonableness. Besides, drugs took away my dreams and left only the black waking times behind. I had always needed flint to strike myself against, which was why sparks flew between Roberto and me from the first moment we met. Once I began to recover even slightly, I knew that I should never succeed in living again while confined in an atmosphere as soft and cloying as marshmallow.

Pittsburgh, Baltimore, Cincinnati: there was no pattern to my wanderings after that. Settling, hoping to God I could settle, failing to settle for more than weeks at a time. Soda dispenser, library clerk, layout drafts-person; I'd quit college to marry Roberto without taking my final architecture examinations and wasn't qualified for a thing.

A wilderness of people flowing around me, ceaselessly chattering. Until, somehow, I forced myself to stay longer in each place, swear I would last another week before running. It became three months at Willimantic, Connecticut, and I was very nearly sorry to leave, though not sorry enough to stay. Keg Bay, Maine, came next and the first Sunday there I swore on my knees: God, this is me, Sally Martin. I promise to stay here longer than I did in Willimantic. A whole month longer, at least.

This pledged me to four months, and as I left the church, subconsciously I was already figuring out how to cheat on my promise. Four months is two thousand nine hundred and twenty-eight hours. One hundred and seventy something thousand minutes. I was in a cold panic just thinking about so much time. Time turned into a cunning and dangerous adversary. I needed all my strength to fight each day and put behind me; unfortunately, terror was still sufficiently strong to exhaust me very easily.

I found a job as a teacher's aide, and the kids were great, although strictly I shouldn't have been hired uncertificated, and in the evenings I learned to sail a dinghy. This began as a way to stop myself from fidgeting about the town while putting off my return to a rented room above Mrs Dowell's summer ice cream parlor, but it soon became the best part of the day. Sharp

Atlantic air needled depression into flight, the chanciness of sailing a dangerous coast in a craft I knew very little about – though at least I possessed the sense to stay in reasonably sheltered water – sufficiently absorbing to take my mind off other things.

My four months passed, and I liked Keg Bay even better once the vacationers had gone. The air tasted salty, and most days you could hear the sea booming on the rocks. But no more dinghy sailing now, and long dark evenings to endure, so I took cleaning jobs after school to help hurry my continuing enemy, time, along. Somehow to mop up an eternity of days. Think of tomorrow and tomorrow, until memory might eventually rest with Roberto and leave only a stain of horror where it once had been. Or so I hoped, scouring and polishing like I'd never heard of electricity: New England home pride had nothing on me. Between teaching school, cleaning like crazy, and the harsh salt air, I began at last to sleep most nights and sometimes without dreams. Soon I shall be able to handle anything that comes, I thought.

By then I had met Royston Leavis. It was on the evening of the last Keg Bay regatta of the season, when the wind leaned hard against my dinghy sail and spray hissed cold and clean. An edged man, difficult to judge. Reserved, sensual, and sharp; a rising Boston lawyer with all the assurance associated with that city. I could visualize him dropping on hapless witnesses like a puma out of a tree and winning the most complicated case without betraying a single flicker of satisfaction.

Roy traveled up from Boston most weekends even after the sailing season ended, and it wasn't long before I realized he could be coming only to see me. The Maine coast is harsh in winter and no place for a rich corporation lawyer to relax.

7

Panic-stricken, I felt victimized, angry, and delighted by turns. Several times I nearly ran again, except, of course, I began to look forward to the next time he would come. Also to dread and fear it, which, after more than three years by then, just shows how much of a mess I still remained.

So each time Roy went back to Boston I expected he wouldn't return, since I couldn't figure a single scrap of pleasure for him in toiling up to a gale-shot Keg Bay only, like as not, to find me swirling in the treacherous currents of tentative happiness and ludicrous virginal dread. None of which I had yet brought myself to explain. Weeks passed in this unsatisfactory way, and it was the end of February before I nerved myself to let him make love to me, only to lie afterwards in Mrs Dowell's upstairs room engulfed in wretchedness and listening to waves exploding on the rocks. By then he was sleeping, tidily and without a sound, a completeness about him that made even minor inadequacies like snoring seem unthinkable.

What a fool I am, I thought. He has none of Roberto's bravado or lightness but, yes, he is the same: I have chosen to strike myself against flint again. Just because I thought I must – surely I must – be ready for a man again, I had to choose a hard bastard who follows his own way and kindly allows me to gallop along behind if I should happen to feel inclined.

Except, of course, he had showed surprising patience during the weeks when I could scarcely bear to let him touch me. No patience at all though when . . .

Yesterday evening I had finally let Roy come to my room, three months after I rammed his yacht and we met in poorish circumstances out in Keg Sound. But at last he had made me want him, or so I thought. Want a body of straight lines and angles, and the feel of that cool barbed mouth on mine. Perhaps enough time had passed for me also to accept desire once more. I suppose my own clinically grudging attitude should have warned me of what was almost bound to happen.

But, because of those months when happiness had begun to grow, I was nearly as unprepared as he to discover that once he lay with me, his caresses triggered utter terror. I fought his arms and thrust my elbow in his throat, felt my teeth sink into his hand and his blood sticky on my breast. It was then his patience broke and his common sense as well, an act of love changed into a war that inevitably he won. He thought, maybe, I had bitched him all the way.

Tears ached in my throat as I lay in the dark and grieved over what had happened, and that, too, was another first after three dry-eyed years. Much later I slid out of bed and felt for my clothes; it must be very early still.

'Where are you going?'

'Nowhere.'

The bedside light flickered on. He was leaning on one elbow, golden shoulders and back, face in shadow. 'You haven't lied to me before.'

'How do you know I haven't?' Childish futile bickering.

A movement of shoulder, shadows changing shape.

'My dear, I know. You've done most things else to keep me away.'

'No.' Blindly I pulled on a sweater. 'I've been myself. I can't help any of it, although God knows I'm trying. I wanted you to stay away.'

He turned back the bedclothes and came over, naked in a drafty bedroom while an Atlantic gale beat outside. 'You could have fooled me a few times recently. In fact, I don't believe it any longer. If you really intended to live

9

the rest of your life under glass, I shouldn't have wanted you from the moment you rammed the *Moonstar*.'

I studied him a moment and then smiled. I couldn't help it. I felt sick and drained and ashamed of myself but better than before. Whatever else had happened that night, and most of it unpleasant, something I thought dead inside me had snapped alive. 'You ought to try cross-examining with your clothes off in court one day.'

'Sounds like a tough life if that's what it takes to make you laugh.'

I bit my lip. 'So damn you, too, Royston Leavis. Listen. Go back to your fancy law firm and forget last night. I guess this is the first year you kept coming to Keg Bay after the regattas finished, so where should you be weekends instead? Skiing in the Adirondacks by now?'

'I don't get rammed by a dinghy most regatta weekends.'

'I was nowhere near the regatta! Well, not very near. I mean it, Roy. I thought it might . . . after these weekends when we've . . .' I felt myself flounder and took a deep breath. 'For heaven's sake, I sound like a kid trying to talk sex. I thought I'd learned about loving again because I began to love you. I thought if only I could start, then everything might be simple, like it used to be. I was wrong, that's all. How many women have you taken to bed who screamed when you made love to them?'

There was the movement of laughter in his face. 'None, but then, I'm pretty choosy. Once is enough, but if you would give us another chance to try together, then I hope once would be all it was.'

He made no move to touch me, but stood, hands hanging at his sides, as if sharply to remind me how the body's ecstasies could offset its terrors, while I stared at the taut muscles and flat belly of a man who would despise mental as well as physical flabbiness, and felt horribly confused. Quite possibly he was right; next time I might – somehow – be able to stop myself from screaming. What I couldn't forget was how much I had loathed instead of loved him, once the abscess of guilt burst open under the violence he forced on me. The pus of guilt flooding everywhere, in its true bleak colors. The relief of pus no longer trapped, so it felt like I was thinking clearly for the first time in over three years. 'It isn't as simple as that,' I said slowly. 'But you helped last night, however else it seemed. You see, I didn't know before.'

'Know what?' Calm voice probing doubtful evidence, but I was simply thankful for his detachment.

'The horseman, galloping across the pampa. You see, when I dream . . . no, I can't explain. But I thought I was remembering happiness, when all the time I was trying to reach . . . *desaparecidos* they're called: the disappeared ones. Vanished, gone, no graves, nothing; but, of course, they'll never be back. Some women go on hoping, write letters to themselves and pretend they come from a husband or son who's dead. I'm not like that, but two of them were mine and so . . . of course I have to go back.'

Even the thought of going back made my senses spin with fear.

But now that I was finally thinking clearly, I knew I had to go. Had to. Precisely because I had somehow snapped alive again, the unshed tears of vanished love became the last barrier I had to cross.

Distractedly, I began piling clothes into a valise. February in Argentina is about the hottest time of the year, and very little I owned would be of much use there.

'It's five o'clock on a Sunday morning in Maine. Unless I drive you, you won't get far for a while.' Roy's voice splintered through again, and I saw he was pulling on pants, flannel shirt, a thick yachtsman's sweater. Lawyers are used to recognizing unprofitable lines of questioning, and he saw at once that physically he could no longer hold me. Slightly frowning, though, annoyed by rejection. Or sorting through such fragments of evidence as I had offered him? I still didn't know him well enough to tell, and caring slipped swiftly out of reach.

'There are always ways out if you want them badly enough.' I turned, smiling like I was in love with going away, really to hide how very much afraid I was.

He was shaken. There wasn't any doubt about it: For the first time since we met I saw Royston Leavis's assurance shaken. Only a few years before I had been used to this reaction, since as long ago as I can remember there were boys, and later men, looking at me in ways that showed exactly what they wanted. At college I ended by paying very little attention to them, which just made them madder. Instead, I fell in love with architecture for a while: the simplicity of line and grace and calculation. I dreamed I would build differently from anyone ever born, which is the kind of dream a lot of people have when they choose a career that is more than just a job of work. Sure, I liked admiration, the attentions that singled me out most places I went, but the more I enjoyed them, the cooler I became. Both my parents were divorced, remarried, divorced again, which, rather surprisingly, left me a romantic. I hated the idea it would be like that with me. Anyway, millions of women have fair hair, gray eyes, and a passable figure; it was merely an agreeable mystery that in my own case these happened to be arranged in a way that jerked at male corpuscles.

All this, of course, was before I met Roberto.

12

Now Royston Leavis, partner in Blainey, Rosenthal, & McGeown, was looking at me as if he, too, were back at college, just for an instant before he caught himself. I was alive again all right.

He drove me to New York, a vile journey through snow squalls, and all the way tried different ways to discover where I was going and why. I wondered afterward how he fared the next day, hard at work while still trying to figure what other tricks he might have used to trip me into telling.

'You can let me down here,' I said as soon as we reached somewhere I recognized: I scarcely knew New York at all.

'Where can I reach you?'

'I don't want you to try. You couldn't anyway.' I reached for the door handle. Really, I hated finishing with him. A man who wasn't only flint, although guarded with his own emotions. Persistent, too, God knows, as soon as he saw something in me he thought he wanted. Keg Bay winter weekends layered with color because he came and began to teach me that time need not always be an enemy, force my rusty intellect into disputes I enjoyed, also with wit and cunning to make me laugh again. And why should he have bothered, after all?

'Isn't it possible you're prejudiced?' he said now.

'How do you mean?'

'Think it over. Because you're set on whatever it is you decided in the night, you want out. Cut loose and off. But like you said, God knows how many hours ago in Keg Bay, I helped. Even though I made one hell of a mistake acting how I did. Okay, so you're thinking of one thing at a time, but I've seen other people in your state of mind. Sometimes they end up shooting someone, other times they win a jackpot.'

'I'm not planning to shoot anyone,' I said, annoyed.

'You're sure?' He pulled into the curb and turned to face me.

'Of course I'm sure.'

He looked down at his hands; he seemed tired and preoccupied. 'Something was set off in you last night so I can smell the smoke. No, don't answer. Whatever you're off to do, I suggest that when you've looked where you have to look, you say yes, that's tidied, finished, and then leave it how it was.'

'Drop it, good dog,' I said silkily.

He leaned past to open the door. 'If you like. A call to my office will always find me when you get back.'

I climbed out into slush on the sidewalk. 'I haven't thanked you for driving me down, with most of a long way back to Boston. I'm truly grateful and for some other things as well.'

He stayed very still for a moment, leaning across and staring up at me as if he wanted to say something more. Beaked nose, long mouth, high forehead, green-blue eyes. Then he shrugged and slammed the door, recognizing that in six hours through snow from Maine he had said all there was to say without it changing anything. On the journey I had only gradually realized how carefully he was controlling the conversation, slanting this way and that, seeking information. That slammed door was the measure of his failure. In so much time one of the smartest attorneys on the East Coast had failed to shake anything loose after my one unwary outburst in Mrs Dowell's spare bedroom.

I watched his automobile whirl into Manhattan traffic, wondering whether I had been wrong after all. If Roy meant anything important to me, surely I would have allowed him to chip out the fragments that would have allowed him to keep in touch if he wanted.

Looking back, I think that even before his intuition shocked me into some kind of awareness, I sensed that I might indeed want to shoot someone before I finished. A partner in Blainey, Rosenthal, & McGeown had no place in such ambitions, then or afterward.

Shivering a little in street corner drafts, I picked up my valise and called a taxi. Tomorrow I would discover how much money I had left after buying a one-way air ticket to Buenos Aires.

2

The answer was, sixteen or seventeen hundred dollars at most, after allowing for airport taxis and stop-overs.

A couple of days passed before I was on my way, spent mostly in acquiring a U.S. passport in my maiden name. It was dusk as the Aerolinas Argentinas Boeing banked over the Rio de la Plata preparing to land at Ezeiza Airport, and Buenos Aires looked like molten metal spilled over the dark pampa.

A city sparkling with light from the air; a nervously tense metropolis roaring noise from the moment we landed. The trembling that started in my stomach as we took off from Rio de Janeiro had by then spread to my legs, and, shamingly, I found difficulty in standing up from my seat, let alone walking into the terminal. Hatefully familiar gray and blue police, and khaki military uniforms waited for me there: during the years away I had forgotten how uniforms jostled everywhere here.

The Argentine I sat next to on the flight had drunk scotch all the way from Rio; he was going back after two years spent in exile. 'They say the military are more careful of appearances now, señora,' he told me several times – cheerfully as we flew over Brazil, with melancholy over Uruguay, in maudlin fear as Buenos Aires slipped into view. 'Ah, my city is so beautiful, but do you know what a friend told me when I visited him in Washington?' I shook my head. 'He said, "When the police arrested me and gave me the prod, I screamed and talked about everyone. Friends, shopkeepers, even priests. You as well. I cannot even remember what I accused you of any more."'

But when I asked him whether this was why he had gone into exile, he shook his head. 'I was a professor of archaeology. I ask you, señorita, what could be more innocent? I went across the Brazilian border when two and then three more of my students disappeared. I had seen one of my colleagues arrested after his class began to disappear: who knows what anyone will say once he is at the mercy of barbarians? No . . . this friend in Washington . . . they release people after torture sometimes. Then others will be the more afraid because they see with their own eyes what can happen.'

'They don't often let their victims reach the outside world.' Probably some general had been bribed, but I knew that Argentina's military rulers sometimes seemed simply not to care what outsiders thought, and added, 'Perhaps you should have stayed with your friend in Washington a little longer.' It was then the trembling in my legs became worse.

'My family, my livelihood, my soul, are here. And they say the police are more correct now, providing you give no trouble.' His lips twisted. 'I have not come to give trouble, I assure you. Excuse me, please.' He lurched out of his seat and bolted for the toilet.

We did not speak again, and he was some way in front of me when we waited for immigration and passport control.

Elegant officers flicked imaginary dust off their uniforms in between offhandedly slapping at files and rubber stamps. I knew their kind well – men who spent longer in front of the mirror than their wives, the more brutish among them prepared to kill the prisoner who

17

bled inconsiderately over their boots.

By the time my aircraft acquaintance reached the front of the line, his face looked dirty green from fright; anyone must have thought him worth questioning. But no, apparently not. His knees buckled as an officer hissed something rude, almost threw his passport back, but he was allowed to dart past the table and disappear into the crowded terminal. This was 1982, not the seventies during the height of the 'dirty war', when I had last known Argentina. Perhaps the military really had become more careful of appearances.

When I was a couple of steps away from the table, a man in airline uniform came up and whispered to the officer sitting there. Instantly his eyes lifted, searched, settled on my face, his mouth a small tight pucker under a thin moustache. My stomach immediately snarled into knots as I stared back, even more terrified than before. What they whispered I couldn't hear, but they were whispering about me.

Too late to change my mind. Nowhere to run to now, nor anyone except myself to rely on.

The officer snatched my passport as soon as I reached him, fingering the new pages as if he expected to detect a forgery. The airline man stayed standing behind him with a smirk on his face: He was one of the cabin stewards, I decided.

'Why have you come to Argentina? How long are you staying here?'

I shook my head as if I didn't understand. The way he spat his words, it certainly wasn't easy. Argentines speak a distinctive version of Spanish, and Porteños, as the inhabitants of Buenos Aires are called, mix this with a slang all of their own. Even half-paralyzed by fright, I realized no American fresh out of the States could be expected to grasp his meaning at the first attempt.

'Come now, bitch, don't pretend not to understand. Why have you come?'

Every Argentine in earshot stopped what he was doing and stared; Porteño manners are excellent, not to say elaborate, and they couldn't believe they were hearing right.

'I shall report you to your general,' exclaimed an old gentleman behind me. '*Teniente*, you disgrace your uniform.'

Mercifully, his intervention diverted attention while my brain zigzagged. He called me bitch hoping that shock would reveal I understood what he said. The steward must have watched me talk to my neighbor on the way from Rio and run to squeal to the police. Because he expected a reward for discovering an American who spoke local Spanish, or an American familiar with exiles? It scarcely mattered which, since both would interest the authorities. I had been criminally careless. This was the kind of error that took you into the nearest military cellar, or would do if, after checking, they decided I wasn't American but an Argentine citizen after all.

'No, wait,' I said in Spanish to the eldely gentleman, who by then was practically offering to fight a duel on my behalf. 'I heard that, *teniente*, and I'm sure your ministry will be shocked to receive my complaint through our embassy here.'

'You do understand!' he shouted, and slammed his hand on the table.

'Why shouldn't I?'

'You pretended not to, that's why!'

'I learned from someone who doesn't speak water-front Porteño,' I explained sweetly, this being generally regarded as the least-educated speech in Argentina.

The lieutenant jumped and swore, and this time I

really didn't understand. Roberto was reared to watch his tongue in front of females.

He waved my passport in front of my nose. 'Your name?'

'Sally Chaffee Martin.'

'You have been to Argentina before?'

'No,' I lied.

'I say yes!'

I shrugged and didn't answer. There was a doorway behind him leading to a customs search area, and in the entrance stood a bulkily unpleasant woman, staring as if she couldn't wait to get her hands on me.

'Answer, Señorita Martin.' His voice dripped contemptuous courtesy.

'I have never been in Argentina before,' I said steadily. 'If you want to know how I speak your Spanish, I learned from a cousin. Señor Cortazar, who was president of the First Bank of Buenos Aires. He is now with the World Bank in New York, and I was studying Spanish at college. Under a professor who also came from Buenos Aires.'

This was the best I had been able to think up in a hurry, and we stared at each other in mutual hatred while he digested it. In police states it is even more vital than elsewhere to know important people, and a bank president under a corrupt and spendthrift regime is a very important person indeed.

'I am acquainted with Xavier Cortazar,' exclaimed the old man behind me, as if that clinched the explanation. 'Permit me to say you have a great look of him, señorita. Welcome to Argentina.'

'Thank you, señor.' I saw his eyes flicker as I made my second mistake: the curve of wrist and hand with which the women of certain Argentine families instinctively accept a compliment or acknowledge a service. Fortunately the lieutenant lacked the upbringing to notice anything out of the way.

After that official interest waned, but not before I had been ordered to report to central district police headquarters the following day, in case anyone thought of more questions to ask. Inevitably, they would use the time to check my story.

I felt dazed as I walked across the very insubstantial-feeling floor to reclaim my single valise. They hadn't finished with me, might still call me back, and all this within half an hour of landing. From now on I would figure in official memory as the undesirable American, Sally Martin, as well as in older, fatter files under the name of Señora Roberto Esquilar: the risk of the two becoming one infinitely increased.

The space in front of the terminal building was bustling with taxis, buses, and chattering elegant people. Everyone appeared carefree, although Ezeiza had been a word to chill the blood when I flew out of here three years before. Not because of the airport, but because the woods and rough ground around it had become a dumping ground for bodies after the police had battered the life out of them.

Solid heat thrown in my face, the everyday scene remote, as I stood staring into the distance with glassy eyes struggling against an enormous temptation to turn right around and take the next plane back to the States; struggling, too, to free myself from fright and decide what to do next. I had intended to go straight to Avenida Callao to discover whether my mama-in-law was there or away at the Estancia Santa Maria; now I must first make sure I was not followed and then doubly sure, because probably I would be. Two mistakes were enough, if I were to have any chance at all of keeping out of jail.

21

'Would the señorita care to share my taxi?'

I jumped and turned. The elderly man who had stood behind me at the immigration desk bowed with a flourish and added, 'Hernan Alvarado, at your service.'

I hesitated and then gave the same flick of the wrist he had noticed before. 'Señor, I thank you. So long as I am sure you understand, as I believe you do, that I am not cousin to Xavier Cortazar.'

'*No importa*. In any case, it may be so, for how can we know every one of our cousins? And, for my part, I am happy to inform you that in truth you have no likeness to him at all, since poor Xavier reminds me of a marmoset suffering from double vision.'

We both laughed, and after that there seemed no question of refusing his offer of a taxi. I looked back several times, but the traffic was too intense to guess whether we were followed. Since I was last in Buenos Aires, new thruways had been built, the city only hurling memories at me as we reached closer into the center. There I glimpsed the *café tertulía* where Roberto used to drink with his friends, and the fountain where we often met. Heavens, I bought the same pattern of fabric still in that shop window for new drapes at the estancia!

'It is too soon for anyone to be behind,' Señor Alvarado said quietly.

'I'm sorry. I didn't realize I was being so obvious. Señor—'

'Not here. Later you may tell me how I can serve you further.'

He lived in a very grand apartment off the Plaza Congreso, two maids bobbing pop-eyed curtsies in the hallway as we entered before being peremptorily sent about their business. One of them showed me into a room that contained a purple silk bed about ten feet square, the bathroom leading off it well suited to one of the more dissolute Roman emperors. Even the bidet had gold fittings.

Marble and gold or no, elegance was very welcome after the long flight. I showered and changed leisurely, examining doubts which told me I ought not to be here. My host showed every sign of knowing how protection worked in a military state, but until I tested the mood of Argentina again, I disliked taking unnecessary chances with the lives of others.

However, it was too late to change anything tonight. Optimistically, I decided to enjoy the luck which had turned an airport fracas into a free night's luxury lodging. Señor Alvarado must be nearly eighty, and however dubious the furnishing of his guest room, this stay promised amusement rather than danger.

Quite apart from anything else, when I returned to the main salon his stamina in the matter of flourishes and compliments was truly extraordinary. I had forgotten the sport of witty extravagances offered by males to females everywhere in Argentina, including strangers in the street. Only practice prevents you from laughing when you are likened to Aurora rising from the waves, or to flamingos in the dawn, and inevitably I laughed.

'Ah, that is better,' he exclaimed. 'If I was dictator in Buenos Aires, I would build a statue to so fair a lady's laughter. Sherry, señorita?'

The sherry was chilled and very dry, another sign that this man belonged among Buenos Aires's Spanish-blood elite, a small but powerful clique within a polyglot society. I sipped, teeth on edge, wondering how to phrase the questions I longed to ask.

He talked amusingly throughout an elaborate meal, about horseracing, literature, buttered asparagus (for some reason I cannot now recall), and architecture, once he discovered the subject interested me. Anything

23

except matters of current importance, in true Argentine fashion. The two maids regarded me with a kind of jocular interest and wheedled portions from dish after dish onto my plate, as if I was a foie-gras goose.

Eventually they were dismissed, after carrying in a silver coffee urn decorated with the twelve apostles around the rim and assorted devils at the base. Coffee piddled tepidly from somewhere I couldn't see, although imagination suggested a vulgar answer. By then I felt thoroughly revived, as much by my bizarre surroundings as by the meal, and as soon as the coffee was safely gathered into tiny enameled cups, I asked point-blank what Argentina nowadays was like.

'Like, señorita? Why, not so different from when you were here, although our masters tell us their dirty war is won.'

'I was here just over three years ago,' I said after a pause.

'I guessed at two. You have forgotten some of your Spanish but not too much yet.'

'You are so easy to understand, señor. In all Buenos Aires I cannot believe there is anyone who speaks Spanish more elegantly.' I knew how to play the compliment game, too, and he bowed, looking pleased. The effect was slightly spoiled when I returned directly to the point. 'I was married here – not in Buenos Aires but down on the pampa near Dos Bichos. My husband was Roberto Esquilar of the Estancia Santa Maria.'

He nodded slowly, parrot nose pecking over the rim of his coffee cup. 'I have a slight acquaintance with the family.'

'The Cortazars are cousins of theirs, and I remembered one of them was with the World Bank when I had to think quickly at the airport. Do you expect the police will check?'

24

'*Sí*, Señora Esquilar, those sons of mules spend their lives checking. But so long as Xavier is still in Washington, they may not find anything quickly which does not sound right. Powerful bankers refuse to answer routine questions. It is a matter of honor, you understand, whether you know the reason for the questions or not.'

'Even if he's never heard of me?'

'Xavier would kick out a policeman before he finished saying *buenos días*, so long as he possessed the power to do so. And in Washington he is safe and has the power.'

Señor Alvarado ought to know, I reflected. He would certainly kick policemen out if he could, as Roberto had the first time they came. 'I expect to be here for two or three weeks, so—'

He drew down his lips. 'Three weeks? That offers a great deal of time for checks. Can you not leave sooner?'

'I don't think so. It might be longer.'

'You must go to the American Embassy tomorrow and sign their book. Then you cannot simply disappear, as the wife of an Argentine subject might. Tell them—' He drew another trickle of coffee out of the urn. 'What will you tell them, señora? It would be wise to inform your countrymen as fully as possible of all you intend to do, for your safety's sake.'

I stared down at the dark wood of the table. 'Why should I feel unsafe if the dirty war is over?'

'Because it is not over. The Montoneros and left-wing brigands may be destroyed or driven out of sight, but everywhere there is danger. The anger of police and military who enjoyed their bloodsport and want more. Anger of a people beginning to demand justice, bread, and work. Anger of women, too, who shout each day in the Plaza de Mayo for their loved ones, the *desaparecidos* who have vanished. I think soon the police and *militares* will say again, "This people have forgotten how

25

much we should be feared. We must teach them another lesson before they become too daring."'

'Or perhaps there will be good news of the *desaparecidos*, and the women at least can be happy.'

'The *desaparecidos* are dead, señora. Only their graves are unknown.'

'You can't be sure. Without the graves no one can be sure.'

'Is that why you came? Look at me, Señora Esquilar.'

After three years when I could not weep, suddenly I had begun to weep too easily. His face sliding and shimmering through tears that felt chilly on my skin.

'You know I am right,' he said evenly. 'Men, women even, do not stay alive in the hands of police who refuse to acknowledge their existence. If a prisoner is a number in a book or has been sentenced, however corruptly, then perhaps he stays alive. But those who disappear in the night—'

'They took my husband in daylight and in front of his men, not two hundred paces from our estancia.'

'It makes no difference. Did they even acknowledge that they had him?'

'No.'

Alvarado's voice changed to savage mockery. '"You must be mistaken, señora? Perhaps brigands or Montoneros wanting money kidnapped him, or your husband has a *puta* he visits in the city, señora? Do not fuss, men will be men."'

I nodded. 'Then nothing. Not a word, ever. I couldn't believe it, the Esquilars are well known, after all. Roberto—' I had never spoken about how I'd felt before, but found it surprisingly easy to tell a stranger whom no cruelty of life was likely to surprise. 'I couldn't believe a man as vital as Roberto would simply vanish.'

'And you never heard anything more?'

'Not while I was in Argentina.'

'But later, yes?'

'His mother wrote me once. Once only, she had to be careful I suppose. Or perhaps she blamed me a little, I'm not sure. She said a friend had seen Roberto dead.'

'So?'

'So you wonder why I have come back when it's years too late?' I hesitated. 'I'm sorry, señor. You've been very kind, but I don't think I can tell you any more.'

'I see you will have to be careful what you tell your embassy,' he answered dryly.

How much more did he guess? Not much, I think. Most likely he jumped to the wrong conclusion, since Spanish literature bulges with bitter feuds over inheritances, and if you happened to think that way, then the Esquilars owed Roberto's widow a share of their wealth.

We talked for a long time, until exhaustion struck me like a blow, as much a consequence of dredging through emotion as the long flight from New York. I must ceremoniously have taken my leave, undressed, and plunged into the soft vast bed, but the next thing I remember is waking to the din of a Buenos Aires day. The sun was high and hot; the clock by my bed said eleven-thirty. I stared at it stupidly and then leapt out of bed, but there was no mistake. From the window, by squinting across a courtyard, I could see sauntering crowds in the Plaza del Congreso, which had an indefinable midday look about them, when thoughts begin to turn toward café tables or a siesta.

I stretched and twirled on warm polished boards, feeling good. And nearly jumped out of my skin before I realized all the naked women dancing around were me. Mirrors reflected my body from every angle: I grinned, visualizing the scenes this room must have witnessed

27

down the years. Soft lips laughed back at me, multiple eyes bright after sleep, a lecher's delight of breasts provocatively tilted. Sun spilled sensuously across my limbs and stomach showing – No. I turned away abruptly into the bathroom, slamming the door behind me.

I found Señor Alvarado dozing in the salon, a newspaper open on his knees. A NEW ARGENTINA STRONG AND TRUE proclaimed the headline, below it the usual picture of a general opening something. Very little seemed to have changed in three years. 'If you are imaginative, it is possible to discover a little news among the propaganda.' He sensed my presence and straightened, crumpling the paper into a ball. '*Buenos días*, señora.'

'I'm terribly ashamed of sleeping so late, but it was lovely all the same.'

'*De nada.*' Apparently unbidden, the maids arrived carrying jugs of coffee and a kind of green tea called maté, trays piled with croissants, English marmalade, cold sausages, and fruit. 'Seat yourself, señora. I broke my fast earlier.'

One croissant is about my limit for breakfast, which would have seemed boorishly ungrateful; fortunately I was hungry enough to manage three and even so was scolded. By the time I finished I had begun to negotiate my departure, another protracted affair, since convention made my host protest every step of the way. Semi-circular waves of the hand offered me his apartment, his substance, everything. *Su casa*, señora. He would, of course, have been disgusted had I accepted. Eventually a bargain was struck. He would accompany me on my call to the police station, since they were certain to want a permanent Buenos Aires address, and at dusk I would leave by a way, he assured me, that would deceive any watcher into thinking I was still within.

'But what will happen if the police demand to see me again, and blame you once they find me gone?' I asked uneasily.

'You are entitled to leave the house of a friend, are you not? If an idle policeman dozes and fails to see you go, it cannot be my fault. They do not look for trouble over an American, I assure you. As for the rest—' He shrugged, enjoying a dramatic scene and yet meaning it too. 'I am old and no longer troubled by matters of safety.'

That day dragged past because all at once I was in a fever to be gone. Now that my journey into an agonizing past had begun, any delay seemed intolerable. A dozen times I nearly telephoned the Esquilar apartment, and each time it became more difficult to take the prudent course and refrain, in case it should be bugged. Señor Alvarado and I strolled out for *aperativos*, sat in the shade of a sidewalk café watching the well-dressed throng, then visited the U.S. embassy and the police, where no one seemed in the least interested in me. Even the duty sergeant was more occupied trying to look down the front of my dress than in asking questions.

'It is clear to me that any papers from the airport have not yet arrived,' observed Señor Alvarado as we came out.

'Or if they have, no one read them.' I felt ridiculously lighthearted just to be out again into the sultry Buenos Aires air, as if I half expected them to lock me up there and then. Police precinct paint, furniture, and uniforms had been hatefully familiar, the same smell as in Matias Grande three years before. A smell which, for all I knew, might be common to every police post in the world, compounded of fear and filth inadequately disguised by cheap disinfectant, and paper moldering in files. In fact, once I knitted my nerves back into place, I had to admit that Buenos Aires central district police headquarters looked reassuringly torpid, tunics unbuttoned in the heat, even argument muted. But, once safely on the sidewalk outside, my knees began to tremble again and I found myself staring at the flagstones; any police building would have cellars.

I was glad when Señor Alvarado called a taxi for the short distance back to his apartment, thankful for the safety of his spare bedroom, spent my siesta time sweating and staring at those mocking mirrored walls.

Slowly the sun dropped toward the decorated roofline of Buenos Aires, people strolled in the street again, and the oppressive heat eased. A week ago I had been driving through snow to New York.

'You should go soon,' Señor Alvarado said at last. 'For a woman alone the city is best before it is completely dark.'

I nodded thankfully and rose, my grip packed long ago. 'I am more grateful than I can say for so much help to a stranger.'

'It was nothing. I enjoyed your company and shall feel rewarded if you do not remember my country only with hatred.'

'Of course I shan't! I was so happy here! Roberto, the pampa, that year we had together, seem like a wonderful dream.' I stopped abruptly. Dreams are for romantic innocents, the light of day often very different. 'I could never hate Argentina, only what your government allowed to happen here.'

'Life has never seemed so important to us, and you should remember it. In my father's day, when they killed a man on the pampa, if they could, they killed him as they would a sheep, the point of a knife slowly into his throat, the edge outward and a foot in his back. So the blood drained from his carcass as he died. A sheep is killed this way so its meat tastes good, a man—' He shrugged. 'He is not eaten, so there was no purpose to it. Except it seemed more natural to think of killing well than to consider pain. This the victim also understood, and to offer one's throat like a king was to die respected.'

'No,' I said fiercely. 'I could never accept that.'

'You are American, señora. But you understand what I am saying?'

'Oh, yes, I understand it. Roberto didn't act so differently when he boasted that he, an Esquilar, had friends who were guerrillas. To brag of danger and loyalty to friends is behaving like a king; whether you actually are loyal or in danger is unimportant. And because it seemed like a game, I didn't take him seriously, believed him when he said that in Argentina the police understood these things, and anyway seldom touch the rich.'

'Ah, but when kings are killed, their power falls to the assassin. Good, it is safer if you understand a little of how we are. This way, if you please.'

Black rage drummed behind my eyes as I followed him down the servants' passage; anyone can understand wickedness, stupidity, cruelty, once it is explained. My trouble was, no one explained anything of importance until too late: Twenty-two years old and ignorant of life outside Montana and architecture school, I fell in love with Roberto's swagger. I came also to love his grace and tender amorousness which made each day as his wife a joy, took care not to linger over a few characteristics which I was fairly sure I should dislike if I did. By the time I was forced to face all that Roberto truly was, I was lying on the floor of a police car with a pair of boots grinding into my back.

All finished long ago and must be kept forever

finishcd; yet not finished since here I was, following Señor Alvarado down steep stairs from his apartment kitchen. He ignored dirt, cockroaches, and curious faces popping out of other kitchens as we passed, as stately as a butler except he didn't carry my grip. In South America women are rarely offered assistance with mundane tasks.

I expected that at ground level I should have to cross a back courtyard to reach the street, with all its attendant dangers if indeed there was a watcher. Instead, we went on to the basement, out of which branched a maze of heating pipes and passages. There Señor Alvarado halted, leaning rather heavily on his cane. 'Go with God, señora. You will find that from here there are entries to the street from every apartment building in the block.'

To this day I am not sure whether Señor Alvarado's apartment was watched or not, whether a radical or dissolute life first prompted him to investigate the basement. Either way his forethought served me well. If I had been followed from the airport, then on that second night the trail was lost. After groping quite a long time among cobwebs, I chose an exit that led up through a baroque archway to a side street. The lights in the street were dim, and what I could see of it looked deserted. There was no point hesitating, so after brushing off the cobwebs I walked briskly toward reflected illumination from the Plaza del Congreso.

A taxi took me across the city to the Avenida Callao. It was the hour of late promenade, when everyone shows off their finery, tosses compliments back and forth, talking, talking endlessly. I looked at the crowds and wondered how safe talking was nowadays; I still hadn't the feel of this different Buenos Aires, where police cars no longer screeched past with guns poked out of the windows and darkness did not bring the sound of shooting. On the other hand, there were still a great many uniforms on the streets, people stepping delicately past heavily armed men as if they feared contact with the plague.

Traffic was moving slowly, sweltering ill-temperedly from one intersection to the next, until at the end of the Avenida Bolivar my taxi finally stuck in a solid jam. The night was airless and humid, Porteño tempers brittle.

'What is holding things up?' I called to my driver.

'*Las Madres*, señorita.' He slammed his hand against the Klaxon, not in anger but tunefully, jerking his head at neighboring drivers. Instantly everyone began to sound off and shout in anonymous sympathy, the noise confined by exhaust fumes and buildings. Some police who had been idling by the corner unslung their guns, others began doubling out of wherever they'd been held in reserve, holding riot shields and long night-sticks. A closed van shot out of a courtyard, its back doors slamming open to reveal more men. People began to run; when a boy of about fifteen tripped near one of the policemen, he was kicked into the gutter and beaten while he curled up, yelling and trying to shield his head. The police, too, began to run, striking out at anyone they could reach.

The change from normality into chaos was so swift that instead of being terrified again, I stared at it, astonished. Then, as quickly as it began, it was over. Klaxons stopped, the police slowed to a trot, passersby vanished. The traffic moved forward with a jerk and we turned into the Plaza de Mayo, an enormous space in front of the Casa Rosada, the pink presidential palace. There a crowd of women stood their ground, the police jostling rather than charging them. Banners tore, a woman screamed, several more shouted; a group of them linked arms and charged in their turn, holding their banners high. GIVE BACK OUR SONS! I read. RETURN THE DISAPPEARED ONES! and, most tragic of all: RAUL, MY HUSBAND splintering against the steel sides of a police pickup.

My husband, my son, I thought; and wept inside.

'The women of the *desaparecidos* become fiercer every day,' shouted my taxi driver over his shoulder as we crawled through the crowd. 'At first the government hoped they would go away, then they were ordered away and now the police take any excuse to drive them out of the plaza, but still they will not go. Some are always here, a few or many. I do not know what will happen.'

'I would like to join them,' I said.

'*Perdón*, señorita?'

'It doesn't matter. Except I am happy to see women at last demand an end to madness.'

'The señorita is *norteamericana* and finds such things entirely natural, but at first we felt disgraced to see our women make a spectacle of themselves.'

'And now?'

'Now we hope they find their *desaparecidos*. The men, too, are beginning to march, but their demand is for work and bread. Prices rise each day and life is very hard.'

There is anger now, Señor Alvarado had said.

'What will they do?' I said aloud.

'The government, señorita? Attack, of course. Soldiers only understand war. But who to attack first? That is what we want to know; they have so much choice nowadays.' He winked and laughed.

The Avenida Callao was completely normal, uproar in the Plaza de Mayo might have been on another continent. After my taxi had driven off, I stood for a moment looking at the apartment block I knew so well, calculating carefully. The fourth floor, I remembered. Those must be the windows there.

A light shone out and shadows moved in the room beyond, one at least of the Esquilar family must be in residence. The question was: Who?

3

The familiar steel mesh elevator carried me slowly up to the fourth floor, empty marble hallways jerking into and out of sight. I couldn't remember the apartment number, but it didn't matter; once the elevator stopped, instinct took me to the right door.

I rang the bell and was inspected through a spyhole before the door opened partway on a chain. '*Por favor,* señorita?'

'Is Señora Renato Esquilar within?'

'*Sí*, señorita.'

'Will you tell her Señora Roberto asks if she may enter?'

The maid was unknown to me and saw nothing unusual in the message. But neither did she take off the chain while she went to speak to her mistress, which suggested that beneath its calmer surface Buenos Aires remained a dangerous city.

She came back faster than she went. 'If you would enter, señora.'

Roberto's mother had always dressed exquisitely, even away at the estancia. In the yellow and gilt salon which, for all its splendor, I had always privately considered gaudy, she looked smaller, older, and even more exquisite than before.

'Mamina,' I said. This was Roberto's name for her, which he had insisted I use too.

She nodded, very cool and distant. 'You came back.'

'You thought I wouldn't?'

'America is safe, and you are very much an American. No, I did not expect you back.'

'I found . . . in the end . . . there were some answers I needed from Argentina. Answers I had to have if the past was ever to rest. Tell me, Mamina, do you blame me for any of what happened?'

'We are our own judges of our actions.'

'Yes, oh, yes, we are.' Impulsively I went closer but was stopped by her icy detachment. 'I blame myself, you see. Not for Roberto, he did exactly as he wished – always – didn't he? Nothing I said would have changed him.'

If I spoke no more than the truth, it was also the right truth. Male pigheadedness is a source of pride rather than exasperation in South America, and Mamina's manner warmed perceptibly. 'So, you do not blame yourself for Roberto's death and cannot be blamed for our politics during the dirty war. For what then do you hold yourself responsible?'

'Afterward, for just about everything, I guess. For running off to Matias Grande after you warned me what might happen and losing the baby because of it. For quitting like a skinned rabbit most of all. Once I could look at myself again, that's why I had to come back.'

'*Por qué*? It is expensive to come all the way from the United States, only to say goodbye.' Her glance flicked from my plain, crisp dress to my shoes: When Roberto asked me to visit Argentina and then to marry him, Mamina had been quite as scandalized by my student clothes as by my lack of dowry.

I touched the paper-thin hands folded on her lap. 'It would be worth it to say goodbye properly to you. But I need to say *adiós* to Roberto, too. He haunts my dreams, and often I still turn and expect him to be there.

All my memories of him are so full of life, I can't accept he's dead. I thought if I came—'

'He is dead,' Roberto's mother said harshly. 'I wrote you he was dead.'

I put my head in my hands. 'I know. I hope I wouldn't have scampered straight back to the States unless I believed in my heart they had killed him. But it's more than three years ago, and most of that time I haven't been making a lot of sense. I'm better now, and just being told Roberto's dead isn't enough any more. I want to hear what happened from a truthful witness. I want to kneel beside his grave and pray rest for his soul.'

'If that is what you want, then all you will achieve is to make a parade of grief and stir up danger for yourself and others, like the women of Plaza de Mayo,' she said contemptuously. 'Why not be truthful and admit instead: You desire to marry again?'

I was instantly scarlet, as though I had been dipped in boiling water. Through the confusion of my darkened senses the shape of Royston Leavis seemed to stoop over me, before sharp, instinctive recoil jolted me back to awareness.

So, I thought; love did happen in Keg Bay after all, and a single hateful night hasn't killed it. Now I have to admit to myself that love, for me, is unlikely to be enough.

I looked up, smiled, and stood. 'I think I shall never marry again, but that's my business. For the moment the best I can manage is one step at a time, which makes it even more important—'

'To make sure my son is dead?'

'No! For he and I to be at peace together.'

Slowly she nodded, as if this made sense at last. 'Aldo Paez saw him after he had been questioned and terribly beaten. Two days later all the men in Roberto's cell were taken out and shot, Aldo said. Roberto had to be carried because his leg was broken.'

My lips formed Roberto's name and no sound came.

'I wrote you he was dead.' Mamina's voice like dry sand blowing. 'Why should I tell you more? But now you want to know. Very well, you go and see Paez, and give thanks that unlike him, Roberto did not survive.'

'I know what the inside of an Argentine prison is like.' I couldn't prevent my voice from jumping. 'Of course I'll visit Paez. Perhaps there is some way I can help him, since he was Roberto's friend.'

'Americans,' she said sourly though not unkindly. 'They always think there is something to be done, wrongs righted, questions truthfully answered. Busy, busy hands, stirring up more trouble. Whereas we Argentines know the best you can do with wrongs is to avenge them or leave them alone.'

'No,' I said obstinately. 'I wouldn't know where to start on vengeance, but this time I'm not quitting without some answers.'

Mamina's black eyes searched mine. 'There is something you have not told me.'

'What do you mean?'

'I am old but not a fool, Sallí. You did not come in a hurry all the way from the Estados Unidos just to discover terrible things about Roberto's death. Things it is better you do not know, now only Jesucristo will bring the *desaparecidos* alive again. You are not *una histérica* in the Plaza de Mayo, brandishing a placard that demands the impossible. And yet, after more than three years you have come back to a place where you are in great danger, since your consul promised you would leave forever if only the authorities would release you. Naturally I ask myself why you should take this great risk, and so far you have given only part of an answer.'

I must have gazed at her for quite a long time before my thoughts spun into a pattern again. A pattern of tears again, when I hoped I had conquered tears.

'Sit down, Sallí, while I send for coffee. Then you shall tell me why you really returned to see us.' I felt Mamina's frail birdbones touch me as she passed.

'I'm sorry,' I groped for a handkerchief which, of course, I couldn't find. 'I never cry. I haven't cried for years and now these past few days—'

Mamina uttered a sound between a snort and a chuckle, an echo of the skeptical tolerance she used to show toward me, and whisked a tiny embroidered scrap out of her sleeve to give me before turning to make a bustle over the coffee. Would Mamina have wept for Roberto? Yes, but never in front of others.

'You are better now?' She sat stiff-backed again as the maid left.

I nodded.

'*Bueno*. Now tell me why you returned to Argentina.'

'You said I'd told part of the answer, and truly I would have come about Roberto, but—'

'That is understood. It is the other part that interests me now.'

'The baby,' I said baldly. 'I think I must have begun to miscarry in the police car; they threw me on the floor and put their boots in my back. But I was half-crazy with fear and rage, and when the pains began, at first I scarcely noticed. I've tried and tried to remember everything I can, but it's all such a nightmarish mess. When we reached the barracks I had to wait on a bench for hours . . . there was a dirty green wall and some policemen laughing. A woman waiting with me was raped before she was even questioned. I must have been pretty far into labor by then and remembered only being kicked and slapped. In between I kept trying to ask about Roberto, which infuriated them, so in the end they must have hit me hard enough to knock me out and break my arm, because the next thing . . .' I stared down at my cup. 'I never told anyone this. They knew at the Greer Clinic . . . I spent six months in a psychiatric clinic in the States, and they knew I was hiding something they needed to reach, but I fought to keep sympathy out, and won.'

'But now you want to tell me, because the child was mine as well.'

I nodded. 'Your first grandchild, and I don't even know whether it was a boy or girl. I remember a filthy cellar next, five of us in there – three men, two women. One of the men was delirious with fever, one a terrified boy, the third a brute called Jaime. He was the kind you'd find in jail in any country, and the quicker the better. The other woman besides myself was called Manuela, a Communist. She didn't give a shit for anyone – sorry, Mamina, but that's what she said and meant. Rape, beatings, a criminal locked up in a cell with her; she expected it all from capitalists. She told me she had been an urban guerrilla, so I suppose she deserved to be in a cellar, but she was kind to me. Because as soon as I came to, I felt my flat belly. My breasts wet and aching but no baby any more. Manuela even tried to fight off Jaime when . . . when he said he was hungry and needed to drink my milk. She didn't succeed, of course.' Words spilling, spilling, now that I had begun, like blood from a cut artery. 'You do see, don't you? Afterward, prying was the last thing I could bear. Oh, God! They'd killed my husband and my child, and at the time even Jaime's foulness didn't matter.'

My hands were shaking so badly that coffee slipped on the yellow carpet. Jaime's foulness had mattered a great deal ever since. 'I asked Manuela about the baby, and she said it was stillborn and taken out in the slop can.'

'Why-have-you-come-back?' Talon fingers closed on my arm.

'Three days later I was handed over to our consul. I think that must have been your doing?'

'I spoke to your consulate in Bahia Blanca, yes, and told them by your law I believed you were still American.'

I nodded, found I couldn't stop, and leaned forward, head in my hands and elbows on my knees. 'The consul said at once that Roberto was dead, and I believed him. It doesn't take long in that kind of prison to realize someone like Roberto wouldn't leave alive. The consul didn't approve of me, an American mixed up with Reds, he thought. To him, the military cleaning up Argentina wasn't a dirty war but necessary sanitization. I remember him saying he got good information from the chief of police when they played golf together, which seemed kind of crazy, so I giggled when he said it. I was crazy, too, by then, and my arm . . . all of me hurt like hell, so a doctor shot me full of drugs for the flight back to the States. That's all.'

'No, Sallí. Because you came back it cannot quite be all.'

The room was closing in on me, sight dissolving into sickly sepia images. 'Yes. I mean, no. Of course you're right. Ten days ago I slept with a man, the first since Roberto. It was more horrible than anything you could imagine, because Jaime was in bed between us, and afterward I had to face the fact that even a few days in an Argentine prison put some kinds of recovery forever out of reach. But . . . horrible though it was, that night triggered a cure I'd tried a long time to reach on my own: I dared to remember exactly what happened, when for three years I had been surviving by slamming a padlock

41

on my mind the instant I started to remember. Then running from the place it happened. But when I lay beside Roy in the dark remembering and remembering . . . thinking back to that cellar, too . . . as I thought back I seemed to hear my baby cry. *Una histérica*, you'd say. Because you can't have a man, you invent fables about a dead child. Well, perhaps. Manuela swore it was stillborn and . . . taken out in the slop can. But as soon as I began to wonder whether I truly did remember it crying, which would mean it hadn't been stillborn after all, I knew I had to be sure.'

'So that was why you came,' she said flatly.

'Yes.'

'But how can you possibly discover what happened to you in a police cell all those years ago? The mothers in the Plaza de Mayo want to know about their loved ones, too, but no one answers them. You cannot even admit you are back in Argentina.'

'I have no intention of walking around with a placard, begging the military for a handout. I am going first to contact the Communists,' I said harshly.

Mamina threw up her hands. 'They are driven into the sewers. Those who survived the dirty war are exiled or well hidden, I promise you.'

'But some still exist?'

'Naturally, they exist. When did any campaign of extermination poison all the rats? But, Sallí, if you try to contact them, you will be caught. Our military have not finished, only tidied their worst actions out of sight.'

'The Communists are my only chance. If Manuela should by any chance be alive, then she knows the truth. She was both Communist and an urban guerrilla; someone here in Buenos Aires ought to be able to tell me whether she survived. What I've got to do is find the someone.' Quite suddenly my horrors lifted, leaving a feeling of muzzy cheerfulness: perhaps because after years spent crawling, slipping back, crawling again up the slimy walls of my stinking introspective pit, I had found a clear purpose again.

'I do not see how finding this Manuela will help,' said Mamina coldly. 'A Communist is never to be trusted, but if in such a personal matter perhaps she might be, by your own admission she told you the child died.'

'Yes, she did. I might have said the same to a mother whose baby went out with the slops to a garbage heap in Matias Grande. If I thought it might help to keep her sane.'

'And if you cannot find her?'

I hesitated, terror again not too far out of sight. 'Then I shall travel down to Matias Grande. Garbage gets carried out – by prisoners or guards, I don't know. There can't have been many babies born in the Carmesi Barracks: someone will remember. A priest perhaps, since the military like to call themselves devout.' As soon as I said it, this seemed a promising possibility. If a child should have come alive out of those barracks' cells, and if it then survived being shoveled on to a truck along with kitchen filth and excrement and beaten corpses, then quite likely it would be left as a foundling on a convent doorstep or taken to a priest for baptism.

A name, a date in a register; a single clue that hinted the life I sought might still exist; that was my hope against all hope.

I stood and went over to the window. Out there somewhere, in a hovel on the pampa or in a teeming *barrio*, my child could need me more terribly than ever I had needed deliverance from prison. Below, frenetic Buenos Aires traffic was beginning to calm down. Lights were going out except where music blared from night-clubs or bars, the gray bulbous trunks of *palo borracho* trees like a ghostly bowling alley between the decorated façades of the Avenida Callao.

In all of this vast and secret country, where could I begin to look?

I turned. 'Where does Aldo Paez live?'

4

I slept that night in Mamina's guest room, although quite determined to leave next morning. I could not guess where my search would take me and had no wish to run anyone else into danger; questions, too, each night on my likely lack of success, would be unbearable. All the same, my few hundred remaining dollars wouldn't last long since I was dependent on my own resources.

Mamina did not kiss me on parting, had only ever kissed me on the day I married her son. She made the sign of the cross instead: 'Go with God, my daughter, but do not squander your life. A single scrap of humanity among our millions, which, if it should have survived, you will not recognize. You have set yourself a hopeless task. But are you sure you never asked whether it was a boy? It would be natural, after all.'

'Quite sure.' Annoyance made the parting easy. I understood her thinking; a boy, the eldest son of an eldest son, was worth even a hopeless search. Maliciously, I added, 'I guess I hope it's a girl, they're tougher as babies, my mother used to say.'

I simmered down outside, the broiling morning quite uncomfortable enough without internal heat as well. Automobiles raced suicidally across intersections followed by shouts of invective, the spindly branches of jacaranda traced lacework across wide pavements, smart image-conscious Porteños swaggered past, the working population long since in their offices. The shops were crammed with imports, the price tags showing mind-rocking zeros. Graffiti had vanished from the walls. I hate graffiti, but in Buenos Aires clean walls seemed to symbolize a people gagged. It was odd that the city should feel so tense when the surface was more normal than three years ago. A few young men were loitering as they would not have dared to loiter when the police cruised openly in unmarked cars, machine guns poking through the windows; women still kept vigil in the Plaza de Mayo, watched by steel-helmeted police, and only the need to avoid attention kept me from joining them.

I rode in a taxi to the Constitución terminal of the Argentine Railroad, where I placed my valise in a locker. Mamina had said Aldo Paez lived only a couple of blocks away from the terminal, in one of those barrios its inhabitants consider neighborly and which to outsiders look menacingly uninviting. Because I am interested in buildings, the way they look affects me, and I disliked the area around Constitución on sight. Behind the blank façades would be courtyards where families gossiped in the shade, but from the street all you saw were dirty walls, fly-spotted bars, and an occasional jaundiced store. Footsteps clicked oddly on tiled side-walks and all those closed shutters made me think of a morgue. Only men were to be seen, lounging at bar tables, asleep in corners, heads together in discontented groups. The women would have marketed and be home again by now.

One glance was enough for me to decide to take another taxi even the short distance to Paez's apartment, and bribe its driver to wait while I went inside. I had already left most of my money in the locker with my valise, and while in the taxi I slipped the rest into the hem of my dress. Where money was concerned, I wouldn't trust anyone here.

I had a hazy recollection of meeting Paez once with Roberto. In the bar of the Plaza Hotel, after the kind of Esquilar party that went on forever and made Roberto need a proper drink afterward. He and Paez had been at college together and in the same outfit for their military service, then drifted apart. 'Aldo's the serious kind, not like me at all,' Roberto had said. 'Do you know he read law because he wanted to win cases in court?'

'Isn't that why everyone reads law?'

'*Queridita, no!* Only deadbeats leave their cases to chance in a court.'

I remembered Roberto's amusement as I climbed five flights of stairs to Paez's apartment; it didn't look as if taking the law seriously rather than bribing judges had helped him with many cases.

The door of number fourteen was ajar, its paint bubbled, the floor gritty underfoot. The whole building smelled as if everyone had eaten onions cooked in rancid oil for breakfast, and I wondered how someone I remembered as cultured and amusing existed in such a place: not a slum by South American standards, but so stripped of hope that only the bones of existence remained.

A man's hoarse voice answered my knock. 'Who is there?'

'A friend of Roberto Esquilar.'

'Enter then, the door is open.'

If the smell in the passageway was bad, inside it was enough to dehydrate your eyes.

'Open the shutters, comrade, and see what you came to see,' added the same voice mockingly.

I flung back shutters and a window to admit heavy city air, freshness itself compared to the atmosphere inside, then turned to look across bare boards at a man lying on a bed. He was covered by a stained sheet, under which

47

bones poked sharply, his eyes sunk into an unfleshed skull so I could not guess their color or expression.

His lips drew back. 'Aldo Paez, at your service, señorita.'

'We met once, oh, over four years ago. Do you remember? I was Roberto's wife.' I hoped my voice sounded steady; routine acceptance of his condition the only way to avoid retching, which would humiliate him even more unbearably.

The eyes narrowed. It was difficult for him to adjust to light after dimness, and I moved closer to the bed. *Jesucristo*, I thought; Spanish prayer more appropriate than English expletive. This man is rotting where he lies.

'I remember. Lucky Roberto, we all said. Selfish *bastardo*, I also thought, who brings an American teenager to Argentina at the beginning of our very dirty war.'

'I was twenty-two,' I said indignantly, and then laughed. 'Did I really look fresh out of the cradle?'

'You did, and still the same, I think. Anyone with sense would know it is too dangerous for a woman to come here.'

'I bribed a taxi to wait.'

'So I should hope. I expect you want to hear the things I did not write to your mama-in-law about Roberto?'

I nodded and watched him clench his jaw. 'Then you have come to the wrong place. I am not going to tell you, do you understand? Look how I am when the military finished with me. Then give thanks they lost patience with Roberto and shot him after only a week.'

There was a bottle of wine and some bread on the floor beside him and, without answering, I went to find a glass. Paez's shoulders felt dead when I lifted him, slumping from his neck like sacks, and he fell back after a couple of gulps. '*Gracias*. Go now, quickly. There are plenty of wagging tongues eager to earn a few pesos by telling the police I have a visitor.'

'Not yet, when I've come all the way from the States to learn what happened. But first of all, who looks after you?'

'A comrade from the next block when she remembers. I don't want you helping me, Señora Esquilar, if that's what you are thinking. Leave me the privilege of lying in my own filth without insisting on charity, if you please.'

I could see he meant it, and also that the effort of talking had nearly burned him out. 'Can you tell me where Roberto is buried?' A board creaked outside and I tensed, imagining policemen listening there.

'*Muy fácilmente.*' The jeer came back into his voice and with it a spark of strength. 'In the city pit outside Matias Grande. They threw all the prison corpses there, for the rats to eat.' His hand jerked on the sheet, reached out to clutch mine. 'How a man dies matters, not where his body lies. I was in the next cell, and Roberto died as well as any man can who is tortured and shot for a cause he never cared about. He liked to boast, didn't he? The rich estancia owner with dangerous friends. Enjoyed riding out sometimes with guerrillas after an evening drinking with them? At least the *militares* caught the right man when they caught me; I could feel a little pride when I refused to speak. Roberto could only scream he knew nothing, knew nothing, knew nothing. Once they believed him, there was no point keeping him alive. With me, they always hoped another day hung on wire or drowning in shit might loosen my tongue. Until any information I possessed was stale and somone decided to release a shambling skeleton, to teach Communists the meaning of fear.'

I stared down at Aldo Paez's hand in mine: knobbled joints, vanished nails, mauve folds at the wrist where wire had flayed it. *They release people sometimes, so others may see with their own eyes what can happen and be the more afraid.* The terrified professor of archaeology who sat beside me flying into Buenos Aires had said that, and here was one of their pitiful beings making me want to howl with fear. That loathsome shudder back in my guts again and spreading to my brain, dislocating thought. But passing out would be the ultimate disgrace, when only courage might, just might, offer Paez a little comfort. So I stopped and kissed those hideous fingers, vomit locked somehow in my throat. 'Roberto said you were one of the few men who learned law so as to fight deadbeat cases. I hope you won some before they took you.'

'Two.' His hand dropped but he was smiling. 'That's all, but I never regretted my choice.'

His voice was slurring, I had to be quick before his senses went. 'Did you ever hear of a woman called Manuela? She was a guerrilla here in Buenos Aires, before being imprisoned in Matias Grande.'

'Manuela? Manuela Guischetti? She was one of us but as for prison . . . Once I was arrested I knew only the poor devils in the cell each side of me. Like Roberto.'

My heart leapt. 'If this Manuela Guischetti is alive, where might I find her now?'

'I don't know where to find anyone any more.'

'Please think! It's terribly important.' God forgive me, I nearly shook him.

His lips moved, gasping for breath.

'You won't get anything out of him,' a voice said from the door. 'A man who withstood army butchers won't squeal to you '

I whirled around, my first thought that I had indeed heard a sound outside. A woman stood watching me with an impatient, excited look on her face, as if she couldn't wait to fire the pistol in her hand. She was small, quite dainty, and about my age, restlessly shifting from one foot to the other. We stared at each other, each surprised not to be facing an enemy who looked more sinister.

'I wasn't trying to make Señor Paez betray anyone,' I said at last, staying very still. 'I came to ask about my husband who was a friend of his and in prison at the same time.'

'I heard you demand information about Manuela Guischetti.'

'You know her!' I cried, overjoyed.

'Everyone knew Manuela when she worked with our night-riding squads.'

'Tall, pointed chin, a quick temper? Lips so beautifully shaped they'd be the first feature anyone would describe?'

'A quick temper? *Ayí*, I could tell tales of Manuela's temper!' the girl exclaimed, laughing. Her manner seemed so odd I began to wonder whether she was high on drugs, except the idea scarcely fitted Communist comrades on the run.

'Where is she now?'

'Dead, I should suppose.' Her gun prodded the air, decisively downward. 'All the *desaparecidos* are dead.'

'She never came out of prison?'

'What is that to you?'

I glanced at Paez, but he was slumped into semiconsciousness. 'Manuela's whereabouts mean everything to me. We were in the Carmesi Barracks together and—'

'Now I know you are lying! You have never been in a barrack prison in your life! See how people look if they come out from those alive.' The gun jerked toward Paez.

'You must be the comrade he told me looked after him,' I said contemptuously, disgust almost overcoming

51

fear. 'When did you last come? You ought to be ashamed of yourself, leaving him like this.'

She did not answer, looking at me out of glittering brown eyes in a way that made me prefer being threatened by her gun.

I had to say something fast, before she tore my throat out with her teeth. 'I swear I was in a cell with someone named Manuela in Matias Grande. I don't know whether she was your Manuela Guischetti, but someone will. That's why I came to ask Señor Paez about her as well as about my husband, who is' – my voice caught – 'was a *desaparecido*.' No doubt now that Roberto was dead.

'If you were in prison, how is it you weren't *desaparecido* too?'

'Can't you guess from my accent? I'm *Yanqui*, and our consul got me out.'

She let out such a screech I nearly laughed; for all its latent violence this scene was farcical. '*Yanqui*! Accursed *Yanquis*, whoremasters of our people!'

'Not me,' I said firmly. 'All I did was marry an Argentine. Now, for heaven's sake, will you tell me where I can find someone who knew Manuela Guischetti well?'

She looked from me to Paez, fingering her gun as if debating whether Marx would insist I should be killed at once.

'If you come with me, then maybe I could ask,' she said sulkily at last.

'Of course I'll come.' When this was the single gossamer thread that might one day lead me to my child, I simply felt relieved she had agreed and no alarm at all at going into some undercover Communist lair.

Before we left I insisted that we clean up Paez while he remained semiconscious. The woman – she said her name was Juanita – was not exactly callous, but it was clear that among her many other enthusiasms, she often forgot him. There is no extremity of imagination that can prepare a normal, squeamish human being for the reality of unlimited atrocities perpetrated on a man's body, and long before we finished I was, this time, most comprehensively sick.

How many thousands in the world suffered such cruelties at this very moment? No one to know how they suffered; no hope, no end to it, no pity. Cruelty breeding a momentum of its own and worshipped for its power: driving the sane insane, turning those who practiced it into madmen too.

My child, my child, are you also bleeding somewhere out of sight? Your belly empty, lacking shelter, hit casually and hard each time you whimper? As I walked down the stairs with Juanita's gun aimed at my back, I scarcely knew how to exist another day in such uncertainty. Yet I must. Put love and longing behind me with gentle hands, and concentrate all my faculties on following a trail more than three years old.

Not surprisingly, my taxi driver had pocketed his part payment and vanished, but accompanied by Juanita I was safe. Everyone in the barrio knew her, and also presumably that she possessed a gun and a disposition that yearned to fire it. In fact, not many people seemed interested in us. Some handsome deadpan policemen stood holding submachine guns in the Plaza Constitución, everyone else seemed in a hurry to get out of sight.

'Another work-and-bread march!' exclaimed Juanita eagerly. To me, her gun seemed very imperfectly disguised under a shawl.

'Do they happen often? There was trouble in the Plaza de Mayo only yesterday with the mothers: perhaps the military are really beginning to loosen their hold. I never remember any protest at all when I was here before.'

'It depends. Not for weeks perhaps, and then, poof! Trouble every day until one of the pigs gets killed. Then they go mad.'

Around the next corner the road was filled by a colorful crowd milling aimlessly. I could also hear the distant clatter of breaking glass above mob noises that sounded like a giant cauldron bubbling. Before we could even begin to work our way through the crowd, some khaki came into sight, which suggested the army rather than police. Not standing for any nonsense either, but advancing with guns held slantwise across their bodies.

'This way,' said Juanita violently, her eyes dancing more than ever. 'We'll be caught in a minute.'

She dodged down a side street, and then another. At one intersection I glimpsed armored cars, at the next a troop of soldiers dropping out of trucks. The military were far from losing hold.

'Perhaps they will bring tanks in next, that'll be good, won't it?' Juanita positively skipped with delight while keeping up far too fast a pace for such a sultry day. 'It is never difficult to organize demonstrations while work is scarce and prices high, but tanks turn demonstrations into battles. Then the whole Fascist system begins to blow itself apart.'

'Bare hands against guns? Do you want a massacre?'

'We have guns and *explosivos* too! If only massacres will awaken the people to their power, certainly we want them. Otherwise we die alone in cells. Come, I think this way is quiet.'

A great deal of shouting continued not far away, but by dodging down alleys we soon reached wider *avenidas*, where traffic moved normally and people strolled, chattering nervously, as the siesta ended.

54

'Slow down,' hissed Juanita. 'Do you want to be stopped?'

I was melting in the heat and thankful to slow down but jumped violently – everyone in sight jumped violently – as shooting broke out behind us. Juanita clapped her hands and then dug her fingers into my arm. *'Bastardos, ah, bastardos!'*

'One of the massacres you wanted,' I said sourly.

'Soon, perhaps. One or two killed is nothing, nothing! They have tanks, regiments, airplanes. So many of them. We must rouse everyone before we win. Everyone!'

By subway and bus we followed an erratic course across the city; I did not know Buenos Aires well enough to decide in which district we ended up, but suspected it wasn't far from our starting point. There we entered a sawdust-floored bar, its paper tablecloths rustling in tepid drafts. Inside, the proprietor dozed by his cash box, a jerked thumb directing us through bead curtains to the back.

'This isn't anywhere particular, but comrades come here sometimes,' Juanita sounded uneasy, as if she knew she ought not to have brought me.

First through the curtain was a swarthy workman who picked his teeth the whole time we were there without uttering a single word. Next came two middle-aged women of such overpowering respectability, they never seemed to get over being in a bar; they sat together sipping maté like two molting birds in a cage.

'No good,' Juanita said succinctly.

I nodded, relieved to discover that the shared horrors of tending Paez and a chancy journey across Buenos Aires seemed, temporarily, to have put the idea of shooting me out of her head.

'The young men are out in the streets this evening.'

'Demonstrating?'

'Different things,' she said vaguely. 'Ah, here is Matteo, he is better. *Hé*, Matteo!'

A man came over without haste to greet us. He was tall, with a long head, small nose, a mouth like a knife cut. Juanita kissed him on both cheeks, which reassured me, since I expected a clenched-fist salute. 'See, Matteo, who I have brought. A *norteamericana* who says she was a Communist in prison with us! I don't believe her and I am sure you will not either.'

She slapped her gun. Though her other hand lingered on Matteo's cheek, I could see the idea of killing me had just hopped back into her mind again.

Matteo looked me over appraisingly. 'You really are American, señorita?'

'Yes, but married to an Argentine.'

'*Sí?*'

'He died in Matias Grande prison, where Aldo Paez saw him.'

'Where did you pick her up?' His eyes shifted back to Juanita.

'At Comrade Paez's apartment. She was trying to pump him for information. I heard her.'

'What kind of information?'

'About Manuela Guischetti. I find that suspicious, don't you?'

'Very. You risked too much in bringing her here.'

'But I thought you would not be at all pleased if I shot her in Paez's apartment! Don't you remember how angry you were when I shot that troublemaker in the Bar Gran' Fortuno and we had to finish going there?'

'Ah, but I do not wish to finish going here,' he answered mildly. From the way they spoke, I might have been dead already; the worker picked his teeth faster and the middle-aged ladies stared at me reproachfully. The least I could do was tidy myself someplace else to die.

The curtain clashed and a bunch of students came in shouting at each other in the way people do when the adrenaline is still flowing. They gathered around Matteo, hunkering on table edges, jostling to tell him about some protest or other.

Soon the tiny place was packed. The atmosphere so thick with heat and smoke and wine, I wondered that everyone wasn't stupefied. Far from it, however. They talked more loudly as time went on, while I began to wonder whether all Argentines hadn't become deranged by twelve years of terror, counter-terror, and crackdown.

'It isn't true!' one of the boys shouted suddenly. 'They're just a bunch of crooks! One push will send them flying across the Rio de la Plata.'

'And you are just a fool,' another answered scornfully.

Immediately everyone yelled at once as the first boy seized the other by the throat, snatching a knife from the table.

I could have run off easily then. No one seemed bothered by a fight, but the melée spread until the two women had to retire with their maté to a corner, screeching angrily at intervals. But where could I run? And why, after all? If I died, I died, but I was damned if I was letting go my single thread of evidence.

Matteo watched the scene with apparent satisfaction, as if fighting proved the virility of his followers, until eventually everyone sprawled back exhausted, dabbing at cuts.

In the comparative quiet that followed, Matteo turned to me. 'Well, señorita spy, you are still here, eh?'

'I am not a spy. I came to ask a question, hoping for some help.'

'You are perhaps a journalist?'

'No.'

'An American comrade, you told Juanita.'

'I am not a Communist, and I never said I was.'

'Ah.' The thin mouth twisted. 'Those evil un-American Communists; of course you could not be one of them.'

'I've never been political; in these kind of struggles most sides seem the same to me. The information I want is personal and not for any cause.'

'So, what is this information you desire so much that you dare visit Communists to find it?'

Haltingly, I explained, while his fingers tapped impatiently. I could see a child meant nothing to him, only children of a revolution, en masse and abstract.

At least he listened, but snapped his fingers before I finished. 'Rosa!'

One of the middle-aged women looked up. '*Sí*, Comrade Matteo?'

'Did you ever hear of a *norteamericana* in Matias Grande jail?'

'I was held in Carmesi Barracks, not the town jail,' I interposed.

'When, comrade?'

'Three and a half years ago. Fall, 1978,' I answered as Matteo raised an eyebrow at me. 'They arrested me after I made a nuisance of myself, demanding to know what had happened to my husband. They dragged him into a car in sight of our home but never admitted having him, you see.'

Rosa scratched her lip thoughtfully. 'No, I never heard of a *norteamericana* in the Carmesi.'

'I was there only three days before our consul got me out,' I said desperately.

'You said you married one of us.'

'By U.S. law I kept my citizenship, and my mother-in-law told our consul in Bahia Blanca what had happened.'

'The *Yanqui* big stick, I see.' Matteo smiled malignly. 'No dollars if you lock up our citizens; plenty of dollars if you lock up your own.'

'At least we look after ours,' I said evenly.

'As we do, too, señora. If comrades are in jail, we try to discover where, but Rosa says she does not remember you.'

'Not many people stayed only three days, and I'm not Communist. She might have heard about my husband though, Roberto Esquilar, who died there although he wasn't Communist either. Señor Paez, who is one of yours, wrote his family afterward about how Roberto had been beaten and shot. Then there was Manuela, who shared my cell.'

I saw Rosa nod imperceptibly, and hope, which had almost died, immediately revived. 'Please, señor. I only want to ask Manuela about my child, and she knows I was in the Carmesi.'

'Manuela is dead.' Rosa spoke quickly, as if she wanted to tell me as much as she could before being forbidden to speak.

Matteo spread his hands. 'You see, señora? You wasted good dollars, flying from the *Estados Unidos*. But I am sure we can offer you one of our own orphans to rear instead, there are so many after all.'

I sat, graven, surrounded by the debris of my hope.

The rest of the evening passed in a mist of smoke and argument; I remember only that Juanita was not allowed to shoot me.

'There is a bed upstairs,' Matteo said offhandedly at last. 'Tomorrow a comrade will take you to the Plaza de Mayo; alone in this district, you would not pass two corners. Roberto Esquilar was a capitalist swine, but since he died in the Carmesi, maybe we can rely on you not to squeal anything you learned here to the police.'

'Yes,' I said dully. Until hope vanished, I had not realized how unreasonably it had grown since I returned to Argentina.

Rosa took me upstairs to a stuffy cubicle papered with newsprint but surprisingly clean. 'Señora Esquilar?'

I turned and saw she had closed the door behind her.

'Listen. I know of six people who so far have come alive out of the Carmesi Barracks. Perhaps one of them could help you. You have a pencil?'

I nodded and fumbled in my purse, as dazed by the return of hope as I had been by its death.

'Quickly then. These are the names, perhaps you will recognize one of them: Raul Gavilan, Rocco Cortese, Aldo Paez – you have seen him. Regina Ventura, she is addled in her mind after torture and could not help. Teresa Cruz, she is living as an exile, I do not know where. Jaime el Toro . . . Jaime the Bull. He is not one of us, and the pigs used him as an informer. We kill him one day I think, for the blood he helped to spill.'

Jaime. Oh, God, Jaime.

'There was a Jaime in the same cell.' My voice beat inside my skull as I wrote JAIME in straggling capitals across the back of an envelope addressed to me in Keg Bay. Keg Bay, a different planet compared to this. 'A foul brute . . . and yes, I would expect him to be an informer.' Jaime el Toro, even the nickname fitted his headlong animal lusts.

'His is the only name you recognize?'

'Only the four others who were in my cell might be able to help, and one of them died of fever while I was there.'

'A pity. Of them all, only Regina Ventura's poor wits would be of less use than he. Jaime is dangerous, too.'

'I know.'

'Not a comrade, an animal.'

'Yes.'

'But you will go to find him?'

'Yes!' I said violently. 'If my child should by chance have lived, it will be growing up in a slum somewhere, preyed on by brutes like Jaime.'

'Then you must seek him in Matias Grande. El Toro was last heard of there.'

'But you don't know where!' I exclaimed in dismay. Matias Grande might be only a provincial capital, but I wouldn't know where to begin finding Jaime in its barrios.

'Oh, quiet!' she said pettishly, as if I had spoken in church. She opened the door and added more loudly, 'Good night, señora.' She dropped her voice again. 'Try Padre Sebastian at the Church of San Ignacio. He tends all the dregs of Matias Grande.'

The door shut behind her.

My hands were trembling so I could not write. Padre Sebastian at San Ignacio. Jaime el Toro. The thread was still there but the way I must now follow led directly to a degenerate called Jaime, who had been worse than the police, worse than a beating that broke my arm, worse than boots in my back. In labor as I was, and unpolitical, perhaps the police lacked time during my three days in Carmesi to be more than routinely brutal. Jaime . . . It was the memory of sharing a cell with Jaime that had haunted and destroyed me, kept me running for so long trying, vainly, to outpace horror.

5

I traveled south to Matias Grande by railroad, as more anonymous and cheaper than flying. Soon the pampa stretched on either side, the ceaseless wind I remembered stirring waves in grass that was green in spring, then yellow, now as brown as a scuffed saddle. A few dark ombú trees and dusty settlements rose slowly into sight and as slowly disappeared, as if they had been ships at sea; isolated estancias in their groves of poplar or eucalyptus were islands floating on distances so vast and flat that the horizon showed the earth's curve.

How often Roberto's tales had made me wish I'd seen the pampa before automobiles, telephone poles, and barbed wire cut it into sections men could grasp. I stared and stared out of the train window, reliving the year when these great spaces were my home and held my love. An hour before we reached Matias Grande, the Estancia Santa Maria slipped past, just over the horizon.

Always when I had lived there, I found the pampa invigorating. I delighted in its mighty skies and the wind which seldom rested. Perhaps that was what helped Roberto to love me, because most Argentines hate it. But as the pampa reached for me again in the train that day, its infinite harsh distances seemed to mock the single life I had come to find.

In Matias Grande everything appeared more tranquil than in Buenos Aires, the heat less oppressive, tangos sounding more softly – though quite as gloomily – across the cobbles, the post-siesta promenade keeping pace with the shadows. The police, too, seemed more intent on sunning themselves than anything else. Only I was out of step, scampering mindlessly as a kitten chased by bees as I searched for the Church of San Ignacio.

Matias Grande harbored too many ghosts for my thoughts to settle; even the train had passed the municipal garbage dump as it pulled into the station, heaving with scavengers both animal and human. There, so Paez said, lay Roberto's bones. Here, somewhere, was my child, living or dead. And wherever I walked, the Carmesi Barracks seemed close by, its flaking plaster glowing in the sun. To an unprejudiced eye the building was worth a tourist photo, with its wrought iron gates and colonial-style roof. In me it kindled such a witches' brew of rage and fear and loathing that each time I glimpsed it I raced to put it out of sight again. Perhaps the military government for the moment had ceased to kidnap its citizens in broad daylight, to kill them at its leisure and throw their corpses out with the garbage. But there would be prisoners in the Carmesi still, degraded as I had been, longing for death as Roberto must have done.

Then, no matter how preoccupied I was, there was also the Latin curse of importunate men, exasperating, rasping further at my nerves.

The center of Matias Grande was physically safe for a woman walking alone, but I could not move without being harassed, when what I actually needed was to search the town undisturbed, trace to their source the few clues I possessed.

A couple of hours must have passed in this frantic fashion before I paused in the central plaza and took a hold of myself. If in Matias Grande I remained more fragile emotionally than I had hoped, then the only answer was to snap out of panic fast. No indulgence, no running from pressure any more.

I swore at the next man who came up: one of Roberto's choicer expressions which no Argentine woman would have dreamed of using, and he practically leapt out of his socks. 'Señorita, if I decided to compose a dictionary, I would worship at your feet. You used a word I never heard before.'

I had to laugh; the Argentine compliment survived anything. 'I want to be left alone, is all. I'm looking for the Church of San Ignacio, can you tell me how to reach it?'

'*Pero sí!* But it is not in a place where a señorita could go alone.'

'I'm going,' I said firmly. 'There are taxis, aren't there?'

'Then I will accompany you.' He bowed and offered his arm, delighted by wrenching success from defeat. His name was Ernesto and I didn't trust him a yard. He had dark, slicked hair, a mustache that reminded me of a very young Hitler, and smelled of scent. On the other hand, he might have been much worse. Though he spent the whole time in the taxi boasting about his apartment, since he assumed that after this expedition I would return there with him, in practical terms he behaved with typical Argentine generosity. Nothing was too much trouble. The taxi was mine, some flowers I admired on a stall, the town of Matias Grande itself if I should have a whim to possess it. *Su cuidad*, señorita.

'Señora,' I said.

'Ah, what is a husband when he is not here?' He made another of those splendid motions with his hands. He realized I was a foreigner, which intrigued him, and soon would ask more questions.

'Mine is a grand and jealous señor who rules a

hundred peons,' I said firmly; Roberto would have relished protecting me from beyond the grave.

Ernesto nibbled his mustache while he thought about that, darting looks to decide whether I was serious. Grand señors defended their women in any way they thought fit, and I judged this boy as a government clerk who spent the bribes he took on his oversmart clothes. 'In that case, señora, he will be very angry with you for entering this part of Matias Grande,' he said at last, triumphantly.

'I have a holy obligation that can be discharged only at the Church of San Ignacio,' I answered glibly, but he was certainly right about the district. Matias Grande prospered modestly on the products of the pampa, and most people probably lived adequately there, a few very well. But, of course, there were barrios, and barrio slums anywhere in South America are atrocious.

Streets became alleys that lost the regular pattern found in the center of town. Washing looped across tumbledown façades, stench increased, the road surface became a series of potholes which would fill with water whenever it rained. There was more color and noise than in the better areas, but naturally it was the children who wrung my heart. Many of them merry enough, but others huddled on doorsteps or hunkered over trash, often coughing savagely. They stared at our taxi with huge dark eyes, their thin bodies poking out of their clothes.

'Here is San Ignacio, señora.' Ernesto interrupted my thoughts, his tone suggesting he had built it himself.

'Then I thank you more than I can say for your escort, and take leave to fulfill my vow.'

'But, señora! How will you return? Of course I am happy to wait until you complete your prayers, and then you shall come to visit my apartment.'

65

We stood wrangling on the sidewalk, and by the time I'd decided to say my husband was coming to pick me up, of course he didn't believe me. A crowd began to gather, including several characters a great deal more unsavory than Ernesto. He was getting rattled, too, perhaps worrying over the price his clothes would fetch in a barrio, and in the end we both bolted into the church with our argument unresolved.

Inside it was cooler and nearly dark. Pinpricks showed where vigil lights and offertory candles burned, otherwise small, obscured windows reflected incense-laden gloom. Nor was it the kind of church where there would be pews to sit on while I figured out what to do next. I didn't want to pray, because it would have been a sham. At the moment I was simply going from one thing to the next, down a tunnel that shut other considerations out of sight, and just now I wanted to see Father Sebastian. Until I found him, I couldn't concentrate on anything else.

Annoyingly, Ernesto followed behind me, chattering anxiously about the terrible inhabitants of the barrio outside. Almost at once a priest came up. 'This is a holy place, not a *café tertulia*. Behave yourself, my son.'

'Father.' I grasped his sleeve. 'I have a vow to fulfill. May I see Father Sebastian, please?'

'He is not here.'

'But he will return later?'

'Perhaps.' He gave me a graveyard smile. 'If you desire a priest, I shall be hearing confessions in an hour, time you should use to seek a state of contrition.'

'I wish to confess to Father Sebastian.'

'Indeed? Then I will inform him you are here, and he must judge your need.'

I was angry then, but more determined than before. Partly to escape Ernesto and more particularly because I had ceased to care about hypocrisy, I went closer to the altar and knelt at a priedieu. Which, after a while, began to seem a good place to be, in a remarkably evil world.

A long time passed. The dimness of the church became darkness, and I no longer heard Ernesto's new leather shoes fidgeting on the flagstones. Outside, the barrio became more strident; there was no easy way now for either of us to leave San Ignacio before daylight.

'You wanted to see me, my daughter?'

I looked up, but saw only thicker blackness than the rest. 'Padre Sebastian?'

'*Sí.*'

I stood up stiffly, knees creaking after so long. 'I have come from Buenos Aires to find you.'

'And before that from the *Estados Unidos*?'

'I know my Spanish is bad,' I said ruefully.

'Forgive me! I was merely reflecting that your need must be urgent. On the contrary, your Spanish is most agreeable.'

'I heard about you from a woman called Rosa in Buenos Aires, but yes, I have come a long way to ask some questions that are very important to me. I hope you may be able to help.'

'We will go somewhere more private, then. Even in God's house I have learned not to trust listening shadows.'

'Ernesto!' I said guiltily. 'Heavens, he's still here somewhere.'

Hastily I explained about Ernesto and heard this unseen priest chuckle. 'Let us see what has become of him.'

He lit a candle and moved down the church, peering in corners until he found Ernesto, fast asleep up on what looked like a pile of old vestments. 'Did you know your cavalier was a policeman?' he asked softly.

'No! I thought . . . I placed him as a clerk who used his bribes to buy snakeskin belts and silk shirts.'

'Hmm.' Father Sebastian slid his fingers into Ernesto's pocket. 'You can usually recognize them even off duty, and this one I have seen around.' He tipped the bill-fold he had palmed with such unexpected skill so I could see a badge and card inside. 'Well, we have to hope he continues to cool his passions on the flagstones.'

'I don't think it matters,' I whispered anxiously. 'I mean, it was only chance he came with me. It could have been anyone, depending on when I lost my temper in the plaza.' I was taken aback all the same to discover Ernesto was police.

'It is in the hands of God. This way, señorita.'

He led the way up some steps into a bare presbytery. When he lit the oil lamp hanging there, I was able to see him clearly for the first time. Perhaps because of his reassuring voice I had expected an ascetic; in fact he was small and round. Questing, up-swooping eyebrows his most remarkable feature, otherwise a mop of stiff gray hair, red cheeks, and brown eyes gave him the look of a university professor in one of the jollier disciplines.

He brought some bread, cheese, and a bottle of wine from a cupboard. 'Sit down, señorita. You must be hungry.'

I sat, amused to notice that even a priest was not immune to the all-embracing wave: *su iglesia*, señorita. Of course he did not say it. 'Thank you, Father. You seem to be used to people who visit to ask questions secretly.'

'It depends on the questions. *Sí*, some of us have become used to many things these past twelve years. First the Montoneros and guerrillas, then the military behaving like Montos and guerrillas. Now . . . who knows? There is something brewing and I am not sure what.'

'I am astonished by your frankness, Father.'

'Ah' – another wave of the hand – 'I cannot help anyone if I am too careful.'

I leaned forward, gripping the table edge. 'Then listen, Father, please. Did you ever visit the Carmesi Barracks when it was a prison?'

'Often. I still do, and it still is.'

'More than three years ago, in the fall of 1978?'

'Are you asking because one of the *desaparecidos* was yours?' He looked at me compassionately.

'Yes, but that's not it. Roberto . . . my husband . . . I'm sure he's dead. Roberto Esquilar, did you visit him?'

'*Un momento.*' He left the room and came back holding a tattered notebook. 'So many, you see, señora. So many years, so many suffering souls. I write down whatever messages and names I hear as soon as I return, though at the time I may not understand. My visits are watched, curtailed, and usually I am allowed to see only those who have betrayed enough to be left alone or brought to trial. The military do not like me, I am afraid.' He turned the pages, lips moving. At first I thought he was praying for the sorrows each word recalled, then realized with a shock that he was barely literate. 'Nineteen seventy-eight you say? No, I did not see Roberto Esquilar, nor hear his name. I do not see many, you understand.'

'Aldo Paez?'

'*Sí!* They did terrible things to him, but he lived, I think.'

'I saw him two days ago in Buenos Aires. Yes, he lived. More's the pity.'

Father Sebastian nodded without answering, so I liked him even better than before. He knew too much to mouth priestly phrases about the sin of craving death.

'Paez told me Roberto died and I'm sure he told the truth. I was sure even before I met him, but . . . Well, I wanted to know what happened. But there's more to it than that. You see, I was in the Carmesi, too, but for only three days. I had a child there, who died. Or so another woman said, who was in the same cell. I don't remember a lot about it myself, and afterward . . . I guess I was too sick to think. It's only since I've gotten better I began to realize how I, too, might have told a mother her child had died if it had been thrown out in a shit can. I'm sure about Roberto; now I have to be certain about my child, believe in my heart it couldn't somehow have survived.'

'My daughter,' said Father Sebastian, and stopped. 'Very well. I will find out if I can. The priests of San Bartolomeo would most likely baptize any infants born in the Carmesi and certainly there were one or two, to the great scandal of us all.'

'I'll come with you.'

'No. Often I am watched, because my sympathies are known.'

'I have to come. That other woman in the cell, she was good to me and I told you how she said my child was stillborn; now, after three years, I find that isn't enough. Don't you see? I must question each witness myself if I am ever to accept there isn't any hope.'

'A longing heart is seldom satisfied, I fear,' he answered gently.

I stood up. 'You said if you were too careful, you'd never be able to help. I'm the same. If I'm ever to discover anything, I can't afford to be careful.'

He brooded, a hand to his chin. 'San Bartolomeo is church to the military and I would call its priests corrupt. I should learn nothing, be made unwelcome if I visited there by day and also stir up a great deal of trouble by asking questions. If you were once in prison, then you are not here legally, I think?'

I smiled and shrugged. 'I'm not sure. I came on a U.S. passport, but under my maiden name.'

'Then you would be lucky only to be deported if the *militares* caught you a second time. An Amercian comes to Matias Grande seeking her child born in one of our torture chambers? That would make big headlines in the *Estados Unidos*. I think while our government seeks to look better in the world, there are men in high positions who would prefer an unexplained murder to such a story in the newspapers.' He lifted his shoulders in a parody of apology. '"Our profound regrets, señores. How unwise are women in these feminist days, who wander side alleys alone, where our police cannot always guard them."'

'I can't help it. I have to go to San Bartolomeo myself.'

He flung up his hands, a gesture expressing male irritation as well as priestly understanding. 'We must go tonight then, and you will dress as one of our Sisters of Mercy, and so walk safely through the barrio.'

I didn't argue, but was superstitious enough to dislike the idea. I also felt dismayingly confined in sweat-thick robes. If anything went wrong, I should be incapable of fast movement.

'Your wimple is incorrect,' snapped Father Sebastian when I rejoined him in the church. 'Here, let me.'

A nun's wimple is not made to go over a full head of hair, and I think, also, he found touching a woman difficult; while we were struggling with recalcitrant cloth I heard a sound behind him, opened my mouth to whisper a warning, and felt his fingers on my lips. 'There,' he said clearly. 'Pin it so and all is well.'

Another sound, and this time I identified it as the creak of Ernesto's shoes. Ernesto, who was a policeman.

By then it must have been quite late, most candles guttering, the barrio noises less than before. Very gently Father Sebastian pushed me into an alcove near the altar. Whatever happened, Ernesto must not see a woman he, like Father Sebastian, knew instantly as a foreigner, now dressed as a Sister of Mercy.

I felt Father Sebastian leave me and move back into the body of the church, moving lightly for so solid a man. Again that stealthy creak away to my left, perhaps Ernesto was too vain to take his shoes off while investigating circumstances that were only mildly doubtful.

'May I help you, my son?'

I jumped at the sound of Father Sebastian's voice, unnaturally loud after our whispers.

'I am looking for the señora I escorted here.' Flame flared and died as Ernesto flicked a lighter. 'She said she came to fulfill a vow, but couldn't have left alone.'

'That is true. I called a taxi for her some time ago.'

'But I was waiting! She knew I was waiting.'

'Ah, perhaps that was why she preferred to go alone.' Father Sebastian's voice was bland.

There was silence while I felt Ernesto's suspicions grow. Whether he had been suspicious before and was ashamed of sleeping, I don't know, but Father Sebastian must have been pretty notorious in police circles. The moment I mentioned his name I could see Ernesto thought it odd that I wanted to come to such an inaccessible place to fulfill a vow. Now he felt in his policeman's bones that he was on to something. 'I don't believe you. Even in a taxi, after dark it is not safe for a woman to go alone through the barrio. So, I ask myself, why would a priest lie?'

Ernesto sounding quite different now, filled with the menace of his power. Somehow I had to scramble out of incriminating black robes while argument still raged, lucky indeed that I had kept on my own clothes underneath. With infinite care I moved away from my niche, felt for the steps leading to the presbytery. Ernesto would hear the rustle of cloth if I pulled off heavy skirts so close to where he stood. Superstition had been justified; dressing as a nun had brought bad luck.

At that moment two things happened. As I reached the presbytery steps Ernesto snatched up a branch of candles, and one of the many drafts blew more strongly, driving the flames higher. They guttered again at once, but he had seen another person standing close. He plunged forward with a cry, his hand diving toward a holster under his shirt, before Father Sebastian tripped him and the candles went out as he fell. His pistol must have been partly drawn, because it went off with one hell of a report, the bullet howling end over end across the flagstones.

For a moment no one moved. I think we were all so astonished, each of us waited for blood to pump out of a hole we hadn't felt. Then, simultaneously, we realized we weren't hurt. Ernesto swore and scrabbled to pick up his gun, Father Sebastian kicked out like a mule and sent him flying. I went to help and tripped over my skirts. A great many people began pounding on the church door, roused by the sound of a shot.

I felt my arm grabbed. 'This way!'

The Church of San Ignacio must have been very old, the barrio having grown inside the original colonial town. One crumbling space led to another, up steps and down, through straw where people seemed to be sleeping, until we reached cloisters outlined against the night sky. Father Sebastian was sure-footed, myself an

73

encumbrance in the dark. A pause at last, the sound of bolts being pulled, and we slipped into a narrow street. 'A pity we can't lock the door behind us, but I doubt whether a policeman will fancy walking through the barrio at night,' said Father Sebastian coolly. 'Fold your hands into your sleeves, look at the ground, and follow two steps behind me.'

There were scarcely any streetlamps, which made a few corners' start a great advantage, but we did not dare to hurry. A smooth, purposeful walk took priests and nuns about their business, and anything faster would attract attention.

The discipline of walking even-paced in those circumstances and without being able to lift my eyes to look for danger, ought to have driven me crazy, but, oddly, I felt quite calm. Perhaps I couldn't afford to be driven crazier than I was. Even so, I strained to interpret the sounds I heard. Shouts, moans, whimpers, scufflings. As a stranger to the barrio, I found it difficult to disentangle threat from normality. Once a drunkard lurched against me, only to recoil in terror of the evil eye when he saw black cloth; to the poor, blessing and cursing are two sides of a single image.

Then a man came running down a stair and threw himself at Father Sebastian. '*Padre!* My woman is dying! Come and bless her, I beg you.'

By then we were nearly out of the meanest alleys, but Father Sebastian couldn't ignore a plea. As I climbed behind him up a staircase through layered heat, I felt tension clamp tight again. Surely, Ernesto would never tamely wait in San Ignacio until daylight, but once I was in the right part of town and wearing my own clothes, the police couldn't prove I had not innocently left San Ignacio in a taxi. There would be questions, of course, and even thinking about police interrogation made those dreadful gut shudderings begin again, but that was a worry for the future. The priority now was to get out of the barrio unseen, for Father Sebastian's sake as well as mine. Ernesto could not be sure whom he had glimpsed in such poor light, would not have grasped that if it was me, then I was wearing nun's clothes.

But Father Sebastian had different priorities, and once he was called to a deathbed, I could only wait. Dip my head lower among a crowd of wailing relatives, then kneel in prayer for an unknown woman who lay as still as marble on some straw. And all the time tension was winding tighter, until soon it must reach snapping point and break.

6

Because everyone accepted me as a nun, they did not look at me, which was as well, since my wimple and bearing might not have passed more than a casual glance. There must have been twenty people crammed into that space under the tiles: six children from a few months to about ten years in age, ranged in height order where their mother could see them as she died. The father weeping beside them, friends and neighbors flapping cloths at the stifling air and between wails discussing who had milk in the breast to spare for the baby.

As I knelt as far out of the way as possible, watching covertly between my fingers while an unknown woman died in a barrio attic, a quite different thought slipped into my mind. *We can offer you one of our orphans,* Matteo had said in Buenos Aires. *We have plenty.* Here were six more, not orphans, but very small children who would find great difficulty in surviving the loss of their mother in a place like this. I looked from one to another as if in a dream; which would die, that one or that? What was the tie of blood after all, if the search for it only endangered others? In this case, Father Sebastian, a man desperately needed by his people. Perhaps it was the habit I wore that made me think like this and for the first time faced the likely failure of my search: if by a miracle my child should be alive, then too much time had passed ever to discover a single life among Argentina's millions.

But I might find others if I wished.

As quickly as they came, such thoughts vanished. Blood did matter. Nothing less could have kindled such unreasoning hope for a child I had never held in my arms, nor have brought me such a long, strange way already, only to take me farther yet.

I saw Father Sebastian make the sign of the cross, copied by everyone else in the room as wails changed into sobs. The three-year-old alone among the children did not weep, but took his fist from his mouth and put it on his knee without a sound. There was something beyond sadness in his tiny unformed face, a conscious abandonment of warmth. I went over and picked him up without thinking how I might expose myself to view, but small though he was, he made himself as inanimate as iron, rejecting comfort.

'Leave him, Sister. These good people will see to him later.' Father Sebastian spoke warningly, and turned to the husband. 'My son, have you work?'

He shrugged. 'Sometimes. My wife used to clean for the military, and she found tasks I could do.'

'Come tomorrow to San Ignacio and I will see what I can arrange.' He blessed him, and everyone knelt again as we went out.

'What can you arrange?' I asked on the stair.

'I shall send him on errands for others worse off than he, in return for pesos from the offertory. I never offer alms, for at San Ignacio there would never be enough. Only help while a soul in need decides how best to help himself. Wait here while I look outside.'

Obediently I waited, hands back in my sleeves but eyes not yet fixed on the ground, while he studied the alley outside.

'I think there is someone watching at the corner,' he breathed.

'Ernesto?'

'I am not sure. If so, he is mad to follow and watch alone in a place like this. Wait, I will fetch Ramon.'

Ramon must be the bereaved father, because Father Sebastian disappeared back upstairs, leaving me in a stinking passage. And while I waited I became aware of movement, of stealthy steps using the darkness to surround an unwelcome intruder. Instinctively, I opened my mouth to shout a warning, and if I had, then probably I would have been killed as well. But it was already too late. With a pouncing rush four or five men ran out from the shadows and I heard a scream as they knifed their victim, followed by a long, bubbling moan. I had never heard such a sound before but could not think what it meant: Ernesto or no, the watcher is dead.

I whipped around as wood creaked behind my back, but it was Father Sebastian with Ramon. 'Wait,' he said, and walked past.

'The padre will be all right.' Ramon stood back so I could see Father Sebastian walking steadily up the alley without attempting to hide.

Five minutes later he was back. 'It was Ernesto. His assassins stripped and left him.'

I thought of the slick youth in his smart clothes coming unwisely into the barrio, more because afterward he hoped to lure me to his apartment than in response to his policeman's curiosity. Ernesto stripped and dead in a gutter because of me.

Father Sebastian gripped my arm. 'You must not blame yourself for the world's evil, but pray for his soul instead. And then give thanks for God's mercy, because once you are out of here no one will be waiting to make more trouble.' He turned to Ramon. 'The sister has to reach San Bartolomeo without being seen. I had thought we would be safe once we left the barrio, but I think we cannot chance it. When the police discover one of their colleagues was killed tonight, they will ask many questions. And since someone may tell them about a shot in my church, I do not want to be seen, very late and without good reason, in the plaza. Once they think about it, a sister out of her convent in my company will seem strange as well.'

Ramon flashed a look at me. 'Our back ways are too difficult for her to travel.'

'Not as difficult as arrest in the Carmesi, where this sister has already been. Tell us what we must do to reach San Bartolomeo secretly. I know it can be approached across the roofs. I never needed to climb there before, but once inside we can wait until daylight and leave among other worshippers.'

Ramon scuffled bare toes in the dust. 'We have to walk a wall as well as roofs, for a sister in skirts—' He spat. 'I am sufficiently accursed already without being responsible if a woman of God should fall.'

'Blessing and cursing are not your business. Obedience, faith, and courage are. Show us where we must go and leave the rest to God.'

I was not surprised when Ramon sullenly turned and led us through the passage into a yard: Father Sebastian's tone conjured up too many papal battalions to be withstood. Within minutes of starting on this new and much worse journey, I was lost. The barrio was not large and we had been quite close to the wider streets found near the middle of Matias Grande, but here every courtyard was full of sleepers, passages were blocked off by shacks and became a maze where generations had squatted, built tumbledown shelters, met disaster, and built again.

'Here,' said Ramon at last, and began to climb.

At first I wasn't quite sure what we were climbing

when it seemed so rough, until a fitful moon disclosed a stairway sagging out of a broken wall. A hundred years before, this house might have belonged to a beef baron; fragments of moulded plaster and wrought iron hung dizzily over voids as we climbed higher, tall ceilings crumbled above subdivided dens. Now dozens of people sheltered at every level; I saw the bodies sprawled in sleep as we climbed past.

I wished then that I knew less about architecture and the precise techniques on which staircases depend for their strength, because I saw at once that this one was suspended on little more than dust and air. Wedge-shaped blocks slanted unsupported out of rotten walls, the occasional gap showing where some had already crashed down. I bent and felt where a step had vanished: the wall was cut less than three inches deep to accept the narrower inside edge of stair. A groove that was entirely adequate while the whole structure remained intact offered no security at all once its integrity was lost. There was also the matter of three people climbing where a prudent cat would refuse to go.

Five steps later the inevitable happened.

Just ahead of me Father Sebastian stepped on a small sloping landing and it gave way with a crash. The floor planks folded slowly downward past me while he tried to slow his fall by clinging one-handed to a joist that was also pulling loose. For the fraction of a second his feet were level with the end of my stair. 'Quick!' I shouted, no longer caring about the noise, and grabbed at him.

He landed across the outer edge of my wedge-shaped block, almost winded, but still holding the joist as the planks he had been standing on crashed to the ground below. Then I felt my own stair also shudder to a steeper angle under both our weights while I scrabbled for a hold, anything that would stop us from sliding into the gulf below.

'Let me go,' breathed Father Sebastian.

I grinned, teeth painful against my lips. 'I'm damned if I'll pray for two souls, both dead in a single night because of me. Climb past, using me and the joist. But for mercy's sake, be quick.'

It was a strain. Until he was up I could not move, could scarcely help him. A shower of dust fell from where the other end of the broken joist he held, on which he depended for his balance, remained precariously embedded in a crumbling wall, my own fingers clawed through plaster in a desperate effort to reach the rubble wall behind. This offered an illusion of support, really no support at all. Pebbles, flakes of stones shifting as I fought for a grip among perished mortar joints, while slowly he crawled past and even more slowly stood, trying for fresh balance while he reached up. Of course the landing was gone; there was a gap of several feet between him and where Ramon waited. God knows what held our stair into the wall. An edge, perhaps, tilted against that cut niche, which the slightest unwary movement would shake loose.

'Ramon?'

'*Sí, padre?*'

'Go on up. I shall have to jump.'

I heard Ramon's breath whistle through his teeth and he needed no second telling. The hazards of jumping four-foot gaps on such a staircase did not need emphasizing. I felt Father Sebastian gather himself; he was not the kind of man who would waste time over a disagreeable necessity. Then he jumped; the stair creaked, showered dust, and held. 'Come on,' he said, and it was my turn.

My turn slowly to balance myself, to hesitate longer than he had while I looked at that gap, which was nothing really if it hadn't been for the drop and

81

sloping, perilous foothold beyond.

'Wait,' I said, and untied the cord at my waist before cautiously slithering the nun's robe over my head. It had brought nothing but bad luck and I was thankful to be rid of it. A pity I wore a dress rather than pants underneath.

The gain in freedom of movement was enormous and I half stepped, half leapt the gap without giving myself more time to think about it.

'*Bueno.*' Father Sebastian was smiling a fierce unpriestly smile. 'Up as fast as you can go. I think we have tried the good Lord's patience enough for a single night.'

I wasn't arguing, and went up like a kid into a candy store, to find Ramon waiting on a cracked tile roof. He looked at me queerly when he saw my dress and bare legs, and instinctively crossed himself.

'You said you did not want responsibility for a sister.' There was a laugh in Father Sebastian's voice. 'Just accept from me that you are helping God's cause and not the devil's.' He was panting, probably as exhausted by fear as I was, and also too short and round to scamper easily up ramshackle stairs, but I received the impression that Father Sebastian was enjoying himself.

Ramon muttered something under his breath and turned. 'See, it is there. Bartolomeo's cloister is at the end of this roof.'

At first I couldn't see much, it was so dark. Then I picked out an irregular line against darker sky, which gradually solidified into the bulk of a church as we walked circumspectly toward it. By then the sky was very slowly lifting toward dawn; we would have to be quick over this last lap.

Ramon gestured, finger to lips, thumb pointing down. Here alleys straightened into streets, the roof on which we stood jutting to reach an archway. Long ago a monastery must have been attached to San Bartolomeo; now only the shell remained. Tufts of grass grew in jagged stone and I could see where the ruin had been breached by a road, leaving a single arch to connect it with the church roof.

'It's narrow,' I said, that masonry edge between where we stood and the church roof was about nine inches wide and twenty feet long.

Ramon wasn't listening. 'Police,' he said, and gestured again.

I couldn't see anything, but not too far away heard boots on the cobbles and a mumble of conversation. For whatever reason, there were indeed patrols around the edge of the barrio.

'The arch is safe for one to cross at a time; someone used it only a month ago.' Ramon turned to leave, and I couldn't blame him for feeling that on the night of his wife's death he had done more than enough for a stranger.

'Remember, I expect you at San Ignacio whenever you cannot find work.' Father Sebastian gripped his shoulder.

'I pray I may find you there, padre.' He vanished into the shadows.

He didn't sound too convinced, and the longer I studied that wall, the less convinced I felt too. A nine-inch path would be an easy walk if painted on an interstate, but twenty feet above cobbles, when police patrolled not far away, it looked narrow. Very narrow. The light, too, was in that deceptive stage between night and the coming of day. Outlines were hardening even while they remained insubstantial as mist and as difficult to judge.

'We have to go at once,' I breathed, and saw Father Sebastian nod. Saw him. Within minutes the police couldn't miss us whichever way we tried to leave this roof.

I was standing nearest the edge that abutted on the wall but had to lower myself over the eaves to reach it. A warm wind was blowing out of the dawn, snatching at my dress and making matters even more difficult. The temptation simply to melt back into the safety of the barrio was enormous, when I feared arrest far more than injury in a fall. Arrest in Argentina again. The thought kept hammering on the soft damaged surfaces of my mind.

But if Father Sebastian believed San Bartolomeo might hold the information I needed, then getting there was what I must worry about, not possible arrest. He had also said the church had to be entered at night. Quite why, I wasn't sure, but any night entry meant secrecy and walking this goddamn wall successfully would make the most secret entry of all.

With one hand spread to hold my weight against the tiles I wriggled inelegantly and very fearfully over the eaves, the other hand groping for any hold to keep me steady while I turned. Damn Ramon! There must be easier ways to leave the barrio unseen. But not, maybe, to reach San Bartolomeo. My feet touched wall and slowly I lowered my weight, skinning my arms on the way. Now to turn. I waited for my breathing to ease, just the tips of my fingers offering an illusion of balance. Almost level with my eyes was the white blur of Father Sebastian's anxious face, easy to hear his whisper. 'You can trust the sacristan who keeps the church at night. No one else.'

I stared up at him. 'You aren't coming?'

A flick of his fingers was answer enough: Look at the light. Only if I hurried might he, too, have time to cross. Ramon had hardly needed to warn us to cross only one

84

at a time: dangerously distracting to hesitate and feel someone behind you urging greater speed, perilous to risk doubling the inevitable trickle of falling grit, suicidal to chance a scrap more weight than necessary along that unsupported length. One near disaster on precarious heights was more than enough for a single night.

I pivoted while a sense of urgency made movement easier, and at once the narrow masonry edge stretched in front of me, the roof of San Bartolomeo beyond. The coping was even more weathered than I had realized, but I could walk it, of course I could. All I had to do was place my feet squarely and softly, take balance for granted, and think of it as less risky than hiking in Glacier National Park.

Only, my terror was so intense, it made every risk a nightmare.

Slowly I took my hands away from the wall, the most reluctant farewell of my life. It would be best to go quite fast, resist the temptation to hesitate over each step in case my balance faltered. Fragments of mortar shifted under my feet and I could hear the rustle of falling dust. The police might hear it too. No wonder, no wonder Ramon said only one must cross at a time. Astonishing no one could ever have fallen if this way was often used, because if they had, then the police would have pulled down this slender remaining stretch of arch: they would want to keep their eyes on who left the barrio at night. Three, four paces, no problem at all. Suddenly I was filled with confidence, unable to imagine why I had thought this so impossible. The trouble is, confidence needs watching. The very next step I caught my toe on a tuft of weed and nearly fell. For an instant I wavered there, arms outflung, terror exploding from every nerve. Sheer instinct drove me the last few paces at a teetering run as momentum alone kept me from falling,

85

until I slammed into the wall of San Bartolomeo.

No time to waste. The thought that within minutes it would be too light for Father Sebastian to cross almost instantly banished panic, the most important thing to get off that wall so he could start. I remembered San Bartolomeo as imitation colonial, fronting the main plaza: there were high parapets hiding guttering, plaster hiding brickwork, florid decoration distorting perspective, and I didn't trust any of it. By the time I had scrambled over the parapet by way of some molding and a couple of faceless gargoyles, my curses on the architect must have whirled his bones in his grave.

But I had reached the next place in my search.

As soon as I caught my breath, I looked back. It was still too dark to see much, but I saw a shadow move to the edge of the roof and turn to lower himself from the eaves. Father Sebastian would be just in time. Then the faintest of clatters drifted across the gulf toward me, a slither followed by a clink. Not loud, but distinct in the predawn hush. A pantile off the roof probably, its fall muffled in weeds below. Away to my right a voice called out, followed by the sound of boots. My mouth opened, shut again. A warning would confirm suspicion and those boots were prowling rather than certain there was anything to find. Anyway, Father Sebastian was gone. He had done the only possible thing and melted back out of sight behind the roofline.

'*Quién está?*' The sentry was directly below.

Minutes ticked past while the light strengthened and none of us moved. In the barrio I could hear the business of the day beginning. Soon the night sacristan of San Bartolomeo would go off duty, the only man who could be trusted there. This must be why a normal daytime visit to inspect the registers was out of the question.

Step by step I retreated from the parapet edge, the

86

church roof nearly flat and offering no obstacle to silent movement. Father Sebastian would not be coming now, I must manage the best I could alone. Somewhere there ought to be a door that led to the church below. I found it set into the high false front of the church, which curved against the sky and carried a single bell. Inside, a flight of stairs led up to the bell, and also down. After most of a night, as it seemed, spent in negotiating crumbling buildings in the dark, the Church of San Bartolomeo was a steal. The interior solidly maintained, rich, smelling strongly of incense.

A door at the bottom of the stair opened to show a gleam of candles, some of them guttering after a night's burning, others freshly lit. As I watched I could see a figure near the altar, taper in hand, lighting more. Given any luck at all, this should be the night sacristan preparing for early mass. It was not, I suppose, entirely natural to be as single-minded as I had now become, but already the terrors of the night had whisked away and I felt only triumph because success seemed close. I was also very tired.

So far as I could tell the church was locked and, apart from the single figure, deserted: I would just have to assume he was the man Father Sebastian considered safe. Though I tried not to startle him by appearing too suddenly out of nowhere, inevitably he was startled.

'Father Sebastian sent me to you for help,' I said quickly. For help, for help, the echoes whispered eerily overhead.

'Father Sebastian?'

'Of San Ignacio. He came with me most of the way here.'

The sacristan shook his head and eyed me warily.

'He said you would help me,' I repeated, too weary to think what else to say. Conscious, too, that I was grazed and dirty. Once daylight came, where could I safely go to rest?

'Help in what way?'

I breathed with relief. 'It's very simple. All I want is to see the church register of baptisms.'

'*Ay de mí!*'

'I know it sounds strange. I can tell you why if you like, or would you rather not know?'

He considered, torn between prudence and curiosity. And, as I hoped, curiosity won. 'I would have to know before I considered showing anyone the church's books.'

As briefly as I could, I told him, the tale sounding disagreeably commonplace after so many tellings to people who found horrors instantly believable.

'Early mass will begin soon,' was all he said when I finished.

Too commonplace by half, I thought wryly. 'I swear it's true. What I'm asking is nothing to do with politics at all.'

He shrugged, as if to say: What are words? And he was right; *los militares* called everything politics.

'Will you help me?'

The taper shook in his hands, conscience most unwillingly prodding him along a path he did not wish to tread. I didn't blame him. Anyone would think carefully before risking savage interrogations for a stranger.

'*Sí*,' he muttered finally, the look he gave me pure dislike. 'Return tomorrow and I shall try to have it for you to see.'

'Tomorrow!'

'It is too late now, and in any case the registers are kept locked away.'

I wasn't sure I believed him, but there seemed nothing I could do about it. 'Then is there anywhere here I could stay out of sight today?'

88

'No, no! Certainly not!' He flapped his hands. 'Go away, then stay to meet me again after last mass tonight.'

But by then I didn't feel charitable. 'If I go out into the plaza looking like this, I shall be taken up for questioning. In fact, the police may already want to interview me. And if I should be arrested, they are bound to squeeze out of me that I was given your name as a contact by Communists in Buenos Aires.'

He flinched. 'It isn't true!'

'No, but you will have deserved it by turning me out to be caught again.'

'I didn't ask for you to come here!' he said angrily.

'You are just unlucky,' I agreed.

The taper dribbled a gout of grease. 'After tomorrow you will go away?'

'If I discover what I want in the register, yes, probably.'

He muttered rudely and scuttered away down the church, leaving me to follow. If this was the only priest in San Bartolomeo for whom Father Sebastian had a good word, the rest must be pretty awful.

He found me a splendid place to pass the day, though, not a corner of the belfry as I half expected, but in a small hospice run by nuns which communicated with the church. Here they tended all manner of unfortunates without asking questions, an exhausted woman accepted as nothing out of the ordinary.

I slept for hours, oppressed and uneasy under layers of darkness. A certain kind of pain striking through the dark, the pain of fear and my child calling, while I stayed moaning in my pit. A cold wind blowing, too, which hurled me from edges of crumbling wall into the place where children sucked their fists as their mothers died, and said good-bye to warmth. When, dazed and sweating, I woke up at last, the bare room where I lay looked threateningly unfamiliar. The Carmesi! was my first thought, panic subsiding only as memory seeped back. This lime-washed space bore no resemblance to the Carmesi. I was at one end of a half-empty ward, the bed was hard but clean, a white-robed sister hurrying past. Evening light lay like an amber pool high up on the wall as leisurely promenade noises drifted through the window, and I was famished.

No one took any notice of me, and, impatiently, I pulled the sheet around me before climbing out of bed. I had already discovered I was naked, so finding my clothes and some food became the next necessity.

Outside, I found a bare hall with four similar wards opening out of it, and a corridor leading to a courtyard. The door to San Bartolomeo, I remembered, was set in the farther wall of this, while on other sides I discovered hearths, stewpots and sheds.

'You feel rested?' A sister emerged from a passage.

'Yes, thank you. It was good of you to take me in.'

'From your voice you are *extranjera*. We do not succor many such.'

I nodded, wary of offering any information. 'I'm looking for my clothes.'

'Ah, they will have been washed!' She went off at a trot and returned almost immediately with everything meticulously ironed and folded. 'When you are ready, there will be bread and coffee.'

A scrap of mirror hung on the ward wall and I smothered a laugh as I caught sight of myself. Most decidedly, this wasn't one of my better moments. The nuns had pressed my dress ruthlessly into squares, there were tired lines under my eyes, and for all my efforts with a comb, my hair looked dull. Still, I would have looked worse after a night in the belfry, I reflected cheerfully. A wash and clean clothes had done wonders for my morale.

A bowl of *dulce de leche*, which is a kind of unset jam, a mug of coffee, and a flat loaf of bread waited for me on a table in the courtyard, although when I thanked the nun in the kitchen, she put her fingers to her lips. For them, a time of obligatory silence must have begun. Actually, I was relieved by this. Clearly everyone was bursting with curiosity to find a foreigner in their midst, and there is nothing like closed communities for gossip. I needed time to consider what, if anything, I should say in answer to more questions, and besides, I was too hungry to talk until I had wiped my plate clean, licked the last scrap of *dulce de leche* off my fingers.

'I must go,' I said at last. 'Sister, if you cannot answer because of your discipline, will you listen, please? I am searching for a child. A particular child who was born three years ago, in prison, during the dirty war. I am going back into San Bartolomeo as soon as it is dark, but would you allow me to return here later? I don't fancy the Plaza Mayor of Matias Grande at night.'

She hesitated and then nodded, her soft, bumpy face full of speculation.

'Thank you. I have found great kindness in Argentina, as well as sorrow. Tell me . . . Do you ever take in foundlings here if they should be left on the steps of San Bartolomeo?'

She shook her head, so that hope, which had briefly flared, flickered down again.

I touched her hand and smiled. 'Pray for me.'

Later, when it was dark, she went ahead to the door in the wall, stood watching as I slipped back inside the church.

7

At first I couldn't find the sacristan anywhere. I searched
with growing exasperation, believing he had chosen this
way to be rid of me, quite rightly chancing my threat to
embroil him with the police.

But in this I wronged him.

Some priests came late to say mass, and while I hid I
realized his vigil must begin only after they had finished.
Quite what he was meant to do, I never discovered. I
suspect it was to pray through the night rather than
secure the church, which anyway was locked; in practice
he had hidden a mattress under one of the side altars and
I followed him there after the mass finished.

'Have you managed to get the registers for me to look
at?'

His eyes glittered at me in the candlelight. 'All the
barrio is in an uproar because the police arrested Padre
Sebastian.'

'No!'

'Sí,' he mocked. 'A policeman has been murdered and
a shot was heard inside the padre's church.'

'But the policeman wasn't shot, but stabbed!'

'You seem to know a great deal about it.' Naturally,
he remembered I had said that Father Sebastian had
come with me the night before.

'I didn't do it, if that is what you mean.'

He shrugged and refused to answer, while I stood
biting my lips, flooded by remorse. What had I begun by

returning to Argentina? If I had been innocent before, already this search made me guilty of wrongs I couldn't have imagined. Ernesto would be alive if I'd stayed in the States, and Father Sebastian . . . I could not bear to think what might be happening to him now. Yet to give up my search was impossible and betrayed the help that he had gladly given.

'Have you got those registers?' I demanded.

He nodded reluctantly. 'They are in the sacristy.'

Probably they had been there all the time. Three large volumes gathering dust among the jumble of inkwells, thumbtacks, and string. I carried over a branch of candles, anticipation still curdled by the dread and guilt I felt for Father Sebastian.

The second book seemed to be the one I wanted, and I turned the pages until I reached the first week of October 1978, finding sloped Hispanic writing enormously difficult to read. *Huérfano*; orphan. That was the notation I sought, and did not find. Father Sebastian had told me that several foundlings were left on his step every week; in rich San Bartolomeo, none in early October 1978. I turned more pages, desolated by disappointment. *25 octubre Pedro, huer:d:Cm.* The hieroglyphic fairly leapt off the page. *Huérfano de Carmesi*; it must be, surely. I stared transfixed, before doubt struck. The twenty-fifth of October; by then I was back in the States, the child born to me three weeks old, or dead. How could Pedro, *huérfano*, have survived unbaptized for three weeks after being carried out with the trash? A priest would have baptized a baby immediately if someone took pity on a child left to die and brought him out of the Carmesi. And if a guard should have taken him home, then he would hardly bring him back to rich and hostile San Bartolomeo for baptism.

In an attempt to double-check the meaning of that

scribbled *huer:d:Cm*, I studied all the pages for the years of 1978 and 1979, when the 'dirty war' was at its height, and found three children marked the same way – a boy in February 1978, Pedro the same October, and a girl in March 1979. There have been a few to the great scandal of us all, Father Sebastian had said, and here they were. Only in these cases was there no clue as to parentage or to where they had gone, although with ordinary foundlings an orphanage or foster family was noted in the parentage column. Surely this confirmed my guess as right: these three had been born in the Carmesi and survived. And of them, only Pedro just possibly could be mine.

I went back to the side chapel and shook the sacristan awake. 'If a baby is left on the step, what would the priests do while his relatives are sought?'

He yawned. 'How should I know?'

'Who would, do you think?'

'Father Damien is the priest in charge here, but you can't ask him.'

'Why not?'

'Don't you know anything?' He settled back on his bed. 'He's in the pocket of the military.'

'He's still a priest, isn't he? I'm not a spy or a criminal, why should he run to the police the moment someone asks an innocent question?'

He closed his eyes. 'Because he would, that's all.'

I sat with my back against stone and tried to think about what I'd learned, while all round me darkness pressed in close. I couldn't afford to make misjudgements now.

Someone had brought a boy called Pedro out of the Carmesi.

That person, or another, brought him to be baptized. Argentina is a strongly Catholic country, so this in itself was unsurprising.

The same person, or another, took him away after baptism.

Facts. But within those facts such an infinite variety of circumstance I could not guess at. He might next have gone to an *asilo de huérfanos*, or orphanage, to a family, or been boarded out with a wet nurse. Yet guessing wouldn't help. Facts. I must coolly weigh and discard facts, without distraction.

But . . . My son, my son.

I sat for a long time, considering ideas about how I might question men who had worked or still worked in the Carmesi, but I couldn't really imagine how to start without inviting arrest.

Yet the more I thought about it, the more convinced I became that this was my best hope. Those three weeks though. Once an ordinary soldier, policeman, or clerk took a child to his home in a poorer district, he could not reasonably be expected to bring it back to San Bartolomeo for baptism.

I couldn't figure it out at all. An ordinary person . . . what about an officer? That might fit. Three unexplained weeks remained worrying in a country where baptisms normally took place within days of birth, but an officer would very likely bring a child to San Bartolomeo. I jumped up and fled back to consult the register; an officer would pay a fee, offer alms for the services of the church, perhaps leave some clue of identity behind. And if this last guess should be the right one, then at least my son would not be suffering in some slum. My son. Already, dangerously, I assumed that Pedro must be mine.

But the register offered no further information.

Other entries gave names of parents, godparents, heaven knows who. Dozens of people sometimes, when a birth was socially okay. Pedro had nothing beyond that cryptic *huer:d:Cm*. The earlier boy was the same, although oddly enough the girl some months later had created quite a stir. No parentage or named sponsors but a flourish of indecipherable initials and almsgiving in the register there – I should have missed the telltale notation if the priest had not scribbled it between exclamation marks in the margin, as if he considered the matter a huge joke. I didn't get it, but could see why Father Damien roused dislike.

I put back the registers where I found them; if I should discover Pedro, I might one day need their evidence, such as it was. For now I'd already decided to break away from churches and priests, establish as innocent an identity as I could in Matias Grande, and search the city for Pedro, *huérfano*. Which sounded quite hopeless unless you looked at it optimistically and realized the progress I'd already made. I knew now I was looking for a boy, so half the city's three-year-old children could be left out of account, and his name was Pedro. Stupidly, I wished he'd been called a name I liked: Pedro conjured no answering image in my mind.

How much better to think of progress than the immense task that remained, the inevitability, sooner or later, of police interest in my activities. Gossip travels fast in provincial cities. So think of Pedro, alive and waiting for me, instead of Father Sebastian, whom I had helped lock in a cell.

I spent the rest of the night sitting on the edge of my bed in the hospice ward, too unsettled to sleep. Outside, the silent city seemed to seethe with possibilities, my earlier, calmer mood impossible to recapture. The all-important fact remained, however; I had seen evidence which almost certainly proved that babies came alive out of the Carmesi. The question was, where should I begin the next stage of my search?

As it happened, I started quite differently from anything I'd imagined. I began by helping to fix a riot.

When the serving sisters' silence finished the following morning, I asked for advice over a hotel, and they decided a place called the Magnifico was best. Though not magnificent at all, it was, they said, the kind of place a foreigner in difficulties would like. I was suspicious of this, since it suggested expensive folksiness, but obediently went to fetch my valise from the station locker once the plaza filled sufficiently to make walking around seem reasonably safe.

It was great to be out in the sun, to walk without concealment again. The police were hung about with guns as usual but didn't look interested in me – or in anyone else particularly. A murder in the barrio wouldn't be too unusual. The sidewalks were crowded with people strolling to work, my fair coloring unremarkable in a country where German and British settlers made up a significant fraction of the population. A sense of security an illusion all the same, because if I should be stopped, then my story needed to be good.

The Magnifico was not how I expected it at all, but a mahogany and plush survival from the past. The patrona squatted like a molting fur seal behind a desk in the hall, otherwise the place seemed deserted. Perhaps solitude was what the sisters had in mind when they considered it suitable for a female foreigner, since it possessed no other obvious virtues.

'*Buenos días, señorita, qué quiere?*' The patrona poked her head to study me from every angle, rolls of fat making her look more like a seal than ever.

'Can I rent a room for a few days?'

'Why not?' The wave included the entire building and its contents.

We haggled briefly about prices, but once translated

into dollars they were absurdly cheap. Which was a relief, although the rooms were depressing. Dark green paint, huge furniture, and a plastic crucifix above each bed.

'All right, I'll take it,' I said about one of the dimmer and cheaper rooms, quickly, before I could change my mind.

'*Bueno*. Always there are sandwiches if you come in hungry. Good beef sandwiches, anytime. You want to try one?'

I declined as tactfully as I could, being familiar with Argentine beef sandwiches, a yard long and as thick as a fist.

She shook her head sadly. 'Anytime, like I said. Shout at the kitchen and they come. *Los señores* like women they can hold, eh?' She pinched my arm disparagingly and gave a bark of laughter. Really, seals wouldn't even have noticed if she joined them someplace on a beach.

Outside again, the streets were clearing in the heat, but a policeman stood at the first corner I had to pass. I heard my steps hesitate, but I would become a prisoner in the Magnifico if I allowed myself to fear every policeman with a gun across his arm. I felt my head turn slowly, stiffly, as I reached him, nerved myself to nod civilly as I passed. He stared back, the black third eye which was the muzzle of his gun staring too.

Then he yawned, and I was past.

Not long after that the riot began.

Inconsequentially, without my noticing it at first. Instead of thinning for siesta, the crowds thickened, cars fled down side turnings, heat and noise increased. Soon I was wedged in the crush, which smelled sharply of sweat and onions.

'Why haven't you bolted with the rest?' demanded a

woman packed against me. 'That's what your kind do when trouble starts.'

'I didn't notice what was happening until too late,' I said truthfully. 'Is this a work-and-bread march like I saw in Buenos Aires?'

'What's it to you? The pigs have taken Father Sebastian, and that is why we march.'

'Then it means a great deal to me.' The noise was growing all the time, so I needed to shout, but shouted gladly because I was among people fighting Father Sebastian's arrest. Around me women began to stamp their feet while the men shook their fists, the crowd picking up speed like a river in spate. I was borne along with the rest, nervous I might trip and be trampled, but exhilarated, too. After Roberto was arrested I went alone to protest, demand information; murder and more murder drained everyone's courage. And because I was alone, they arrested me too. Now it was different. The murderers had tried to turn respectable and take their killings out of sight. Well, we wouldn't let them; even Pedro would have to wait while I paid this debt. As we trotted and stamped and linked arms, I was shouting louder than anyone: *'PADRE SEBASTIAN! MILITARES ASESINOS! LIBERTEN TODOS LOS DESAPARECIDOS!'*

Down a road with trees on either side we went, glass shattering as we passed. Just in front of me an elderly peon stumbled and in a moment whirled away out of sight; on the fringes of the crowd, boys catapulted stones at hastily shuttered buildings lining the street.

'The Carmesi!' a voice yelled.

'To the Carmesi!' we shouted back. 'Padre Sebastian is in the Carmesi!'

The square in front of Carmesi Barracks was quite full before our part of the crowd reached it, jammed solid soon after. No one seemed to know what to do because the gates were shut, and behind them soldiers stood on sandbags beside machine guns, blue and white Argentine flags flapping above their heads.

Pedro, I thought again. If I am killed, there's no one left for you. But if Pedro was indeed Roberto's son, then the tie of blood would one day tell him that some debts of honor must come first. As Father Sebastian would have said, this is in the hands of God. The Carmesi too. As soon as I joined in shouting defiance at its hated walls, I began to ride a high. My stomach in its hatefully familiar knot, my mouth almost too dry to shout, but I was still exalted, vindictive, too, once I found myself shouting at the Carmesi.

Some boys trundled up a handcart full of cobbles and we began to throw them. I knew this was a bad idea, although I enjoyed watching stones fly through the air and chip the Carmesi walls. The soldiers were becoming rattled, and though respectability demanded that they should not massacre civilians, soon they would open fire. Closer to the barracks a truck carrying watermelons had been stopped when the riot began and I tried to work my way through the crowd, hoping to suggest they drive it at the gate. But before I could reach close enough, the crowd tipped it over and set fire to the gas. Melons bounded in every direction, bursting on the cobbles and making the soldiers jeer as yelling people skidded on the mess. What with the flames and red watermelon, the space in front of the Carmesi began to look like carnage had already taken place. As laughter mingled with fury, the mood of the crowd poised in the balance. At any moment people would begin to drift away with nothing accomplished.

'Padre Sebastian!' I shouted again at the top of my voice, grabbing those nearest me to make them shout,

too. 'We mustn't stop! I just heard, they've mur␣
him!'

The cry was immediately taken up, putting fury␣
in control; perhaps because everyone had imagined ␣
the police might do to Father Sebastian, now t␣
believed they had seen his corpse thrown out through␣
gates. Packed humanity surged forward and a knot␣
men put their shoulders to the wheels of the burnii␣
truck to thrust it, bodily, toward the barracks gate. Th␣
soldiers inside wavered between derision and consterna␣
tion, then the bang of high velocity bullets slammed␣
across the din: one-two-three-four. Before the echoes␣
died, everyone was fighting to reach cover, and I found␣
myself among a dozen others crouched behind the␣
burning truck.

'Come on, another heave,' said a curly-haired man␣
beside me, and they put their shoulders to the wheels␣
again. Unfortunately, by then the truck was so well␣
alight, they were quickly driven back. We crouched,␣
panting in the heat, wondering what the hell to do next.␣
As quickly as my exhilaration had come, it ebbed,␣
leaving behind only helpless rage.

I must have been crazy to get mixed up in a riot, when␣
my purpose in Argentina was clear and very different.

Through shimmering heat I glimpsed the untroubled␣
façade of the Carmesi, flag blowing mockingly above␣
barred windows. No, not crazy, never crazy to attack␣
torturers in their lair; but now I had to get away before it␣
was too late.

The soldiers had stopped firing; in fact, I think they␣
had fired in the air since no one seemed to be hurt, which␣
just showed how respectable the *militares* wanted to be.␣
The space in front of the barracks was empty except for␣
the burning truck, a lot of squashed watermelons, and a␣
knot of us hoping to God the flames would leave enough

101

of the truck to give us some cover. Because if it didn't, respectability alone would never stop those soldiers from firing to kill the ringleaders of a riot.

The crowd hadn't gone far: they were in doorways, up trees, and down side turnings, still shouting, which was good. Better still if we had run with the rest.

Everyone behind the truck was male except for a black-clad peasant woman and myself; a tough, nervy, stubble-shinned bunch arguing among themselves. The woman and I exchanged looks, rueful acknowledgement that none of these macho guys would listen to us, even supposing we could think of anything useful to say.

And since human contact is one of the best defenses against fear, instinctively we crouched together as far from the heat as possible without breaking cover. Her name was Carmen and she worked in a bakery near the railroad station. I said I was American and had gotten mixed up in the riot by mistake, which she accepted with a shrug. *Estranjeros* and their foolishness were beyond her comprehension.

'Why are you here?' I asked, and ducked as another part of the truck crackled up in a spurt of flame.

'For the good padre. He helped my man to leave the barracks.'

'Your man? Your husband was a prisoner in the Carmesi?'

'No, señorita, God be praised. He served in the kitchen, which was almost as bad as prison for a man who desired only to do his work honestly, and provide for his family. I tell you, he came close to taking his own life before Padre Sebastian spoke with him and found him other work. For less money, of course, but work which allowed a Christian to hold up his head.'

'When? When was your husband there?'

She wiped sweat from her face; the flames were less

but the heat still frightful. 'Two summers ago it must have been.'

'How long in the kitchens before that?'

'Two, maybe three summers.'

'It was terrible you say?' I was praying now the truck wouldn't burn too fast. This was twenty-two-carat luck, and in our mutual peril, questions wouldn't seem intrusive.

'Señorita, I cannot tell you how terrible. Even in the kitchen my Rodrigo heard the screams. Saw brave men – and women too – dragged out and shot. Thank God, he used to say. Men were shot and he thanked God their sufferings were ended, that is how bad it was. Carmen, he would say, one day I hang myself because I cannot stand it, then you and the children will starve.'

When I was in the Carmesi I dimly imagined friends or family worrying about me, never a kitchen help on the floor below. 'Did others feel sick like Rodrigo?'

'If you work in the Carmesi, you don't talk about feeling sick. At first Rodrigo was just quiet.'

'And later?'

She rolled her eyes. 'Too sick to keep quiet with me. I don't know about no others, but he said they get . . .' She gestured, seeking words. 'Rougher, you now? Bad jokes, bad thoughts, bad laughs about bad things help them to keep from wanting to hang themselves. So in the end they began not to mind so much. Inside perhaps they still feel bad, but better not to show it, *hé*?'

'It took a man to show it, surely,' I said into the crackle from a burning truck. 'Did – did Rodrigo ever speak of babies born in the Carmesi?'

'I think the smoke may thicken enough to let us escape.' Carmen looked over her shoulder, the nearest tree some fifty paces distant. 'Babies? *María Madre!* I never heard even the pigs torture babies.'

'No. Babies born there after the mothers were arrested.'

She frowned, darting a sideways glance, beginning to wonder about my questions. '*Sí*, he say he find one, *pobrisimo*.'

'How . . . what happened?' Words as light and dry as ash.

'It was dead. What else when a newborn babe is thrown out for the dogs?'

She was staring at me openly now, but I didn't, couldn't, care. 'Some . . . Padre Sebastian told me one or two left the Carmesi alive.'

'I never heard, señora.' Automatically she changed señorita to señora as if she understood. 'There was a story once. God forgive me, I laughed at that one. *El Carnicero* desired a child after he wed a wife young enough to be his daughter, because all the world whispered he couldn't bed her like a man. Everyone waited to see what would happen, laughing up their sleeve, and poof! Nothing. How we mocked, but secretly, since all Matias Grande feared *El Carnicero*.'

El Carnicero. The butcher.

'What happened?' I grabbed her arm and shook it. 'What happened?'

But at that instant the crash and whine of a shot ricocheting off the smoldering truck made everyone sheltering behind it fling themselves flat. 'What happened?' I shouted, my mouth full of dirt. Instinct might make me grovel for cover, but shooting simply didn't matter until Carmen told me what she knew.

'Fellow citizens of Argentina!' a loud hailer rasped abruptly. 'This is Colonel Marqués speaking to you. You will not have heard the announcement of our national triumph, because of your foolishness in the streets. Today our country found its destiny! The Malvinas are ours! After stern fighting, at last our full heritage is gained. So, because this is a day of glory and not a time for us to be divided, I forgive your wickedness. Go and dance in the plaza with the rest of Matias Grande, and Padre Sebastian shall be released before sundown. You have my word of honor. *Viva Argentina! Viva las Islas Malvinas Argentinas!'*

'The Malvinas?' I said blankly.

One by one people were standing, coming out from behind the truck, from trees and buildings, staring at one another and at the helmeted officer standing, hailer in hand, beside the machine guns. Smoke continued to drift above the squashed melons; no one spoke, the turn of events too weird to grasp.

Then shutters crashed back against a wall across the square and a head poked out of an upstairs window. 'It's true! I heard the announcement on the radio! Our troops have landed and the Malvinas are ours! *Viva Argentina!'*

And in an instant everything was higher than flags on the Fourth of July. Men were weeping and kissing one another (which would be frowned on most Fourths of July), people cheering, laughing, snapping their fingers. As for me, all I wanted was to keep hold of Carmen in the crush. Whatever those Malvinas were which had probably saved our lives, they suited me only after I heard the end of Carmen's story.

'Carmen.' I plunged through the crowd after her. 'Carmen, wait!'

'It is all right, the padre will be freed,' she called back.

'I hope so! Yes, I expect he will.' I squeezed past soldiers who had come out to be feted by a crowd which had wanted to kill them only moments before. 'You have to finish telling me about El Carnicero.'

She flapped her fingers. 'That to El Carnicero! This is

victory day! Didn't you hear? Our men have taken the Malvinas.'

'That's good,' I said soothingly. Chilean, were they? Or British? Dimly, I remembered Roberto speaking about some islands Argentina wanted. 'Carmen, if you wish to dance in the plaza, all you have to do is tell me quickly what I want to know. Otherwise I swear I'll hold on your skirts for as long as it takes.'

She looked confused, a little frightened too. 'All I said was how El Carnicero swaggered everywhere like the brute he is, without being a man for his new pretty wife. How he was—' She hesitated, then used a word I'd never heard. 'Señora, I can't explain, but Rodrigo said everyone in the prison knew that only foulness with his victims pleased El Carnicero, not women any longer. And so they laughed when he wed this bride who was only twenty years old.'

'You thought of him because I mentioned a baby from the Carmesi.'

'*Sí!* El Carnicero was commandant, and governor of Matias Grande.'

'And?' I was shaking, physically shuddering with frustration.

'But, señora, that is all.'

'It isn't all. You began this story because of something about a child and El Carnicero. *Digame!*'

She looked relieved. 'If that is all. You see, in time the Señora Valdez had a child and the whole city was invited to celebrate, so the joke ended for a while. But some in the prison knew it was a sham and, of course, the rumor spread. The babe came from the torture chamber, not El Carnicero's loins, or so Rodrigo said.'

'Rodrigo could tell me, too?'

'That is all there is, I think.' Her work-twisted hands touched me tenderly. 'This matters to you?'

I nodded.

'It is not good for any child that it should be raised in the household of El Carnicero.'

Oh, God, I hadn't thought of that. My spirits, which had lifted dizzily on the hope that after all my child might have been raised away from the slums, slumped again as I imagined him corrupted by the Butcher of Carmesi Barracks. Out of the slums came brutes like Jaime but also women like Carmen; El Carnicero must be evil, unredeemed.

All around us blue and white flags were appearing, the crowd beginning to dance and sing, their mood surrealistically changed. At a stroke, *los militares* were heroes, the junta adored instead of hated; murder, misrule, and stinking jails forgotten. Those Malvinas were magic, all right, the easiest way out of a dead-end street you ever saw.

Carmen bent close. 'The little one was of your family? *Sí*, I see it in your face. Of course, that explains El Carnicero's choice. He is too proud to pretend a peon's brat was his. Go with God and find her then, before she believes a monster is her papa.'

'*Gracias*. Where is . . .' I began, then stopped. 'She? El Carnicero adopted a boy, surely. A macho hog like that, of course he would adopt a boy.'

She shook her head. 'No, señora. He has a true son, fully grown, of his first marriage. He wanted to prove himself still a man, not break an inheritance. He chose a girl.'

It fitted, as I'd realized it did from the moment Carmen said girl. The entry in San Bartolomeo's register, all those signatures and Father Damien's nasty little snigger in the margin. A girl, newborn in March 1979, could not possibly be mine.

I cannot write about my desolation. Before, I believed

107

I was hurting, but this was so much worse. Only minutes ago the thread I held led directly to a child who could, just possibly, be my son, though he lived in the house of El Carnicero. No more. Pedro was still lost.

'Okay,' I said numbly; in English, I was so disoriented. 'Enjoy yourself in the plaza.'

'Señora,' she hesitated. 'Any little one raised by El Carnicero needs help. That was a bad joke, too, we should not have laughed at it.'

I shrugged; Carmen was like that Communist in Buenos Aires, who couldn't see why I fussed after one particular child when the world was full of orphans. But blood counted even more now that I'd seen Pedro's name on paper, and anyway, the idea of meddling in El Carnicero's household was quite horrific.

By the time I reached the Plaza Mayor, it had become a crawling cheese of happy people. Goddamnit, all they'd done was take some rocks off Chile, or maybe Britain. Had Roberto said people lived there? I couldn't remember and doubted whether most of those around me knew much more; perhaps there were only fur seals who would welcome a common citizenship with their cousin, the patrona of my hotel.

So snap out of desolation, Sally Martin; there's this city to search for Pedro, *huérfano*.

Yet I felt oddly tired. The riot had not lasted long, two hours at most, but during it I had spun through a dynamo of emotion. Getting anywhere in such a crush was hallucinatory too: the entire population of Matias Grande seemed to be whirling past eyeball-high, slamming into me on their way. So I decided to go back to the Magnifico to rest for a while, and think out where to search during this most favorable of times, when the police celebrated along with everyone else, and hope that soon the crowds would tire.

The hotel door was open, the patrona vanished; alarming to think of her undulating bulk tangoing in the plaza. I lay on my bed surrounded by chipped green paint and listening to uproar, thinking: what next, where next? And for the first time felt an echo in my thoughts. There was something definite I ought to do. Before I had been floundering, now something I'd heard or seen or thought pointed in a new direction, if only I could remember what it was. Frustration niggled at me. Last night or today, among the dead ends and irrelevance, I had learned something that made no sense but stayed in my mind because . . . because . . .

When I woke, it was dusk. A strong pampa wind rattled the shutters and the noise in the plaza was louder than ever. Tapes belted out tangos, radios amplified patriotic speeches, cafés and cantinas spilled customers across the sidewalks, automobiles blipped their Klaxons. How I had slept through it all, I don't know, and . . . Even as I woke, recollection of that something I'd missed slithered from where I'd understood it in my sleep, and hid again out of reach.

I washed and changed, trying not to worry at it, but worrying all the same. Let it go. Get out there and start looking, and whatever it is will slip back again, unasked. I ran down the stairs to find the patrona snoring across her desk, which at least meant one less in the crowd. I had decided to visit the section where I remembered officers and the well-off living; whenever we stayed at the Estancia Santa Maria we used to visit a starchy aunt of Roberto's who lived in Matias Grande, and she reckoned only a single street had an address she recognized. I suspected this was harsh, but not too much so, the city having certainly seen more prosperous days. If Pedro had indeed been adopted by an officer, then this street or its close neighbors was most likely where he lived. Provided the officer wasn't in the Malvinas, or Buenos Aires, or wherever by now.

It was both a bad and a good time for questioning mamas and the *niñeras* they paid to watch their children. Normally, Argentine women, and particularly the country peasants often found looking after children, are reticent with people they don't know; that evening reticence went up in smoke. The difficulties were children howling at the hubbub and fragmenting conversation, the near impossibility of shouting more than banalities above the uproar. I guess not many islands give as much pleasure as those Malvinas, if the rest of Argentina was like Matias Grande.

Hours later the party was still going on and I had gotten nowhere, except negatively. I had questioned, as casually as I could, more than a dozen women minding boys whom I guessed as about three years old: none was called Pedro or possessed circumstances that sounded remotely right. In fact, Pedro seemed a distinctly plebeian name in the neighborhood, scraps called Augustino or Gabriele were much more common. One child I really thought looked like Roberto as he slept in his *niñera*'s arms, the corner of his mouth twitched upward like Roberto's when he used to sleep in mine.

I looked at him and thought, Yes. Oh, Christ, yes, it could be him.

And instantly was swept into such a tangle of emotion that I stood paralyzed. Surely I ought to *know*. And if I didn't, then he couldn't be mine. While I watched he yawned and snuggled deeper into sleep, and the likeness of Roberto vanished.

The *niñera* laughed when I steadied her next time the crowd eddied. '*Gracias*, señorita. Though the little one grows heavy, on such a night I do not wish to leave the streets.'

'I'm not surprised! I have never seen anything like it in my life before.'

'The señorita is not one of us? Americana? *Bueno!* We all dance together because today we won our Malvinas.' She twirled me around a fountain, the little boy nodding like a puppet on her shoulder.

'He'll fall!' Immediately I was anxious. 'Here, let me hold him.'

And hold him I did while Angelica linked arms and danced furiously on the sidewalk, his drowsy limpness feeling very unfamiliar in my arms.

'I am grateful, señorita.' She came back laughing with a soldier.

'What is his name?' I touched the sleeping child's face.

'Nando, señorita.' She giggled as the soldier squeezed her waist; on any other night she would have rejected open familiarities with scorn.

'Nando?'

'Ferdinando Alessandro, what a mouthful for a mite to live with! Here, I must take him home.' The soldier whispered in her ear and she hesitated, nose in the air but only pretending to refuse.

'I'll take him if you tell me where.' At this time of madness I was afraid she would lie with her soldier anyway, and forget the child.

'*Bueno*, take him,' said the soldier, and winked.

'You would?' said Angelica doubtfully.

'Where to?' I answered, and took back the sleeping child.

The soldier's hand was digging into the folds of Angelica's skirt, both of them hardly able to wait until they reached the shadows. 'Number twenty-four,' she shouted as they vanished into the crowd.

'Well, Nando,' I remarked. 'We'd just better hope she meant this street.'

He grunted drowsily, showing small pegs of teeth in a ferocious grin, so my heart melted with renewed conviction that he must be mine. I would have liked to walk off with him, then and there. I admit it. Temptation a peculiar, uncertain lightness that needed physically to be thrust away. To help control it, I decided quite coolly that he looked too young for three and half, which would mean he couldn't be Pedro under another name.

Number twenty-four was divided into apartments, and I hesitated, peering at the list of occupants. Nando was sufficiently heavy for me to shift him from my arms to across my shoulder; perhaps he might be three and a half after all. The names meant nothing to me, but the top apartment was occupied by Teniente Gomez. *Teniente*, or lieutenant. An officer, who, if he had been in Matias Grande three years before, must then have been very young. Compassionate perhaps.

I went up in the elevator and rang the bell.

'Who is there?' a frightened, disembodied voice from a grille above the door.

'Am I speaking to Señora Gomez?'

'Who is it?'

'My name is Martin. Have you a son called Nando?'

'Nando . . . My Ferdinando! What has happened?' The door crashed open and a girl leapt out to snatch the sleeping child from my arms and cover his face with kisses. Immediately he began to wail. 'Ah, I was so worried. That Angelica! I will kill her when she returns.'

'She certainly isn't to be trusted with a child.' I watched Nando's face become red with rage at being mauled: Roberto had occasionally thrown such dreadful rages, I hadn't known whether to be alarmed or cross. 'He's a charming child, señora. Tell me, how old is he?'

She thought, while my heart squeezed tight. 'Three years this very month.'

Disappointment filled my throat, as solid as unswallowed food. 'You must have been young when he was born.'

'*Sí*, I suppose so. Now I have two more *niños* and it seems a long time since I was young.' She gave a swift, unhappy smile. 'Señorita, how can I thank you for bringing Nando home?'

'I enjoyed his company. You're sure . . . Señora, I will be honest with you. I am collecting impressions for an American magazine about how women live in Argentina today. If you want to repay me, will you invite me in for a few minutes and tell me about yourself?'

She bit her lip, clearly torn between obligation and refusal. 'If you would be quick, señorita. You see, my husband is out with his friends but should soon be home. Me, I shall be very angry with Angelica tomorrow but I would not like . . . he will have celebrated well, you understand. It is better if he does not hear tonight how Angelica has misbehaved.'

'I will be quick, and wouldn't tell him anyway,' I promised.

'Then welcome, señorita. What is it you want to know?' She stepped aside to reveal a pleasant apartment, bulkily furnished. I sipped sherry while she fussed Nando into bed, and as I waited sneaked a look at some photographs on a table. Groups of suavely uniformed officers mostly, but one of three children: Nando in the middle looking smug, two babies at his side. There was sufficient likeness virtually to make it certain they were all one family.

Señora Gomez returned to the room. 'Forgive me, Señorita—?'

'Martin.'

'Ah, the same as our national hero, General San Martín! That is good. So, what can I tell you?'

I took her through a rigmarole about her life, slipping in questions which might help. She had been married at sixteen; yes, it had seemed glamorous at the time. Yes, her husband was older, *muy valoroso* . . . provincial appointments were hard on such a man. I gained the impression of a selfish, awkward-tempered bastard, soured by lack of promotion and very different from my imaginings about compassion.

But I had been fortunate to find an army family left to stew in Matias Grande longer than the usual two-year appointment. 'Was Nando born here?' My pencil poised; look casual, Sally.

'No, in Buenos Aires at my mother's house. He was my first and I was so happy to be home.' She sighed. 'How we pray soon to be sent back there ourselves.'

'So Nando is Porteño by birth?'

She brightened. 'I had not realized it, but that's nice, I think.'

I couldn't detect a crack of doubt; I liked Señora Gomez and found no reason to doubt she spoke the truth. Nando was hers.

Perhaps, then, it was time to risk a different kind of question. 'Since I have been in Matias Grande, I've heard stories about political prisoners kept at the Carmesi Barracks during the dirty war—'

'My husband had nothing to do with that.'

'Of course not, he's army, not police, isn't he? Army officers would never be concerned with things like that.' Wouldn't they, hell, I thought. In Buenos Aires the navy was rumored to provide the worst torturers, in Matias Grande Carmen had said El Carnicero was an army colonel. 'But since you've been here several years, I thought you might be able to help over a particular story I've heard, that's all.'

'What story?' She was on the edge of her chair. She

114

suspected her husband had enjoyed a part in the dirty war, all right.

'My editor likes the personal angle, and we always protect our sources. You needn't be afraid you'd be named. You see, I've been told several times that some babies were born in the Carmesi after their mothers were arrested. You're an army wife, and that's the kind of terrible thing women would take more notice of than men. I thought you'd know if it was true.'

'How could it be, when only criminals were taken to the Carmesi? It is just lies anyway, to call arresting terrorists a dirty war.'

'Would you expect women criminals to be put in the Carmesi?'

'Everyone there is criminal. How do I know if a few were women?'

'Other people in Matias Grande seem to think so, if they tell me that babies were born in there.'

'Who said so? What wicked person told a *norteamericana* this?'

'We protect our sources, remember? And though you may call them lies, I think you've heard them too.'

'No!'

'*Sí*. Your husband—'

'My husband wasn't concerned—'

'Hold your tongue, woman. What wasn't I concerned in?' A man in army uniform stood in the doorway: dark, butch, moderately drunk.

I recognized him, that was the trouble. The years rolled back, and I was crouched on the floor of a speeding car, boots in my back, and in the front seat this man, moderately drunk. The voice was the same; distinctive, off-key. The shark's nose and heavy jowl, deeply cleft; very painfully I remembered that Nando had a dimple in his chin that might grow into a cleft like that. One day would he, too, laugh while a woman knelt in terror?

I wasn't afraid, but blazingly angry then. The kind of foolhardy anger that seizes any chance to disconcert an enemy. 'I'm an American journalist and your wife was just assuring me – for the third time, I think – that you were not concerned in the dirty war.'

'God curse all journalists!' he said violently. 'How did you get in here?'

'We met when your son tried to run away in the crowd.' I could believe he might nearly kill Angelica if he learned about her folly with a soldier. 'Señora Gomez was kind enough to invite me in for a sherry and we were talking, generally, about women in Argentina.'

He grinned, clearly wanting to say something crude about women but not quite drunk enough to do so to an American reporter. '*Su casa,* señorita. Now that I am here, perhaps you would like to ask me, instead of her, about the dirty war, *hé*? Or does your journalism consist of interrogating wives behind their husbands' backs?'

'I would very much like to ask you questions. Perhaps you could suggest how many people might have died in the Carmesi for a start.'

'Señorita, you should not read communist leaflets. We disciplined those who needed discipline and sent them to repent.'

'Sent them to where? To hell?'

He sprawled in a chair. 'Ah, that would be telling. There are people who say the *desaparecidos* will be back. Ask them, not me.'

'I'm asking you. As I asked your wife whether women as well as men were imprisoned at the Carmesi.'

'If there were female guerrillas, why not prisoners?'

'No reason at all, if they were tried and sentenced fairly. Without torture.'

116

'Wine,' he said to his wife. 'Can't you see I'm thirsty? Sure, they were sentenced.'

'And shot.'

'Good riddance, too. If there is one thing worse than male guerrillas, it's their bitches.' He gulped about a half pint of wine. 'You're wasting your time, *periodista*. Everyone's happy with the army now that we've taken our Malvinas. There won't be any witch hunts.'

'Were you beginning to be afraid there might be?' I said softly.

His eyes, which had been glazing, flicked open and stared at me with surprising lucidity. 'Why did you come?'

'Just to research some background.' I was tense, watching his mind fumble toward a familiar answer. Violent killing had been his answer to any problem for so long, he'd ceased bothering about alternatives. And by then he guessed that probably no one knew I was here: a body found in the street after such a fiesta as tonight's was unlikely ever to be properly investigated. 'For instance, I was asking your wife whether any children were born in the Carmesi. My magazine likes human, perhaps occasionally inhuman, stories.'

Unexpectedly, he laughed. 'There was a good story once, but I don't think *norteamericanos* would appreciate it.'

'The one about El Carnicero and a child?'

He jerked his legs up, ready to stand. 'What do you know about El Carnicero?'

'Not much, but I can see you do. There were other children born in the Carmesi besides the one El Carnicero took, weren't there? Two boys at least, or so I'm told.' I didn't want to mention San Bartolomeo's register, in case Father Damien's telltale notations should be destroyed, or the sacristan arrested.

117

He shrugged, hands grasping the arms of his chair. He would be at me any moment, clumsy with drink perhaps but inflamed to kill. A nosy female *Yanqui* deserved it, he would think.

'Do you remember any others?' I repeated, trying to decide which way to jump.

'Guerrilla spawn weren't my affair.'

I believed him. He would no more think of taking a baby found in the trash than he would turn down promotion to Buenos Aires. Nando was his all right.

Poor Nando, who had lain so warmly in my arms.

'There was this good story about El Carnicero,' I said deliberately, after a pause. 'Why not see if you remember any others I haven't heard?'

And he began to tell me, just like that. Boastfully jeering instead of wary because he was drunk and becoming drunker, had made up his mind it was safer to kill me than wait for headlines in the *norteamericano* press that might persuade his superiors it was best to keep him more years away from Buenos Aires. He would enjoy killing me. Safe on this night when no one knew what was happening in Matias Grande, flesh under his boots a release he craved and perhaps found less often during recent policies of respectability.

The stories he told were bad enough to make a real reporter shiver, although few were new to me. I shivered all the same. 'The children,' I said, when the bottle was nearly empty and his voice slurred to a mumble. 'There was the one El Carnicero took; where did the others go?'

He waved strong-fingered torturer's hands. 'Out with the garbage; to an *asilo de huérfanos*; how should I know? I shit on guerrilla spawn.'

The room darkened, so I saw him through mist. 'You never heard of anyone – officer or enlisted man – who took one home?'

'*Concha de cotorra, no!* We all shat on guerrilla spawn.'

'Then God curse every one of you,' I said clearly.

The mist interfered with seeing him come. If he hadn't been so drunk, he would have killed me easily, and finished the task he didn't remember beginning three and a half years before. As it was, his clumsiness offered the fraction of a second in which to throw myself sideways out of my chair. I had spotted where an electric cable hung loose along the wall, leading from a wall plug to the single lamp, reached it with my fingertips and pulled. For a moment nothing happened. I gave another savage, despairing tug as I scrambled to my feet, not an instant to spare before Gomez came after me. The lamp rolled off its table and smashed, the wire gave me a hell of a shock, and all the lights in the apartment went out, a strong electric smell suggesting the current hadn't been properly fused.

I heard Gomez crunch lamp fragments where he thought I was, but by then I'd felt my way behind the chair where he'd been sprawled, dazed from the shock I'd received and scarcely daring to breathe.

He was straining to listen, too, though the wine he'd drunk made it difficult. '*Puta!* Whore!' he said violently. 'Come here, you bitch.'

My foot touched his empty wine bottle, which rolled, making the faintest of sounds on the rug. I recoiled, and sour breath filled my nostrils as Gomez went past so close, the cloth of his tunic grazed my breast.

With infinite care I bent and felt for that bottle; when I found it, the smooth thick neck fitted easily into my hand. I intended to kill him. I still didn't feel afraid, which was extraordinary after fear had for so long been part of me. But revenge works a cure all of its own. That is its strength and danger. Fleetingly I remembered

Roy's expression as he left me on the sidewalk in New York; he'd sensed then that revenge was part of what I wanted.

A twanging crash told me Gomez had knocked over a guitar I'd noticed in a corner. 'Take care,' I said, and laughed. 'It's your furniture that's getting smashed up this time.'

He swore and came feeling his way toward me, but before he reached close, I'd moved to where I hoped I would see him outlined against the shutters.

At once he outsmarted me. Kicked the windows wide and fumbled the shutter open, so reflections from the street reached into the room. But then it was very late and the municipal lighting of Matias Grande extremely poor, but sufficient to show when shadows moved. His head and shoulders bulked back against long French-style windows, the middle pair flung open. Those windows could solve most of the difficulties I was now, belatedly, considering. If I wanted to kill Gomez, then his death would have to look like an accident after he drunkenly attacked an interfering journalist; a fall from those windows the kind of accident police might possibly accept. But what would his wife say? Inevitably her evidence about my questions would help the stupidest investigating detective make a great many connections I couldn't afford to have him make. And most Argentine police aren't stupid. It was at this point that sanity reached down and seemed to peel away a curtain inside my head: I could not safely kill Gomez by making him fall from a fourth floor window, or any other way.

Pedro came first, not revenge, and the moment I realized it, my euphoric, single-minded lack of fear vanished. I wanted only to get out, but was terrified of making any move at all because the moment I did, Gomez would see me.

The silence was intense. Gomez stood quite still with his back to the window, I think trying to sober up sufficiently to tell one shadow from another. I had been crouched behind a chair but, tentatively, still on my knees, now I crept sideways to where a screen offered cover between me and the door. I reached it as Gomez belched, covering any small sound I made, and from there could see him silhouetted against the sky. He had pulled a gun but held it slackly, either aware that an accident would be easier to explain to the *Yanqui* consulate than an American with a bullet in her skull, or because he anyway preferred bare-handed killing.

The realization of how nearly there had been little difference between us jarred me from fear into self-disgust. He and I, torturer and victim, both contemptuous of the law, both wanting blood.

Gomez moved away slowly from the window, head probing from side to side. He went over and flicked the light switch. Nothing happened. 'Luisa?' he called to his wife.

'I am in the passage.' She sounded scared and I didn't wonder. In the time since the lights went out, her husband and I must have spilled enough hate into the atmosphere to set anyone's warning system jangling.

'Don't just stand there, fetch a lamp.'

'I tried, but everything is out.'

'A lamp, woman. My military flashlamp is under my cape in the bedroom.'

I heard her go and knew I had a minute at most to get out, my fright over moving counterbalanced by certainty of death if I stayed. It seemed unfair that just because I had decided against revenge, all my horrors should come hurtling back. But Pedro; what mattered was to remember Pedro.

Without giving myself the chance to think about it, I

121

stood up under cover of the screen and flung the bottle I'd picked up through the window. There was a quite appalling crash, and instinctively Gomez whipped round, though he must have known I couldn't have reached behind him. By then I was out of that room faster than current through a laser, only to run into Señora Gomez returning, a powerful beam of light between me and the door to the apartment. Behind, Gomez was yelling at her to stop me, a splitting noise as he kicked something out of his way.

The beam went out.

The passage completely blanket-dark while Señora Gomez screeched like she was being murdered. Screeches contradicted by her hand on my arm, guiding me to where the door stood open, her hand thrusting me out, slamming the door behind me. A shot splintered the panel behind my back, which helped her scream louder, while Gomez raved at her to stop making such a shitting fuss and get out of his way.

By then I was sprinting down the stairs, shouting. '*Ladrón!* Thief!' when someone tried to stop me. He was so astonished by a woman, he not only let go but gave chase beside me, panting imprecations about thieves. Perhaps thirty seconds after Señora Gomez thrust me out of her door I was three levels down, and on the sidewalk. Late revelers still milled around and I plunged among them, to be almost instantly jostled out of sight.

Señora Gomez, may your son Nando inherit your mercy and nothing from his father.

8

The hour was late and the streets had become unpleasant as drunkenness took over from celebration. I stayed as inconspicuous as I could and hurried to the Magnifico, very glad when I glimpsed its light still on outside. The patrona herself came shuffling to answer my ring. 'Even *norteamericanos* should know better than to stay on the streets so late, unless they seek wickedness in doorways,' she said without preamble. 'And so I told the señor.'

'What señor?' It was too much. I couldn't cope with any more tonight, had been certain Gomez would fall into a stupor the moment I left and wake confused in the morning.

She cackled. 'The señor who waits for you. If you belonged to my family, I said, he could charm how he liked and still wait outside until morning. But a hotel is a hotel, and who am I to stop a man from hiring my best back bedroom?'

By then I had stopped listening, because Roy was standing just behind her. Roy. 'For God's sake, how did you find me here?'

'I asked,' he answered cagily, so I could see he had been cursing himself all the way from Boston to Matias Grande for being insane enough to come.

'Asked who?'

'Does it matter? You mentioned *desaparecidos* at Keg Bay, which suggested the Argentine to me, and you signed in at our Embassy in Buenos Aires.'

'So I did. What made you decide Matias Grande came next?'

'I didn't ask the police, if that's what you're afraid of. Your mother-in-law said you might come here.'

'*My mother-in-law?* How could you know I'd married here?'

'Since the Freedom of Information Act, you need to know only which questions to ask. You filed your nationality on marriage, and lucky you did, from what your father told me.'

'You've been to Montana?' I said dazedly.

'Telephoned.'

'And he told you my life story, just like that? How dare he! How dare you come prying after me, when all I want is to be left alone?'

'Yeah?' he said, unlawyerlike. 'Sally, stop looking fit to bust and come up where we can talk away from flapping ears.'

'The patrona doesn't speak English.'

'I don't speak Spanish, come to that, but grabbed a fair notion of what she said when you came in just now.' He watched me color up: I always blushed too easily. 'I've been given a great room: green paint and a brass bed.'

Involuntarily, I laughed. 'So have I, except I'm farther from the smells. She tried me on the first floor back, but I wasn't having that.'

After which it seemed childish to refuse to go up with him; after all, he had come a long way to sleep in a brass bed in Matias Grande. Unasked, the patrona brought beef sandwiches so she could size things up: Roy hadn't wasted his time waiting, with or without the Spanish language. She thoroughly approved of him.

'Don't you think she's just like a seal?' I asked when she flippered out at last.

'Sure, the sort with whiskers. God, look at the size of those sandwiches.' He unstrapped a valise and dug inside. 'Bourbon?'

I nodded. Because of the way my life had run, I'd never drunk spirits, but today surely seemed like a good time to start. 'Roy—'

'Wait. Steam off while you drink and see how things look then.'

'I shall still be angry.' The bourbon went down so I scarcely noticed it, which shows how taut I felt.

He sat on the edge of the bed, springs rustily creaking, rolling his glass pensively between his fingers. He was wearing casual clothes but looked Boston professional to the backbone. Sharp, rich, and arrogant.

'What do you think this is anyway, a movie?' I said edgily when he didn't answer.

'It would make a script.'

'A farce, now that you've come meddling. Have you any idea what a fool you make me feel, galloping like the cavalry to the rescue? A fool or a freak, I don't know which, and all I want is for you to get the hell out.' I was pretty wound up after Gomez and a riot.

'Why?'

'Why? How would you feel if you lost a pushover case all the way to the Supreme Court and I came shimmying in, saying, never mind, I'll fix it. And if I can't, then how about forgetting everything in bed?'

He grinned faintly. 'Now, that might help.'

'Well, you can't help down here any more than I could in court. Goddamnit, you don't even speak Spanish, or understand what I'm after. I nearly killed a man tonight, and wanted to very much.'

His eyes lifted from his glass, intent, the mix of blue and green stranger than I remembered. 'But you didn't. Why not?'

125

'Because . . . oh no you don't. I haven't forgotten how you worm out secrets given half a chance. Go back to the States and leave me alone.'

'I'm on a trip to South America at the moment, after no proper vacation in a raft of years. Eighteen days before I'm expected back.'

'Look,' I said reasonably, or so I thought. 'You're a danger to me here. I've some facts to check, places to go, people to see. If you follow me everywhere, I can't do any of them without attracting attention.'

'That's bullshit. You're safer as soon as the authorities see you aren't alone, as you would realize if you were thinking straight. You wanted to kill a man tonight, you said. How long before anyone would know you were missing, if he'd killed you instead?'

'Months, I suppose. I'm thinking straight all right. Because it wouldn't matter if I disappeared, none of it matters if I can't find . . . if what I'm looking for doesn't exist. Or if it exists and I can't find it.'

'It matters, if only because the wrong side won.'

I was surprised. I hadn't expected clinical judgement after he came so far to find me, and liked him better for it. 'Roy, I'm being unfair to you, but I can't help it. I guess you came down here—' I stumbled. 'You wouldn't have come unless—'

'Unless I loved you? I guess I wouldn't.' Nothing in his voice, eyes on his glass again. Tigers are humiliated, too, when they're made to jump through hoops.

'But why? I mean, how could you . . . I'm damn sure I wasn't lovable in Keg Bay. Or now, for that matter.'

'I happen to like courageous people.'

'But I'm not! I ran like hell for three years before I managed to stick a while in Keg Bay. Here, I've been terrified all the time.'

'Which might be part of what I mean. So far as you're

126

concerned, I'm not into the business of analysis.'

'Then – then, of course, I owe you some explanations.'
Bourbon on top of exhaustion made me drowsy. 'Roy, I
don't know how you felt after that night in Keg Bay—'

'Ashamed. I made one hell of a mistake thinking the
time had come to gamble. I guess I hoped to cut through
something I couldn't get you to explain. And then, next
time, we'd get better than good.'

'But you did! Though I – I hated you for – I mean I
didn't think we'd be better than good next time. I'm still
sure we wouldn't. But as soon as I straightened out even
a little, and I did in Keg Bay, I began to think I'd get
over the rest as well. Now I know I'll never get over . . .'
I felt tears on my face and that didn't matter either,
because he wouldn't risk comfort now. 'I'm making such
a mess of this. I don't want to explain, you see. You
wouldn't like it if I did. You must have worked out some
of what happened, and may think you wouldn't mind,
but—'

'Jesus, I'd mind!' he said flatly.

'No, not like that. You think you'd be angry whatever
I told you happened to me here, but you wouldn't be.
You'd be disgusted. You'd never look at me without
imagining . . . I'd never want you without remembering . . . things. After that night in Keg Bay this was the
truth I had to face, and now you have to face it too: some
injuries don't heal. Some of mine won't. That's all.'

There was a long, long silence.

'Thank you,' he said, drier than the driest legal dust.
'Now suppose you tell me some other truths you faced,
which I figure sent you racing here.'

'No.'

'Look, Sally. I accept your right to keep private what
you wish, when just thinking about them flays you raw.
What you're doing here is different. You could use some

help, and I'm a tricky bastard with witnesses who refuse to plead.'

'Okay, you win, as usual, I dare say.' I felt so unutterably dreary now that he understood our relationship had to stay impersonal, that further fighting hardly seemed worthwhile. I told him quickly and baldly about the child, how I didn't know whether it was alive or not. Strictly facts only: I went to prison, I had a child and believed it died. Until, once I began to live again (after you started coming most weekends to Keg Bay, and we slept one awful night together, although that I didn't say), I dared at last to look those same facts squarely in the face and discovered I wasn't sure enough. So I came back here, period.

He listened without showing surprise or any other emotion beyond meditative interest. Some kinds of training help, when it comes to wearing masks.

His detachment certainly helped me, and my own tiredness which numbed emotion, so by the time I finished a rundown on my antics since arriving in Argentina, most of my hangups were tidied out of sight again. 'I think unless Gomez trips over me in the street, he'll decide to nurse his head and hope I didn't learn anything a *Yanqui* editor would think worth publishing. If he should happen to remember how he bragged some nasty stories to me, there are now two of us instead of one and he'll probably leave bad alone,' I finished optimistically, feeling full of ginger again once the telling was all over. Or the part I intended to tell was over.

'I told you I'd be useful.' He sounded abstracted. 'Jesus, you've stirred things up in a short time, haven't you? You're not sure if the police might want to question you about Father Sebastian, or the fracas when you flew into Buenos Aires. You could have been spotted among the leaders of a riot. This guy Gomez may still think it's easier to kill you.'

'Have some more bourbon. Because all I'm really bothered about is looking for Pedro.'

'Meaning, to hell with the police and Gomez.'

'Well, once I start worrying about what I stir up, I shan't have time for anything else.'

His expression softened and, unfortunately, this time I knew what he was thinking. What I really couldn't afford to worry about was seeing the inside of the Carmesi again. Once I began to think about being arrested, I wouldn't be able to stop. Then I'd get the shakes again, and last time it took three years of running before they left me.

'Yeah, maybe, but if you want to go on looking for this Pedro, you have to get out of here. You're lucky everyone beat the drum over invading the Falkland Islands when they did, and tomorrow may be okay while they sleep it off, but after that—' He shook his head. 'The risk of meeting Gomez, or the police picking you up for questioning, is too great. You have to get out of Matias Grande.'

'I told you, I can't worry about them. I have to check out Pedro first.' Falklands, I remembered. Yes, that was the other name for the Malvinas, which meant they must have been British rather than Chilean.

'If I remember right, you said his date is wrong. And haphazard looking is always a waste of time.'

'You think since I've been here I've just skittered around like a singed prairie dog, don't you?'

He stood up, smiling. 'That's my Montana girl. As it happens, no, I don't.'

'Pedro exists, and could quite easily fit. He's the only one who could, and if in the end he doesn't, then I just have to start again. I'm not going back to the States until I'm completely sure.'

The muscles of his face tightened; he was too intelligent not to guess there was evidence I hadn't told him. Jaime. If I couldn't find Pedro, or if he didn't fit, then I was going to have to seek out Jaime. And that was one encounter I'd make sure Royston Leavis didn't gate-crash.

But apparently he decided that further questions then would only make matters worse, and soon afterward I stumbled upstairs to bed, beat.

'Sleep well.' He came to my door but stayed a pace clear, not touching, all the way.

'I'm asleep already. Roy—' I longed for a little softness.

'Yeah,' he said very cold and deadly. 'Would you be wondering whether you might want it both ways after all? But like you said, the world is wrong, and I can't change it. So you go have your sleep, because I sure as hell don't bet twice against the table.'

I did not reply. I knew how alone he felt.

This was the heart of our problem; I knew, because I felt the same.

9

We met again at breakfast, though I'd hoped to eat and go out before Roy woke. However, I slept rather too well and, regretting the beef sandwich I'd left untouched the night before, when I went to look for food I found him pensively drinking coffee at an oilcloth-covered table in what passed for a dining room.

'The coffee's okay.' He avoided my eyes, both of us embarrassed by what had been said, and not said, the night before.

'I shall want something more than coffee.'

'And less than a T-bone steak?'

We laughed uneasily and greeted the patrona with relief. For anyone so large, she moved with remarkable speed when driven by lustful speculation. She also understood ravenous appetites.

'Naturally the señorita is hungry after a night she has enjoyed. I remember fancying fresh-killed sheep every morning for a year when I was young; my Alfredo was a man to wear out any woman who didn't take care of herself. And we lived in Patagonia, where there are too many sheep. You'd better warn your señor he'll need more than bread on his plate if he's to please a healthy señorita like you for long.' She went out again, snickering.

I shot a look at Roy and chuckled.

'What's the joke?'

'Lucky you don't grab Spanish as easily as you

thought. I think the patrona may be about to revive your strength with a fresh-killed sheep.'

The atmosphere eased a little and loosened further with the collection of dishes shuttled out from the kitchen. 'Pretty weird,' commented Roy, about chorizos, beef, *dulce de leche*, onions, and maté arriving in succession.

'Usually breakfast is the one meal without beef. I'm hungry, though.' I couldn't remember when I had last eaten.

'Have you decided where to go first this morning?' he inquired after waiting for me to demolish most of a plateful. 'There's a potato you missed under the onions.'

'I hoarded it to go with the chorizos.' Keep loose, and we'll be okay. 'I'm going to visit the Sisters of Mercy at San Bartolomeo again. Looking back, I can't remember quite why I was so sure Pedro must have been adopted, and probably by an officer, except it seemed to fit the circumstances best. But Gomez was quite clear last night; only El Carnicero adopted one of the children, a girl, and he's so foul, everyone simply laughed at the joke.' Without warning, disgust choked me. Anyone who laughs at such a joke is fouled as well. I put down my fork, breathed carefully, and added, 'I have to go next where I should have started, to the *asilo de huérfanos*.'

'How would it be if I went to the – how do you say City Hall in Spanish?' He was sharp-eyed; also sharp-witted enough this morning to avoid emotion.

'*Ayuntamiento*.'

'How would it be if I went there, then, and asked the question? Said I was acting for a client in the States and showed my card. Without official help you'd be lucky to turn up anything if you stayed a year.'

'No!' I said in alarm. 'I came as near authority as I

132

dare when I approached the church, and even that is risky. Argentine police can be very efficient. At the moment, in Matias Grande they're not worried. Even though Gomez may tell about a nosy female American, perhaps a journalist, who he suspects of liberal sympathies. That's not much when they need U.S. dollars, especially while everyone is feeling happy. Once you start asking about a particular child, there's a lot of ends they could pull together in a hurry if they wanted. For instance, I don't know what Father Sebastian may have been forced to say; they could arrest him again as well as me. And all for nothing. Officials never admit anything. *Desaparecidos* don't exist, the Carmesi is just a barracks, and if you think differently, then you must have been listening to Communists or guerrillas. That law firm of yours would run pretty scared, I guess, if one of their partners was deported for mixing with left wing terrorists.'

He didn't answer, but neither did he mention visiting officials again, and we went together to San Bartolomeo. The plaza was emptier than on a normal day, most of Matias Grande suffering from a collective hangover after the night before; in spite of my sleep and gluttonous breakfast, it was still early, the sunlight thin and chilly. April had come, the beginning of winter in the south.

The newsstands were stacked with inch-thick headlines, few passersby gathered there to enjoy their triumph once again.

Roy bought a *Prensa* and was hammered on the back just for being American. 'Now we have beaten the British, too, like you in your revolution. The century of the Americas, *hé*?'

'Sure,' said Roy, who disliked being jostled. 'The British had people over there, did they?'

'We'll be good to them, give them everything muc}

133

better than before! *Viva las Malvinas Argentinas!*'

There were pictures on the front of the paper of some furious-looking British marines held under guard and shiploads of grinning Argentines pouring on to a dock. 'U.S. marines wouldn't care much for that, and I guess the British won't either,' Roy observed, fingering the paper thoughtfully.

'They will get over it because there is nothing they can do,' another bystander answered in English. 'Señor, England is thirteen thousand kilometers away and we have the islands. They are realists with many business interests here; soon we shall be friends again.'

There were British families in Matias Grande I knew, but no evidence that anyone had vented Argentine patriotism on them; yesterday's sunny humor prevailed everywhere in the city still. Only Roy kept looking at those pictures as if he were hesitating over selling bonds.

The hospice of the Sisters of Mercy was harder to get into from outside than the way I had used before, through the cloisters of San Bartolomeo. Only after a great deal of tugging at an iron bell was there the sound of felt-covered feet and solid bolts being drawn. A wooden panel slid back to reveal a pair of cautious eyes. 'Señorita?'

'I ask pardon, Sister, but I stayed here two nights ago and was offered further help if I should need it.'

'What is your desire?' Her eyes swiveled to Roy.

'A question I forgot to ask while I sheltered here. If you called Sister Felicia, I think she could answer it.'

The door swung open to reveal a meek-faced porteress. 'If you will enter, señorita. The señor must stay outside.'

As I knew, the sisters were far from cloistered in the ards, where they tended castouts, drunkards, and the

134

insane, male and female alike. This made no difference to the principle: fit men stayed outside.

Sister Felicia was unable to leave a dying child, so I went into the ward to find her. '*Asilos de huérfanos?* There are two where we send children,' she said in answer to my question.

'Where are they?'

She considered, her hands continuing to sponge a tiny boy with pus-filled eyes and a swollen face. This one, too, could be mine. 'There is our sister house in the Calle Santiago. Also another out in the country, I am not sure where, but the children are taught to be industrious. A state home, you understand, where nowadays soldiers drill ten-year-olds, which I find a great impiety. Sisters from the Convent of Our Lady look after the infants.'

'Then where is the Convent of Our Lady? The home must be nearby.'

'In the campo, near Dos Bichos.'

Dos Bichos? A town less than a dozen miles from the Estancia Santa Maria, of course I remembered the government training school. I had even looked at its peeling walls and dusty ungrassed square and thought flippantly: I bet they don't learn much there. Everyone thinks things they regret, and since I settled into life at the estancia as Roberto's wife I did resolve to call one day at the foundling training school to see if I could help. But I never did. We went to Buenos Aires on visits, back to Montana and New York, galloped the pampa together, and within a year Roberto was dead. Facts, not excuses. But yes, now I learned that Pedro might be inside those walls, I needed some excuses.

'Would a child of only three . . . three and a half be sent there?'

'A boy might be, particularly if he promised to be strong and healthy.'

I hope I thanked her and gave alms for the hospice, but I'm not sure. *Mea culpa*. I'm not Catholic, but the phrase bobbed out of my Esquilar past and struck where it hurt.

Inevitably, Roy disagreed with most of the conclusions I'd jumped to. 'You haven't any more evidence than you had before. From what you say, a young child is less likely to be placed out on the pampa than in the convent orphanage here.'

'Pedro will be at Dos Bichos,' I answered. It had the authentic feel of fate; the next step on a pilgrimage, which would not let me avoid the Estancia Santa Maria. My child confined to the place I had meant, but failed, to visit.

But when we went to rent an automobile, the Calle Santiago was around the corner from the Hertz depot, so we went first to the convent there before driving to Dos Bichos.

This proved to be a pleasant place, filled with unbelievably well-behaved children who crowded around me with the starved curiosity of those whose lives contain little variety. The reverend mother was shrewd, a little hard perhaps, but several children of *desaparecidos* had passed through her hands and she made no difficulty about checking the records: one boy had been admitted in February 1978, marked *huer:d:Cm* by a priest from San Bartolomeo.

I expected nothing more, but disappointment fastened a small hard claw into my heart. 'Thank you, Reverend Mother. I saw this boy's entry in the church's register, too, but the date is too early for the one I seek.'

She inclined her head. 'I regret it if that is so, but you may like to know that this one is well and promises intelligence, although he isn't spiritual, I fear.' She squeezed a small wintry smile.

In a dream I gave her half my remaining dollars to be kept for him, a gift for when he must go out alone into the world. A child of the Carmesi, but not mine.

Roy started the engine as soon as he saw me returning, the look on my face enough to tell him this search had failed, and neither of us spoke until he needed to ask for directions to reach the Dos Bichos road.

How well I knew that road! A hundred and fifty kilometers of shredding tarmac, scuffled over by blowing dust. Black cattle crowded round the wind pumps, the grass yellow after the summer. A wide sky lacking color, the occasional stream lost between banks of willow and reed, a sideways wind beating at our Japanese auto-mobile. Occasionally we passed grandiose gateposts which marked the estancias of people I once had known. None of them raised a finger when Roberto disappeared. Would I, if one of them had vanished?

Roy drove almost without speaking, and after about an hour a pattern of undulations, streams, and tracks I would have known among a million others began to appear on either side. Over there Roberto and I drew rein after a race, here we had a blowout and skidded into the ditch. In that straggle of brush we made love, laughing at our slippery wet bodies, when caught by a storm that flooded the stream we needed to ford.

'Dos Bichos.' Roy slowed to a dawdle as corrugated roofs lifted over the horizon.

'This side of town, turn right and you'll see the building straight ahead.'

'Have you thought what you're going to say?'

'That's the difficulty, isn't it? This is a state home where a military training unit drills the older boys. It'll be risky to take chances.'

'You can't take any chances at all. I guess even

137

unsympathetic nuns hesitate to lay evidence with the police, but a state official more likely will than not. To keep his nose clean, in hope of promotion, to sweeten bureaucracy. He doesn't have to be hostile.'

I scarcely heard him, as Dos Bichos opened out in front of us. I remembered it as an easy-paced gray town, apart from painted tin roofs. Today Argentine flags snapped at every corner and the streets were full; celebration reached the campo a day later than it did the cities. We turned down a track and stopped beside a tall blank wall.

'Well?' Roy slewed to face me for the first time since we left Matias Grande.

I stared back; the feeling I had for him without a name. Things happen sometimes before you can give them a name. Unsafe things, like wanting and not wanting a man like Roy.

'Have you any ideas?' I asked, and looked away.

'Only one. If you can't afford to be checked out, then you have to pay for information. Out here, fifty dollars would make a hell of a lot of pesos.'

I thought for a moment. 'It wouldn't work. If we bribe someone and they produce a child, how could I know he was Pedro?'

'How will you know anyway?'

'I shan't, unless whoever we see really wants to be helpful, looks up the records, and says, "*Sí,* that is Pedro over there." So I haven't any choice. I take a risk and ask.'

We batted it back and forth, both of us growing exasperated for different reasons, but without coming up with any different answer until Roy looked in the mirror, and tensed. 'Don't turn, but there are some soldiers coming up behind us.'

'We aren't doing anything wrong.'

138

He grunted derisively. 'I guess you can answer that one better than me.'

I could, of course. We didn't have to be doing anything wrong if a patrol happened to dislike us.

There were five of them in khaki fatigues; their corporal gave a routine double thump on the roof of our automobile as he passed, then stared over his shoulder through the windshield and came back. Thrust his head through my open window. 'What are you doing here?'

'*Nada*,' Roy answered shortly; four days after he landed in Buenos Aires, his Spanish had grown enough to guess at questions like that.

'How nothing? You are here, aren't you? So you are doing something.' He unslung his gun while his patrol leaned wide-eyed on the hood: mere boys, lost in their uniforms, almost certainly from the training school.

I smiled at stubble inches from my face. 'We want to visit your excellent training home for children, but feared it might be siesta time. And so we waited out of the way.'

'The training school? It is military. You can't go there.'

'Why not?'

'Because you can't!' He withdrew his head and thumped on the roof again, this time with his gun. '*Es militar!*'

'It can't all be military; the nuns told us they look after the infants. Perhaps you'd better take us to your officer.'

'No officer!' He turned on the boys. 'Stand straight, you clumsy slobs.'

Roy was beginning to simmer, but it was no good blasting off at a man of this type: poorly trained and educated yet in charge of others greener than himself, enjoying his power over them and us. The first thing a military government does is ruin its army; certainly the officers would be enjoying themselves while underlings carried out patrols.

'Then you are the man we want, sergeant,' I said conciliatorily. 'You could send to find out if the principal had finished his siesta, couldn't you?'

'*Es militar!*' Thump on the roof.

Roy leaned across, billfold in hand. 'Tell the swine to come round this side.'

He went across like a shot, pesos palmed instantly out of sight although his scowl hardly shifted. 'If the señor will follow to the gate, I will pass you through.'

'Now, why the hell should an orphanage have a guard on the gates?' Roy looked at uniformed boys slouching at the entry, their guns bigger than themselves.

'In a military state there are guards on the oddest places. Water company, fertilizer works, you name it. If there's a training squad for the older boys, they'd put a guard on the gate.' I gripped my fingers hard together until they hurt. Uniforms frightened me very easily, even when they had kids inside them.

Roy's hand fastened over mine, the first time he'd touched me since Keg Bay. 'No risks. Leave this to me, and I'll try to make money do the work.'

Wrought iron gates gave on to a grit square surrounded by buildings, where an old man dozed on some steps.

He blinked at us sleepily when we pulled up beside him. 'Señor?'

'*El Señor Director?*' Roy demanded, but intentionally or not, the peon refused to understand, so I had to intervene, although he would more easily refuse a woman.

Once the curse of Babel was sorted out, we discovered the director was indeed enjoying his siesta, and it was more than a peon's life was worth to disturb him. 'That's not bad news,' observed Roy. 'Tell him we'll stroll around while we wait.'

'No, no, no!' shouted the porter. *'Es prohibato!'*

'Soy American, no es prohibato,' Roy answered blandly, pulling my hand under his arm. 'Tell him his director will be pleased we have come all this way to see how well the Argentine government treats the children in its care.'

I told him, and he tore at his hat, trying to convince us otherwise.

By then we had reached up the steps to a bleak, unfurnished hall that led in turn to a refectory filled with grimy tables and benches. Several doors opened out of this, some clearly leading to corridors and classrooms. Roy made straight for an archway, beyond which we could see more dusty yards and buildings.

The porter hesitated, then ran off down one of the corridors, boots flapping.

'Okay, so let's make sure we see as much as we can before he turns out some help.' I could see Roy was beginning to enjoy himself, probably for the first time since he reached Argentina.

The whole place seemed empty as we put our heads around a succession of doors, discovering sacks of stores, slatted washboards in a laundry, some workshops equipped with little more than mallets. 'Perhaps the children are having siesta, too,' I suggested.

This seemed to be the case, because the next door opened into a dormitory. Perhaps forty beds sprawling with children, very little room to move between them. A few looked up disinterestedly, the rest were asleep: unventilated fustiness flowed out through the door. Nothing was dirty or neglected precisely, but neither was anything clean or well repaired. The children looked reasonably fed, but institutional apathy lay in stagnant pools, sticky to the touch.

We shut the door and went on again, up some stairs,

141

through a chapel, and down into a second courtyard. Beyond it rows of beans and squash and corn stretched into the distance. 'I did them an injustice,' I said, surprised. 'I remember thinking, oh, a long time ago, that children wouldn't learn much of use out here. Those crops are good.'

'They sure look better than the workshops,' Roy agreed. 'Which probably means someone is making money out of them, and I don't mean the state. It's an old trick and a good one.'

Around us the buildings were beginning to come alive. A bell jangled, a line of boys filed into the wind, carrying hoes. Others went up to the classrooms; there must be two hundred children here, but none we saw looked younger than five or six.

'Can I help, señor?' A white-haired man carrying some books stopped politely.

Roy went through his American act and I added that we were waiting for the Señor Director. 'You have a fine place here, so industrious,' I added mendaciously.

'You think so?' the old man said doubtfully. 'I, too, like to see children industrious, but my love is to feed their minds. Only one lesson a week for all the great writers of Spain and Hispanic America! But everyone tells me I am an enthusiast and they would not appreciate a longer time.'

'There are infants here as well, I believe?' Difficult now to keep my voice steady. Pedro; if he wasn't here, then I didn't know where next to look.

He waved his hand across the courtyard. '*Los pobrecitos, sí*. My heart sorrows for them.'

My breath seemed to stop. 'Why?'

'Señor, would you like your child to grow up knowing only a place such as this?'

'No,' I said somehow. 'No, I wouldn't.'

142

A thin shout from behind us heralded a squad of boys clutching guns and shooed on by the porter.

'Christ,' said Roy. 'They don't give kids bullets as well, do they?'

The white-haired teacher said something I didn't catch; it is pretty terrifying and also tragically sad to find yourself on the wrong end of guns held by school children. They enjoyed it of course; the oldest, who might have been twelve, already strutting like a bully and screaming abuse as he skidded to a halt. 'Hands up!' he yelled. 'Hands up, offspring of fucked whores!'

And jabbed the muzzle of his gun, hard, into Roy's ribs.

I heard him grunt, the teacher and myself cry out. Then Roy took hold of the barrel just above the trigger and jerked it so the boy sprawled on his knees, reflex sending half a dozen bullets over our heads. For a moment we all stood petrified, Roy and I instinctively turning to see if the other was alive. His hand still thrusting the boy's arm at the sky, all those other guns with ten-year-old fingers on the triggers pointing at us.

'Boys, remember what Cervantes said: *"Paciencia y barajar,"'* the teacher exclaimed. 'Great minds never lie, and patience is indeed the highest of virtues. Miguel, if you would aim a little farther to the left, and you, Jesus-Maria to the right . . . ah, that is better.'

I let out breath in a long, slow sigh, which seemed to have been held forever.

'We were sent here,' the twelve-year-old said indignantly.

'But not, I trust, to behave discourteously toward guests?'

An understatement, I considered.

'We have orders to take them back to the gate and throw them out.' The boy tried to tug his gun out of Roy's grip.

Roy simply chopped at his fingers and held it up out of reach. 'No,' he said sharply. 'And if you weren't a kid, I'd shove it back where it hurts.'

I didn't translate, but it wasn't necessary. The boys all understood that their leader had been humiliated. So did he, that was the danger.

'I'm sorry,' Roy added to me. 'He riled me up, and I didn't really believe they'd give kids live ammunition.'

'Señor, I think I had better accompany you to the principal, if that is where you wish to go. I should not care to leave these little ones to take you, not now. Señor Beruete, at your service.' The teacher flickered a smile. 'I am right, am I not, when I say they would indeed benefit from the influence of great minds more than once a week?'

I began to laugh, found it difficult to stop. 'I wonder if *Lord of the Flies* is translated into Spanish.'

We were a strange party trudging to see the principal, Roy and I uncomfortably conscious of half a dozen schoolboys kept from shooting us only by Beruete's gentle presence. As for him, from the moment I mentioned it, his main interest became to discover more about the unknown great mind who had written *Lord of the Flies*, and why, in this situation, a particular book should have occurred to me. Actually, I couldn't remember too many details, but surely made the moral come over with a punch.

'You're good at keeping cool the worse things get,' Roy said, and smiled.

'I don't feel in the least cool, in fact—'

'I know, which is another answer to the question you asked last night. I'm not giving you up easily, you know.'

You have to give me up, I wanted to say and couldn't. This isn't real. Here we are, walking across a courtyard a hundred kilometers out in the pampa while searching for a child, and all we can talk about is *Lord of the Flies* and love. 'It's all so crazy I just can't worry. Sure, I'm scared, terrified, if I'm honest, but the moment fright is over, I forget it. This one thing I have to do . . . afterward it may be different.'

'What exactly does this Lord Fly say about his boys on an island?' demanded Señor Beruete inexorably, beside us.

I answered somehow, thoughts about Roy and Pedro and guns and police whirling like charred paper in a draft, hypnotically distracting until I beat them out of sight. Pedro. I must stay fixed to the job in hand. As Beruete said, I should not like a son of mine to grow up here.

We came off bare boards and, at the top of some stairs, on to red tiles spread with rugs. 'You stay on guard, boys, while I take our guests to El Señor Administrator,' said Beruete.

'I'm a soldier under orders, not a boy, and we come, too.' The twelve-year-old shoved rudely past.

We trailed along a pleasant passage, past polished furniture and prints on the walls. 'I said someone was making money,' observed Roy.

Our boy-guards froze, blank-faced, as we filed into a large salon. 'El Administrador Caproni,' announced Beruete.

The shutters were half closed and lace drapes stirred in the wind; bright Mexican rugs on the floor and uphol-stered English furniture scattered about, from Buenos Aires's Harrods probably. A man slouched in one of the chairs, regarding us out of bright green eyes set in a coppery face. Long blond mustaches and luxurious surroundings irresistibly suggested an earlier century. 'Well done, boys. Leave them here, and except for Sargento Luis, wait outside. You, too, Beruete.' He might have been speaking to dogs.

'The señora and señor are guests from America.' Beruete shifted his pile of books from one arm to the other.

'No guests of mine,' answered Caproni. 'You forced your way in here, señor. May I ask why?'

'Señor Leavis does not speak Spanish,' I said.

'Oh? Then it is odder than before. Beruete, I already reminded you of your duties.'

Beruete bowed to us anxiously. 'I have to go, but may I wish you a pleasant visit with us? William Golding, you say, was this great English writer?'

'You have been more than kind, señor. When I get back to the States, I'll see if I can find the book translated into Spanish, and send it to you. Do you live here or in Dos Bichos?' I searched my purse for a piece of paper to write down his address, dumbfounded by how nearly we had missed the chance to pinpoint the whereabouts of a potential ally.

'What is this?' demanded Caproni.

Between Beruete trying to explain about a book he hadn't read, my determination to disentangle the location of his lodgings from the flood of words, and the boy sergeant deciding it was time he offered his account of events, in a very short time Caproni had packed everyone except us outside. But by then I'd formed a good idea of where Beruete lived, in rooms above the courtyard where we'd met.

'Now, Señor Americano, it is time you explained yourself,' Caproni said, lying back with a sigh.

I translated, a process which gave us some advantage, since Roy had time to consider each word. We would be unwise to rely on the *administrador* not understanding English, all the same.

'He's a goddamn discourteous swine,' Roy observed

146

conversationally when we weren't offered chairs. Which might or might not mean he, too, wanted to know how much Caproni understood. 'Make yourself comfortable. Sherry?'

Before Caproni could decide whether to leap out of his seat, Roy had poured us a glass each from a fluted flagon and pulled out a chair for me.

'Don't you understand you are under arrest? *Sargento Luis!*' squealed Caproni.

The boy sergeant bounded back through the door. '*Sí, Señor Administrador?*'

Roy sat down carefully. There was blood on his shirt where the gun muzzle had gouged his ribs. 'Tell Caproni we have come all the way from the United States with an offer of more dollars than he's made illegal pesos in a year, but if he likes to arrest us instead, that's up to him.'

I just hoped Roy knew what he was doing, and translated a tactfully edited version.

Yellow afternoon light poured through the shutters and fell in a striped pool between the two men: Roy sipping sherry, the administrator bolt upright in his upholstered chair and regarding him with a mixture of stupefaction and covetous disbelief.

'Dollars, señor? Why should you bring dollars to Dos Bichos?' he said at last.

'He'll have to throw out that pint-sized guerrilla before I'll explain.'

Caproni gestured. 'Shut the door behind you but wait with your squad. Now, señor,' he added as the boy reluctantly went.

Roy set down his glass and took out his billfold, selected a card, and handed it over, together with his passport. 'You will see that I am partner in the Boston firm of Blainey, Rosenthal, & McGeown. I have come here because one of our clients wishes to establish a fund

147

in memory of her husband who lived near Dos Bichos until he died three and a half years ago.'

I'm not sure my voice was steady when I translated, but Caproni wouldn't have noticed anyway. He had begun to believe in those dollars. 'Ah, I understand. You – you had in mind to place this fund here?'

'It was an idea my client had. One among several, of course.'

Caproni waved his hand. 'Such delicacy! A living memorial is infinitely to be preferred above a pile of stones.'

'Nor are there many places near Dos Bichos where such a charity could satisfactorily be administered,' Roy added pensively.

'Indeed, no! It has to be near Dos Bichos, you say? Excellent! May I inquire in whose memory this fund is to be established?'

'In memory of Roberto Esquilar of the Estancia Santa Maria, who died of torture in Matias Grande prison.'

Roy's eyes stayed carefully away from me while I struggled through the translation. Remotely, I was angry, suspected jealousy drove him to use Roberto, now of all times. A clever lawyer ought to be able to think up less hurtful lies, surely. But truth, or near truth, helps any tale, and as I spoke I saw the tentacles of an avaricious soul fasten on the essentials of the situation. Fine lines I had not previously noticed puckered Caproni's skin; the green eyes squinted at imagined moneybags, heavy lips protruded in calculation. 'Señor . . .' he stammered. 'Señor, I cannot establish funds to the memory of traitors.'

Roy lifted his eyebrows. 'No?'

'It isn't possible! *Los militares* . . . señor, you must see it isn't possible!'

'If you say so. I'm sorry if I wasted your time, and mine. But then, fifty thousand dollars are worth a little time.'

'*Fifty thousand* dollars?'

'It might be more,' said Roy maliciously. 'Or a little less. Investment values change all the time.'

There was a long, considering silence.

'This fund,' Caproni said carefully. 'What had you in mind?'

'My firm thought we might set up a trust and pay the income twice a year to sponsor boys into better training than hoeing vegetables.'

'Our boys are very well trained! It is good to hoe vegetables,' said Caproni peevishly, but his mind was elsewhere. 'Señor, one problem would remain.'

'Yes?'

'Such transfer of dollars will be noticed, and the authorities inquire about the reason. We cannot name the fund after this Esquilar.'

Roy tucked card and passport back in his pocket. 'Then we can't do business. The Esquilar Memorial it has to be, and I don't intend to advise placing the principal in an Argentine bank.'

Caproni wasn't insulted by the innuendo, his mind scampering after possibilities. 'This school sells many, many things. Vegetables, corn, meat. Payments would be easy, and call them what you will.'

'I didn't come from Boston to Dos Bichos simply to pay you a fee.'

'Ah, but you did!' exclaimed Caproni. 'Your client wishes to spend much money because of a widow's caprice, and you perceived I might be the man to help you, since this fund must be administered in the name of a traitor. In Argentine today that is a very hard caprice to accommodate without help. *Los militares* would be delighted by an excuse to impound dollars for themselves, and where will you be then? So you ask me to take a chance, and yes, for a lady I am willing to take chances.' He gave a small, smug bounce in his chair. 'But both of us sell advice, eh, señor? And good advice sells dear.'

The haggling went on and on, becoming more sordid as it progressed. I suppose he hid it from Caproni, but I could tell how much Royston Leavis of Blainey, Rosenthal, & McGeown detested even pretending to do business with a man who wouldn't have passed the doorkeeper of his Boston office. Worse still, he must allow himself to be outwitted by a crass and third-class crook.

By then I had grasped most of what Roy was after: greed and the taint of treachery would keep Caproni quiet about our visit, the negotiations protracted because he would have been suspicious if they were easy. Then, gradually, came the grudging concessions that allowed Caproni to dream of cozy profits, the digressions that pried information loose.

Of course there wasn't any fund, and neither of us would have trusted Caproni with a paper peso if there had been, which made the whole affair seem more degrading. The children here lacked so much that this particular deception, even though it might help find my son, seemed obscene.

I glanced at Roy. He was leaning forward, fingers laced, eyes hooded, energetic mouth compressed; two vertical furrows above his nose. He looked white and disagreeable; several times I'd noticed him shift in his chair. That goddamn kid could easily have cracked a rib. Still, fragment by fragment, with infinite skill, information was sought and gained.

Yes, some money could be used to sponsor children.

Young children?

If that *puta* of a mad widow wants it, why not? Infants attend first grade from five years old.

But, señor! Even a mad señora couldn't expect reports on every sponsored child!

Well, perhaps I could make up some reports.

No, it isn't easier to keep records! We know which of our children are poor workers, I promise you.

But so many children sponsored from each year would use up all the money! We need funds for so much else, señor.

Jesucristo, that señora!

Ah, who knows such things? Possibly the nuns could say which among the infants seem intelligent.

Señor, you have a golden brain. What a truly excellent idea. If we choose only infants, then the nuns may keep the records and also write to the señora. Meanwhile, the school uses the money while the infants are too young to need it.

There was an Esquilar who was an admiral fifty years ago? A hero I am sure! What a joke, indeed. Who is to know if we say the fund is called after him.

I think we have eighteen infants, let me see. Your widow will be rewarded just thinking about so many infants.

Roy sat back disinterestedly while Caproni produced a stiff cardboard register to count up the under-fives. As for me, I couldn't take my eyes off his finger stabbing down lines of slanting handwriting; if he had looked up, he could have read my soul.

But he didn't. I was just the translator and good for a leer when he thought Roy wasn't looking; business was male, and this the most important tradeoff in his life.

'Fourteen,' he said. 'I remember, two died of a fever some months ago.'

151

'Eighteen, you said.'

'I return eighteen to the government.'

'But two died. That's sixteen.'

Caproni hummed a little tune and then grinned. 'So it takes a long time to complete papers. Between ourselves it is fourteen, and only one of them is old enough to be sponsored in the coming year. Under five years old and they stay with the nuns. But meanwhile the nuns can write to acquaint your señora with them, and the dollars be used for other, more important things. Señor, we have solved most of our problems.'

I don't remember translating, because my eyes had reached an entry which read: *Pedro Bartolomeo, noviembre 1978*.

At last! At last as much fitted as could be expected to fit, down to the surname they gave him. Pedro was here, and my search, one way or the other, nearly over.

I don't intend – even if I could – to describe the rest of our time in the *administrador*'s salon. To feel I was close to the child I had lost yet still be unable to reach him is an experience best forgotten. I had to continue to translate, to appear normal, or we would never get out before I flew to pieces with longing. It was like a play. I was acting in a play and after a while I managed, more or less coherently, to think again, spurred on instead of split apart by Pedro's nearness.

At weary length the negotiation drew to its end, Roy saying casually, 'Then that's most heads of an agreement roughed out. I'll give you a postdated draft for five hundred dollars to set up the accounts and cable my firm to start preparing documents for signature. Of course, someone will be down each year to check the payments.'

'Of course.' Caproni's green eyes widened guilelessly.

We walked down the stairs, trailed by the sulky squaddies who had been waiting outside the door all this time, across the hallway, past the refectory, where benches of children were eating almost in silence. Silence seemed so unnatural for a room full of boys, it roused me for a moment. The food looked reasonable, and no one was telling them not to talk. They were simply too tired, too numbed by monotony to chatter.

Like a sleepwalker, I went past. When this was over I would try to do something for the boys of Dos Bichos. God knew how or what, with the military riding higher than ever in power. But once I'd smuggled Pedro out of Argentina, I would do something.

10

I couldn't believe it when Roy, far from slipping in some last minute request to visit the infants, told Caproni adios and held the automobile door for me to get in. Since this afternoon's performance, I'd trusted his ability to negotiate almost anything he wanted, and was unprepared to set this up for myself. In fact, I was afraid to interfere in case I spoiled some deception I hadn't grasped. But Pedro was here, all we had to do was talk our way over to the nuns and ask which one he was; any excuse would do.

'*El Señor Administrador—*' I began.

'We both thank you for your help, Señor Caproni. I hope a local notary will deliver the trust documents for signature within two or three weeks.' Roy's voice clashed with mine, bore it down. His strength hustled me into the automobile, the door slammed, lights switched on. I had not noticed it was nearly dark. I could have refused to be silenced, wound down the window, and announced myself as the *puta putana* señora who wanted to see the infants. But out of nowhere an image flashed on the dark screen of my mind: of a laughing Roberto patting my stomach a week before he was arrested, and saying, 'If I ever crash head-on, I know you'll have love to spare for him from us both.' This had been the only time I could have guessed he'd begun to feel worried. Yes, already I loved our son for both of us, but somehow must force myself to realize that at this most agonizing of moments, love demanded patience rather than emotion. Above all to remember I couldn't afford another mistake. Our child, if it indeed survived, had only one life to lose.

I was tired, overstrained, excited. I knew I wasn't thinking clearly. So the window stayed up and we drove around the dusty courtyard to the gate, past a child leaning sleepily on a rifle, out into a darkly blowing night.

A hundred yards down the road Roy cut the engine. Neither of us spoke. The monotonous wind said it for me, a sound between a moan and a sigh.

'You were too eager,' he said at last. 'God knows it wasn't your fault, but if Caproni had looked at you, really looked, I mean, he must have realized we'd spun him a pack of lies. I was afraid he would look if we asked a favor he couldn't understand.'

'Yes.' I ought to have thanked him, expressed delight because we had discovered so much, but I was tired, so tired, of caution.

'Sally,' he said gently. 'What would you have done if you'd reached the kid?'

I should have given myself away to everyone.

Which would have left Caproni calling the shots and Pedro marooned in Dos Bichos. Extortion, blackmail, betrayal; once Caproni understood what we were really after, he had a dazzling choice before him.

Success followed by such disappointment can't be conquered in an instant, so, since Roy's efforts deserved a better reward than recrimination, I waited to answer until I could smile again. 'What next?'

'My dear—' His voice sounded oddly rough. 'My brave love. Next comes food and rest.'

'How are your ribs?'

'Like after I skied into a stump. Are there hotels in Dos Bichos?'

'Only one, and it never looked good from the outside. There's also a risk someone would recognize me, and the police are quite as curious as everyone else about strangers in a place like this. I think we'd better go to the estancia.'

Call it fate or what you will, but ever since I'd heard Pedro was probably in Dos Bichos, I knew I should see the Estancia Santa Maria once more.

I could tell Roy didn't like the idea, whether because of Roberto's ghost or the danger, I'm not sure. Come to that, I didn't like it either. 'That's the last place to go, and keep from being recognized.'

'No one there would run to the police.'

'You can't be sure. It's over three years since you left.'

'I'm nearly sure. Pampa people are an exaggeration of all that's best and worst in Argentina. Someone could pick a quarrel, kill for fun even, but never dream of betraying a guest. A man I met in Buenos Aires called it "offering your throat like a king", and I knew at once exactly what he meant. To me, the estancia seems the safest place to lie up while we decide what to do.'

'If you say so,' Roy said grudgingly, after a pause.

'Yes. Yes, I do. I'll drive if you like. I know the way and it'll be pretty rough on your ribs.'

And so, once more, the Estancia Santa Maria lifted like a lovely and familiar ship above the silver horizon. First the moonlit tops of eucalyptus, then roofs and white walls, the shadow of cattle scattered across the plain. All drifting close on a rippling tide of wind while we might have been rooted into a petrified landscape.

Last of all, the straight track we followed vanished into an avenue of trees, and when we came out from beneath them there was the house. Dogs barked as we reached gravel, there's never any chance of reaching an estancia unnoticed. The main building, with its green shutters and low-sweeping roof, was in darkness, as I expected. Of all the Esquilars, only Roberto had liked to live for months at a time on the pampa.

'It would be best if you stayed here,' I said to Roy, and got out to speak soothingly to the dogs. Old One-eye was still there, and Lion, Roberto's favorite. They remembered my voice and how my fingers found the places they best liked rubbed, and changed in a moment from menace to sentimental lolling against my legs. Estancia dogs are not pets, and I never saw anyone except myself treat them softly; consequently Roberto used to tease me about my posse of admirers. This time it was the same. One-eye and Lion snapped the rest into silence and the whole pack followed me to the overseer's door.

This was already open, lamplight stretching toward me.

'*Quién está?*' Jorge's familiar voice took away the last element of uncertainty.

'Señora Roberto,' I answered. The dogs, the wind, the sounds of the estancia: three and a half terrible years might never have existed.

The door opened wider, was flung back. 'Señora! Señora! This happy day!' Jorge rushed out and kissed my hand, weeping.

I wept, too, and neither of us felt ashamed. 'Jorge, I am only traveling through, but it might not be safe if the government learned I was back.'

He threw up his hands. 'Since when have we invited *los militares* to the Estancia Santa Maria?'

'Since never, but they don't wait to be invited.'

'The señora need never worry she might be in danger here.' His hand touched his *facon*, the gaucho knife, like a small bayonet.

'I shouldn't have come if I did. Jorge, I bring a guest,

my American lawyer, with me.'

'I will bid my wife open the house immediately. The servants, the gauchos, too, are in Dos Bichos, drinking. Such celebrations! But I, Jorge Montezillos, stayed at the estancia with only my maté kettle for company, because everything is in my charge.'

'Señor Roberto always said he would trust you with ten thousand cattle,' I answered, and he beamed. It is insulting to say you trust a gaucho with your life, since in some circumstances his honor might be engaged in taking it.

I went back to Roy. 'It's all right. Jorge is here and everyone else grogged out of their minds.'

'Jorge?'

'The overseer. He's going to open the house, but I think we'd better put the automobile out of sight.'

Already lamps flickered behind shutters, and when we walked across, the outer door swung open, disclosing the bent figure of Jorge's wife, Guadelupe, delight transfiguring her face. I kissed her on both cheeks. 'Guadelupe, how marvelous to see you again.'

'Oh, señora, how could you come back and find the estancia shut up! Shame on you for not warning us, so meat could have been roasting on the hearth.'

'The welcome is what counts, and I hope Jorge told you we had good reason for coming without warning.'

'You are safe with us. Not that I would trust some of the new men who have come since Señor Roberto's time; you will need to keep out of sight.'

'*Verdad?*' I was disconcerted.

She nodded vigorously. 'Young men nowadays hate the *Estados Unidos* so much, and the new ones never knew you. I have heard them laugh and say—' She broke off, confused.

'Say what? Come, you have to tell me.'

158

'Oh, señora, one said Señor Roberto deserved his death for bringing a *norteamericana* to the pampa as his bride! Jorge knifed him and he ran away but there were others who agreed that indeed it was so. Señora, why must things happen so cruelly and our happiness rot in the sack?'

'I don't know,' I said slowly, looking about me at familiar faded wallpaper, spur-gashed chairs, and glinting chandeliers. 'I wish I did, Guadelupe.'

She shuffled away and almost immediately the smell of cooking began to drift through the rooms, while I stood like a forgotten guest, surrounded by shrouded furniture.

'What have you told them about me?' Roy asked, I think as much to break the silence as anything else.

'That you are my American lawyer.'

'I fancy your Argentine retainers dislike me in your husband's home, and I don't blame them.'

'I'll explain so they understand,' I said wearily.

'You won't be able to. It isn't safe here, Sally. We made a mistake to come.'

'I'm afraid you could be right. I hadn't realized how three more years of nationalistic military government could change things everyone used to take for granted.' I told him what Guadelupe had said.

'And Jorge?'

'He said we were safe.'

'Do you believe him?'

'I did. Now I'm not sure. I'm ashamed of not being sure when he was so pleased to see me.'

'Oh, I shouldn't think he would betray you, but the lights he's turned on already must show for twenty miles. And what are they roasting, a whole ox? Because it hasn't occurred to him you might not be safe on your own estancia, he isn't taking any precautions at all. Then

159

there's me. I've a nasty feeling that once Jorge and Guadelupe start talking between themselves, a *norte-americano* in their master's home and with their master's woman might become the reason for not minding too much if things went wrong.'

'We have tonight,' I said. 'Surely we have tonight, while everyone is drunk. God bless the Malvinas.'

He shrugged, and winced. 'Perhaps. We'll eat anyway; if we don't, they would probably feel so insulted, it would screw things up for sure.'

It was a strange, almost surreal meal. Roy insisted on turning out the lights and we ate by moonlight and a single candle in the small salon Mamina had used for sewing. Steaks, cheese, and bread were washed down by the splendid Argentine red wine all the Esquilars kept in barrels. The house creaked about us, the wind hummed strongly against the walls, and from down the passage came the sound of Jorge and Guadelupe, drowsily gossiping. It could have been the past, and was not.

'I'm glad we came,' I said abruptly.

'To exorcise more ghosts?' Roy's voice was neutral.

'I've seen for myself that the ghosts have gone. There's no love here any longer. It's a place farmed for profit by absentee landlords. One day I expect the Esquilars will lose it, and deserve to.'

'No more gauchos offering their throats like kings?'

'Oh, sure, but for themselves, don't you think? Not the Esquilars.'

'Which brings us neatly back to a decision about tonight.'

I considered. I felt enormously restored by hot food, the wine, and even a short time of rest. 'I think we should stay. You said yourself they'd be insulted if we didn't eat, and it would be worse if we walked out now: there's nothing like wounded honor for loosening

tongues. I told Jorge we were on our way to Bahia
Blanca to fly back to the States. It would seem natural to
leave in the morning, darned odd if we rushed away now.'

'How far to Bahia Blanca?'

'Three hundred kilometers.'

'Okay, so we say we have to leave before dawn, to
turn in the automobile at the airport. I shouldn't care to
stay after the hired hands report for work.'

I ran my finger along the edge of Mamina's sewing
table. 'So we fetch a circle and still get back to Dos
Bichos early.'

'Sally, all through that damned rough journey out here
I tried to think, but haven't come up with any ideas for
getting at the infants in that school.'

'And taking one out with us afterward.'

'You mustn't make up your mind too soon. The most
likely thing is you'll never be completely sure if this
Pedro is yours or not. Then what will you do?'

'If he is mine, I can't imagine I won't know. What
matters is to get in there. We saw where they keep the
infants; it shouldn't be too difficult. The place is fenced
to stop the crops from being stolen, not tight enough to
keep kids in. Caproni doesn't care if one goes missing
when all he does is leave the name in his register and
pocket some extra pesos.'

'Sure you can get in. What then? Your Spanish sounds
good to me, but I guess you speak like a foreigner. No
one would swallow the bluff if you pretended to be a
government resettlement worker or whatever.'

'That's where I stick, too,' I confessed. Because, once
in, we had to find a nun willing to point out Pedro. Then
take him away with us, hundreds of miles to the nearest
frontier, without raising any alarm. After a moment, I
added, 'I think our best chance is to tell the truth. You
said yourself that even nuns unsympathetic to the

161

desaparecidos' cause might not run easily to the police, and I'm a mother looking for her son. If I simply tell them what happened, I believe they might help.'

'Not they. She. I never met a nun to speak to, but out here I'd expect them to be pretty simple. They're also under discipline. You can bet that faced by a serious problem, most would run straight to their superior. It isn't piety or pity you need to find, but one nun out of all the rest who trusts her own common sense.'

'Beruete.'

Roy burst out laughing, then stopped, holding his ribs. 'Curse that kid. I bet Beruete despises nuns for only reading Israelite great minds. It's an idea, all the same.' He tilted his chair, frowning, and suddenly my heart was torn, because Roberto used to tilt that same chair, spurred feet thrust any way on the table when his mother was away. How would Roberto have reacted in this situation? The question took me unawares, the answer slipping past my guard. Disastrously. He would have bawled threats and shaken Caproni until his face turned blue, have been so savagely jealous . . .

I pulled my thoughts up short. I had dragged Roy into a position Roberto would, point-blank, have refused to occupy. He loved me and we were happy, but if I had asked his help to cut free from a dreadful past in which he had no part, to find my child by another man, he would have seen me in hell first.

A very natural reaction.

It was only as I sat, fleetingly at peace in Roberto's home, that I saw how monstrous my demands on Roy had become. And since I hadn't changed my earlier judgement of him as a self-willed and sensual man, presumably he felt the same anger and jealousy that Roberto would have thrown in my face.

He hid it well. I found myself straining to see his

features in the moonlight, thinking: This is a different love from Roberto's. Not softer, as perhaps it seems, but tougher, more enduring. A fact which, subconsciously, I'd already recognized by telling him to go. When did I first understand he could not go, no matter how unreasonable I was, once he understood how desperately I needed help? I searched through my memories without finding any answer. Certainly I no longer believed he'd only begun to find out my past when I left him in New York. Once something about me – courage, he said, which was nice but odd – had intrigued him in Keg Bay, then he would have made it his business to discover more. That was the way his mind worked. Unluckily for him, in my case discovering more made it less easy for a scrupulous man to walk away next time I was tiresome.

Roy was watching me, too. The dim light, the shadowed room, this place with its memories, all were deceptive, but at least I oughtn't to make the easier mistakes with him again: he grasped very well that the tide of my thoughts about him had changed.

A change which would not help, since the Carmesi Barracks was the specter standing between us and not, after three years, Roberto's ghost.

I looked away to stare resolutely across moonlit pastures, conscious now of Roy's every movement, each bone in his body. Yet when at length he spoke I was relieved. His patience held and he had no intention of asking yet how much had changed, how much remained the same.

'It's an awkward problem, Sally. Are you sure you want to try to get in at once?'

I nodded.

'Then Beruete it has to be. He surely must hate a louse like Caproni.'

'We'll have to—'

'Bed now and decide the details tomorrow.' I saw his mouth twitch into self-disparagement. In this house we would have slept apart, though an earthquake changed my feelings.

'I'll take a look at your ribs first. There are always accidents on an estancia, so I learned a little of how to cope, and the emergency kit is good.'

'No.' He stood abruptly.

'Okay, be a martyr—' I began crossly, and stopped. Only minutes before I had thought I wouldn't make easy mistakes with him again. 'I'll show you the medicine chest and you help yourself, then. Or get Guadelupe along if you need some strapping.'

'Yeah,' he said dryly. 'I don't think I'll be tempted into wild grabass with Guadelupe.'

11

I expected to sleep badly in one of the estancia's many spare bedrooms, but exhaustion stunned me into instant unconsciousness. Here, where I should have been racked by nightmares, I rested easily, the years of hate and terror wiped away. Roy roused me before dawn and only then, just for a moment, was I disoriented, the dark mass of thoughts inside me ready to uncoil.

He touched the scream on my lips. 'Hush, time to get up.'

I relaxed, distressed that he had found himself cast in the role of ogre again, and reached to curl my fingers into his. 'Sorry. What time is it?'

'Half past four.'

'Heavens! Didn't you sleep at all?'

'Sure, but I can't guess what time stewed gauchos might roll in for work. I want us over the horizon before they do.'

'We can't go without seeing Jorge and Guadelupe.'

'All right,' he agreed reluctantly. 'I'll raise some coffee while you go to say thanks and please keep your mouths shut tight.' Though only a voice and warm fingers in the dark, he wasn't an intruder in this place any more.

The moon had vanished behind storm clouds, and when I went in search of warm pants, sweaters, and boots still in the cupboard of my old room, the blackness was so complete I must have tripped over every piece of furniture on the way. Rain spattered in the wind as I went over to Jorge's cottage. No one else was stirring, although a battered automobile in the yard suggested some of the revelers had come home. A hound snarled as I pushed open Jorge's door but quieted when I spoke: Jorge roused, too, and when he realized we were leaving already, he and Guadelupe knelt by their hearth to bless our departure. It was, quite literally, unthinkable that they could betray us.

'Señora, will you truly never be back again?' he asked.

'I'm sure this time will be the last,' I said gently.

'It is so sad here now, señora, so sad.' He wiped his nose. 'How I remember the days of old Señor Esquilar, and then Señor Roberto and his brother! The *asados* we had! The rodeos and races! The Estancia Santa Maria was a place of happiness, and now it is dead.'

'You and Guadelupe have made this last memory a happy one for me.' I kissed his cheek. 'Take care of yourselves.'

As we drove away there was just enough light to see them, still standing in the doorway of their cottage. By then, columns of gray water were falling out of a predawn sky. Slowly thunderheads and grass turned crimson as a sign that the sun had risen, but rain soon stained everything gray again. I didn't watch the estancia drop out of sight, but once we were over the horizon Roy pulled up. 'Is that the only telephone wire?' He jerked his head toward poles beside the track.

I stared at them, thinking. 'Yes, I'm sure it is.'

'Then I'll get over close enough to reach.' He edged the automobile into the mire until one of the poles was alongside.

'Jorge and Guadelupe won't betray us,' I said flatly.

'Maybe not, but would you bet he won't gossip down the wire, whiling away a long, wet day? I'm cautious, I guess, but I'd like to give him time to settle down. I don't suppose they mend wires too quickly out here.'

'I'm cautious, too, but—'

He grinned. 'You'd never guess it.'

'Well, I am. I suppose breaking a wire makes sense in case anyone beside Jorge might have seen us; it happens often in the winter, and this is the first big storm. I'll climb up and do it; I've seen how stiff you are today.'

The wind practically snatched the automobile door out of my hand, and just standing on the roof was difficult. We were drenched within seconds, while the wire remained maddeningly out of reach.

Roy looked carefully up and down the track; visibility was poor, but in such flat land we could see for perhaps a mile. 'Nothing coming. I'll lean forward and hold the pole while you climb on my shoulders.'

'Your ribs?'

'Damn my ribs,' he said impatiently. 'Let's get that wire down. I'm itchy just looking at it.'

I am light and reasonably agile, but reaching up that pole in a tempest was tricky. The automobile swayed underfoot, Roy's ribs something I needed to avoid. Our clothes stuck in clammy folds and the pole was slippery. All the same, I found it exhilarating perched above a plain that stretched in most directions for a thousand miles: a giant in seven league boots with thunderbolts in my purse. No point wasting time though. A moment later I was precariously balanced on Roy's shoulders, the wire tantalizingly swayed up by the wind and still inches out of reach.

I looked down. 'Are you okay?'

The answer was impolite but affirmative and, very cautiously this time, I drew up first one leg and then the other until I was kneeling. This time I was able to grab the wire one-handed, and saw at it with Roy's pocket knife. At first it resisted; knives don't cut wire easily and I couldn't put much strength into the job. But those wires weren't great quality and, as I'd said, often parted in winter. After half a dozen jabbing saws it sprang apart and I came down with a rush, both of us landing heavily on the roof.

'Maybe I'll take your word on gaucho honor next time,' Roy commented once we were back in the shelter of the automobile. He glanced at his watch. 'We've all the time we want now, so I suggest we talk over those details we left to look after themselves last night.'

There was nowhere to pull out of sight, so we drove on slowly to the next arroyo and drew up beside some scrub. From there the track ran straight as a ship's wake back to the estancia and on to Bahia Blanca. Nothing moved, the few cattle motionless, tail on to the wind. I remembered these fall storms on the pampa: Once a big one set in, everyone hibernated until it blew over.

And gossiped over the telephone; perhaps Roy's precaution had been sensible after all.

I had brought a bottle of Esquilar brandy and some bread and beef, so once we were dry again, the day began to look up.

'We couldn't have chosen a better time to reach the school unseen,' I observed. The brandy formed a puffball of warmth in my stomach, and as soon as we began to talk about reaching Pedro that same day, I was filled with anticipation.

'We'll buy some ponchos at the first store we pass. They're nondescript and good cover even though nothing would keep out so much wet.'

'It's going to be a lucky day.' My confidence riding as high as anticipation, fueled by brandy and adrenaline after climbing that pole.

'It's easy to miss out if you rely on luck to take you

through,' Roy observed, a capable man more at ease using his brains than sloshing across the pampa in a poncho. 'Sally, suppose you manage to see the child, what then?'

'If he's mine, we take him.'

'I thought that's what you'd say, but it isn't possible. One, you're unlikely ever to be completely sure he's yours; two, even if you're personally convinced, you'd never get him out of the country without proper documentation. Or into the States. Three, it's goddamn unfair on Beruete and a nun, if they agree to help, to leave them afterward to explain where a kid, age three, has vanished.'

'What do you suggest: we see him and go meekly away again? And if you really want some answers: One, I expect to be nearly certain he is mine; two, we drive for the Uruguayan or Brazilian border – I went up there once and they're impossible to guard properly. Three, who will know or care who is to blame? Caproni won't, and kids disappear all the time, even in the States, as the Missing Persons Bureau could tell you.'

'I'd expect the nuns to care, and you missed the bit about getting him back home to live.'

I stared at him, gripped by my demon of unreason. Yet again I was fighting blindly, the only way I knew how, for this child who only might be mine. 'You're a lawyer. You tell me.'

'I'm not the sort who might launder stolen kids. Once you're satisfied this boy could be yours, we have to do it right. Go back to New York and begin the legal processes from there. I bet the Argentines will be glad to shift an orphan; it shouldn't take long.'

'That may be your way, but it isn't mine. Argentine law took away my child, remember? Put me in jail and could put me there again. If they did, I suppose you'd go

169

quietly back to Boston and start the legal processes to get me free. It shouldn't take too long, six months is fast in South America.'

His face tightened with temper. 'If it was the quickest way to get you out, then yes, I might. I'm not so good at storming jails single-handed. But at the moment we're talking about judging risks so you don't land back in there, chasing forlorn hopes. We cut some corners reaching as far as this, and plan to cut some more to get you in to look at the boy, but so far there isn't much anyone could prove against U.S. citizens. Probably the worst the Argentines would do is deport us. Trying to take the boy out is plain crazy. Apart from what I just said, he's never seen you and would very likely scream every step of the way.'

Roy had treated me as I deserved, for behaving like a bitch. Used the sledgehammer of logic to force me into sense. Except I didn't feel sensible, couldn't imagine walking away from Pedro once I believed him to be my son. I knew Roy had been wrong to suspect Jorge of anything worse than gossip; quite likely he was wrong over this as well. We stared at each other across the clammy interior of the automobile while rain drummed on the roof, each groping for hurtful things to say.

A truck spattering past brought us to our senses. We had been too preoccupied to see it coming and the driver climbed down to ask if we'd broken down. I thanked him and exchanged news about the road, but the incident shook us both. We couldn't afford to take on each other as well as the whole of Argentina.

'I'm sorry,' I said insincerely when we set off as soon as the truck vanished into rain.

'I meant it, Sally. Apologies won't make any difference. Unless you tell me you mean to leave the boy where he is for the moment, we don't go in.'

'Maybe you don't go in. I'm going anyway, and there'll never be a better time than while this storm lasts.' I put my foot down, reflecting it was lucky I happened to be in the driver's seat as the automobile practically submerged in the next pothole. I was frightened even so that Roy might try to take control unless I kept going fast; scared he would find a way to stop me anyway.

Roy didn't answer and I stole a look at him: pointed nose and thin-lipped mouth made a furious angle, our predawn warmth a fable from imagination. Then I didn't want to look any longer; my emotions swinging like a weathervane, a quarrel the last thing I needed now. My fault? Yes. I was the one who had used a quarrel deliberately to hurt, not him.

'Roy—'

'No,' he answered sharply. 'Physically I could stop you until you gave me the slip tomorrow or next day, of course I could. If you have a taste for cheap violence, that is, and I know damn well it terrifies you. Or I could swallow pride and sense, and come with you after all. But I'm not going to, and I'll tell you why. If you seriously mean to try to take that kid out, then you'll be caught. Unless one of us stays free, this time you'll be in jail for most of your life. You can't prove the boy is yours, and kidnapping is a serious crime in any country; our embassy wouldn't do more than watch the Argentines lock you up.'

'I have to try,' I said obstinately. We might have been driving across the sea instead of rich farming land, and I was glad of the excuse to keep my eyes on the road.

We reached the outskirts of Dos Bichos toward midmorning, after a four-hour journey, when the trip to the estancia had taken one. We spoke occasionally and even laughed, needed to shove the automobile several times

171

out of mud, but spontaneity had vanished. His mind was made up and so was mine; nothing remained to be said.

We didn't turn down the lane that led to the main entrance of the training school, but drove on until we reached a ruined hut dissolving in the rain, where our small Japanese automobile could crouch out of sight.

Roy glanced at his watch. 'Only ten o'clock. You have to wait until siesta.'

'What are you going to do?'

He shrugged. 'Wait.'

We waited for what seemed an age while time dripped past. I felt sick when I tried to eat and didn't dare drink any more brandy; I longed for hot coffee and drank rainwater instead.

Roy scarcely moved all of that long time, staring through the windshield at soaked countryside, a frown cut between his eyes.

'Time to go.' I looked at my watch for the hundredth time. 'Are you taking the automobile?'

'You know I goddamn wouldn't,' he answered shortly, and followed me away from the shed. 'I'll come with you to the wire.'

Suddenly I knew I was incapable of leaving him while, out of the many tangled emotions between us, only strain and resentment remained. After several hours of waiting, I, too, was beginning to get a disagreeable feeling about what might happen to me as a result of this expedition. 'Roy—' I turned to face him, held his shoulders so my fingers dug into muscle under his sodden clothes. 'My dear . . . I know apologies can't make any difference and words make everything worse, so I won't try either.' I kissed him quickly then, which was the very first time.

Of course we'd kissed before: on his yacht, on a headland beyond Keg Bay, in my room above Mrs

172

Dowell's Ice Cream Parlor that disastrous night he made love to me. But each time, he kissed me, while I tried or did not try – or tried and failed – to respond. Today I was the giver and it felt good. We clung together without speaking, rain-wet lips to rain-wet lips.

Then I set off into blowing scud and never once looked back, although I knew he followed quite some way.

The poncho we had bought was welcome, though I was too keyed up to feel the wet. Anyway, I had my own winter gear from the estancia and weather never bothered me much. The barbed wire strands of the perimeter fence were six inches apart, the highest above my head. Although I looked carefully, there was no sign of juveniles with guns, the fence designed to keep out thieves rather than keep in children who had nowhere else to run.

Very gingerly I began to climb, a foot either side of a post to gain maximum stability. Fortunately, Argentines are reared on the idea that fences are for stock; if those wires hadn't been strung tight enough to keep bulls from charging out, the climb would have been more difficult. As it was, I reached the far side with nothing worse than a punctured hand, but I couldn't help thinking Roy had a point: taking a three-year-old out this way promised to be very difficult.

Well, I had made that particular decision and wasn't going to change it now. All the same, I would need the hell of a start before chancing a home run.

The wire protected unexpectedly large paddocks of vegetables. From the school yesterday it had been impossible to gain any clear idea of how much Caproni was producing with his free child labor, since scrub windbreaks had been allowed to grow up to protect the crops and, almost certainly, to deflect inquiring eyes from the extent of the enterprise. I fingered glossy well-

173

sprayed leaves as I passed: Caproni might be a lousy school principal, but he surely knew how to make a profit.

I walked from the fence to the school buildings between rows of corn rattling in the wind, but there were acres of tomatoes, squash, and fruit as well. At last I stood where cultivation gave way to open ground, and then courtyards between buildings. A few lights showed between drifting drapes of rain, and to the left I could see the wing where Beruete indicated the infants were housed. I stared and stared at the lights there; so near and still so far. And whatever Roy said, the Argentines would never admit a child from here could be mine, if by so doing they also admitted their military's activities during the dirty war.

On the top floor of the main building, where Beruete had indicated that he lived in rooms, another light shone. I would have to gamble that this marked where he read great minds while others slumbered through the afternoon break, and get up there unchallenged.

Fortunately, estancia hounds are too chance-tempered to keep in schools, or I couldn't have hoped to approach the buildings unseen. From cover at the edge of the crops to the stuccoed wall of the school, the distance seemed immense. Nothing stirred, the buildings wearing the same deserted air as yesterday during siesta. I may have been seen, there must have been a good many watching eyes behind so many windows, but if so, then no one thought a bedraggled peon huddled under a poncho in any way remarkable. All the same, it was an enormous effort to use an unhurried, shuffling pace, not to look up or hesitate, but I managed it and at last I'd crossed the courtyard, the next obstacle a choice of doors, all made of ironbound timber. This place could once have been a monastery. I decided on a door directly

174

below the light I hoped marked Beruete's room: of course, his quarters might face out the other way, or he could be dozing with the light switched off. Never had appearances been more deceptive. Though this whole place might have been deserted, it housed more than two hundred children and their teachers, not to mention servants.

I slipped inside. No sound, nothing. I took off my poncho and scraped the worst of the mud off my boots; I needed to move quietly and fast, and not look too absurdly out of place to a casual glance. I grabbed at my scampering thoughts. I should look out of place to any glance; the only safety lay in never being seen.

In front of me was a hallway, one side stacked with empty packing cases, the other almost filled with mops and pails and brooms. The scent of stale, unappetizing food hung in the air, the kitchens couldn't be too far. Pray God I shouldn't find a fat chef snoring under that light upstairs. The seconds rushed by and became minutes while I stood listening, until eventually I couldn't persuade myself there was any reason to stay in the shadows a moment longer. By then I was feeling really scared. Edgy, too, but very conscious of Pedro waiting for me.

And yet this task I had set myself seemed so preposterous, Roy refused to come with me.

I slammed my mind shut on Roy. He was trained to figure probabilities, in a way my stripped emotions no longer could.

I nerved myself and left the corner where I had been standing, threaded past buckets just waiting to clatter over. Ahead stretched an unlit flagged passage that led to a flight of stairs. I was about to reach these, when a sixth sense stopped me, one foot in the air. Someone was there. A woman resting at the very edge of my vision, her ample buttocks tucked against the banister. She had only to turn to see me. And, somehow, those buttocks looked as if they belonged to the kind of woman who screamed first and listened to explanations afterward.

What in heaven's name was she doing, goofing on some stairs? I didn't dare retreat to look for another way up in case I made some sound, time ticking relentlessly toward the moment when even on a wet day, the school would stir about its work again.

A creak of basketwork, a grunting sigh, and the woman heaved slowly out of view; she must have stopped to catch her breath under a heavy load. Which meant she would take several minutes to get out of earshot. Impatiently I kept my eyes on my watch, forcing myself to wait.

No sound now. Slowly, stiffly, I moved to the stair and began to climb, keeping close to the wall. The first landing I reached was filled with baskets on wheels, of laundry, I supposed. Shut doors stretched either side of a passage, between each a wooden bench. The impression of a monastery became stronger, reinforced by the lack of comfort. No shades on the lights, the lamps dim and sparsely set; no furniture except those benches; no carpets, and bone-chilling damp condensing on the walls. In an odd way, this bleakness helped my flagging courage; any risk must be worthwhile to snatch my son away from such surroundings.

I took the next flight of stairs faster and at the top found the same arrangement of passage and doors but without the laundry or benches. Just bare boards and drafts. I paused, counting off doors. Under the fourth from where I stood, a strip of light gleamed. Very softly I began to walk toward it, freezing as a board creaked underfoot. As if in reply, behind one of the doors I heard a body stir, call out sleepily. I waited, trembling with tension, praying that whoever it was would go back to sleep.

He didn't. I'm not sure whether he hoped to find a servant he could send for coffee, or a trespassing boy, but bedsprings rasped again, and I knew he was coming to investigate. Without any choice except to gamble on my guess that Beruete would read rather than sleep during siesta time, I stepped swiftly to the door where a light showed, turned the handle, and slipped inside.

A table lamp threw light on a littered table beside which Beruete sat, wrapped in a flannel robe against the drafts. I put my fingers to my lips as he looked up, jaw dropping to see me there. Simultaneously, the same board snapped sharply outside and I stepped behind the door, staring at Beruete as if I might hypnotize him into doing what I wanted.

The handle scraped and the door opened so it nearly hit my nose. 'Still reading, Carlo?' said a voice, and yawned. '*Dios*, don't you ever relax?'

'I prefer reading to sleeping,' answered Beruete, ostentatiously using a finger to mark his place. 'If you don't mind, I've just time to finish this before I have to teach.'

'Unsociable bastard, aren't you? I thought I heard someone skulking in the passage, but I suppose you were too nose-down to notice.'

'It was probably Esteban. He brings up a kitchen woman sometimes to share his siesta.'

'He does? *Jesumaria*, the sly fartface! You watch while I walk in on him.' The head withdrew, chuckling, the board creaking again as preface to some thunderous knocking farther down the passage.

'You'll be in trouble with your friend Esteban,' I said shakily.

'Then I'll lock my door,' answered Beruete. 'Sit down,

please, señora.' He turned the key in the lock and turned to shovel paper off the only other chair in the room.

'I don't know what you must be thinking,' I said feebly. To tell the truth, I was glad to sit down, as reaction thinned my blood.

'Perhaps you bring a copy of Lord Fly,' he suggested, chuckling.

The doorhandle rattled. 'Carlo? What do you mean by saying I bring kitchen sluts to my room?'

'Go away, my dear Esteban, and see if you can think of a better way to clear out an unwanted visitor,' called back Beruete.

There was a hiccough of laughter. 'I'll cut your throat one of these days, *amigo*.'

Feet retreated down the passage, doors slammed, a transistor began to wail tangos. Getting out of here wasn't going to be as simple as getting in.

'Will you ever forgive me for coming here like this? I thank you from the bottom of my heart for your gallantry in protecting me.' The Spanish language is good when gratitude needs some flourishes added. But there wasn't any time to waste, and without waiting for his answer, I plunged into yet another explanation of the past I wanted to forget.

I shall never forget that setting. An attic room furnished with only an iron bedstead, a washstand, and hundreds of books in piles and on shelves. The single pool of light where Beruete's face registered astonishment, anger, compassion. Books had become his escape, until he ceased to feel more than mild disgust for the place where necessity compelled him to accept employment, but as he listened I could see that in his youth he had been different. His eyes began to smolder, his hands to clasp and unclasp, his knees twitched. 'Señora, this is monstrous!' he exclaimed as I finished.

178

'Oh, quietly, please! These walls can't be very thick. Señor, I am ashamed to ask you, but I don't know where else to turn. Would you – could you – do you know any way I could get to see Pedro Bartolomeo?'

He stroked his chin. 'It will be an honor to assist the señora.'

'If anyone found out—'

He waved his hand, the same gesture of hospitality that might mean nothing and this time signified my cause was his. 'I am old, your child is young.' He squinted down his nose and laughed silently. 'Also, I fought Peron long ago, and shall enjoy to ride against *las fuerzas antidemocráticas* one last time before I die.'

'How can we do it?'

He reflected. 'Your señor is not with you?'

I flushed. 'No.'

'Then the best way will be for me to pay Encarnita.'

I tried to look intelligent.

'She is the linen woman, the—' He shot me another sidelong look. 'The go-between, you understand. If Esteban should have wished to hire a woman, Encarnita must be paid to bring her up. A fee which includes making sure she is not diseased.'

'I see.' Absurdly, I was embarrassed.

'There is no rule, but by employing Encarnita matters arrange themselves with delicacy. Thus it was that Esteban felt insulted by my suggestion he might himself have hired a peon from the kitchen. You do not mind, señora?'

I shook my head. '*Bueno*. I will speak to her first and then to Sister Pia. I agree with you that one of the nuns must also help us. You wait here until Encarnita comes to take you as far as the kitchen entrance. As you leave, turn left.'

'Left? Wouldn't that take me into the road?'

179

'She will be watching. Curious, you know? She isn't used to me courting beautiful señoritas she has never seen.' He smacked his palms on his knees, clearly relishing the image of a caballero who could still attract women who were not whores.

'So when I reach the road?' I persisted.

'Before you reach it, there is a yard, much garbage, boxes everywhere. You enter the building again and at the end of the passage is a hall. More boxes but a good place to wait. Meanwhile I will see what I can do.'

'I think I must have come in that way,' I said slowly. 'Buckets and mops on one side, crates on the other?'

'That is the one. Afterward you could slip away down the kitchen passage to the road. It is safer than the way you came across the courtyard.'

I nodded noncommittally. It was clear there was considerable traffic in women through the rear quarters of the school; which, since a military training unit was located here as well, wasn't surprising. But if I could just walk down a passage and out to the road at the cost of no more than a lewd joke or two . . . Roy had been wrong after all. I could get Pedro out, and once we were out we'd take our chance together along Argentina's northern borders.

The endless waits that punctuated that day! I fidgeted around Beruete's room, picking up books and dropping them again. Rain fell unabated from a dark sky and spread a stain on the ceiling; in the courtyard below some boys were on parade, khaki insects cowering from the elements. No officers in sight, I noticed; they would be warm and dry inside. Only a couple of sergeants sheltering in a doorway, who sent a corporal scurrying out whenever drill showed signs of wavering into chaos. Inevitably the boys became confused, since the corporal preferred to aim blows and kicks rather than take control. I watched, incensed, as one of the sergeants eventually ran for a rowcrop tractor and, after twisting up the spray bar into a weapon, began to use it to simulate attacks. The boys were expected to crouch, throw imaginary grenades, scatter as the tractor drove straight at them, showering grit and chemical as it passed.

My muscles cramped into tension as the boys became exhausted and demoralized, began to mill in circles like sheep chased by a Dobermann. Soon, very soon, one of them would be run over.

It happened only moments later. The tractor slewed into a turn and caught a tiny foreshortened figure as he fled. The sergeant stopped, climbed down, and lit a cigarette, walked back quite slowly to where the boy lay writhing.

I was craning down at an angle, the details of infamy unclear, but several minutes later the boy was carried away, legs trailing. A training accident, the sergeant would say. You can't roast a cockerel without plucking it first.

My spine felt like that child's legs when I turned away from the window: flame shot into bone. Some Argentine hospitals are excellent, but very likely no one would bother to send an orphan to Matias Grande in this weather: if they didn't, then he might never walk again. No one had dreamed of bothering when a blow at the Carmesi Barracks broke my arm; if I hadn't been out within days, gangrene would have set in for sure, American doctors said.

As I stood in the middle of Beruete's floor I discovered I had begun to wring my hands, wrenching at the fingers until pain made me stop. I remember looking down at them and thinking: you read about people wringing their hands and never see it. Now I'm doing it

181

myself, in helpless rage and anguish.

Quite how much time passed after that, I'm not sure, but eventually I became steadier. Pedro. I had to concentrate on him. I should never achieve anything once fury drove me now against this injustice, now against that.

And what, by now, would Roy be thinking?

I had supposed success here would depend on speed, quick in and out while siesta lasted, and probably he had, too.

Serve him right for not coming?

Well, perhaps. But as it happened, this was easier without him. Better to smile than weep, and so, painfully, I smiled at the thought of Encarnita's face if she had been asked to show a man out of Beruete's room.

She came at last, wheezing breathily up the passage and thumping on the door for me to open up. She was nearly square, with a fat, sly face and hair worn in a shiny bun. Imaginatively, I decided I recognized her buttocks from the stairs.

She considered me out of scavenger's eyes. 'A fine thing when Señor Beruete brings a friend in for himself and then leaves me to show her out!'

'He didn't want to cheat you,' I answered, my heart beating fiercely now. Pedro, I am close.

'*Digame—*' she began indignantly, but I wasn't listening; simply gave her more pesos right away. No time to haggle.

'All right,' she said, and laughed. 'You need to scuttle back to your own house before you're missed, *hé*?'

I shrugged; if I spoke only monosyllables, she might never guess I was foreign. To my surprise, once we left Beruete's room she made no attempt at concealment, Encarnita and her women presumably an accepted part of the school. In fact, she swaggered in front of me like a maître d' showing off, hoping perhaps for offers. If I hadn't been so tense, I would have laughed. As it was, I remained as jumpy as a flea: there were several people here, including Caproni, who would demand instant explanation of my presence if they saw me.

Fortunately, this domestic wing seemed almost deserted after siesta and we reached the ground floor without much incident – a peon carrying rugs clicked his tongue at me, a couple of boys clattered past on some errand. At the bottom of the stairs I offered more pesos to avoid curiosity in the kitchen: there seemed a wilderness of pantries and storerooms opening out of each other here, some of which would have their private exits.

'*Qué hay de nuevo?* So what's new about curiosity?' demanded Encarnita.

'Nothing. I just paid to avoid it.'

'Ah, señora, you have been watching romantic *cines*. Señor Beruete should burst with pride and walk with you on his arm for all to see.'

'It's me who isn't bursting with pride to be seen with him.' I answered rudely, and pushed past her.

After that it was easy. As Beruete said she would, Encarnita stood to watch me out of sight. Rusting gates hung at the entry to the kitchen compound, beyond them a muddy track leading to a small wicket in the wall, where some boys were jumping in puddles wearing heavy army boots. Nice to see them having fun for once, but if they were a kind of guard, then not so nice at all; I hoped to go out that way with Pedro.

I glanced over my shoulder to check that Encarnita couldn't see me any longer before I turned back into the yard Beruete said would be there. Almost immediately I was stumbling over garbage carelessly thrown in heaps and disintegrating in the rain. A door stood on the latch beyond, a quite filthy passage showing this was the way trash came out. I fumbled in the gloom, gripped by humiliating panic. Rats never worried me before I went in the Carmesi, but there they ran over prisoners' faces when they slept, gnawed at those too sick to defend themselves. I've loathed them ever since. And here, among piles of stale opened cans and leaking sacks, I heard the soft thuds and squeaks I remembered with such dread. There was only just room to squeeze down the passage past the trash – I suppose on this wet day no one cared to carry it outside – and when something soft flowed across my foot, I snatched too late at a scream of terror exploding from my throat.

I stood, petrified, straining my ears for calls of inquiry or running feet, the rats forgotten.

'Señora?'

My brain shuttered, went limp with relief. 'Señor Beruete?'

He appeared out of the gloom, aiming a healthy kick at a bucket as he passed. It landed with a clatter and the rats dived temporarily for cover. 'They do not care for noise,' he explained in a voice pitched so Caproni could have heard it. 'This way, if you please.'

I followed him, wondering how to phrase a warning about the need for quiet. After all, I had screamed, not he.

Between fright and anticipation my wits weren't as sharp as they needed to be, and soon I wasn't sure of the way we had come. This end of the building was a warren.

Eventually we came out into a hall I recognized, where I had entered God knew how long ago, and Beruete turned to face me. 'I have spoken to Sister Pia.'

'She works with the infants?' I answered in a whisper, hoping he'd take the hint.

'*Sí*, and much loved by them, I think. A woman of sense whose mind has not been addled by superstition.' He spread his hands. 'I am a freethinker who agrees with your Bernard Shaw, you see. Have you ever met him?'

'Shaw?'

'They nickname him GBS, I think.' He looked at me hopefully.

I swallowed a laugh. 'No, he lived in England, not America, I think. Quite a while ago.'

'I always felt especial sympathy with him ever since I read he disliked going to France in case he was tempted to run over the first priest he saw. So you see, señora, I truly am a freethinker,' he added triumphantly.

'I'm just grateful to everyone who's helped me, including priests and nuns. Sister Pia, for instance.'

He struck his forehead with his hand. 'Forgive me. If I take you across to the infants' wing, she will bring Pedro Bartolomeo for you to see.'

'Now?' I said joyfully.

'You will have to wait until a safe time for her to bring the child, of course. The other sisters are stupid hens who would run tattling to their superior.'

Oh, God, more waiting.

'I understand.' My lips felt stiff.

'This way, then.' He turned and held the outside door ajar, stooped theatrically double, his eye to the crack. 'Two of those accursed soldiers are out here talking.'

We waited.

'I have to supervise the evening meal soon,' Beruete observed.

'If you have to go—'

He straightened. 'They are moving. I count twenty and you follow me.'

I flicked on my poncho, most marginal of disguises, and waited. Probably we counted twenty because

185

Beruete fancied melodrama rather than in rational calculation that this was an adequate time to wait.

'Now,' he said, and stepped outside.

Rain and wind snapped into my face, but to the east a lighter gray was spreading across the sky. By the time I needed cover most, to get Pedro away, the storm would have blown itself out.

The infants' wing lay diagonally across the courtyard but, sensibly, Beruete kept close to the wall in preference to crossing open space, temporarily deserted though it was. We reached the corner where the rowcrop was still parked as mute reminder of witnessed crime, when some boys burst out of an entry. They immediately became goggle-eyed and passed us with their chins on their shoulders.

'Hey, you there, come back,' I called. 'Can you tell me how the boy is who was run over?'

They shuffled and stared at their toes. 'He is sick,' one said at last.

'Has he been sent to the hospital?'

They looked at one another uncertainly, the workings of bureaucracy beyond their powers of speculation.

'Hurry to your meal now,' ordered Beruete, and they went thankfully. 'Señora, are you crazy?'

'I begin to wonder! But they'll think less about me now that I've become part of authority in their minds, don't you think? Anyway, I wanted to know.' I told him quickly what I'd seen from his window.

He threw up his hands. '*Los militares* are, of course, barbarians, but they would answer that you cannot train soldiers without blood.'

'Yes, I thought they might,' I answered grimly. 'I guess the boy was about thirteen years old.'

Beruete stood aside. 'In here, señora.'

I followed into a kind of shed, beyond it a passage

leading to a tiny chapel. Beruete's nostrils flared at the smell of incense but he made no comment, the need for silence apparently greater here. When he spoke I had to strain to hear. 'The infants live through there with the nuns, who take turns to reside away from their convent – perhaps they think if they live here long we might corrupt them.' He chuckled gently. 'If we wanted to, of course.'

'Sister Pia will bring Pedro here?'

'*Sí*. The nuns have six years to train children to be good Catholics, then—' He snapped his fingers. '*Los militares* take over. I ask you, who do you think wins? But if you wait, Sister Pia will bring the boy to say his prayers.' He opened a cupboard door, his whisper getting louder all the time. 'There is room to stand, and you are safer out of sight in case others come.'

'How shall I know if it is Sister Pia?'

He gestured, wickedly sketching curves. 'She is the one who remains feminine under her robes.' Which, as a description, left a good deal to be desired.

There was only just room to stand between tottering piles of ecclesiastical brass and books and vestments. I touched Beruete on the arm as he turned to go. 'I have no words to thank you.'

He bowed and kissed my fingers. 'The honor is mine. Shall I return when it is dark?'

It took a moment to grasp that he was offering to help me get out. 'Encarnita showed me how her other women leave. I might be best on my own. But thank you again for offering.'

He looked relieved, but after he left I felt horribly guilty over deceiving him. Once I was convinced Pedro was my son, I intended to seize the first chance I saw of taking him out, with or most probably without Sister Pia's connivance. A disappearance nuns would never

187

casually ignore, however slack Caproni's habits. Then the thread of evidence leading from me to Beruete and Sister Pia would become painfully clear, the consequences to them very serious. This Roy had foreseen and I had not.

I waited waited waited.

The cupboard was claustrophobic and my head began to ache. The sense of Pedro's presence never left me, but became overlaid by anxiety; chafing at my composure, shredding the plans I tried to make. This was the time I would have given anything not to be alone, for a fleck of humanity in the dark, a more detached intelligence than mine to take over figuring the percentages that mattered.

But I had to have some kind of plan, even if I left kidnapping Pedro to the chances of the moment. Should I try to break out through the kitchen, or across the fields? And what about those consequences for Beruete and Sister Pia? I had felt excited by those apparently easy exits out of the domestic quarters, but from here they lay across the courtyard and down a tangle of passages. If I should meet Encarnita – and I guessed she spent a great deal of time with her eyes round corners – then she would know I had no business with a child. And if I did get out that way, I should have to walk a greater distance to reach Roy and the automobile, all of it along the road. Too great a distance for a three-year-old to manage.

The fields then. I bit my lip, thinking about all those paddocks and water-filled gulleys across which I had come. The distance was less, the cover better, but the terrain totally exhausting. A child would never make it, and nor could I carrying a child. A screaming child, so Roy had said.

It was then that a possible solution occurred to me

and I turned it over, examining every facet. The only snag seemed to be that I would need both hands free. A struggling, frightened child made it look impossible.

Feverishly I tried to imagine what else I might do, but nothing except darkness came. Darkness pressing closer, until I heard footsteps and a voice using the tone a woman keeps to speak to children. I eased the cupboard door fractionally open and saw the flicker of candles vanish into huge shadows as a nun moved between me and the chapel altar. A child held her hand, a small stocky silhouette with his back turned to me.

I had thought about this moment for so long, been so certain I would know my son the instant I saw him, my senses blurred. He was there and I was here, yet the world still turned. I still needed to stay hidden until I was sure this was Sister Pia, and I still did not know whether this was Roberto's son.

As candlelight fell on the nun's face she looked down at the child and smiled. No doubt about it, she was most gracefully feminine. I should just have to hope that Beruete's prejudices hadn't led his descriptive powers too far astray.

'Sister Pia,' I said softly, and stepped out of hiding.

'Señora,' she answered composedly.

'This – this is Pedro Bartolomeo?' My voice shook. The boy had hidden his face in her skirts.

'*Sí*, señora. Pedro—' She stooped. 'Do not be afraid, little one. Remember what you have been taught and bow to the señora who comes to visit you.'

Pedro's stern twitched in the motions of a bow, while his face stayed hidden.

I knelt, fumbling in my pocket for some raisins I had brought from the Estancia Santa Maria. Esquilar raisins. Roberto's son's raisins by inheritance. 'Look, I brought you a present.'

All I could see was dark hair. So he took after his father rather than me! He was hesitating, curiosity overcoming shyness, though I guessed the idea of a present meant little to him, since he was unlikely ever to have received one before.

Gently Sister Pia took both hands in hers and eased him out from her skirts.

I stared and stared, while my heart cried into the empty air.

I had believed I would know my son if I found him, and I did.

Pedro was not mine.

12

'He is not your son.' Sister Pia spoke into the silence, stating a fact rather than a question.

I shook my head. Still kneeling, staring at a small boy's averted face. I am fair and Pedro was dark, but that alone didn't offer the knowing that is beyond knowledge. The Esquilars might have some Indian blood, as many old Argentine families had, so straight, strong hair and a suggestion of the Andes in his face would not alone have convinced me Pedro wasn't mine, although he made me think at once of the mask behind which Indians hide their feelings.

Even now it is easier to describe Pedro's negative qualities than the positive. Already he possessed the instantly recognizable faculty that comes to some, but only some, of the generations born to oppression. A kind of expressive, sly elusiveness that takes protective color from its surroundings. Adequately fed and clothed by kindly nuns, yet the stamp of past and future was already bred in his bones. When these things ceased, as they would as soon as he left the infants' wing, Pedro Bartolomeo would survive by thieving if he could and bragging if he dared, through being servile if he must.

How did I know all this?

How did Sister Pia also know?

We had both, I suppose, in our very different lives already endured enough to accept some of the snap judgements instinct and experience offered. At the

Estancia Santa Maria, certainly, there had been a type of gaucho exactly how I imagined Pedro would become.

The disappointment was devastating. Over the past week my son's existence had grown from remote possibility to near certainty in my mind, his personality conjured from memories of Roberto. Now Pedro Bartolomeo existed, and by existing annihilated the image I had put in his place.

I remember clambering up from my knees and trying to thank Sister Pia for her help, while tears fell faster than I could brush them away.

'I brought him because you would not have believed a message sent through Señor Beruete that this child was unlikely to belong to you,' she answered. 'Pedro's true mother, I fear, would never persist in searching for her son for years. Nor his father either.'

'He hasn't a chance, has he?' I said wearily. 'Pitiful innocent spawn dredged out of nowhere into nowhere, while no one even cares.'

'God cares, and gives His gift of love. Go now, señora, while you can, and may His blessing attend your search.'

I looked again at Pedro. He was chewing the last of the raisins I had given him as if it tasted of dust: without apparent enjoyment or in the hope of receiving more. Yet probably he had enjoyed them and did desire more. 'Pedro, would you like me to write and send you pictures perhaps, when I get home? Then one day you might like to come and visit.'

Stupid, futile sop to conscience.

His answer was the one I deserved: no single flicker that might suggest response.

I will write, I thought, and see afterward whether it is futile.

On my way out of the chapel I collided with a wall and tripped over a chair, although it wasn't so dark I couldn't have avoided them by exercising ordinary care. But I was beyond care, unable to pick myself out of the pit where my hopes had been thrown to rot. Instinct brought me to the door that gave on to the courtyard, the least creditable kind of instinct that wants to find a place to hide. Just then I had forgotten completely about getting away, or starting to search again.

I opened the door carelessly, my face lifting gratefully to the evening air as I stepped outside. The rain had stopped and a blustering wind blew out of an angry sunset. It must have been only seconds later that I became aware of footsteps coming toward me: two sets of footsteps arrogantly crushing stones beneath their soles. My brain zigzagged awkwardly to life, uncertain still but working again after a fashion. There wasn't any cover; those footsteps between me and the door I had left. The entry back into the school some thirty yards away, the tractor, which was scarcely cover, somewhat nearer.

'Who is that?' shouted a hard, bullying voice.

I turned, my back to the sunset, face in shadow; it was the sergeant I had seen from Beruete's window together with his sidekick corporal less than a dozen paces away.

'Who are you, what are you doing here?' he demanded again when I didn't answer.

Molten fury must be one of the best antidotes to the demoralization that follows shattering defeat. I know, because it rescued me in the courtyard of Dos Bichos Training School, sweeping aside confusion, replacing mindless despair with a cool compulsion to teach this brute a little of what suffering meant. 'I have come to find out whether the boy you ran over with a tractor this afternoon has been sent to the hospital,' I answered, and watched him recoil.

'*Qué!*'

'Are you trying to pretend it wasn't you who ran over him?'

'A boy was accidentally hurt, but that was nothing to do with me.'

'Then perhaps your corporal drove the tractor that ran him down?' I said maliciously.

The corporal immediately began to jabber a denial and was cursed into silence. The sergeant turned back to me; he had curly hair, teeth that would have turned a film star green with envy and ridges of blubber above his eyes. 'I demand to know who you are.'

'In case I'm from the judge advocate's department? Or don't you expect a court-martial for killing an orphan?'

'He wasn't killed—'

I smiled. 'So you do know about it. He may not have been killed but he was seriously hurt, so let's go back to my first question. Has he been sent to the hospital?'

'He was not bad enough, when we have a sickbay here.'

'One leg broken, or both?'

The sergeant's eyes narrowed. 'Just who the hell told you all this?'

I turned to the corporal. 'One leg, or two?'

He licked his lips. 'Both.'

'But he hasn't been sent to the hospital,' I said flatly, and glanced at the tractor close to where we stood. In the chapel, my idea for escape had been to use this to carry Pedro and me across the fields; my doubt then, whether I could control it while struggling with a possibly screaming child. Reluctantly, I'd decided the chance of an accident might be too great. Now I wanted to fix an accident and the idea turned, transformed.

The sergeant elbowed the corporal aside. '*Jesucristo!* So the boy slipped! Accidents happen in an army. We would never have taken the Malvinas if all that mattered was to keep our soldiers warm and dry.'

'We aren't talking about an army, but of a child brutally run over in the courtyard of an orphanage. Because you lost your temper when his squad drilled badly. Because boys don't know how to drill if officers and sergeants stay in the dry to watch.'

All I needed was a few spare seconds to reach that tractor and start it up before he grasped what I intended. Instead, he shot out a hand to grab me. 'You still haven't said who you are!'

I dodged, and he didn't yet dare to use his full strength against the authority I'd assumed. 'I told you, I came about the boy.'

'Then I know your kind, bloody interfering pious bitches.' His scowl cleared as he finally decided I couldn't represent the judge advocate.

But this time I was ready for him, wanted him to lunge. He came after me fast, an ugly smile showing most of those white teeth. I made as if to duck left, went right instead, and ran for the tractor, leaping the extended spray boom; feeling cool, very cool still, as if it wasn't really me dodging an Argentinian sergeant around a John Deere rowcrop in the dusk. He came after me but I'd gained a start and the corporal seemed happy to stay on the touchline: Keep your own nose clean was his motto.

Once I saw there was a key in the tractor's switch, I fled toward the school, letting the sergeant come quite close before I jinked again. I could hear his breath whistle between curses; a soft appointment in Dos Bichos would produce flabby personnel.

He stopped swearing as a bar of light reached out toward me, breath too badly needed if he was to head me off from vanishing into one of those many passages.

195

As his hand snatched at my jacket I flung myself aside again, my own lungs beginning to burn. He would have me pinned against the corner of the building soon, whichever way I went. His lips peeled apart in satisfaction as he realized it too; his hands went wide and he came more slowly, relishing his victory. With only seconds to spare, I snatched up a handful of grit and threw it in his face.

He shouted a string of oaths that gauchos use and flung up a hand to protect his eyes. The corporal shouted, too, as heads began to peer out of windows, but already I was running back toward the tractor, my unnatural calm shredding into panic.

What if the tractor wouldn't start? It was years since I helped plow out potatoes with a John Deere at Shuckatee Falls, Montana.

I flung myself into the cab, snatching for the controls: the layout seemed different from how I remembered it. The engine caught, but roughly, throwing out a cloud of smoke. I took a chance, too late for anything except taking chances: engage first gear, let in the clutch with a hell of a jerk, change down before the brake was off. The tractor shot forward like a cork shaken out of champagne, snapping my teeth on my lip.

The sergeant reached the front wheels as they bit on gravel, rubbing his eyes with one hand and drawing his gun with the other. I spun the wheel violently and he leapt to save himself, leapt again as the spray boom scythed past his knees. Tractors may be slow, but they're handy on the charge. Dimly I heard the corporal screeching as I passed, advice, I think, which his colleague took in bad part, because as I straightened up the first shot kicked dirt between his feet instead of punching through my cab. Foot hard on the throttle by then, the John Deere in road-running gear. Considering the small size of that courtyard, we were traveling fast. A metallic clang as a bullet struck somewhere in front, but by then that sergeant needed to run for his life with me riding herd behind him.

I didn't precisely aim to kill him but reckoned it was up to him whether he got hurt or not. A reckless, joyful, explosive feeling that this one time powers of evil were on the run. I'd found the spray button, too; the nozzles still turned up and from the smell were squirting sewage. He lost his footing next time we cornered, and I sprayed him as I passed. The corporal had ventured from cover to watch, and I soaked him, too, before he fled. I found the headlights next and as I wrenched the wheel to come at the sergeant again, pinpointed him in the beam. He was back on his feet and running for the nearest wall, where he must have calculated I could reach him only if I crashed. A shot went through the cab above my head before I could swerve, braking so I scraped the spray boom along the surface of that wall. He tried to leap for the cab as I lost speed but the boom caught him first and tossed him head over heels into the swirl of fumes in my wake. One boom snapped off as I straightened up with a jerk, aware I'd made a mistake by leaving him where he could shoot me in the back.

Where had he gone to? Headlights sweeping round again, lighting up white blobs craning out of windows. There! There he was, the beam over and beyond him before I could check the tractor's momentum. Brake, for God's sake, brake! Up a gear, there he was again.

He was brave. I hated him, but had to admit his courage as he stood on wavering, bloodstained legs, this time knowing he could not move fast enough as I raced to run him down, but waiting to make as sure as he could that his remaining bullets went where they hurt. I all but lost control as the first struck a headlight and ricocheted with a vicious whine; jacknifed down instinctively so I could just see past a spoke of the steering wheel. The next hit with a solid thud followed by a hiss. Fuel? Water? By then I was on top of my quarry again, dragging the wheel around anyhow because I no longer wanted to join the brutes by running him down. Aware, suddenly, of exhaustion too. But as it happened, this particular maneuver couldn't have been bettered, because I caught him in the face with the full force of my remaining spray, sent him sprawling back so the last bullets went into the sky.

I shook my head to try to clear it; those unsilenced shots would bring Caproni and everyone else running. Get out. Get out fast; the decision already made as I heard myself speak out loud, felt my hands make the movements that turned the tractor toward the cover offered by paddocks of vegetables, one headlight insufficient to avoid God knew what: nearly thrown out of my seat when a wheel jarred into a ditch. My speed dropped alarmingly, the engine sounding very sick. Chasing an enemy around a confined courtyard, with walls, grit, bullets, and leaping figures spinning past had been a psychedelic high, this wet darkness and spitting motor was reality again. I craned over my shoulder but couldn't see any pursuit: from the moment the sergeant stopped me to his final sprawl away from the tractor's spray, probably no more than four or five minutes had elasped. Given ordinary luck, it ought to take longer than that to scream hysterical explanations at quarter-trained kids and gather them into a posse, above all to decide exactly what had happened.

With no more warning the engine crunched to a stop. I had reached into the crops but back in the courtyard they must, surely, have heard that engine stop. Figures still milled about, shouts and flickering lights suggesting that no one had yet taken control.

I clambered down slowly from the cab, stood on ground that seemed ridiculously remote. There might be time to reach the automobile ahead of the chase, but I would have to hurry. If only I didn't feel so tired; I looked back again, remembering Pedro. And as I looked, most of the lights vanished, reappeared again. I blinked, confused, before the explanation hit me. Between where I stood and those lights, someone was already moving close.

It was too much. While rage drove me at that sergeant I hadn't cared what happened afterward; now all I wanted was time in which nothing happened. In the wind and dark I held on to the hot hood of that tractor and very nearly gave up.

'Sally?' It was Roy. Roy calling my name, low-pitched but clear, from the direction I had seen that shadow move.

'Yes.' A single syllable was all I could manage, an enormous, simple relief to see him. Even more of a relief to discover he wasn't Argentine soldiers; but at the same time very neutral over finding him again after the worst of the night was over. 'You're closer in than I expected.'

'Then let's go.' His hand on my arm without more words, hurrying me between rows of corn, across exhaustingly sodden furrows. I lost count of how many ditches we struggled through, how many paddocks, they hadn't seemed so many when I crossed them coming in. Preoccupied, too, by keeping on my feet. Without Roy's hand I would have fallen several times; when we reached the fence I apologized, in a rush while the mood for apology was there. 'You were right. I wouldn't have made it with the boy.'

His hand jerked, as if a nerve snagged tight. 'You might have if I'd come in to help. Can you climb up?'

I looked at that hateful fence, six feet of barb wire, and nodded. 'Just watch me now that we're nearly out.'

We were over and within reach of the ruined cottage where we'd left the automobile, when a truck swept past on the road beyond. 'Soldiers?' I breathed.

'Can you tell me what happened?'

I told him, without expression, in not more than a dozen sentences.

'Jesus,' he said, and grunted a laugh when I reached how the sergeant learned a lesson he wouldn't forget. 'I stayed close to the buildings in case you needed help, but when the fuss began, I couldn't see clearly enough what was going on to chance a shot.'

'A shot?' I said blankly. 'Since when did you have a gun?'

'I thought tonight we might need one, so I searched around until I found a guard asleep. I think the automobile ought to be okay, don't you? Now that I've heard what you did, I guess if they can't catch us themselves, then neither Caproni or that sergeant will want to explain to headquarters.'

I began shakily to laugh; I hadn't thought of it like that before, but of course they wouldn't. Caproni was bound to wonder whether a female on his premises had any connection with the Americans of yesterday, but his likeliest reaction would be fear of losing his dollars if we'd seen a boy run over. I couldn't imagine any explanation to a general that might leave him in the clear. As for the sergeant, he would have killed me if he'd caught me, but a macho Argentine n.c.o. wouldn't fancy telling too many people how he'd run from a woman in a tractor and missed with six bullets out of six.

Half a minute later Roy had the automobile's engine

running. 'Back to Matias Grande,' I said sleepily, eyes watering after the slug of brandy he'd made me drink.

'Matias Grande? Bahia Blanca surely, and the morning shuttle up to Buenos Aires.'

'Matias Grande. Pedro wasn't my son; I have to start from the beginning again.'

'Sally,' he said carefully, and turned off the engine. 'You have to face it sometime.'

'I faced it in there, before I remembered I hadn't finished yet.'

'You told me only one boy in the register might fit what you knew, and we just finished checking out your leads on him.'

I gagged showily on another mouthful of brandy, but Roy simply sat and waited until I recovered breath to speak. No sign of haste despite the fact that the sooner we left here the better. Like he'd waited with a gun in case I needed help. As my sense of proportion returned, his reasons for waiting made more sense. I was also beginning to feel the American Bar Association might find a good deal to disapprove of in one of the partners of Blainey, Rosenthal, & McGeown. 'I have one other lead to follow,' I said flatly.

'What kind of lead?'

'A man I have to see.'

'Then maybe you'll tell me what kind of man outside the police might know anything useful in this particular situation.'

'I may not be able to find him,' I said defensively. 'But I have to go back to Matias Grande and look.'

'It seemed a good place to get away from a day or so ago.'

'If you're right and Caproni won't alert his superiors to some odd doings at Dos Bichos – perhaps we could phone a few legal queries to make him feel his dollars are still around – then Matias Grande should be as safe as ever it was.'

'There's that lieutenant . . . Gomez, was it?'

'He thought I was a journalist,' I pointed out. 'A nice quiet murder would have suited him, but he can't tell the police much that would interest them. In fact, I'm beginning to think Argentina is pretty safe for Americans while the junta wants international approval for taking the Malvinas. That would explain why no one followed up the fracas at the airport.'

As if to add emphasis to my words, another truck went splashing past, blue and white flags flapping madly above the cab.

'Sally . . . oh, God!' Roy said in exasperation, and turned to hold me. 'You aren't going to interview some torturer, are you?'

'No! Whatever made you think so?' He was too smart for comfort, and Jaime was not a torturer precisely. To me, worse than a torturer. He was also the one lead I had left.

'I'm not thinking, I'm asking,' he answered roughly. 'There can't be too many men who could give answers about this mess, and torturers are one kind who might.'

I looked at his face close to mine; the frown that had betrayed hurt before was back between his eyes. How abominable this whole business had become, sucking him deeper and deeper into a foulness he could not have guessed at when the alchemy of attraction so fatally touched both our lives in distant Keg Bay.

More than abominable if he should learn about Jaime.

'My dear . . . my dear, I'm sorry,' I said helplessly. 'So sorry. But I have to go back to Matias Grande.'

'Can't you even try to tell me?'

202

'Tell what?'

He kissed me lightly and turned back to restart the engine, perhaps the most disturbing of all the restraints I had so far seen in him. 'There's still a way for both of us to go. Matias Grande it is then, and God help the fools of this world.'

13

Roy drove through the night while I slept intermittently, my brain filled with demons wearing Jaime's face, until we reached Matias Grande in the early hours of the morning.

The familiar squares and streets lay deserted under a moon that floated out serenely from the storm clouds; it seemed impossible to imagine we had left here only two days previously. An occasional police patrol walked the streets, but though we looked carefully, we saw no sign the Magnifico was being watched. We had kept our rooms, since the trip to Dos Bichos was unplanned, and the night porter let us in without any fuss.

Roy came to the fourth floor with me, and kissed me quite naturally without expecting any recoil. After all, only hours before I'd wanted him to hold me. But I recoiled, although I'd been nerving myself not to since halfway up those stairs. It didn't make it any better that this time I knew the reason: all the way from Dos Bichos the image of Jaime had swelled in my mind until it poisoned everything. Passion, tenderness, love, and longing among the rest.

Roy drew back as if he had been slapped, and left me without a word.

I slept again, pitched across my bed, too sick and exhausted to undress. And woke some four hours later as Matias Grande stirred into deafening life. I hadn't slept my fill but the hours of dozing on the journey helped, and my mind seemed to be functioning adequately again. I eased over on my back, creaking with stiffness. The first thing to do was scrub from head to toe, the second to set about finding Jaime while Roy still slept.

Six o'clock by my watch. He couldn't humanly be around for a while, when he'd scarcely slept at the estancia and last night driven all the way while I rested.

Whatever the need for haste, I was incapable of hurrying over my bath. The Magnifico possessed vast enamel tubs and boiling water, and by the time I was through I had come slowly and pleasurably to life again. I even managed not to think most of the time: about Pedro waking solitary in his crib, or Jaime, whom I had to hope was part of Matias Grande's morning uproar. I chose a fresh, crisp dress, dried and brushed my hair in sun streaming through the window, finally crossed to a mirror hung in the darkest corner of the green wall. The view was encouraging, considering what I must have looked like last night. There were tired lines under my eyes, but my hair shone and terror was decently tidied out of sight.

Jaime. The monster in my zoo of hateful memories.

I grimaced at myself for luck, and turned away.

There weren't any creaking boards along Roy's passage and his first floor faced away from the Plaza Mayor's din, but I went past his door like a wraith; too much to hope I should escape the patrona as well.

She pounced from her desk as I went by. 'I did not know you weren't coming back the night before last.'

'I'm terribly sorry if you worried about us. We hired an automobile and then got ourselves caught in a storm.'

'A trip in the country is best for *magica negra, hé*? The power of a woman to rouse her señor in whatever ways she wishes.' She shook her head disapprovingly, so that

205

pins like skewers fell out of her hair. 'But afterward he sleeps alone in my Magnifico again! Señorita, you can go too far with the art of touching and not being touched. Like I told my Alfredo, fencing is for sheep, not men.'

My cheeks were still burning while I called a taxi. The old harridan! But surely she would have told me if the police had called to ask any questions.

The taxi driver was helpful when I consulted him: there were, he thought, three bakeries near the station. The second he took me to was the one I wanted; as the taxi drew up outside I recognized Carmen, the friend I had made in the riot, standing behind the counter.

I asked the taxi to wait and went in, my stomach growling hungrily at the smell of fresh bread.

'Señorita!' Carmen recognized me at once. 'I am happy to see you again.'

'Me, too,' I answered warmly, and waited until the only customer had left. 'Goodness, I forgot I was nearly starving until I smelled such delicious bread!'

Immediately she bustled about finding butter, a knife, and a plate, and selected more sugar rolls and croissants than a rhinoceros could possibly have eaten to set on a table in the corner. 'I can't stay long! I've asked the taxi to wait,' I said between mouthfuls. 'But do you remember how I asked you about the children born in the Carmesí, and you said your husband had been a guard?'

'Good men were never guards. He was in the kitchen.'

'I'm sorry. Of course I know from what you said he wasn't the kind to be a guard, that's why I've come for help. Is he here?'

'Sí, señorita. Shall I call him?'

'Could I see him in the back?'

She nodded, her eyes shifting from me to the sidewalk. Good-hearted though she was, no one wanted to look for trouble.

So I went and asked the taxi to return in half an hour, no point attracting more attention than I could help. By the time I went in again, there were other customers in the shop and, in answer to Carmen's jerked head, I went straight through to the back. Work was clearly over for the moment, a couple of boys scrubbing up while a tubercular-looking man stacked loaves into trays. He looked up as I entered, wiping sweat off his face. After hours of work, the heat out here was fierce.

'Señor Rodrigo?' I asked uncertainly.

'Señorita,' he answered, surprised.

'I know this will seem a dreadful intrusion to you, but I met your wife when we demonstrated for Father Sebastian's release a few days ago.'

'I remember, there was trouble and they let the good padre out because we took the Malvinas. A gesture, no? Nothing to do with our demands, or justice either.' He lit a cigarette, and coughed.

'She told me you used to work in the Carmesi kitchen.'

'To my shame. Father Sebastian helped me leave and find this work.'

'I was a prisoner there.' I stopped, began again. 'I want to trace someone who was in the same cell with me, and, of course, I can't go to anywhere official for help. I'm not even meant to be in Argentina. I thought – When Carmen said you once worked there, I thought you might know who I could ask.'

He drew hard enough on his cigarette to make the cheap tobacco crackle and regarded the glowing tip intently. 'I was only a cook, you understand.'

'I know, but you would hear gossip, see faces you recognize around Matias Grande. It isn't large, and a lot of people must have worked in the Carmesi. If you were willing to help, I think you could.'

'Who is it you want to meet?'

207

The smell of bread seemed nauseating now. 'A man called Jaime; he's nicknamed Jaime el Toro.'

'Half the barrio knows the son of a bitch. You're better without him, señorita.'

'Much better. But I want to ask him a question in such a way I'll get a truthful answer.'

Rodrigo scratched his head. 'You'd have a job to get truth out of Jaime.'

'I know. Can you help find him for me?'

'I could tell you which bars you're likeliest to see him in.'

I clenched my hands, revulsion as hard as a brick inside my ribs. 'Which?'

'Beyond the freight yard,' he said reluctantly. 'Jaime's gang mostly live off truck pickings nowadays. But, señorita, you can't go into such places, and if you wait long enough, you might see him here. Occasionally he buys a loaf to float on a bellyful of alcohol.'

Here. I could find him here.

'Yes,' I said softly. 'Would you mind if I saw him here?'

'I don't want trouble. Jaime would smash the place, carve Carmen with a knife for a word he didn't like. He's crazy, you know. Too rotted up with liquor even to thieve properly any more.'

'Not here, then. Would you give him a message next time he comes?'

'What message?' Rodrigo lit another cigarette, fingers fumbling nervously.

'Tell him . . . no. Ask him whether he remembers Manuela Guischetti, who was in a cell with him, and then say Manuela's mother will pay American dollars for information about whether she is alive or dead. He ought to jump at a chance of such easy money.' I hesitated. What I really wanted was to question Jaime at the wrong end of Roy's gun, but then I'd never be sure if he spoke the truth. 'Once he's interested, tell him to come to the Church of San Ignacio just before it closes, the next evening after you give him the message.'

'Jaime won't like going in a church,' Rodrigo said dubiously.

'*Ya lo creo!* But San Ignacio is in the barrio, he shouldn't feel threatened there. Besides, I can't think of anywhere else it might be safe to meet him.'

Rodrigo promised to do as I asked, and send a message with the single word 'Toro' to the Magnifico immediately after Jaime left the bakery, providing he took the bait. By then my taxi driver was waiting outside again, so I gave Carmen a bracelet I was wearing for her baby daughter, since any gift of money would have offended her, and left amid so many shouts of goodwill, I might have been a friend for years. As another plus I took the taxi driver's name and phone number, since he seemed reliable: altogether a good hour's work, I considered, although I wished that bricked-up dread inside me would stop getting harder and colder with each minute ticking by.

All I could do now was wait until I heard from Rodrigo again.

H.—11

14

More than a week dragged past without anything happening, and I began to wonder whether Rodrigo had decided that Jaime was too dangerous to meddle with.

If I could have thought of anything else I might try, it would have been easier, but there seemed no other possibilities left. Unless I could trick Jaime into some accurate memory of what happened to my child, at the very least whether it had been living or dead when it went out with the slops, then I was beaten for as long as *los militares* ruled in Argentina. And at the moment they were riding higher than ever, the very people who had loathed their loss of democracy gathering in support, waving flags, cheering the junta whenever one of them appeared. Taking those Malvinas had been a crafty move, no doubt about that.

'Provided they get away with it,' Roy said.

'They have gotten away with it.'

'I'm not sure. The British are spitting blood and Washington isn't happy. Al Haig's due into Buenos Aires to try to fix a deal: We wouldn't want our firmest allies in South America and Europe to tear our policy into shreds. Goddamnit, the Argentines are practically broke; we could lean on them if we had to.'

'Not enough to make them give up their Malvinas. If the junta stepped back now, they'd be ripped apart.'

'They aren't their Malvinas,' Roy said irritably.

'They took them, didn't they?'

'The British can talk about the Falklands and say the islands belong to them for as long as they like, it won't make any difference. Roberto explained it to me once, though I don't remember what he said happened . . . Oh, a hundred and fifty years ago, I think. The point is, all Argentines believe those islands belong to them; they've taken them back and now they'll sit tight. Britain's – what? – eight thousand miles away? Argentina's less than five hundred. Al Haig better calm down London, not Buenos Aires.'

We were drinking excellent Argentine wine after dinner on the ninth day following my visit to Carmen and Rodrigo. I knew Roy was baffled over what I was up to, strolling around the plaza and driving out with him like a tourist, but so far he hadn't tripped me into indiscretion. Not that he hadn't tried, and when a clever examining attorney tries to trip an inexperienced witness, it isn't easy to avoid mistakes. I hoped I hadn't made one all the same, though each day my concentration needed to stretch tighter and Roy became more restless. In another three days he was due back in Boston.

He fiddled absently with a fork on the table. 'What I'm trying to say is that the happy time might nearly be over. You remember you said Argentina ought to be safe for Americans while everyone felt good and wanted approval for this Malvinas business?' I nodded. 'I think a lot of unhappy and anti-American people may come out on the streets during the next few weeks.'

'I don't see why. Of course it will take a while for the international dust to settle, but no one's going to get the Argentines off those islands now. They enjoy dramas, and this is one they've won.'

Roy took a grubby note out of his billfold. 'Bet you a hundred pesos you're wrong.'

'You're holding ten thousand.'

'How I hate these goddamn zeros. Ten dollars, then.'

'For what? The Argentines keep the Malvinas, or *Yanquis* get roughed up after Secretary Haig tries to lean on them?'

'Ten dollars says the Argentines lose.'

'It's a bet,' I said promptly, and waited for what I knew was coming next. I had learned a good deal more about how Roy Leavis's mind worked these past few days.

'So if they lose, the junta will be strung up. You said so yourself. Then you could ask the police for help in tracing what happened to your kid.'

'No deal. I could wait thirty years.'

'I spent a postgrad year at Oxford after law college,' he said irrelevantly. 'I mayn't speak Spanish, but I figure this newspaper says the British have fitted out a task force inside a week and begun to send it south. To the Argentines that's quaint and they're gloating over so much wasted effort, but I think the British are coming and coming fast. If they get on those islands, they'll carve up draftees like we've seen goofing around here.'

I don't remember how I answered, but certainly I didn't believe him. To me, England and Oxford were places out of history, not real at all, and the atmosphere in Matias Grande remained too festive for doubt to creep in. I suppose, too, subconsciously I accepted many of Roberto's views on Argentine affairs. This in spite of a very personal experience of how easily his not untypical mix of patriotic fervor and political crassness could lead to disaster.

In any case, the whole matter vanished out of mind when, later the same evening, Rodrigo's message arrived. Roy had gone to fetch our jackets before we went out for a stroll, when the patrona slipped me a folded square of paper with such ostentatious secrecy I was scared he would notice something when he came back. Printed inside was the single word 'Toro.'

Jaime had taken the bait, and tomorrow evening in the Church of San Ignacio I must face him.

In a strange way I was beginning to think of my return to Argentina as a kind of odyssey, my purpose still unfulfilled but forcing me step by step to trace a past which, before, I'd wanted only to forget. This fancy encouraged me, although fear remained close enough to touch, and, unfortunately, it made no difference so far as the humiliating matter of controlling my own emotions was cornered, not to the disagreeable reflexes triggered by emotion. Roy must be counting the hours until he was due back in his office. But, as I was forced relentlessly to face the past, at last it became easier to accept: though I could never forgive and forget, an insult to those who had suffered if I did, the corrosion of hate was less. Less now than when I reached Matias Grande, less then than in Buenos Aires; less again in Buenos Aires than in Keg Bay. I had not given up my search, I would not; instead, my gossamer thread of evidence was raveling into a new and richer tapestry I could not yet completely grasp.

But the next test would be the worst. I loathed and feared Jaime so much, that only knowing I couldn't give up took me to meet him in the Church of San Ignacio.

All that following day Roy never let me out of his sight. Of course he realized events were moving again: I was as agitated as a flea, and I asked to borrow his gun. I'd intended to steal it, but he watched me too closely.

'Have you ever used a gun?' he demanded.

'No. Have you?'

'That's not the point. You've gotten enough on your mind without killing someone as well.'

'I don't intend to kill anyone. Once . . . Yes, I came

213

to Argentina mixed up enough to kill. Now is different, but I surely would feel happier to keep this particular appointment holding the right end of a gun.'

'I don't quarrel with that, except my finger has to be on the trigger.'

'We would both probably miss,' I said impatiently. 'For pity's sake, I'm not setting out to play gangsters in a—' I broke off, biting my lip, but had finally been led into that mistake.

Roy's eyes flickered green and blue in the disconcerting way they sometimes did when his brain shifted a gear. 'In a church,' he said finally. 'Which one?'

'I didn't say anything like that.'

'Judging by your activities since you returned to Argentina, you could plan to meet a contact in a bar, a Communist gathering, a public place, or a church. I've been trying to guess which, and now my money's on a church.'

'Another bet you'll lose?' I said edgily, wishing I'd been able to fix Rodrigo's bakery as a rendezvous. That would have made the joker in Roy's pack.

'I don't think so. You'd need to play gangsters among a bunch of Communists, or in the kind of bar I've been afraid you might risk visiting. You're too scared of this guy to meet him after dark in a plaza someplace—' He glanced at his watch. 'And it is going to be dark by the time you make your move. Which also counts against a bar. So it's a church. San Ignacio?'

I experienced the infuriating feeling of being outwitted; Roy was walking in and out of my mind as if it were his own apartment.

As I hesitated, he added, 'You can read my mind, too, you know.'

I jumped. 'Don't do that! Thought-reading may be professionally okay in court; it makes me nervous.'

He laughed. 'It's a trick people learn when they're happy together, so I doubt I'm much good at it in court. And this week while you've allowed things to drift, we've reached a little closer to contentment. The Church of San Ignacio then. When?'

'I don't want you there,' I said stubbornly. 'If this trick you've learned is any good at all, it'll tell you I mean exactly what I say. I do not want you there.'

'I mean things, too,' he answered mildly. 'Like my finger on the trigger. Maybe you got some wrong ideas when I stayed out at Dos Bichos. God knows what it cost me to stick with that decision, but I did it only because it seemed the best insurance for keeping you out of jail. I sure as hell refuse to let you go into the barrio alone.'

We were in his bedroom at the Magnifico, for the unromantic reason that he insisted I go everywhere he went and I hoped privacy might offer me an opportunity to find that gun. Romance was back among the were-wolves as far as I was concerned, but Roy hadn't taken his eyes off me long enough to look anywhere for the gun. Now time was racing past. Soon my taxi should be waiting at the corner of the Plaza Mayor, and short of handcuffs, I reckoned Roy couldn't keep hold of me once all I needed was a few seconds to bolt around a corner and away.

I shrugged, feigning indifference. 'Okay, no gun. It was only an idea.'

Without a gun I wasn't sure I could nerve myself to meet Jaime.

'A good idea. So, I come, too.'

'No.'

'You can't stop me. All I have to do is go to San Ignacio and wait; it doesn't matter any longer if you won't tell me when your man is due.'

'I'd cancel him rather than have you there. If you

don't understand that, I can't help it.'

Roy was standing with his back to the wall, only the deep strokes of his breathing showing that he recognized this as a crisis in which whatever he did was wrong. 'I doubt if you can cancel him. You could fail to go, but then all your efforts to set up this meeting will be wasted.'

I put my face in my hands. 'Roy, please. I beg of you, do not come.'

He was shaken at last by a simple plea where argument had failed. I sensed him waver, tension winding tight and tighter between us. Then he moved into the bathroom and I heard the clatter of metal from what sounded like the cistern cover: he must have taped the gun inside. I looked up, my hand involuntarily lifting to accept it.

Instead, he kissed my fingers. 'It's time we went, my dear.'

Pointless to quarrel further, his mind was made up. Nor was there time to change my arrangements. I went with him or not at all.

In the taxi we sat side by side without a word spoken, all the way to San Ignacio, each busy with profoundly solitary thoughts.

The barrio seemed further than I remembered it, now winter had begun. I stared at badly dressed children trudging through the mud and tried somehow to pin my mind back to the reason I was here. Not to meet Jaime, though meet Jaime I must, but to find out what he knew.

It wasn't easy. After Pedro I had avoided imagining any image for my child, and the result was a chilling blank; now Roy was coming with me to this rendezvous, the one last thing I'd thought I couldn't bear.

'When shall I tell the driver to come back?' Roy asked when we reached San Ignacio.

I shook my head; I did not know.

Fear growing now like a hurricane: darkening, twisting, feeding on itself.

From the beginning I had decided I must reach San Ignacio well before Jaime, and it wasn't yet dark. I peered around, feeling irresolution grow; early though it was, I couldn't be sure he wasn't loitering somewhere in a bar. I turned and went inside, leaving Roy to handle the driver; already he'd acquired some of the more useful words of Spanish.

A few women knelt in the body of the church as if they hadn't moved since I came last; the smell of incense and damp plaster had punctuated my stay in Argentina. As soon as I received Rodrigo's note I had telephoned a guarded message to Father Sebastian to say I was coming, but when my eyes adjusted to the gloom I couldn't see him anywhere. Well, I wasn't the only soul needing help. I was disappointed all the same.

Roy came up behind. 'Don't let me worry you. I'm not aiming to eavesdrop, just be around if I'm needed.'

'All right,' I said jerkily. 'I'm going to look for the priest now.'

He nodded as if he hadn't noticed how unstrung I was and turned away. Did he understand that I might scream at the first breath out of place? *Don't let me worry you.* I felt giddy with worry just imagining that agile brain deciding why this particular man I had to meet should cause me such distress.

I found Father Sebastian in the little presbytery, sitting on a straightbacked plush chair and looking very frail. His face was cut, teeth missing, and he held himself awkwardly askew. 'Forgive me,' he said apologetically. 'I did not understand from your message what time to expect you.'

I knelt beside him. 'No one said you had been beaten.'

217

He smiled. 'Even a short stay in the Carmesi is not comfortable, as you also know. I shall recover soon.'

'It was all my fault. They took you because of what happened after I came here.'

'They took me because of many things, and anyone who wishes to enter God's church should be free to come. They have wanted for years to teach me a lesson. Do not blame yourself, my daughter.'

'I shall always blame myself,' I said bleakly. 'For coming back tonight as well, and endangering you again. It's looking for my child, I suppose, that makes my judgement so lopsided.'

He laughed. 'Very right, too. How can I help this time?'

'I hope a man will come as it grows dark. A dangerous brute who makes his living by thieving and used to make it, so I'm told, by betraying men for money. I need to ask him a question and get an honest answer.'

'A difficult task.' Father Sebastian's face was noncommittal.

'May I sit in a confessional?'

'Why, my daughter?'

'For protection. I don't want to be recognized, and this man is unsafe even through two-inch boards.'

'This question you wish to ask him. It will help find your child?'

'Yes.'

'Then you are welcome to a confessional.'

I thanked him, and added, 'That's all I want, so please stay away. I've brought someone . . . you needn't feel I'm in any danger, and afterward I shall go and not come back. I couldn't bear to bring more trouble on you.'

He blessed me and said of course I must come back if I needed help, but it was clear that a shorter stay than mine in the Carmesi, and while the military were reputed to be more careful of their image, had left him unable to stand alone.

I sat inside the tiny wooden space of a confessional box for what seemed a very long time. While the last of the barrio women left, the dusk changed to darkness. While my breathing wheezed against the tension in my lungs and protective layers were stripped, one by one, from nerve and sinew. Until I could no longer avoid thinking about every nauseating detail of what Jaime had done to me, in a cell of the Carmesi.

Then I forgot everything else, and sat as blankminded as I had been after Jaime finished with me there. Now as then I even forgot my child. This was the pit of no escape, this the morass where humanity vanishes without trace.

The crash of a door flung open on its hinges brought me leaping to my feet, fingers hooked into the confessional's grill.

'Who wants to pay me dollars *norteamericanos*?' bawled Jaime, adding a stream of profanity that ranged from God to Judas, taking in a score or so of saints in between. I was surprised he knew so much about religion.

Eventually he ran out of breath and kicked the door shut behind him before beginning an erratic progress up the church. He was drunk, of course, and in the darkness collided with anything in his path, kicking what he could against the walls.

The temptation to stay cowering where I was! All I had to do was remain still and silent. Then, unless Jaime stubbed his toe on my box and tore it apart in revenge, he need never know anyone had come to meet him. Staying quiet made sense, after all. I had expected Jaime to come lightfooted and suspicious, to keep his temper checked until he knew this wasn't a trap. Perhaps I even imagined the atmosphere of church and confessional might induce sufficient superstitious uncertainty to help more certain greed along. If so, the manner of his entry immediately proved me wrong. Jaime would charge the confessional like a bull if I tried to speak to him from there, bellowing blasphemies while he ripped it, and me, apart.

I eased back the bolt on the door with trembling fingers and slipped out; as soon as I tried to speak to Jaime in this mood, the open spaces of the church would be safer than a timber trap. Somewhere Roy was waiting, too.

'Jaime el Toro,' I said quietly into a lull in his progress.

Scarcely had the words passed my lips than a hail of hassocks and missals bounced off the wall close to where I stood. I remembered Jaime as brutally violent, but this irrational malignance was new. He is rotted by alcohol, Rodrigo had said, and I'd accepted this as only to be expected, yet without revising any of my judgements. But the kind of alcohol Jaime drank – and he was likely to gulp rocket fuel if he found it – had stripped the remaining constraints from his nature, amongst which quite probably was the memory I wanted.

The need to think fast cleared my mind. I remained very frightened, completely terrified in fact, but purpose had returned. Silently, I moved behind a pillar. 'Jaime el Toro,' I said again, less softly than before.

He spat out a stream of obscenity.

'You have come because I offered dollars in exchange for information.' I moved the instant I finished speaking.

He was coming, quite fast but unsteadily, and passed me like a squall.

'If you look along the altar steps, you will find thirty dollars waiting to be picked up,' I said as soon as it seemed safe to speak again.

He came back with a bounding rush, without tripping over anything. My senses shivered close to panic as I realized he could still occasionally move by instinct, like a thief in the night.

Candles burned on the altar and he found the three ten-dollar bills easily. I had planned this stage to whet his appetite and no more. While his bulk was silhouetted against candlelight, I called to him again. 'You know I'm serious now, Jaime. Stay where you are and tell me what you remember about Manuela Guischetti.'

He turned, head sunk between massive shoulders. 'I don't sniff after bitches. I take them when I fancy.'

'You were in a cell at the Carmesi Barracks with Manuela Guischetti three and a half years ago. Since then she's been a *desaparecido*, and I want to know what happened to her.' I didn't dare ask direct questions about my baby; with Jaime, only what he did not know he was telling might be trustworthy.

'Then I screwed her like I screw all *putas*,' he answered casually. 'Like I'll screw you when I catch you.' He stuffed my dollar bills in his pocket and came down the altar steps toward me. By then I'd moved, but if screwing a bitch who'd had the effrontery to question Jaime el Toro really meant more to him than dollars, then I hadn't many cards left to play.

All I could do was retreat farther into darkness, feeling for obstructions as I went. Twice I judged I'd put enough space between us to chance a question: he simply grunted and came after me as if the clutter I thought might protect me didn't exist.

The first time I escaped by the width of a pillar; the second I was forced to retreat into a sidechapel, safe for the moment but with a blank wall at my back. Above my head grimy gilt reflected a spark of light from the altar; a

tiny red lamp burned not far away. I felt oppressed by
the stench of snuffed candles and incense, by pale plaster
hands, painted wounds, glass jewelry and macabre eyes
glinting out of the dark each time I moved.

I froze, petrified, as I heard Jaime change direction
and begin sauntering toward me, malign intuition
perhaps whispering that this time I was trapped. The
shock of hearing him come close and then closer like a
fist exploding in my face; hands in his pockets, hissing
between his teeth, staggering a little.

Perhaps he would go past.

If I lay flat against an angle of wall, maybe he would
think the instinct that told him I was close must be
mistaken. But if I escaped, lay quiet, asked no more
questions, I should never discover whether or not he
remembered what I'd come here to find out.

'Jaime,' I said evenly, my fingers gratefully curled
around the only weapon I could find: a pole holding
some kind of banner. 'Listen to me and don't be a fool.
Two hundred dollars are hidden in this church, and only
I can show you where they are. After you have told me
something it won't hurt you to tell.'

'*Puta, putana*, that's what you think!' The way he
mouthed the words they were all but incoherent.
'Bitches don't tell Jaime el Toro what to do.'

He was so close, I was back in a cell with him again.
The same rank breath, the same wet smile touched red
by a devotional lamp as he reached for me, the same
tongue flicking spittle through a clotted beard. Even
then, if I'd struck out with my pole, I might possibly have
gotten away.

But I didn't; my choice irrevocably made when I spoke
instead of hid. What a fool. What an indescribably
imbecile choice when faced by Jaime.

And yet, as I stared at the face that had haunted me

for more than three cruel years, there was a spark of satisfaction. This time, for my own purposes, I had chosen to be a fool.

Because, as I remembered from how he had been in a cell, once Jaime knew a woman was in his power, he wanted to savor his enjoyment. Twisted his fingers through my hair, spat in my face, bit my mouth. 'Now tell me where the dollars are.'

My eyes were watering from his grip, terror no longer a description of what I felt. ' . . . Manuela. Tell me what happened to Manuela first.'

'What's another bitch to you?'

'Her mother . . . asked me to find out. She's . . . been *desaparecido* three years now.'

'Then the *puta* is dead. Where are those dollars?' His knuckles bored into my skull, hair beginning to tear loose from my scalp.

My bones stretched by the pressure, words agonizing to form. 'In a cell. At the Carmesi. Three years . . . ago. You. Two men. A woman having a baby. Manuela.'

'I remember,' he said, and laughed.

His breath on my face was foul enough to believe he had gangrene of the stomach. 'Did Manuela die? One of . . . the men did.'

'How do you know all this, bitch?' He shook me and, as more hair tore loose, I felt blood trickle down my neck.

'A Communist . . . in the next cell . . . still lives. Aldo Paez. He said they will come after . . . you. One day.'

His grip slackened fractionally with astonishment. 'Me? The Communists said they would come after Jaime el Toro?'

'For selling their comrades to the police. Those dollars would . . . help you get away. What happened to Manuela?'

223

'She died.'

'You're sure?'

'Bitches are tough, and she was the parrot's bitch of a bitch. But she died.' He sniggered. 'Worn out by Jaime as well as police.'

'Paez said she was sent away with the other woman's baby.'

'Well, she wasn't. She died, I say.'

'If I'm to believe you . . . Who went with the baby? Not the mother.'

He smacked his lips in remembered gluttony. 'Not the mother, no.'

My senses swerved from the hateful pleasure in his voice. In the cell I had been filthy, feverish after a difficult, unsanitary birth, in agony with my broken arm; I had been sure he wouldn't recognize me. Jaime saw only lust where women were concerned. But once he began to gloat, my fear and dishevelment might make a connection in his mind. 'Manuela stayed when the baby went?' I said desperately, anything to kick his thoughts off track. The careful, deceiving questions I'd prepared skittering out of reach.

'Squalling brat, good riddance. I told you, Manuela stayed and died.'

My baby lived, I thought numbly. She squalled and lived. She lived, she lived.

This horror had been worth it, all the risks were worth it. My baby squalled because she was alive. She. Not a boy, but a girl. In Spanish, Jaime had used the feminine construction. And if the child was a girl, then I knew where she was likeliest to be.

Not why or even how, but where.

If three years later she still lived, I knew where to look for her. And if I knew where to look, then I knew who else I should find when I reached her.

While I stood dazed, Jaime abruptly dropped his hands and jammed his palms against the corners of my jaw, forcing my mouth wide before covering it with his. His beard, his rotting teeth, and sewer breath wrenched my fragile purposes apart. Worth it . . . worth it . . . Could anything be worth this again?

Everything whirling sanity away. Blackness and despair, silently screaming in a cell.

15

I seemed to have become two people. One knew what was happening, and the other didn't. One too shocked to move, while the other stopped Roy from killing Jaime. A mad uncomic strip raveling past my senses, leaving reason to blunder along behind.

I had forgotten Roy, which shows how badly I'd been frightened.

I remembered him when I left the confessional, but after that only Jaime was real. Now Jaime sprawled on the floor, leaving me holding like a maniac to the pole I'd used to try to fight him off. When my vision cleared, the light was just sufficient to see him sluggishly crawling across stone slabs, leaving a trail of blood behind. Roy stood over him, gun in hand and murder in his face.

Very slowly the two parts of my mind merged back together, like wet pages with their message blurred.

'Roy, no!' I seized his arms. 'Leave him! You have to . . . They'll arrest Father Sebastian again if anything more happens in his church.'

Jerkily his head turned, showing an expression hollowed into darkness, a consequence of poor light but also a great deal else. 'I had to wait. You wanted me to, didn't you?'

'I wanted you to,' I lied; needlessly cruel to say I hadn't remembered he was there. If I had, I would have wanted him to wait.

'Christ, Sally. Oh, Jesus Christ.' I never imagined Roy

like this. 'How could you do it? Back into hell of your own free will. But that's why I had to wait. If you did that . . . I couldn't destroy your chance of winning.'

'You haven't shot him, have you?' Surely I would remember that.

'No. I was afraid where the bullet might go. When you . . .' He swallowed and turned back to Jaime, who was beginning to waver to his knees. Blood oozing from an injury above his ear, where Roy must have hit him with the gun. He hit him again before he could stand; Jaime pitched forward without a moan and this time lay still.

'We'd better put him out in the street; it might be dangerous for San Ignacio if he was found here in the morning.' My distant self remained disconcertingly calm. What I did feel was drowsy; drowsy, cold, and disinclined to think.

Roy hoisted Jaime's blubber weight fireman fashion and dumped him on the steps outside: I rolled him over to make sure he stayed breathing through the night, and as I did so discovered my former electric recoil had vanished, replaced by that same drowsy apathy.

I looked up at the sky; remote and full of stars. It was good, very good, to be out again under the stars. 'I have a daughter, did you know?'

'I don't understand Spanish.' He had understood plenty I hadn't wanted him to understand; now I couldn't worry about it any more. 'My dear . . . if anyone deserved . . . I'm glad this night saw something won.'

Fortunately, Roy had bribed our taxi driver to wait at an all-night bar, but once on our way back to the Magnifico the image of Jaime came to squat, toadlike, between us where we sat. Numbing the possibility of comfort, degrading feeling by its presence until we

227

crouched in our separate corners, neither of us knowing where to flee for refuge. My chill drowsiness became a shuddering ague, yet had Roy touched me, I would have screamed. My whole body that silent scream of memory. As for Roy, in the flickering light of the barrio his face looked green. I had tried to tell him how he would feel once he knew, really knew in his blood and bones what a South American prison was like rather than simply understanding the probabilities; now this was what he faced.

Maybe he still wanted to comfort me but was uncertain whether I could bear him close. What made him sick was the prospect of never knowing again whether, if he touched me, he touched also my memory of Jaime. His memory of Jaime now as well.

We reached the Magnifico too quickly, before either of us was prepared to leave the anonymity of the taxi, to look the other in the eye, to speak. Barrios are deceptive places, dangerous or torpid as its mood may be. That night the barrio of Matias Grande happened to be brawling drunk and unconcerned with strangers.

I was shuddering so badly in the hall of the Magnifico that though I heard Roy speak to the patrona, I couldn't make out whether he attempted explanation or demanded service.

'I'll go up,' I said; words slurred by the shudder. 'I'll be better tomorrow. Don't worry.'

'I'm worrying,' he answered, and smiled. 'So let's take two flights of stairs to my room first, before attempting eight.'

I longed for bed and the covers pulled right over my head, in my childhood room looking toward Big Baldy, Montana. 'I'll try all eight.'

I don't remember if he answered, and when next I noticed things, I was in his room, wrapped in a blanket with my hands around a bowl of soup.

'You carried me,' I said foolishly.

'Didn't you think I could?'

'I wasn't sure . . . you'd want to.'

'I want to. Drink your soup.'

I drank obediently, too wrung out to argue, and a glimmer of warmth began to circulate with my blood. 'You know now why I didn't want you there.'

'I know why you thought you didn't want me there. But in more ways than one, it was as well I came.'

I finished the soup, avoiding looking at him. 'I suppose I have to thank you . . . for my life.'

He took the bowl from me and crouched, one hand on each arm of my chair, where I couldn't help looking at him. 'Considering I held a gun on the bastard, the only thanks I deserve are for flaying my instincts and holding back while you suffered. Sally, this is the wrong time, wrong everything, but I think we have to straighten out what we can tonight. I know you're exhausted, and I'm not feeling good myself, but tomorrow . . . I think by tomorrow some barriers could be even harder to tear down.'

'I don't want to think about it . . . about anything more for a long time.' I could hear the hysteria in my voice.

'You must, or break in pieces while you're too strung up to rest. Last time you ran you said it took three years to stop. Most people would be running still. Me, I don't want to wait three years, so let's take a hold now, shall we?'

I shook my head. Comfort? Royston Leavis was about as comforting as a can opener.

'Listen to me then, Sally,' he said quietly. 'Sure, I learned enough tonight so I could have killed that bastard and never felt a moment's guilt. What I didn't

229

learn was that any of it was your fault. I guess you tried to save your husband with the same rash courage you've used looking for your child, and outside the movies, courage is most often punished. Maybe there is some other woman who might have done as much to try to find her kid, but Christ, I can't imagine a braver fight than the one you won tonight.' His hand moved from the arm of my chair to where mine were locked convulsively together, gripped them, and refused to let me snatch away. 'Before you sleep, I want you to realize that by facing that bastard you won more than information. If only you'd accept it, you won your own soul back.'

I stared numbly at his hand on mine. 'I've been thinking how strange this journey has become. In spite of everything, since I returned to South America I've found it easier not to hate.'

'Yeah? There's nothing the matter with how I'm hating at the moment.'

'I can't explain it. The way things worked out, as if I had to face and beat them is what I meant.'

His hand uncurled from mine and lay palm-up on my lap. 'This is the next step of that journey then, the last you have to take alone.'

I didn't – couldn't – look up. Ever since Keg Bay, when his patience snapped, Roy had left me most scrupulously free to act for myself. He knew another mistake would be his last, when dealing with hangups the size of mine. Yet he wasn't really like that. If I gave way to him in my present state of mind, it would be unconditional surrender and he knew it. All my frailties, nightmares, and sexual fears disburdened on to him, when over the past two weeks my judgement of his nature had been changing. He could be hard, was certainly self-willed, and possessed a tougher intelligence than any I had met. He was also intuitive, emotional, and possessive, a man who would find the burden I brought with me as difficult to carry as I had. Aloud I said, 'I am afraid.'

He knew what I meant. 'My love, your time of fear is past.'

'Your turn now?'

I looked up suddenly and saw the frown I had come to recognize cut vertically between his eyes. 'Yes, perhaps.'

'And you don't mind?'

'I love you,' he said simply.

He minded; dear God, how he minded.

Yet there was no possibility of remaining separate any longer. I loved him, too, and at this moment wanted him as I had never imagined wanting anyone before. The violence of wanting unleashed by the violence of hate and terror; so intense it seemed a kind of dying. This Roy part understood, part felt from his own confused reactions. Tomorrow indeed might be too late, when inhibition, this time, would be double-locked into place.

Tonight I was worn out yet craved release; so dreadfully alone, I lacked the resolution to travel solitary any further.

'Sally,' he said.

My eyes lowered to his hand and mine, still apart. That was the distance left between us. 'Yes,' I said, and closed my fingers on his, tightly until they hurt.

I woke first, to a somewhat imperfect memory of the night before. I was warm, comfortable, and had lost the glued-up feeling that comes from exhaustion. When I turned my head on the pillow, I was muzzily unsurprised to see Roy beside me; by the time I recollected all the reasons why I ought to have climbed the other six flights of stairs to my own room, the pleasurable rightness of waking beside him surfaced, too. Last night we had been

231

passionate but as unskillful as adolescents, the circumstances for skill entirely lacking. This slow, agreeable waking possessed the permanent feel our scrambling, uneasy urgency had lacked. Sleepily I stared at Roy's face alongside mine. Tiger-striped by the sun, it was spectacularly different from the façade with which I had become familiar: confident mouth relaxed, hair tousled, frown and laughter lines smoothed out, he might have been a college freshman. Which most emphatically he was not; I chuckled at the fancy as my gaze drifted to brass bedknobs and peeling green paint. I doubted whether Blainey, Rosenthal, & McGeown considered squalor as romantic.

Slight as it was, Roy woke to my movement. He felt for me without opening his eyes. 'I never felt better about six flights of stairs in my life. When are we going to get married?'

I clung to him, laughing. As soon as the day started, complications would flood in, but for the moment they did not matter. 'Not in Argentina.'

'In Montana then, and soon.'

'My dear, I would like that very much. But you know I haven't finished here.'

He rolled over and lay staring at the ceiling. 'Will you tell me exactly what you learned last night?'

His arm stayed around me, but I did not need sensitized nerves to tell me: This is where effort begins. We aren't natural any more; it hasn't taken long for the toad to crawl out from its lair again. 'I learned I have a daughter who was still living when she left the cell. And as soon as Jaime said it, something made sense that had been nagging at the back of my mind ever since I saw the register at San Bartolomeo. A girl was adopted—'

'You told me only about two boys.'

'Because the girl's date was too late. I still don't

understand how it was done, but now that I know positively my child was a girl, some pieces of the puzzle begin to fit.' I explained the joke about El Carnicero.

'El Carnicero?'

'The Butcher,' I said flatly. 'The colonel in charge at Carmesi Barracks. He wanted to prove he could father a child on his new young wife. I saw the entry in the register where local celebrities signed as sponsors, but even when Carmen said El Carnicero would never take a brat with barrio blood, I failed to make the connection.

'Why?'

'Perhaps I found it easier to believe I'd had a boy, since Roberto wanted a son so much. But I never really considered this child, because the christening took place six months after I was out of prison. In Argentina, if a baby is to be baptized at all, it happens within days of birth.'

'So there's still no evidence this particular child is yours.'

'You're thinking about how convinced I was over Pedro. I mean to do something for him when I get back home, but I still feel guilty over leaving him at Dos Bichos.'

'You can't adopt every orphan in Argentina.'

I couldn't, of course, but my earlier certainty that Pedro must be my son had left an irrational ache of responsibility. Once I found my daughter, then I would see what I could fix for him, and the child with the broken legs. Just now, a change of subject seemed wise, in case Roy began to visualize a lifetime disrupted by meddling, overgood works. 'Perhaps during the months between October and March El Carnicero's wife pretended to be pregnant, if he wanted a macho fool on everyone. No, that couldn't be right, the child wouldn't look newborn and Father Damien's snigger in the register shows he wasn't deceived. Maybe . . . .' I paused, thinking. 'Well, we know the gossips of Matias Grande thought El Carnicero meant to deceive everyone into thinking he could still father a child. The point is, he didn't succeed. Perhaps the joke seemed too good to stay a secret. It doesn't matter anyway. Then I think the scheme must have backfired. His wife could have grown too fond of the baby for him to get rid of it once everyone knew it came from the Carmesi, so he might have decided to drive derision underground by insisting that everyone who is anyone come as sponsors to a baptism. A godparent's duties are taken seriously here; the child becomes almost a part of the sponsor's family.'

I hesitated, relieved to discover that as soon as I began to consider El Carnicero as a man and husband, the idea of confronting him became less monstrous, and then added, 'The next thing is to discover where El Carnicero's gone. No one said exactly, but from how they spoke I don't think he's in Matias Grande any longer. Once the military junta decided on a softer image, I guess they reckoned he and his like were better someplace away from their former killing grounds. But the junta aren't ashamed of their torturers. I wouldn't think it will be hard to discover his name or where he's gone.'

'The intelligence section at the U.S. embassy in Buenos Aires could tell us, I expect.'

'Over an open telephone wire to people they can't check out?'

'Probably not,' he agreed.

'What you mean is, you have to go back to Buenos Aires anyway.'

'You know, Sally, before I met you, I never believed bullshit about female intuition.'

'You told me a while back you had to be in Boston by

234

the end of this week,' I explained.

'So I did, and yes, I ought to be. We have a couple of cases coming up I shouldn't skip, one of them where I hope to finger a corrupt federal judge.'

'Don't sound so defensive; of course you have to go. I'm all in favor of blasting corrupt judges to hell and back. Anyway, I can probably do this next bit better on my own.'

He turned sharply, and put his arms around me. 'You can't stay behind. It isn't safe. I won't let you, I can't.'

Conversation ended there, and this time we achieved the joyous, slow crescendo that receives and offers more than passion. And afterward lay with laughter as our best weapon against the croak of toads.

Very much later I moved away slightly, listening to Matias Grande racketing with life. 'I shall be all right alone. Really. If El Carnicero isn't here, and I'm fairly sure he's not, then no one outside Matias Grande will worry if a female *Yanqui* tourist bums around. It'll be quite safe, you'll see.'

'Oh, sure,' he said sarcastically, and turned back the bedclothes. 'Let's get after the patrona and see if she knows anything and argue afterward.'

When we went down for breakfast it was immediately clear that the patrona was familiar with our changed relationship. She regarded us with beaming satisfaction and personally brought steak to recruit Roy's strength, observing, 'A señor may be forgiven for picking at his food while *amor* simmers on the hearth, but a grand passion needs to be fed three times a day.'

'Jesus.' Roy stared at a steak twelve inches by nine. 'Tell her to feed the barrio with it, will you?'

I translated exactly what the patrona had said and enjoyed watching Royston Leavis redden with embarrassment. Then he laughed. 'What the hell. At least the

235

old hag didn't waste her night catching cold through the keyhole.'

I laughed, too, this the first of many days in which poison would be drained from the past by the varied pleasures of love: shared absurdities, the unexpected caress, unpremeditated acts of passion. Quarrels, too, I was sure, since we were both sharp-edged; and satisfying reconciliations. Our eyes met, and we gazed at each other across congealing steak, tongue-tied by tenderness.

By the time the patrona returned, I had recollected enough of my purpose to ask about El Carnicero.

She threw up her hands, lips puckered to spit. 'You'd be rotted up just thinking about that one, señora. Enjoy yourselves and leave reptiles to croak under their stones.'

The phrase she used so precisely mirrored my own image of memory squatting like a toad that premonition stirred. 'What is it?' Roy asked, watching my face. It exasperated him not to understand.

I shook my head and turned back to the patrona. 'There are many stories about El Carnicero. Was he really so bad?'

'A devil, except there are some devils I would enjoy better in bed than angels! I ask you, señora, if angels had the strength of men, how could mere feathers lift them into the air?' She crossed herself perfunctorily. 'We were well rid of him.'

'But Matias Grande's gain is someone else's loss?'

'Sí, señora. Now you make sure your señor eats every mouthful of that steak. I tell you, my man stayed lusty only when I fed him right.'

'He isn't hungry for steak. So where is El Carnicero now?'

'Out of the way is all I care,' she snapped. 'Down

south freezing his balls off, so I heard.'

'South? Does that mean the military are really trying to disown what happened at places like the Carmesi?' I said slowly. South of Matias Grande lay only the vast rock desert with its fringe of pasture called Patagonia; Argentine officers bribed generals, married their superior's mistress, plotted coups rather than accept a posting there.

'As to that, who knows? They chose to put their trained savages out of sight for a while. But what I say is, when they come back, they'll be worse than before. Stands to reason brutes like them will be crazier than ever after a spell without blood and tormentings they've grown used to! Not to mention having nothing to do but brood in a wilderness.'

'I'm planning to go south after I leave Matias Grande. I wonder if I shall come across him? I could sell an interview with a man called Butcher to newspapers in the States. What is El Carnicero's proper name?'

She looked scandalized. 'You keep away from shit.'

'He would be on his best behavior with a *periodista norteamericana*, surely. I can easily find out if you won't tell me, when everyone in Matias Grande must have crossed themselves in relief as he went.'

'Valdez,' she said reluctantly. 'Colonel Valdez. And it is true; a crowd gathered to watch him drive to the airport, quite silent, just praying he was truly going.'

It was a chilling picture. 'So where did he go?'

'South, like I said. His airplane flew to Roballos.'

'Roballos,' I said thoughtfully. 'That's near Comodoro Rivadavia.'

'A long way off is all I know, and thanks to the Virgin for it.' She shuffled off, enormous bottom expressing the same indignation as her twitching mustache.

I translated the gist of this for Roy, leaving out the

patrona's opinion of Colonel Valdez, alias The Butcher. He was tensed up enough over leaving me in Argentina without emphasizing the nature of this new quarry. He knew all the same. The frown was back between his eyes as he began to rub fretfully at grievance. 'You would do much better to fly home with me and hire someone to find out whatever you want about this Valdez.'

'What good would that do? I intend to take my daughter away from him, not try for damages in court.'

'She may easily not be there, and all you'll find is that son Carmen mentioned, from an earlier marriage.'

'Which is why I'm going to Roballos to find out. Roy . . . you can't stop me. Don't worry, you haven't offered to marry a headstrong harpy, most times I'm pretty reasonable. But I have to finish this before we see if we can be happy, because that child out there is mine and has already lived three and a half years without me. In an orphanage or barrio I thought, but the household of a man called The Butcher must be worse.'

'Not necessarily. Plenty of criminals are good family men.'

'Oh, sure, in an Argentine colonel's house she could be spoiled by a kitchen full of servants. That doesn't make it a good place to bring up a child, especially not mine.'

'What I meant is, you have time to fly home and check out the facts. If they should fit, we'll pressure the State Department to get her out legally.'

'No.'

'I thought you were most often reasonable.'

'Very reasonable. I'm not stupid, is all. We've had this argument before. You can't make a military junta admit those kind of facts, checked out or not. And the greater the pressure, the more they'd say I was imagining things. Besides—'

238

'Besides what?'

'Putting pressure on the State Department and the Argentine government means using publicity, stirring up a fuss. So we'd have to tell the press as many details as we could of what happened to me in the Carmesi, the nastier the better, before anyone believed I might not know until yesterday that my child was a girl and left my cell alive. I don't think I could bear it, and nor could you. To see in everyone's eyes they remembered what they'd read.'

'My dear.' His face slowly drained of color. 'What am I to say? Except I think you still do not believe that personally I prefer to look facts in the face. Including what happened to the woman I desire to make my wife. Which wasn't the least of several reasons why I insisted on coming with you last night. Other people can mind their own goddamn business.'

'I agree with that. So, no talking to the press,' I said, smiling.

'You wouldn't consider studying law once we're living back in Boston?' he answered dryly. 'Some partners in Blainey, Rosenthal, & McGeown could do with help over tying arguments up tight.'

'I'll think about it,' I said cheerfully. No talk to the press meant no fuss; no fuss, little likelihood of pressure on governments. So I was on my way to Roballos. 'Actually, in between raising a family of our own, I think I might like to go back to architecture school.'

But if argument was over, Roy remained dissatisfied with himself. And with me, because I didn't mind that he had to go back to Boston. It was as if, after defying probability by bringing the woman he wanted to the altar, he felt compelled to abandon her on the steps. In these humiliating circumstances most men would have rambled through excuses, complained about the circumstances, irritably blamed the woman. From such exhibitions of injured pride, good manners and common sense restrained him, but the sense of being at fault remained. I watched this inner conflict sympathetically as we rode out to the airport to go our different ways, loving him all the more because of it. He had to return to Boston, I had to go on to Roballos; after inflicting my own disagreeable moods on him for months I was in no position to complain when he, too, began to confuse bad luck with guilt. Anyway, I really did prefer him not to be around when I met El Carnicero. I hadn't wanted him with Jaime, but lived to be grateful he insisted on coming. I was damned sure I shouldn't change my mind a second time.

That morning I was feeling pretty good. Good about everything that had happened since Roy tipped Jaime down the San Ignacio steps; my confidence soaring and the worst hauntings burned off once I discovered I could offer and receive love again. And not just any love. Things we couldn't help might upset our relationship, but with Roy I had reached my long home.

At the airport there was an immediate setback. All traffic was taken over by the military, and whereas Roy could ride an express train back to Buenos Aires and fly out from there, the only southbound railroad served the Andean ski resorts, which were not much nearer the Patagonian coast than Matias Grande.

'It is the affair of the Malvinas,' explained the clerk, spreading his hands. 'Because the British are threatening us, we must fly in many, many more troops. Soon you will be able to fly again.'

'How soon?'

The clerk shrugged. 'When the British are sensible. A week, two weeks perhaps.'

'Are the roads closed too?' I asked.

'No, señora, naturally not. It is just that ships and aircraft are needed for national purposes, but to drive—' He pulled a face. 'Now, that is a long way.'

A map of Argentina was fixed to the terminal wall, and I went over to measure distances with finger and thumb. 'A thousand kilometers; say seven hundred miles. It isn't really very far. We haven't turned in the automobile yet, I'll drive south and hope Hertz has a depot where I can hand it in down there.'

'It's a hell of a way on dirt roads in the wet.' As luck would have it, a steady drizzle had set in as we drove to the airport.

'It sounds as if there will be plenty of military around. They'll help if I get stuck. They really would; I'm not just saying it. Coming back to Argentina has made me remember how helpful most people are, providing—'

'Providing they aren't in uniform, holding guns, or seeing you as an enemy,' Roy said caustically. 'All circumstances which are more likely than not to be present on the Roballos road.'

He went back to the clerk, who spoke good English.

If driving was the only way to reach Roballos, then I'm damned well driving, I thought. If I stop now, the thread of evidence will snap. All the same, I shouldn't find interstate highways in Patagonia, the absence of aircraft catastrophic in a country of distances and scattered population. If only there had been military using the terminal, I would have backed myself to negotiate a seat down to Roballos, but the airport was deserted. Wherever troops were flying to the Malvinas from, it wasn't here.

Roy came back looking surprisingly cheerful after his glum face on the road out. 'No planes and that's definite. I thought there might be a crop sprayer or something we could hire, but the south is military air traffic control only. Argentines have just begun to wonder whether the British aren't bluffing after all. So that's that. We have to drive.'

'We? You can reach Buenos Aires by train.'

'If you seriously thought I would, then I'll take back my advice about reading law.'

'No,' I said gently. 'I knew you weren't going to as soon as I saw your face just now.'

He laughed and kissed me, filled with boisterous good spirits by the prospect of a round trip of fourteen hundred miles to Patagonia and back before he could leave for Boston. Secretly I was entertained by his reaction: once he realized I actually preferred to do this part alone, modern common sense allowed him to accept that I ought to be all right prospecting around Roballos until he could get back, since taking a child out from Patagonia would need a great deal of planning. The traditional situation of licentious soldiery on the open road sparked different, equally traditional responses, and now he must again most comprehensively put himself out on my behalf; the prospect of virtuous discomfort restored his good humor. Whereas, in a similar position, I should practically have burst with rage.

'But how will you make Boston inside those three days?' I expostulated as we broke the speed limit out of Matias Grande.

'I figure I ought to be able to fly back from Roballos to Buenos Aires. If the military are all travelling south, there must be a lot of aircraft shuttling back empty.'

I laughed. 'I reckoned I could have wheedled my way on a plane if there'd been any here. We'll have to motor if you're to do it in the time.'

We drove fast across the pampa all morning while rain lifted in silver shafts between rolling clouds. The land

242

was as flat as ever but no longer fertile. Thorn scrub leaned away from the wind and white dust streamed off scattered salt pans; the road was as straight as string and still quite good.

Patagonia began abruptly at the Rio Negro, where an iron bridge crossed a gray-green river lined with willows. A brick village lay on the far side, skirted by shanties constructed mainly from packing cases and plastic sacks. We stopped briefly to eat tough mutton, then set out again through irrigated orchards that soon gave way to stones, more scrub, and tussock grass. Occasional trucks roared past in a blast of gravel, otherwise the land was deserted. I like remote places and used to enjoy backpacking in the Rockies, but, to me, the Patagonian desert had little to recommend it. No life, no features, not even the austerity of a true desert; only the sound of wind swishing through the thorns, tearing at brown grass clumps, occasionally strong enough to rattle stones across the road.

'I'd go crazy if I lived around here for long,' I observed as the setting sun stained rain clouds a dismal purple.

'Glad you aren't driving down alone?'

'Very glad.'

And glad, too, to share the driving, because this was terribly tiring country to drive in. The monotony of a straight, narrow road, level horizon, and unchanging land blurred perception, so we needed to change places frequently; the road after the Rio Negro so deeply rutted it required unwavering concentration. We passed several stranded trucks whose drivers had probably dozed at the wheel, and once an entire army convoy which must have pulled off the road and then sunk axle deep in soft grit. The soldiers waved to us, offered cigarettes, and explained they had waited two days for a winch. 'We are forgotten,' one said. '*María madre*, I come from a village

243

where the sun is always hot. I shall die if I stay here another night.'

The whole unit seemed to have been conscripted from the tropical north; pathetically young boys shivering with cold, badly dressed, incapable of imagining what they might do to better their condition.

An n.c.o. eventually kicked them aside so we could drive on; all the time we were held up, I saw only a single lieutenant, as young and green as his men.

'Poor devils,' Roy said. 'This is only the beginning of winter down here. They'll be seasick all the way to the Falklands, and die of pneumonia in a foxhole while their officers keep warm in a bar.'

'The Falklands?'

'Malvinas.'

'Yes, of course. The British can't really be planning to invade, though, can they? It sounds crazy, like something out of a history book.'

'I asked that airport clerk, and he said they will make a show and then sail home again, as soon as honor is satisfied.' His tone was skeptical.

'And you still don't believe it.'

'No, but it's such a hell of a time since we met straight news that anything could have happened. You feel so goddamn cut off when you can't believe a word you read or hear.'

We stopped to heat cans of soup and meat over a primus bought in Rio Negro, and then drove on, taking turns to sleep. By then we had covered over four hundred miles, but the road, in darkness and persistent damp, during the night would slow us to a crawl.

16

I woke up to the touch of Roy's fingers. 'A roadblock,' he said softly.

I rubbed my eyes, astonished to glimpse the sea beyond a bluff of tumbled rocks. 'You never woke me for my turn.'

'I'll sleep all the way back to Boston. See over there?' I nodded. A line of red dots marked where the road vanished into early morning fog. 'They're stopping everything in both directions.'

'Where are we?'

'Sixty miles north of Comodoro Rivadavia.'

A town I remembered from the map as about a hundred miles north of Roballos; considering the conditions, we had made excellent progress through the night. Roy looked exhausted and no wonder; gray, stubbled face and eyes reddened by concentration in the dark.

'I've been thinking,' I said, which wasn't precisely true. The sight of that checkpoint had given my system such a jolt that a whole set of answers were shaken loose without any coherent thought at all. 'We haven't the right papers for entering a military zone, which I guess is what this must be, so only a thumping bluff will get us through. I think we have to say I'm invited to visit Señora Valdez, El Carnicero's wife.'

'So they telephone Roballos and if the Valdezes do live there, they discover that you aren't.'

'You don't understand Argentine hospitality, or the

boredom city women suffer in the campo. It must be quite as bad in a place like Roballos. Visitors are always welcome, the most casual acquaintance pressed to come for a visit. I bet if conscript guards should dare to telephone a colonel's wife at dawn, and probably they won't, then she'll kid herself she must have met me somewhere and jump at the chance of seeing a different face.'

A military police jeep went past, its steel-helmeted crew peering at us suspiciously, which meant Roy couldn't argue. If we backed off from a checkpoint or seemed hesitant, then the most slovenly guard would hold us for questioning. He shrugged. 'Okay, we have to try it and decide the next step after.'

When we reached the checkpoint, everyone piled out to see this unexpected phenomenon of two gringos on the Patagonian coast at five o'clock in the morning. 'But what is your business here, señor?' demanded a guard, flipping our passports. These were green-bereted commandos, dismayingly different from the conscripts we'd expected.

'My friend has an invitation to visit a resident of Roballos,' Roy answered in English, the query easy to understand.

'*Qué?*'

I translated.

'Who did you intend to visit?' he demanded suspiciously.

'The Señora Valdez, wife of Colonel Valdez,' I said boldly.

'General Valdez,' the guard corrected me automatically. '*El gobernador?* The governor of Roballos district? You have a pass, of course?'.

'A pass? No, I haven't.' I tried to look mystified. 'Why should I need a pass? We've traveled all over Argentina and never needed passes. Now my friend has to return to America but I still want to see Patagonia; Señora Valdez invited me to visit – oh, a long time ago.'

He looked at our passports irresolutely and, perhaps fancifully, I imagined him as a sincere Catholic who disapproved of an unmarried man and woman traveling together. 'Very well, I will telephone the governor and ask his permission for you to proceed.'

'At five o'clock in the morning?'

He grinned. 'Definitely not, señorita. If you would drive on to the hotel at Comodoro Rivadavia, I will instruct the police to deliver a pass to you there if the governor agrees. If not—' He shrugged. 'You will be escorted back here and have to return north. I am sure I need not caution you against traveling past Rivadavia without your *permiso*.' He tapped his submachine gun.

The barrier swung up and we were through, free to travel another sixty miles toward my daughter. Then to return without seeing her if the chance I'd taken didn't pay off. In all this bleak expanse there was no cover, nowhere to escape surveillance; the occasional trail into the back country little more than a tire track and most probably ending at a farmhouse. 'We were just unlucky to find an efficient outfit at the checkpoint after all the Johnny Raws we've passed,' I said aloud. 'Here, let me drive now.'

Roy didn't argue, stiff-legged as a camel when we changed places and fast asleep within moments of sitting back. So I drove that section in a sense alone, while the sun came up over the Atlantic between a rugged mass of clouds, and a fringe of grass thickened among stones and scrub. South and ever southward; how very far south I had come. First to Buenos Aires; then Matias Grande, which seemed distant enough at the time; now into a land of wind and sheep and penguins at the very edge of habitation. It seemed unreal and yet most sharply real, as the image of El Carnicero reached over the southern horizon too. *El General Gobernador*. Far from being in disgrace, El Carnicero had jumped a rank and become governor of an important military zone. But, confronted by what looked like a very unexpected war, perhaps he might not bother too much about who his wife invited to stay.

As we came closer to Comodoro Rivadavia the road improved and I was able to increase speed; an Argentine fighter flew low overhead in a shattering rip of sound, waking Roy and emphasizing how different this situation was from any I imagined only yesterday. A real shooting war was something I certainly hadn't bargained for.

'Getting a child out from an armed camp isn't going to be easy,' I said aloud.

Roy stretched and yawned. 'I surely could handle a shower and shave. Am I imagining my Spanish, or did that guard say we had to wait here for a pass?'

'Your Spanish is beginning to take off, señor. *Sí*, that is what you heard.'

'So what if it specifies staying with Valdez and no one else?'

'I hope it does.'

'You'll say next that if we get a pass, we just roll on down and stay with our friends the Valdezes.'

'Well,' I said slowly. 'Why not? But me, not you.'

He sat up with a jerk. 'Now I know you're crazy.'

'Listen, Roy. At Dos Bichos you were quite right. I – I know so little about kids, it simply never occurred to me, but if I am to smuggle a child out of Argentina, then she has to know and trust me first. Pedro would have screamed every step of the way. I don't intend to repeat that particular mistake, and if Señora Valdez invites me I'll accept. *Su casa*, señora. They say it so often, how can

248

they remember everyone they say it to?'

'I doubt if they expect to be taken up on it by strangers.'

'No . . . it's terrible manners to accept a *su casa* gift. But a gringo barbarian couldn't be expected to know that. If I say we met three, four years ago at a party, the most she'll think is that I mixed her up with someone else. There's nothing Argentines hate more than being considered inhospitable.'

Roy stared through the windshield, eyes narrowed against the sun. 'You haven't changed your mind about not wanting me there.'

'It – it isn't going to be easy to face El Carnicero, not from fear but—'

'From fear as well.'

I gripped the wheel tightly. 'It'll be all right, I think. I'm sure I never saw him at the Carmesi.'

'I'm not talking about whether he'll recognize you or not. Goddamnit, you're proposing to share a house with the sonofabitch, for weeks perhaps if the kid is yours. My guess is you'll find it quite unbearable.'

'If my child is there, getting her out will be the only thing that matters.'

'My dear, you've come a long way on your search. I'm not talking about Patagonia, although God knows that's far enough.' He swallowed a laugh. 'It's a place I surely never expected to see. But I mean you. You're nearly cured. You're happy again. You're—'

'I'm in love,' I said, smiling.

'Hey, look where you're going! My sweet, you have to think how staying in the same house with the Butcher of the Carmesi could bring the whole filthy nightmare alive again.'

'No,' I said shortly. 'I won't think about it. I can't afford to. Because if I should be invited to

249

stay, then I intend to do just that.'

This was the greatest, perhaps the last, step on my journey through the past. The measure of my cure that I never doubted I could take it. Obscene though the implications were, I could and would stay with El Carnicero if that was the only way to reach my daughter. And this time I felt a different response to the challenge of necessity without fully understanding it: Excitement.

Hate, terror, and revulsion mixed in with it, but this undertone of excitement was new and pleasurable, even though I couldn't begin to imagine how a child might be spirited out of Patagonia. Excitement represented the belief it could be done, a confidence in the future should I be successful; because then the thread I followed might at last lead me out of the labyrinth of the past.

'I don't know how I'll feel,' I said, and felt my stomach knot. 'Only that this looks like the best way to go, and somewhere along it I'll find out. But if you . . . I'm sorry, but I think I'd give myself away if you were there, all wound up and waiting to catch the pieces if I came apart.'

Comodoro Rivadavia gave the impression of a frontier town temporarily taken over by maddened vehicles, which, roughly, was what it was. Sand blew in the streets, most of the buildings crouched between a cliff and the sea were roofed with corrugated iron, oil rigs belched fire in the bay, a few tamarisks thrashed fiercely in the wind. The place was crammed with military stores letting in the wet, while around them trucks fought unscrupulously for space. There also appeared to be a covert trade in liquor, since quite a few drunken soldiers lounged about, as well as morose hung-over soldiers from the night before; the sober majority looked bewildered, bored, and cold.

The hotel was crammed with officers, but after we told

250

the police we were waiting for permission to visit the governor, they turned out a couple of captains and gave us their room.

I slept, I suppose, for about five hours, aware from time to time of a constant racket without ever surfacing fully into it. Roy woke me at midday, leaning over the bed fully dressed, shaved, and showered. 'I have to go now.'

I stretched drowsily and yawned. 'Don't you ever sleep?'

'Often. But this place is full of generals and I found one who spoke English. There's an aircraft flying to Buenos Aires in an hour and he's fixed a seat for me. I'll arrange up there to pay Hertz for the automobile so you can keep it as long as you want.'

'What about the police? The guard at the checkpoint said we had to stay in the hotel until they came with a pass. Or not, of course.'

'It's okay. A policeman came and you're invited to visit Señora Valdez, the papers are on the dresser. I explained I'd brought you down only because you were so goddamn obstinate, you wouldn't accept a war as good reason not to visit Patagonia. The cops were most sympathetic. They said it was notorious that gringo women were *muy testerudas*, which didn't sound to me like a compliment.'

'It isn't. Roy—'

'If you run into trouble, I can fly down inside two days, so keep in touch, will you?'

'What about your possibly corrupt federal judge?'

'I'd get him another time. You want to be alone for this, and maybe you're right. But alone won't be easy either. I'd say impossible if I hadn't come to know you rather well. Once you're convinced the child is yours – if you are – then you may give yourself away for quite

251

different reasons. Promise me that if things start to come unstuck, you'll fetch me back at once. The telephones are open, I checked.'

The frown deeper than I'd ever seen it between his eyes. I had an unpleasant feeling that by insisting I was best alone, I might have damaged something I thought was safe. 'I promise.'

He kissed me then, and the feel of him told me something else: If he met El Carnicero, he would kill him.

'Now, listen.' He gripped my shoulders. 'I ought to be home sometime late tomorrow. When I reach my office, I expect to find you've telephoned the Valdezes' number through. Say it's from Sally Martin. If I ever get a message just from Sally, I'll know something's wrong, okay? We'll be in touch each day and if you say, sure this is Sally answering and everything is fine, I'll understand at once it's the reverse. If incoming calls should get snarled up by the war, then I'll come anyway, unless you cable or phone each day.'

'Calling in or out of Patagonia mightn't be that simple. I don't remember the Argentine system as too good.'

'You're staying with the governor, aren't you? His telephone will work. If you can't get an international call, then use the U.S. embassy in Buenos Aires. There's a second secretary there called Huron, leave a message with him.'

'Like Huron the Great Lake?'

'That's right. I'll speak to him on my way through. So I expect to hear every day even if I'm unable to get through myself. You can tell anyone who wonders that I'm fussy about you living too close to a war.' He kissed me again, hard on the lips, and was gone.

I was glad to see him go. I loved him, I had needed and would need him again, already missed him dreadfully, but I was glad to see him go. It was disconcerting to

252

discover from that frown and his distant manner that he knew how I felt. I wasn't used to being understood before I understood myself. Roberto would have considered trying to understand any woman as a tiresome distraction from the art of mutual enjoyment, an attitude that helped keep most things simple. In an odd kind of way, marrying Roy would require more adjustment than marrying self-interested Roberto; we hurt each other too easily and, because of my experiences in the Carmesi, would always lack completely solid ground on which to build the relationship we wanted. As I finished dressing I couldn't help laughing at myself: *muy testeruda* Señorita Martin was hankering to be ridden over roughshod again. But that was Roy's weakness; I need never fear losing my independence because he would always force it back on me. But neither would he yield up his, as his attitude at Dos Bichos showed. The successes we achieved together would always rest on some very delicate compromises.

Roballos lay eighty miles beyond Comodoro Rivadavia, scattered grass becoming pasture as I drove into a bleak territory of sheep and scouring Atlantic wind. Once, out of curiosity, I turned off the road and bumped several miles to a headland, where I saw a colony of penguins heading out to sea. I wasn't sure whether they found the land too comfortless now that winter had come, or they preferred genuine Atlantic blizzards. Here it would merely be wet and immensely windy for the next seven months, so they said at the hotel in Rivadavia.

To me the long, gray breakers and fast-moving clouds emphasized the isolation of this place, locked between the Andes to the west and ocean to the east and south. While to the north, the few roads out were taken over by the army.

I shivered and climbed back in the automobile to drive the remaining miles to Roballos, passing neat farms nestling behind windbreaks. When I stopped just short of the town to ask directions to the governor's house, I was answered by a man who spoke Spanish with a Scottish accent. Here many of the sheep farmers were of British descent, another irony. Herbaceous borders, tattered roses, and tweed skirts mockingly underscored the strength of blood ties, even three generations on.

The Macpherson family, and their neighbors the Hamiltons, certainly didn't believe there was going to be a war, were horrified by the idea that divided loyalties might endanger the remote otherworldliness of their lives; feeling somewhat encouraged, I drove on. The governor's house, Eduardo Macpherson said, was a white building on the right.

And there it was. Roballos in sight over a shoulder of hillside; another muddy grid of streets and iron-roofed houses around a sheltered anchorage, some aircraft circling overhead as if a military airfield were tucked behind the bluff. A track led off to the right, a white pole across it guarded by two shivering soldiers.

I wound down the window. 'Is this the *casa del gobernador*?'

They agreed that it was.

I produced the pass left for me by the police at Comodoro Rivadavia. 'I am invited to visit Señora Valdez.'

They were pathetically glad to have someone to talk to and only reluctantly swung up the barrier after nearly half an hour of passing around cigarettes and a tin cup of spirits, a delay that inexplicably brought me a bad attack of the jitters. All through the afternoon I'd kept my mind on the scenery, the penguins, Scottish sheep-farms, anything rather than consider that before the day's end I might meet my daughter. Or lose, probably forever, the thread that tied me to her. And, waiting beside her, would be El Carnicero.

Now I was held up in sight of my goal by a pair of homesick soldiers and I could feel myself becoming agitated, my knees beginning to shiver. When I drove on at last amid many exclamations of goodwill, it was all I could do to move off without stalling the engine.

A small sweep of gravel led to a squat white-painted building, two-storied only in the center, where it might originally have been a sheep baron's lodging when he came to inspect his Patagonian flocks. Lights blazed from single story extensions either side, and some military vehicles were drawn up beside the door. I sat for a moment before getting out, fighting to control a cocktail of emotions, most of them destructive. Above all the urge to turn tail and flee. I feared everyone here, including my own child. Because when I met her, if I met her, I must not show by a single flicker she meant anything to me at all.

After what seemed an age, I got out and slammed the automobile door. A gesture of bravado: Here I am and here I stay until success or final failure. Four shallow steps led up to the front door, a thick sky seeming to watch malevolently as I stood waiting for a response to my ring on the bell. When the door opened I suppose subconsciously I expected to be faced by El Carnicero with blood dripping down his jowls; instead, there was a maid who immediately began scolding like a granny. 'Ah, señorita, we were becoming worried about you! The road is so bad and a storm expected this very night! I said to the señora, if she doesn't come soon, I said, we shall have to ask *el gobernador* to order some soldiers to search for her.'

'I didn't leave Comodoro Rivadavia until quite late,' I answered, dazed.

'That's what I said must have happened! Señora, didn't I say the Señorita Americana must have left late?' Triumphantly, she threw open a door at the back of the hallway.

'Señorita Martín,' a voice corrected her languidly. 'I have the name right, have I not? Welcome to Roballos, though why you should desire to visit so dreadful a place I cannot imagine.'

Señora Valdez spoke very precisely, as if every utterance were worth its weight in platinum. The room was hot and crammed with ornaments; furniture everywhere in the way, my hostess reclining on a basketwork sofa behind a minefield of footstools, small tables, and polished stands. My first impression was that she was so slight and delicate that, as with rare china, you might expect to see right through her. Everything, from her elegant jewelry to the rich colors she wore, made me feel clumsy, the fresh air and health I brought with me slightly disgusting. 'It is very good of you to welcome me at all,' I said awkwardly. 'I'm afraid you can't have expected me to take up a casual invitation.'

'Not at all,' she answered politely. 'Our house is yours, señorita. A guest from outside this hateful place is always a pleasure.'

There was a pause during which a clock ticked busily on the mantelpiece. She appeared almost ready to drowse while I stood burning with embarrassment. And if she did, then no one could possibly mistake her meaning, that this invitation was a gesture she expected to hear refused. Somehow I began an explanation that sounded feeble even to myself. 'I have visited most of Argentina and stayed on an estancia in the pampa. It seemed such a pity to go back to the United States without at least trying to reach Patagonia, and then when I came to Comodoro Rivadavia, the army would not let me pass.'

'So you recalled an old, a very old invitation? From my husband, I suppose, since I confess I do not remember it.'

I flushed. 'Yes, I'm afraid so. I will go again at once if you would be good enough to tell me where I might find a bed, now that the army has taken everything over.'

'But as I said, you are welcome. Josefina, take the señorita to her room and see the water runs hot before you leave her. We eat in an hour's time, Señorita Martín.' She closed her eyes.

'The señora becomes very weary at this time of year, when the sun seldom shines,' Josefina confided as she led me up an agreeable flight of waxed pine stairs. 'Ah, Buenos Aires! If the Señor Gobernador is not sent back there soon, we will all go crazy! But life is often hard, is it not?'

'Sometimes,' I said cautiously. 'Do you come from Patagonia yourself, Josefina?'

'*Claro, no!* I ask you, señorita, do I look as if I belonged among sheep?'

I laughed. 'Perhaps Patagonia improves when you know it.'

She pulled down her lips. 'On the contrary, it becomes worse. The first year, yes, it is not too disagreeable to be in so different a place. The second year you think, Never another winter like the last. This is the third year, you understand, and only the Señor Gobernador feels a little comforted, because many soldiers have come to ease past his days.' She showed me into a room that faced over the gravel drive, tested the taps, and bustled out again with an admonition that in Patagonia everyone ate at an hour of unimaginable earliness, since they could

257

not bear to postpone distraction any longer.

I was in, and without arousing more than mild derision as an uncultured American.

It was then I heard running feet and a child's laugh in the passage outside. Thought scrambled and I wrenched open the door, to come face-to-face with a small girl hopping from one foot to the other. 'Is you come to see us long?'

'I'm not sure.' I crouched down to face her. 'What's your name?'

'Lylia. Whatsit yours?'

'Señorita Lylia!' shouted Josefina from the stairs. 'What have I told you and told you about manners? You just apologize at once and get back in your room.'

'All right,' the child said obligingly. She sketched a curtsy and skipped off down the passage. At the far end she turned, mouth slanted into a wicked grin. 'I'se often-often a too very naughty girl.'

My throat locked and I could not answer, stood staring at a shut door long after Lylia vanished.

I had just met my daughter.

17

There wasn't any doubt about it. Once my senses settled,
I could perhaps have discounted the leap of feeling, the
instant tug at my heart. But that confiding, half-derisive
grin made nonsense of doubt: so had Roberto looked
whenever he slid elegantly away from family condem-
nation.

I remember sitting on the edge of the guest bed in El
Carnicero's house, my head in my hands and wetness on
my fingers. I remember saying Lylia's name aloud, the
walls closed in about me. I remember forcing open a
window so the wind surged in to set the pictures swaying.
Mist spun and shifted over the distant town, the sea half
hidden by angry spray; best to imagine the salt on my lips
came from that.

I needed to fight for strength to shut that window
again, turn away from the image of a laughing sprite who
was my daughter, try somehow to calm myself and
change for dinner. But long before I was ready, strength
and courage had vanished again, the image this time of
El Carnicero like an ulcer on my spirit, leaking fear.
Fear I must change to hard purposefulness, and quickly,
before I went downstairs. Convince myself again that I
looked forward to deceiving him. Fear, hate, and love:
all would show under pressure; love for Lylia a fresh and
dangerous weakness. In this supreme test, only purpose
might remain for me to trust.

A rumble of male voices came from the hall and I

hesitated while a group of officers left, although it would have been preferable to meet General Valdez first among a crowd. General Valdez. I must call him that, even to myself, instead of El Carnicero.

As I went down the stairs Josefina appeared, panting and bustling like a locomotive shunting freight. 'That is a pretty dress! Such a shade of blue, it reminds me of my home in the sunshine of Gran' Chaco. Señor, Señora, the Señorita Martín.' She propelled me into the sitting room, so in the end the last steps to El Carnicero were the easiest.

'Ah, you feel refreshed?' Señora Valdez uncurled from the sofa. 'May I introduce my husband, the governor?'

'My pleasure.' General Valdez touched my fingers with his lips. I would like to take some credit for not snatching away, but in truth I stood like a block while words stuck somewhere with vomit in my throat. He didn't seem put out, as if confusion were his due. 'Señorita, you do not know how pleased we are to have you with us. I hope you can stay some while, my wife longs so much for company. Isabelita—'

'Yes, indeed. I long for company,' she answered like a doll, and yawned.

'You see, señorita, Patagonia is hard on a woman who has lived most of her life in Buenos Aires.'

His wife shuddered. 'Don't speak of it.'

'Hush, *querida*. We must not bore Señorita Martín with our difficulties.' He turned back to me and smiled. 'Nevertheless, I beg that you will not rush away like most *norteamericanos* when they travel. You have come so far, take time to savor Patagonia, and perhaps offer my wife a little encouragement to speed the winter past.'

I answered in a dream. I had braced myself to face a monster and found a fussed middle-aged man concerned

260

about his wife. General Valdez was as thin as a spider, with a lined face and priggish demeanor. His manners were excellent and the braided uniform of a general became his spare frame very well. He must have been at least twice the age of his wife, who in his presence adopted so many of the attitudes of a spoiled child that the mighty emotions of revenge, terror, and resolve were replaced astonishingly quickly by a prosaic desire to slap her face. The consequence was hallucinatory: The vortex of menace tamed as soon as I rode its rim of absurdity. I laughed too easily and instead of dreading danger became giddily exhilarated by hurtling round its epicenter on a spume of polite chat.

Sometime during the course of dinner it became taken for granted that I would indeed stay some time, the general waving away my offer to pay for telephone calls to my fiancé in Boston. 'The government will pay, señorita. And why not, when you befriend my wife at a time when I may not be able to share as much time with her as I should wish? Your arrival is a blessing from God.' He bowed in his chair as if in acknowledgement to the Almighty, while Isabelita darted a calculating glance at me from under her lashes. Looking back, I think that the sourest of sour jokes was already beginning to take shape, and my fiction that once, a long time ago, her husband had extended an invitation for me to visit, was rubbing against her easy jealousies.

'I met . . . I think I met your daughter upstairs. If I could repay your kindness by being of any assistance . . .' This another of several sentences that had become hopelessly entangled during the evening. 'It must be lonely for a child here. I should enjoy to help entertain or teach her . . . if I could.'

'You like children? But of course you do, anyone can see it. Señorita Sallí – may I call you that? If you can

261

occupy Lylia a little, I shall be even more indebted to you. I fear she provokes Josefina often with her naughtiness, and my wife's health is too delicate for her to suffer such high spirits for long.'

While he was speaking he peeled and sliced some fruit for her which she ostentatiously failed to notice. When he finished, she negligently pushed it aside. 'Is Chepito coming tonight?'

'He said he would, but the news is bad. He may be kept at the base,' the general answered.

'Chepito cheers me up. I want him here, why shouldn't he come if he said he would?'

'I am sure he will if he can, but all Air Force leave is canceled.'

'It isn't leave if he comes here after dinner. You are the governor. You could order him to come if you wanted to.' Her voice rose.

General Valdez turned to me. 'Chepito is my son, a lieutenant at the Air Force base here. I arranged the posting when I discovered how his nonsense lifted Isabelita's spirits; now I begin to fear the consequences of what I have done.'

'The war isn't real,' Isabelita shrugged. 'A shadow play, a nothing, so you and all the other generals may play soldiers. British generals, too, I'm sure.'

'It is suddenly very real. We heard this morning and the rest of the nation will hear tonight: The British have sunk the *General Belgrano*.'

We looked at him blankly.

'A cruiser. Over seven hundred of our sailors are dead. Soon the battle for the Malvinas must begin in earnest, and Chepito's squadron will be needed to defend them.'

'Generals and their soldiers. Chepito and his airplane, what's the difference?' Isabelita dabbed her lips with a napkin. 'You don't need me to tell you he'll enjoy showing off to the British.'

'That is what I am afraid of,' the general answered.

The door opened and Lylia sidled in on a hiss of admonition from Josefina, all fluffy pink in her nightdress and bathrobe. With a sense of fresh delight I noticed how her coloring was mine; before I had seen only Roberto's smile.

'*Buenas noches, Mama. Buenas noches, Papa.*' She went gravely to be kissed.

How do you react when a man you believe to be a brutal torturer kisses your daughter? When that same daughter leans against his knee and smiles across at you with the eyes of her father, who died in that same torturer's jail? The answers are as impossible as the questions. I don't know how I reacted, nor how I looked at that moment.

I spoke and moved and crumpled linen between my fingers while Isabelita continued to complain fretfully about Chepito and her husband fed my daughter with the rejected fruit, caressing her hair with his free hand.

So, since no one noticed, perhaps it does not matter that even now I cannot truthfully say: This and this is how I felt the first time I saw the man who might well be El Carnicero show affection to my child. If Roy had been there . . . I think I should have come apart under the intolerable pressure of his concern.

And Lylia? She continued to look at me and smile, so my heart was both pierced and uplifted.

Then she was gone, sent to bed by Isabelita, who took no interest in her at all. I remembered how in Matias Grande I had wondered whether El Carnicero's wife might perhaps have become too fond of a Carmesi baby for him to do whatever he wished with it after his pretense at fatherhood became a joke, and glanced from him to Isabelita, who was now maintaining a sulky silence while he pensively finished a slice of peach Lylia had dropped on the table. This whole strange and terrible struggle was becoming more inexplicable the closer I came to it, because one thing here was already absolutely clear: the person who felt affectionate toward Lylia was General Valdez himself.

I made an excuse immediately after dinner and fled upstairs to my room. When emotions were so treacherous they could scarcely function, I longed to be alone. But as soon as the door was shut behind me, I forced myself to stand, burning forehead against cold window glass, and try to think rationally about what I had discovered. Lylia was mine. I was unlikely ever to prove it against the word of an Argentinian general, certainly while the country was ruled by his military buddies, but I was sure. This time the link rang true. And if she was mine, then the decision about her future was also mine. A decision already made: whatever the risks of getting her away, one day they would have to be accepted, since the choice for my daughter lay between America with me or growing up in El Carnicero's home. But was General Valdez really El Carnicero? Could he be? The patrona of the Magnifico had said the two were the same, but in the murky world of dirty war politics, that didn't necessarily mean she knew the truth of who tortured helpless victims, who shut their eyes to torture, and who struggled to retain some decency in impossible circumstances.

I stared at harlequin reflections in black glass, my wits still groggily in shock. Yes, General Valdez could be as bad as Matias Grande thought. Murderers were only sometimes brawny brutes, so torturers presumably occasionally took the form of presentable elderly gentlemen.

But that still left the question: Was Valdez indeed El Carnicero?

If he was, any means were justifiable to get Lylia away. If he wasn't, then for me to come as a guest into his house and steal a child he had befriended, perhaps saved from death and now loved, assumed an ugly form. Even in purely practical terms, Lylia might not then be safe should she reach the United States, against Argentine demands for her return.

So, as well as winning Lylia's confidence, I must discover proof, if I could, of General Valdez's past. Then find a way out of this quagmire for us all.

That was as far as I got before I slept. They weren't, I felt, worth two cents as conclusions, but at least settled my mind enough for a kind of rest to be possible, after an unimaginably exhausting day.

The next week passed quietly and, because every night I had to sit at the same table with General Valdez, to do so ceased to seem quite so monstrous. Or was it because this ordinary man fitted less and less easily into my image of El Carnicero? Certainly I realized my purposes would soon be discovered if I behaved like a terrorized rabbit each time we met. By day I drove out in gray drizzle to look at Patagonia, tried with very moderate success to relieve Isabelita's boredom, spent hours wrestling with the Argentine communications system in order to leave terse messages for Roy, and helped the household prepare food for the increasing number of overexcited officers who burst into the governor's house with tales of victory against the British. Above all, I spent joyous hours making friends with my daughter. This was why time fled past so quickly, as a confident naturalness grew between us that restored my other, more unreliable responses to a condition where they were capable of being useful. This, after all, is how one schemes for victory: by making allowance for matters beyond remedy while building on advantage. My advantage was Lylia herself, because she was so enormously and gratefully responsive to affection in a household where her only previous experience of it was Josefina's scoldings or five evening minutes with the general. As for Isabelita, a slap or malicious pinch was her most usual acknowledgement of Lylia's presence. No one had ever played with her before, told fanciful tales, or chattered about nothing in particular; even her language was quaintly unpracticed for a child her age. Soon, I hoped, she would trust me sufficiently to follow wherever I led, and meanwhile her eager spirit took my heart by storm.

On the eighth day after my arrival Chepito came while we lingered over dinner, bursting like a hurricane into one of my futile attempts to lure General Valdez into talking about his past life.

'Chepito!' Isabelita leapt up and flung her arms around his neck. 'You naughty, naughty boy! Why have you waited so long to come? You know I die of boredom on my own.'

He gave her a hug and patted her bottom unselfconsciously. '*Hé, cara!* Who needs be alone in a governor's residence? I had to go up to Maquinchao, if you must know, to test a new missile. We've brought some back with us to Roballos; you just watch how we smash the English now.' He flicked his fingers, laughing. Air Lieutenant Chepito Valdez looked like every girl's idea of a fighter pilot, from his high spirits to the elegantly careless way his uniform was flung on his bronzed and handsome person: features like a profile on a coin, tilted bones, narrow hips. On a closer view I decided he must be about the same age as his stepmother, twenty-eight or nine perhaps; the same spare figure as his father, in his case emphasizing youthful vigor.

'Have you had anything to eat?' The general rang for Josefina.

'Not likely, once I had the chance to dine here instead of chewing muscular mutton in the mess. Mm—' He lifted a couple of covers. 'No food shortage here, I see.'

'You're short at the base?'

'It's the cooks who are infernally bad and we've three times the usual numbers. Four squadrons flying off one runway, imagine! So everything is spoiled before it reaches us. Josefina—' He kissed her on both cheeks as soon as she entered. 'I swear my belly is scraping against my backbone.'

She immediately began scolding him in a way that suggested she had been his nurse, while Isabelita hung on his arm pelting questions. I had never imagined she could be so animated, and stole a glance at the general. His skin looked oddly yellow, as if shrunk closer to his skull.

'And who is this?' Chepito exclaimed suddenly, although I knew he had seen me the moment he entered. 'Isabelita, how could you fail to introduce me to so beautiful a guest? Señorita, your servant.'

'Señorita Martín is American and has come to stay a short time while she views Patagonia.' Isabelita stared at me from under half-closed lids. 'She says we invited her.'

'Hasn't my father ever hinted how rude you can be sometimes, my pet? You ought to spank her where she'd enjoy it, sir! Really you ought. Señorita Martín, voyeur of Patagonia, welcome!' He detached Isabelita from his arm with ruthless ease and came over to kiss my fingers.

'Strangely enough, I've always avoided voyeurs if I could,' I answered dryly.

He gave a shout of laughter. 'Bravo! Señorita, you must stay a long time and cheer us up. Tell me, have you come to count penguins or look at the house where Billy

267

the Kid once stayed?' He sat down and began wolfing a slab of beef Josefina brought, while she hovered to make sure he finished every scrap.

'Don't tell me he came down here?' I exclaimed, diverted.

'On my honor. The few Americans who visit Patagonia always try to find his house first. So if it isn't Billy, it must be penguins.'

'No, just that I'd seen the rest of Argentina and wanted to see Patagonia, too.'

'*Verdad?*' He quirked a disbelieving eyebrow. 'And now that you've seen it, you've decided to stay?'

'I'm going soon,' I said hastily.

'I bet you are. Now, Isabelita here, she'd give her pretty eyelashes to be back in Buenos Aires, wouldn't you, *cara*?'

'With you, Chepito,' she answered, too angry over the few moments he had devoted to me to care what she said.

Josefina clicked her tongue, two red spots appeared on the general's cheeks, and Chepito, with more tact than I would have expected, began to boast about his Mirage jet.

'*Tío* Chepito! *Tío* Chepito! How'se I missed you!' Lylia burst into the room, squealing with delight.

'And I you, *querida*.' He flung her up in the air.

'Is you stay?' she demanded.

'Not this time. I'm going to fly like a skua just above the waves to catch the big bad British in my beak. Watch out each day and when I catch one, I'll come so low over the roof it will blow away over the hill.'

'Will you? So'se I lie in bed and see clouds 'stead of top?'

'Ceiling, sweetheart. The top of a room is called a ceiling.'

'Ceiling,' she repeated experimentally. 'Will you, *Tío* Chepito?'

'I'll have you court-martialed if you do,' said his father.

'Go to bed at once and stop drawing attention to yourself,' Isabelita exclaimed sharply, her slap this time landing on Lylia's cheek. 'Josefina, that child gets more like an unbroken mongrel every day.'

There was a dreadful silence while we all avoided one another's eyes and I grabbed at all the reasons why I couldn't attack Señora Valdez where she sat. Then I stood up and took Lylia by the hand. 'Come upstairs with me, imp. When we've decided how best to stick down the ceiling, perhaps *Tío* Chepito will come and say good night.'

'*Sí.*' He kissed the red mark on her cheek. 'Of course I will.'

As I closed the door behind us I heard the general say in a low furious voice. 'The child stays! I warned you before, I refuse to be made a fool of twice!'

As for Lylia, she was weeping, but silently, as if she had already learned to stay inconspicuous when casually hit for reasons she could not guess. 'I'se try to be good,' she said in a small voice when we reached her bedroom, and from habit Josefina began snapping at her too.

I took a long, soft breath and knelt, taking her hand. 'You are good, *querida*.'

'That she is not!' exclaimed Josefina indignantly. 'Why, who was it, I'd like to know, smeared *dulce de leche* all over the wall?'

'I drawed a picture.' The child spoke listlessly, the almost limitless goodwill and laughter I discovered when we were alone together beaten out of sight by Isabelita's spite.

I turned. 'Josefina, I'm sure you can't have eaten yet.

269

H.—14

Why don't you let me tuck up Lylia tonight? Teniente Chepito promised to come and say good night and it would be dreadfully rude if a lady happened to fall asleep while waiting for a señor to come and kiss her, wouldn't it, Lylia?' I felt her hand tighten on mine, although she still did not look up.

'If you don't mind,' Josefina said grudgingly. 'Now, Señorita Lylia, you just remember to—' She grumbled her way slowly around the room, tidying up, while I willed her to get out, but also kissed Lylia perfunctorily before she finally went. The trouble here was not Josefina, except her old bones hurt too much for her to be overbothered by a child.

Lylia looked up then. 'I sorry.'

I smiled and stood. 'You don't need to be, except perhaps for the *dulce de leche*.'

'Josefina did getted too very sticky,' she conceded, laughter somewhere distantly reborn.

'I bet she did.' I hugged her as if I could say by touch alone: here is love, this is what love means. Then I supervised teeth and prayers, played some game of hopping into bed, read a story. My knees soft while we knelt, voice aching with effort, hands cold. Too soon, too soon for unleashing emotions I might not be able to control; too soon to risk provoking even more hurtful malice from the woman my daughter had grown up calling Mother.

Never too soon to hear Lylia drowsily say, 'Sallí, isn't you stay long?'

'Yes,' I answered steadily. 'Don't worry, sweetheart. I'm staying long.'

She settled back, satisfied, and slept almost instantly after Chepito came.

I switched off the light and followed him out of the room; I liked easygoing Chepito on sight, and however short our acquaintance, I mightn't have many better chances to pump him for information. 'This looks to me like a difficult household for any child to understand.'

He shrugged. 'So? Life has many harder things to offer.'

'But not too many parents who call their own child a mongrel.'

He grinned. 'I always heard Americans don't duck their punches, but you must forgive me. I'm not familiar with female boxers.'

I laughed involuntarily. 'I've become . . . fond of Lylia. You're able to stand up for yourself when you're fought over. She isn't.'

'There's nothing I can do about it,' he said with sudden venom. 'We live our lives and are saddled with the consequences.'

I thought about that for a moment. 'Would you answer a question?'

'Perhaps.' He lit a cigarette.

'You spoke just now about the consequences of our lives as if you really meant it . . . Were you perhaps thinking about El Carnicero?'

Instantly he froze, cigarette halfway to his lips; his breathing roughened, the knuckles of that lifted hand whitened. Then he turned and walked away without a word, polished boots rapping on boards, and a few minutes later I heard him leave.

Maybe it was anger after that vicious little scene in the dining room that had urged me into chancing a direct question, or an unexpected opportunity to surprise a crucial witness into frankness. I know I suddenly felt consumed by impatience; far more time than I expected had already passed in Patagonia without finding any answers even to the mystery of General Valdez. And chance had paid off, Chepito's shock surely an answer in

271

itself. Nor did I believe he had used those few moments of farewell downstairs to warn his father that Señorita Martín was unhealthily interested in his past. Instead, he had run from a truth he hated to acknowledge – God knows, I ought to recognize those who ran from detestable truth. To grow up as he had, the son of El Carnicero at a time when people crossed themselves if his father passed, would leave scars beneath the most insouciant façade.

And yet, now that this most vital and filthy fact could at last be regarded as double-checked and established, all I felt was satisfaction over another step successfully taken. Fear, even rage, seemed temporarily to vanish, because Lylia rather than El Carnicero preoccupied me now.

The following day the tempo of the household changed. General Valdez stayed in his office, apparently sacrificing even his siesta, while flurried aides swept in and out, trailing mud between there and the front door. He even ate supper off a tray with his staff, as if over the horizon great events were shaping, while on television the Buenos Aires newscaster sounded even more confident than before. The British, he said, had yesterday lost two aircraft carriers to daring Argentine air attacks and their task force had at last turned tail for home.

In consequence, Lylia spent her day skipping on the gravel, waiting for Chepito to fly over and blow off the roof.

I telephoned Roy very late, since the switchboard had been jammed all day, and was lucky to find him waiting in his office: for more than a week I'd been forced to leave messages with Huron.

'It's very formal Miss Sally Martin,' I said.

'Thank God. I was about to reserve a seat for Buenos Aires. My sweet, how much longer are you staying on down there?'

272

'I'm not sure,' I said carefully. 'It wouldn't be easy to get out at the moment; the army is everywhere. I guess you'd find it hard to reach farther south than Buenos Aires.'

'I wouldn't bet too much against it. Say the word and I'll be down.'

'Roy . . .' This was horribly difficult, when I sensed breathing from the extension in Isabelita's room. 'It's interesting here at the moment, and I'm able to repay a little of the Valdezes' hospitality by helping out while the house is busy. I'll make it away the moment the war is over.'

'You may wait quite a while,' he answered noncommittally, as aware as I was that every word needed watching.

'It doesn't sound that way. The British are pulling out.'

'Remember another bet I laid with you?'

'Yes.' He had bet me ten dollars that if the British came, they'd win.

'I expect to collect on it next time we meet.'

Did he, indeed. You surely wouldn't think it, listening to Buenos Aires. 'And are you collecting on your federal case as well?'

I felt his smile reach across six thousand miles of air. 'Yeah, that too.'

'General Valdez won't let me pay for these calls, so I'd better stop.' I hesitated over how to phrase the message I wanted him to understand. 'I'll get back soon, don't worry. It's just difficult to see quite how at the moment.'

'Tell me when you decide to leave and I'll help fix your trip,' he answered deliberately. 'Don't drive the road out on your own. It must be too dangerous for even the most emancipated female at the moment.'

'Yes, I know.' Too dangerous to smuggle Lylia away,

273

too dangerous to make any move at all while Patagonia filled with troops and more troops. Yet that was what I had to do; the last twitch of conscience cleared once Chepito settled my doubts about El Carnicero.

'When you tell lies, you tell them good, don't you?' Roy said tightly.

'I suppose so . . . I didn't really think about it,' I said, confused. Roy was a hard man to fool, he knew I'd disregard his warning if I saw any way out at all. Whereas a listener would simply think his anxiety typically American. An Argentine woman would either never drive alone in a military zone, period, or be provided with the kind of all-protecting papers General Valdez could give me if what I really wanted was to leave for the north alone.

'Even unreally I wish to Christ you would.' The laugh was back in his voice. 'Do you realize we've wasted most of a telephone call without me telling how I love you?'

'My dear . . . and I you.' The oldest of platitudes newly minted on my lips, and I didn't care if Isabelita eavesdropped.

'I never tried to seduce anyone down a telephone line before. I guess I'm not very good at it.'

'You are, oh, you are, my dearest. The only cure for six thousand miles of distance.'

I hung up, feeling serene. No other word for it. The lack of physical contact scarcely mattered when just speaking to Roy made me feel like this. My fear that we might find it too difficult to find a balance in the future seemed absurd. As if, between us, we could put the future on its honor to behave.

18

This conversation, guarded though it was, stayed in my mind because the sense of happiness it brought persisted through the following difficult days. Happiness that contrasted with the deteriorating atmosphere in the Valdez house. The normality of Blainey, Rosenthal, & McGeown was something I enjoyed imagining once Argentine staff officers began to scamper aimlessly, as it seemed, in and out of the house. That was also the last time I reached Roy direct. Next day the gathering battle in the South Atlantic swamped Argentina's unreliable communications system and only General Valdez's influence enabled me to reach as far as Huron at the embassy. The general never commented on my insistence that I must keep in touch, more like a teenager pacifying anxious parents than a globe-trotting *muy testeruda* female, although Isabelita was spitefully caustic; until eventually I began to wonder whether his restraint might be sinister rather than the disinterest of a busy man.

I was becoming jittery as time passed and passed, my excuses for staying wearing thin, while still I hadn't found any way of taking Lylia with me when I went. Alone, I could have left for the north, since the general shipped delicacies from Buenos Aires in military aircraft no matter how serious the war, and he would, I am sure, have given me the papers I would need either to drive or fly out. But it was also easy enough to stay. The war upset household routine, Josefina was old, General Valdez's batman too arrogant for household tasks, the other servants, ignorant. Left alone, Lylia would have been constantly harried to keep out of the way, since Isabelita did nothing beyond languidly entertain visiting officers and lie on her sofa saying she was listening to her spirits: which, she assured us, in Buenos Aires invariably helped her to unravel the latest intrigues. We were given to understand that they, like their mistress, found Patagonia an unsympathetic environment for their activities, for which I was grateful.

Argentine hospitality meant the kitchen must somehow produce enormous meals at all hours as generals, admirals, police chiefs, and air group commanders came and went, often sitting around for hours as if they had come for a party instead of to fight a war. If ever the question of my departure happened to come up, Lylia clung to me in heartwarming entreaty and everyone else except Isabelita begged me to stay: she lay on her sofa watching me out of eyes filled with hatred. A hatred which, as time went on, became ever more obviously rooted in jealousy. She could not bear Chepito so much as to look in my direction, considered each flowery compliment offered me by visiting officers as a personal affront. She also hated me because she sensed – though I tried to hide it – that I detested her. Before I came to Roballos, I guess Isabelita mostly ignored Lylia: not difficult now to realize that the delayed baptism at Matias Grande must somehow have resulted from her rejection of the baby her husband brought out of the Carmesi, the futile, humiliating deception he wanted her to carry through. 'I refuse to be made a fool of twice,' I had overheard him say the night Isabelita called Lylia a mongrel.

After I came and she saw how affection grew between

Lylia and myself, the way she ran to me, our private jokes and instinctive understanding, Isabelita's attitude changed from mostly passive dislike to open malice. And, of course, the more hurtful she became, the more Lylia clung to me, the less easily was I able to hide the explosive mix of love, fury, and gut reaction which proclaims: This child is mine. As the ultimate sick irony, matters would have been easier if General Valdez had not been forced to spend most of his time in his office, even meals often delayed until after Lylia was in bed or out with me. Josefina was exhausted by such upset in her routine, and, for Lylia, out of the whole household soon only Sallí could be relied on not to scream, box her ears, or find her a nuisance. Several times the general thanked me for my care of his daughter and out of an endless array of impossible situations, I think this disgusting incongruity came closest of all to triggering the explosion of emotion I most feared.

As for the war, it was difficult to form any opinion of how that was going. Not far over the windy horizon men were dying and Chepito flew his Mirage jet to attack the British, yet we understood very little of what was happening. This wasn't for any lack of news. The radio and television spoke of little else, showed horrifying pictures of burning British ships and triumphant Argentine pilots, of a garrison secure behind fortifications while the British shivered on a beach. People chattered cheerfully about national triumph and Argentina coming of age through blood; of the invincibility of their men on islands only madmen would invade, in winter particularly. When a Mirage came low over the town trailing smoke and exploded with an appalling flash on the headland behind the base, they wept for the pity of it, but, because it brought the war closer, they also relished their victory with a new intensity.

In the governor's house reactions were more confused. Isabelita's because she was skeptical by habit, the general's presumably because he knew more than the rest of us. As for myself, after Roy's comment I studied the newscasts for scattered clues rather than regarding them as hard fact. For the British had indeed proved to be the kind of madmen who invaded inhospitable, fortified islands in midwinter. Thousands of miles from home and faced by entrenched defense they forced a beachhead on the Malvinas where, so Buenos Aires said, they had now been surrounded and cut off from support.

Each day I took Lylia out, since, whatever her jealousies, Isabelita disliked most of all anyone disturbing her siesta. When I stayed out for the whole time afterward while officers came to call, then at dinner she might almost enjoy talking to me about matters outside Roballos: New York society especially fascinated her. Since it was a subject on which I was entirely ignorant, I enjoyed seeing how bug-eyed I could make her, by drawing on my imagination.

On our daily expeditions sometimes Lylia and I walked down to Roballos, where a deep-sea jetty remained from the great days of Argentina's wool and meat trade. Naval ships were tied up there, so Lylia enjoyed the trumpets and flags, but in spite of the battle a mere five hundred miles away, none showed signs of putting to sea. On other days we drove, ostensibly to visit neighbors or look for wildlife, in reality to test ideas I'd patched together about escape. By then I dismissed any notion of travelling north. Under present circumstances the fifteen hundred miles between Roballos and Buenos Aires could be covered only with General Valdez's help. And yet that seemed the only possible way out. East lay the Atlantic; to the south, Tierra del Fuego and the Antarctic. The high cordillera of the

Andes cut off exit to the west with a jumble of glaciers and peaks, some over eleven thousand feet high. No child could survive a winter journey across them.

Which meant that if I decided to leave that way, we would have to cross into Chile by road. A covert study of the wall map in General Valdez's office revealed three border posts possibly within reach: the nearest some two hundred and fifty miles away, the farthest over four hundred. In a region almost bare of roads, we should need a long start to reach any of them safely.

We would need an enormous start to reach anywhere safely, even though I still kept the rented automobile. Heaven knows what it was costing Roy, though he told me Hertz had agreed it wasn't reasonable to expect me to check it back across seven hundred miles of military zone, so the charges were reduced.

One day Lylia and I drove part of the way toward the nearest frontier crossing. The road was flat, slippery, and unchanging, the wind cold and vindictive. After the military bustle along the coast such solitude was a shock, the melancholy emptiness of Patagonia blending into a smudge of mountain high on the horizon, which by midmorning had vanished into storm clouds. No traffic passed us. Only a few sheep and the occasional farmhouse floated magically above the ground on chimeras of distance.

'I don't like,' Lylia said positively. 'There a nothing to see.'

'I don't either,' I confessed. The idea of escaping along such a road was ludicrous, our vehicle a single intrusion into nothingness. If we reached the frontier, we could be the only people crossing in a day, the guards certain to enjoy demanding documentation for Lylia, the automobile, everything.

'You wanta go on?' demanded Lylia.

'Just a little way. There's a lake here somewhere. Let's reach that if we can.'

'Whasit lake?'

I was explaining about lakes, when we saw a guanaco bounding across scrub like a creature on a carousel, orange coat glowing and white tail held high. We climbed out to watch and instantly the wind leapt at us. I had to clutch at Lylia to stop her from being bowled over.

She hung on my hand, laughing. 'Bump-crash! I like just a sit in the mud.'

I hugged her, laughing too, the spell of my daughter twisting every day tighter around my heart. Pretense always dangerously forgotten whenever we were away alone together, the cankered emotions of the Valdez house more difficult to endure after each return.

The lake when we reached it looked like curdled cream, and all the way there and back the road surface slowed us down to less than fifty miles an hour. Under the circumstances it scarcely seemed worth considering the Chilean frontier any further.

Two days later we drove south, to the tiny port of Santa Cruz. I hoped some coasting vessels might use it since military now forbade these from entering the Bay of Roballos, yet the general said there was still an irregular service by way of Tierra del Fuego to Chile by sea. But the army was in Santa Cruz, too, landing craft stuffed with stores bucking dangerously at anchor in the swell, and, worst of all, a squadron of helicopters squatting behind an abandoned factory. I had climbed one day to the headland at Roballos to study Chepito's air base and been relieved not to find any of these menacing machines there; now I had found some, which probably meant there were more elsewhere I hadn't seen. No use kidding myself any longer; the Argentine forces possessed both the equipment and geographical control to track down fugitives quickly.

But it was worth going to Santa Cruz just for the happiness Lylia and I found there together. The coast was edged by dunes and beyond the port these were unguarded: long Atlantic breakers boomed on to the shore while among the dunes we were almost sheltered from the wind. Lylia tobogganed on her rump down their steep sides and we hunted for yellow harpoon heads carved from seal bone after I'd spotted one lying in debris outside some animal's burrow, which must have been left behind by some vanished Indian tribe.

'Papa just a once told me all the Indians deaded long ago in big heaps everywhere,' Lylia said. 'Then sheeps could come.'

I shivered, thinking also of my home state of Montana. 'There should have been room for both.'

'Oh, no! Gauchos 'joyed deading Indians,' she said earnestly. 'Better'n deading guanacos 'cos if they chased all-all right away, they had to did a battle and the gauchos always winned.'

'Can't you feel even a little bit sorry for the Indians?' It was an effort to keep my voice steady. I ought not to have felt so dismayed to discover that the man who must be El Carnicero had already begun subtly to corrupt even a child for whom he felt affection.

'But they were enemies!' she exclaimed, then paused, hair ruffled by the eddying wind, and glanced uncertainly at the stony Patagonian wasteland which here reached to the coast.

'The Indians must have fought battles they couldn't win because they knew their children would starve, once driven away from fish and pasture, don't you think?' I so detested hearing an echo of El Carnicero in my daughter that I failed to heed inner urgings to caution, and not long afterward, when we found another tiny incised harpoon head, suddenly Lylia almost suffocated me with a hug. 'I think it was *horrid* to send the Indians into the stones to dead!'

I held her tightly, almost in tears. She wriggled after a moment. 'You come 'splain to Papa about the Indians?'

I shook my head. 'I am his guest, and guests have to mind their manners.'

'Here's me to go 'splain then,' she said, in a small voice but without rancor.

Only a short time before, and I had been absurdly upset by callousness she could not help, now I had provoked a situation where for her own safety I must coldly discourage the spontaneous flowering of human pity in my daughter. To General Valdez I was someone who repaid his hospitality by taking his daughter with me while I explored Patagonia; if he ever realized how quickly and strongly the bond between Lylia and myself had grown, a bond which had just led her instinctively to weigh and reject his judgement, then El Carnicero's infinitely more dangerous jealousies might easily be added to Isabelita's. Whether he might also ask himself why Lylia and I were so naturally and lovingly drawn together I couldn't guess, but he might. Begin perhaps to speculate about my motive for coming to Patagonia. And though, surely, he could not possibly suspect the right answer, the easiest way out of unease then would be to end my visit. As governor he could have me sent north, or even deported, tomorrow if he wished.

So I answered Lylia briskly. 'It is kind of your . . .' Oh, God, the effort of even pretending El Carnicero was her father! '. . . your papa to give up his time to tell you stories when he is so busy. It would be ungrateful and rude if you seemed to argue with him.'

'Perhaps he be glad if I 'splained,' she said doubtfully.

'No. No, I don't think he would, do you?' I put my fingers across her lips. 'We'll keep it our secret that we feel sorry for the Indians. Promise?'

She spat on a grubby forefinger and made a cross on my forehead. 'Me promise. Josefina do promises like that.'

In a draft through the automobile window I seemed to feel the chill stickiness of my daughter's spit all the way back to Roballos, while she slept trustingly beside me. I drove almost unseeingly, a prey to a whole set of fresh hatreds churned out of near despair: after this day in Santa Cruz I could scarcely bear to contemplate returning Lylia into a life so surrounded by corruption and deceit for another single day. I was conscious, too, that time must be running out for me, yet I seemed as far as ever from finding any remotely safe way of taking Lylia with me when I went.

'Is a block,' said Lylia comfortably, rousing when we were nearly back in Roballos, and I slowed to join a row of trucks queuing at a checkpoint. You couldn't move far along the coast without passing barriers that appeared and vanished without warning. The papers General Valdez had given me ensured rapid, courteous treatment but also guaranteed that everyone knew precisely which way I went.

I might gain half a day's start before anyone became alarmed or suspicious, but the harder I looked for a way out, the more of a gamble the whole enterprise appeared. A start was useless with every exit closed, and before I made any move, I had to believe my escape plan could succeed, because failure risked not only my chance of taking Lylia out but, quite possibly, her life. These troops fired their weapons easily, and the climate down here was a killer.

We heard a roar just as I parked the automobile on the

gravel outside the house. 'It's *Tío* Chepito!' screamed Lylia, spilling out of the door. 'He's beated an English!'

The Mirage was so low that at first I only heard it coming, then it lifted above some pasture and ripped overhead in a shatter of sound, banked, and came back, waggling its wings. I glimpsed a figure in the cockpit, blue Argentine markings, a line of punched black holes in one wing; then it climbed and decorously lowered its wheels ready for a landing at the base beyond the headland.

Lylia ran inside to see if the ceiling of her bedroom was still there while I followed more slowly, feeling even more oppressed than before, this time by the reality of modern blood and battle when, to be honest, previously I had only considered whether this unforeseen war hindered or helped my own affairs.

In the hall I encountered the general. 'I'll have that crazy boy court-martialed! He could have killed himself, and us.'

I thought of those black punched holes. 'He'd probably been nearly killed in a fight not many minutes before, and can't worry about other kinds of risk.'

'*Sí*,' he said irresolutely. '*Sí*, I suppose so. Thank God he is safe, anyway. Señorita, where have you been all day?'

'Down to Santa Cruz. Did you know that in the dunes there you can pick up old Indian harpoon heads made of seal bone? Look, we found several.'

He peered perfunctorily at the crafted slivers in my hand. 'It is a military zone at Santa Cruz.'

'Well, it is here, too. I thought the papers you gave me were drawn up so I needn't worry about restrictions.' I gazed at him innocently, but inwardly felt alarmed. The last thing I wanted was for him to become interested in my activities. And, as always when I looked at him, really looked, that is, the sense of unreality returned. This was El Carnicero. What infamy had those eyes watched, those hands enjoyed? The ordinary human being I had discovered offered no clue, no clue at all to the nature of an unseen monster who relied on blood for kicks. Only that single unnatural echo perceived today in a child as instinctively generous as Lylia might offer its own warning; or could some part of Isabelita's disagreeable personality, too, be blamed on him? I doubted it. If Matias Grande rumor was right, and El Carnicero impotent away from the torture chamber, then she was more than capable of arranging her own remedy.

'That is so, when I expected you to visit neighbors or take Lylia into Roballos,' he said irritably now about my papers. 'But questions are being asked about a gringo prying into our secret military bases, who perhaps counts our soldiers as they embark for the Malvinas.'

I nearly laughed. 'I promise I'm not a British spy.'

'I should never have entertained you with such pleasure in my house if I had for a moment entertained such a suspicion! But you must see how your journeys would look to our police, when each night you also telephone America or your embassy.' He spread those hands; square, strong-fingered, useful hands.

And for the first time since I came, I shivered, looking at those hands.

'I telephone because the man I am soon to marry is worried about me staying near a war. Isabelita . . . well, she listens, doesn't she? She could tell you I've never said anything about military affairs.'

'*Dios!*' he said, smiling. 'I like women to unsheath their claws, and so far you have seemed too good to be true. I am only warning you, Sallí. For your own safety, from now on I think it is best if you do not drive out of Roballos district. If you would return the papers I gave you, I will have them amended. Then, should our police ask, you will be able to prove you could not have gone where you shouldn't.'

I handed them over at once, since hesitation would have seemed an admission of guilt. 'I could still be accused of spying in Roballos.'

'Yes, you could,' he answered mildly, staring at me out of pitted, rejoicing eyes. A single casual chance of frightening a guest he liked, and he couldn't resist taking it. At last, at last, and as soon as I began to look vulnerable, that other dreadful self slid momentarily out of ordinariness.

I was glad to escape upstairs and then to have my tumbling thoughts calmed by a series of crises in the kitchen. Guests were expected for dinner and there was no time to worry about anything else; worry hit me only as I kissed Lylia good night. I fairly bolted down the passage afterward and into my own room, but, because I had caught that fleeting glimpse of the demon caged inside General Valdez, as soon as I was alone I immediately began to picture horrors again, if possible even more violently than before. In consequence, I had my first bad attack of the shakes since I arrived and was late for dinner.

That was also the evening when the first crack also appeared in General Valdez's suave bearing, although this time I could scarcely blame him. Soon after the meal began, Chepito arrived, still at blow-torch heat after combat. He kissed Isabelita lingeringly on the mouth when she ran to him, in front of a dumbfounded assortment of visiting colonels. '*Querida, queridita,* your kisses bring me luck, did you know that?'

'*Verdad*, Chepito? I like that very much! Then I must come each day to your base and weave my spells afresh, *hé*?'

'If you did, you would have to kiss all the other pilots as well or risk being charged with treason.' He kissed her again, as if they were alone in bed together. 'This luck I keep to myself.'

'Oh, me too,' she sighed.

'Chepito!' shouted his father, and struck an ornamental table with his fist so the china on it bounced and broke. 'Blood of Christ, you have gone too far! What has become of your respect?'

'You tell me if you dare.' Insolently, Chepito flicked his uniform straight.

For several seconds the two faced each other, rage stamping likeness on their faces, then Chepito shrugged. 'Your pardon, sir. I have flown eight missions against the British this last week, and some good friends have been killed since I visited here last.'

'We all admire the courage of our fliers,' one of the colonels exclaimed, sweating with anxiety to defuse the situation.

Chepito looked at him from under his long girl's eyelashes. 'As we are struck dumb by the performance of our army.'

The colonel reddened. 'Our army has lured the English into a trap and is slaughtering them there.'

Chepito laughed. 'On the contrary. Argentina is in the trap and the English are slaughtering my squadron there.'

'I refuse to listen to another word of this treasonable crap!' the general shouted. 'Air Lieutenant Valdez, consider yourself under arrest.'

'Send to the base and arrest me if you can,' snapped Chepito. '*Jesucristo,* didn't you hear what I said? We've lost ten pilots and double that number of aircraft in a week, more the week before. *Claro*, I downed an enemy today and we've sunk more ships than the English

287

expected, but we can't sink the Malvinas. D'you know the bastards sailed a damned great luxury liner right up to the shore and landed all the troops they wanted, while our brave army ran for cover?'

'And what was the Air Force doing?' demanded another of the colonels thickly, his hand on the revolver in his belt.

'Dying! Like the British. The difference is, they've got troops who know their job, and a navy which doesn't skulk in harbor. So tomorrow I'll be flying over the Malvinas again and you can't touch me. The air command is too short of pilots to feel sympathetic toward generals who try to keep their sons safe by rigging a court-martial.'

Isabelita began to whimper. 'Chepito, why are you talking like this? I don't understand, you'll be all right, won't you?'

'Perhaps,' he answered carelessly, and for the first time glanced at me. 'As to why I'm talking like this . . . Let's just say I could have been killed a dozen times last week. Which made me think how much I'd hate anyone to imagine I died to defend shitheads who learned their trade inside the torture chambers of Buenos Aires . . . and Matias Grande.' He walked out of the room.

Isabelita understood the reference to Matias Grande. I saw her hand creep to her throat. The colonels swore among themselves but uneasily, since few of them would be innocent in the dirty war either. As for General Valdez, if ever guilt was written on a man's face it was written on his, although in unexpected ways. Shock came first, that his son should speak with such contempt, then memory followed. His pupils contracted, mouth slackened beneath the soldierly mustache as he peered under the covers of a past he had previously kept tightly wrapped away and discovered – possibly with surprise –

that excitement returned to recollection first. And as he remembered, anger toward Chepito ebbed but his hands began to tremble with desire. 'I'm not ashamed; in fact I'm proud,' he said as if about nothing in particular. 'The task needed doing and we did it. No one remembers now how badly it needed doing.'

'We're all proud,' agreed the colonels. Did they speak of the army they had helped to rot, of torture, or corpses shoveled out with the trash? I'm not sure they knew, but they wanted to feel proud, so pride was what they felt.

As for myself, I watched that flicker of excitement behind El Carnicero's inward-turning thoughts, the deprivation of excitement that hit him now he lingered to remember, and all my fears solidified into a great big certainty that it had suddenly become very much more dangerous for me to stay here any longer.

I realized this feeling was itself dangerous, since haste to find almost any way out for Lylia, provided she left El Carnicero's home when I did, could cloud my judgement of what might and might not be an acceptable risk. Because worse than fear was being afraid of fear. That night, for the first time since coming to Roballos, I locked my bedroom door as if a key could keep evil out, found myself detesting taking so much as water from my bedside jug because El Carnicero might have used the glass before me.

I slept badly on a whirl of hard-edged thoughts, wanting very much to feel Roy's arms around me.

I hadn't wanted him before. His concern insupportable, his knowledge of my past an additional degradation once I was forced to live in the same house as El Carnicero. Without Roy I had in some strange way been able until now to accept General Valdez at face value: that ordinary man, seated at table peeling fruit. Now

289

that the Carmesi stalked my dreams again, soaking the bedclothes in blood and bringing terror moaning on the black night wind, I wanted Roy. Craved the promise of love made slowly and prodigally; imagined the feel of each other, kissing each other; this my last defense against reborn and debilitating weakness.

Next day poor Lylia found me answering her very much at random, my temper as brittle as Isabelita's. Occasionally I saw her watching me uncertainly and tried to grip my sliding will, to chatter lightheartedly as we had before. But it was so hard I often failed.

A week lagged past while mercifully El Carnicero stayed mostly among his huddles of officers, and I became exhausted by nightmares that prevented sleep; each evening it was more difficult not to alter my telephoned message to the embassy and bring Roy flying south. But once he came, my last excuse to stay with the Valdezes would be gone, and still I could not think of any way to take Lylia out.

Perhaps that enormous feeling of danger had been only another nightmare, and I could safely stay a little longer.

Another ten days passed in which nothing particular happened except for worry, fright, and frustration snarling tighter, and then a policeman came to see me. He questioned me while Isabelita watched from her sofa, glinting with enjoyment. He reminded me of a cockroach: scabby, and scuttling in directions I couldn't anticipate. 'You are British by ancestry, Señorita Martín?'

'No,' I said, astonished. 'I'm American.'

'You're sure?'

'Quite sure.' I wasn't about to start speculating with him about a great-grandfather who might have come from Devon.

'But you sympathize with British piracy against our Malvinas?'

'I don't know anything about it, and never expressed an opinion.'

He rustled some papers. 'I have different information.'

'Then your information is wrong.'

'Why did you come to Patagonia, Señorita Martín?'

'Because I—'

'Be careful how you answer. I do not like liars.'

His interruption was designed to rattle me, and succeeded. Out of all my nightmares, interrogation was the worst. 'I came because I had spent time elsewhere in Argentina and wanted to see Patagonia, too, before returning home.'

'How could that be? According to our records you entered our country on March twenty-fourth, spent three nights in Buenos Aires, and then traveled to Matias Grande. From there you came directly here.'

'Matias Grande!' exclaimed Isabelita, and swung her legs to the floor. '*Dios*, did you say Matias Grande?'

'Yes,' said the policeman, annoyed. 'Señora, I must ask you to remain silent or my suspect will have time to perfect her lies.'

'But Matias Grande! That was where General Valdez and I lived before we came here!'

He waved his hand. 'It is a town, is it not? Then of course people go there, I do not see anything strange in that. What I find incomprehensible is a gringo señorita finding excuses to stay with the governor and yourself just as English piracy begins in the Malvinas. Then stays and stays through a Patagonian winter.'

'She said we invited her, but I never remembered meeting her,' agreed Isabelita thoughtfully.

'Well, señorita?'

291

'I have been in Argentina before, in 1976 I think it was.' Isabelita's intervention had indeed offered a few vital seconds to recover from the shock of police precision about my movements. Whatever would they make of Caproni's story if they also discovered about my trip to Dos Bichos? 'You'll find the entry in your records, I expect. On that visit I stayed with friends in Buenos Aires, where I met General Valdez, although I'm not surprised he doesn't remember from so long ago. I admit, when I heard in Matias Grande that he had become governor here, I hoped I'd found a way to visit Patagonia when, because of the war, it might otherwise be closed to ordinary visitors.'

I'd considered this delicate balance of truth and omission many times since I came to Roballos, after discreetly establishing that General Valdez had indeed been stationed in Buenos Aires before being sent to Matias Grande.

'Verdad?' said the policeman skeptically. 'What friends in Buenos Aires?'

'They were called Cortazar; one of them is in a high position in the World Bank in Washington, and he suggested I might like to see the Argentina I'd missed before.' A lie which had served at Buenos Aires airport was far more dangerous now that a serious police inquiry was under way. On the other hand, when I visited Argentina in 1976, I came on a stately pilgrimage to meet Roberto's family after he decided to ask me to marry him, and any mention of the Esquilars was dynamite. The most casual check would reveal Roberto as a *desaparecido*, Sally Martin as his widow; besides, the tale in Matias Grande had been that El Carnicero fancied a brat only with good blood in its veins. Isabelita might easily have been told Lylia's parentage, remember the name of Esquilar. 'You must see I have no connection with the British,' I added quickly. 'The very idea is absurd. The only foreign country I ever visited is Argentina, and my home state in America is in the West. I never met any British there.'

The policeman sucked his mustache reflectively. 'I will check.'

'I wish you would! For heaven's sake, you must see for yourself it isn't likely. When I flew into Buenos Aires two . . . no, three months ago now, the Malvinas were still British and no one dreamed of war.'

It helped that I really wasn't a spy, that he was questioning me about matters where logic remained on my side. All the same, a single wrong answer would unravel my story like a ball of yarn.

Eventually he stood up and put his notebook away. 'You may not leave this house until I say. Any disobedience will make you liable to military law, and being *Yanqui* will not save you.'

'It has already.' I couldn't resist the dig. If that policeman knew that by his law I was Argentine, he wouldn't bother with questions before slapping me in a cellar.

'Then don't count on it a second time!' he snapped. 'Roballos is a long way from Washington.'

'She telephones the American embassy every night,' Isabelita interrupted smoothly, like the slug she was.

'So General Valdez said, which seemed to him suspicious. Prevent her, señora, until we have discovered how many lies she's told.'

'Then they will know there is something wrong.'

'We are fighting a war here, are we not? So. We send messages for her while the exchange is overburdened by military emergencies.' He turned to me. 'Who is it you contact?'

I told him Huron at the embassy.

'What message? Take care to keep it short, when that

293

is the easiest way for us to be sure there is no trick.'

'Just tell him Sally called.'

He glanced at Isabelita.

She nodded. 'Usually she says something simple like that to this Huron if she cannot reach Boston.'

'Then we will speak to the embassy each night until we are satisfied she may leave. Or not satisfied, of course.' He scuttered busily out of the room.

He walks like a cockroach, too, I thought.

Already I was shuddering with reaction, beginning muzzily to calculate how long police inquiries would take in a torpid bureaucracy kicked out of its rut by war. How long for Huron to warn Roy that my message had changed at last; how long before Roy could reach through that same hostile bureaucracy to Patagonia? And when he did, would I already have vanished back into prison?

'That policeman is a fool,' hissed Isabelita by my side. 'Me, I know there is some reason why you came here from Matias Grande. My spirits tell me it is so. Soon they will whisper what the reason is.'

'That will be interesting,' my voice said politely. I marveled it did not tremble as badly as my hands.

'Ah, you may stick your *norteamericano* nose in the air! You despised me from the day you came, because I lie back and give my spirits time to speak. Meddlers like you are so busy running from place to place, you forget how to listen.'

'There's nothing to learn from spirits or anyone else about me, except I made the mistake of outstaying my welcome.' I answered, and left the room before she saw how badly, how suspiciously badly shaken I was. Whether spirits or her own shrewd intelligence tugged at her, where personal enmities were concerned, Isabelita would be quite as merciless as the police.

19

An Air Force major rang the bell two days later. Josefina threw her apron over her head and howled like a coyote as soon as she opened the door to him, which brought the rest of us running. The general from his office, Isabelita from her sofa, Lylia and me clutching floury paws from the kitchen. Since the policeman left, I had lived almost entirely with Lylia and the servants, the atmosphere between myself and the Valdezes so gritty with concealment and suspicion that even minimal social contact was difficult to sustain. Now we ran together and were together petrified by Josefina's sorrow, which, the moment we saw it, made us desolate, too.

The major saluted and put his cap under his arm. 'Major Segal at your service. Señor General, señora—'

'It's Chepito, isn't it?' Isabelita bared her teeth as if she intended to fasten them in his throat.

'I am afraid . . . *Sí*, it is Chepito. He was killed yesterday over the Malvinas.'

'No hope?' said General Valdez hoarsely.

'I'm afraid not, sir. His aircraft exploded quite low over the sea. We . . . the squadron would wish me to say that he was the best of good comrades, a brave man and a skillful pilot. We shall not replace him or our other lost friends easily; I wish only that they could have given their lives for victory.'

'But they did!' General Valdez's staff captain blurted out. 'We had a message from our High Command last night. The British are on the point of capitulation.'

Segal smacked his cap back on his head in a gesture between fury and disgust. 'I assure you, it wasn't British white flags I saw when I flew over the Malvinas this morning.'

'White flags?'

'Yes, white flags. Perhaps you'd better tell the High Command. The British won and I have twelve out of twenty-five pilots dead. May I repeat my regrets that Chepito was among them?' He clicked his bootheels, gently touched Josefina's hand, and marched out as if he expected to be shot in the back.

'Those sons of bitches killed Chepito,' said Isabelita blankly. 'Why didn't you do as you threatened and send a guard to arrest him?' Her voice rose. 'Or did you want him dead because I kissed him? Yes, in the end you wanted him dead like all the rest.'

The general shook his head, tears glittering on his cheeks.

'I loved him and you were jealous and you killed him. You generals killed him between you and I'll never be happy again.'

'Nor I,' said General Valdez jerkily. 'But *dios*, I shall avenge him.'

'Didn't you hear? The war is over!' she screamed. 'Impudent scum like that major are already blaming everyone except themselves: they'll revenge their rage on you! I should have known you weren't fit for anything except gutting criminals and—' She burst out crying, half dreadful and half crowing over the look on his face. Her hair tumbled out of its knot, her hands writhing in her skirt.

Josefina howled again in sympathy, and Lylia wept in panic against my knee.

'Come, señora,' I said quickly, this scene beyond the

stage where sympathy might help. 'Let me take you to your room. Josefina, run and fetch the decanter of brandy and drink some yourself. Lylia, could you manage to roll out the pastry we were making while I take your mama upstairs? I'm sure you could.'

When I came downstairs again, the general was sitting on the bottom step, alone, his face in his hands. I hesitated, unable to pass and swept by pity. The sorrow I also felt for Chepito made hatred seem obscene.

Sally Martin, salesperson of easy sentiment.

He looked up with reddened, unfocused eyes. 'Chepito . . . he was the sort wars always kill. But I'll have that major torn in pieces for defeatism. The High Command proclaims we are close to victory.'

I didn't answer, pity shriveling again. If Major Segal said he had seen white flags over Argentine positions, then I trusted his eyesight above Buenos Aires optimism.

Only seconds later I wouldn't have dared to answer, as, in front of my eyes, a weeping father changed into El Carnicero. The reddened eyes dulled and looked inward; his lips drew back, tongue flickering eagerly between them, while unseen muscles seemed to clench like a fist against his skull. At last, violent shock had shattered the conventional façade I had only recently and occasionally seen cracked, spilling out from behind it the true catharsis of his being: the omnipotent, sweet, destructive release of brutality.

Whatever might once have been the case, I believe he was no more able to prevent this happening than could a drug addict trembling for his fix, which made him more and not less fearful.

A single false move, a breath even, and I would be the first victim of Chepito's death. Let the thought so much as cross his mind and this General Valdez would agree at once that I must be a British spy. I imagined Lylia, tongue gripped between her teeth in concentration, rolling pastry into thinner and thinner strips until eventually she came in search of me, to discover that, like *Tío* Chepito, I had disappeared forever. Which in El Carnicero's household meant quite as great a disaster for her as for myself.

I was saved for the moment by a staff captain, who came hurrying from the governor's office. 'Sir, a message from the High Command.'

The general's head turned, old man's flesh and hooded eyes. 'Well?'

The boy flicked a glance at me. 'It's secret, sir.'

In a stride the general was on him, sent him staggering with a blow across the face. 'I asked for the message, not your opinion.'

'Our – our garrison on the Malvinas has – has ceased to fight! General Menendez . . . the British . . . it's all over!' He touched blood on his cheek where the general's ring had cut. 'How can it have happened? Yesterday they said we had the enemy in a trap.'

'Was that all the message?'

'N-no, sir. You are to take all necessary measures to maintain order when a public announcement is made, but . . . the police say already rumors are sweeping Roballos.'

The general struck him again and kicked him as he tripped. '*Concha de cotorra!* Do you think yourself God to choose what you will tell me?' He snatched up the telephone. 'Give me Commandante Ibanez. Of the police, shithead. *Jesucristo,* that I should be surrounded by idiots!'

While his back was turned and confusion covered any sound, very carefully I inched down the last two treads of stair. Out of sight, out of mind; the platitude beat inside my skull.

298

'Ibanez?' The general bawled down the telephone as if it were a loudspeaker. 'What's this I hear about disturbance in Roballos?'

Four careful paces took me to the kitchen passage. The captain's eyes swiveled as I moved, but he wasn't risking a single unnecessary word; eccentric behavior by a guest no affair of his.

'What the hell difference does that make?' The general paused, violently silent, and then added, 'Call out as many men as you need and seal off the streets. I'll bring down a troop of armored cars, and between us we'll teach a lesson Roballos won't forget. *Jesu, hombre*, yesterday was yesterday and today our government says we were forced to yield before overwhelming force. Our task now is to tighten up at once, or the country will be taken over by scum and Communists.'

The telephone squawked something and the general laughed, a mirthless sound caught on the ratchet of anticipation. '*Claro, commandante.* You and I will see it does not happen.' He slammed down the telephone. 'Captain Ferrer?'

'Sir!'

'Order the squadron of Panhard cars out of barracks, and a battalion of *buzos tacticos*.'

Buzos tacticos. Those were marine commandos, the toughest hardcore professionals. They would unhesitatingly fire into a crowd of fellow countrymen bewildered by a crushing defeat for which censorship had left them utterly unprepared.

I had reached the temporary safety of the kitchen passage by then, stayed flattened against the wall while General Valdez pensively tugged on leather gloves. He looked relaxed, though his eyes seemed to have contracted into small, decomposing insects.

Then he turned and ran down from the front steps

like a boy, shouting for his jeep.

'I got a too very strange pastry, look.' Lylia's head poked round the kitchen door. 'Sallí, one day *Tío* Chepito come back, is not?'

'No, *querida*, I'm afraid he won't.' I knelt and held her. She had to trust someone to tell her the truth. 'We have to remember and be proud of him instead. Will you do something for me before we look at the pastry?'

She swallowed a sob for Chepito, and nodded.

'Peep in at your mama and tell me if she's sleeping yet.' I had poured half a tumbler of brandy down Isabelita's throat and left the decanter beside her bed.

The moment the child vanished I whipped across to the telephone and dialed the number of Roballos's general store. Local calls could still be dialed direct. 'Marcos? Warn everyone to get off the streets at once, the *buzos tacticos* are coming in.'

'*Buzos tacticos?* But why? Who is that speaking?' The storekeeper was a thick-skulled old gossip but the only person I could think of who could pass on a warning in a hurry.

'It doesn't matter, but tell everyone to get inside their homes at once.'

I hung up as Lylia came panting downstairs. 'She asleep and snoring drefful bad.'

Now for the sixty-four-million-dollar gamble, I thought grimly, and lifted the receiver again.

'*Sí?*' The main Roballos switchboard had long ago been taken over by the military.

'I have the governor's authorization, priority two. Señorita Martin on behalf of Señora Valdez. How long is the delay on a call to Buenos Aires?'

'Perhaps ten minutes for priority two. Your reference?'

'One-five, and the number I want is forty-two, eight, seventy-five.' I prayed the procedures hadn't changed

300

since I was last permitted to use the phone. Certainly the police would discover I had used false authorization while under a banning order, but by then I intended to be gone.

'*Bueno*, señorita, my pleasure.' I had become friendly with most of the signalers on the exchange. 'I will call back as soon as I can.'

'I'll hold on.'

'As you wish.' He sounded surprised, but I didn't dare risk rousing Isabelita by letting the phone ring. 'Ten minutes is the shortest time and it could be much longer.'

I bit my lip. 'Just try very hard, will you? Please.'

'Maybe you could be lucky; there aren't many orders coming through today,' he answered cheerfully.

I stooped, holding the instrument against my cheek. 'Lylia, *querida*. I have to go away for a while. One day I'll come back, I promise.'

'No,' she said, appalled.

'I have to, and at once. But remember: I'll be back.'

'Come back really promise?'

'Cross my heart.' We clung together, tears stinging. Ah, she was across my heart.

'Don't go, pleaseit don't go!' Drowned brown eyes, Roberto's eyes, added their own desperate appeal.

'Hush, sweetheart. I've stayed too long already.'

'Soon be back?'

'One day soon.' I didn't dare say more than would seem conventional reassurance, since she was certain to be questioned about my disappearance. 'Run and fetch Dodiebear, and I'll kiss him goodbye, too. Then you hug him instead of me each night until I come back.'

'Dodiebear isn't you,' she said dolefully, but trailed upstairs again to fetch the rubber creature who slept under her cheek at night.

And all the while I was waiting, waiting; willing that

infernal dilatory exchange to connect me. Trying, too, to figure out what and how much I could afford to say when they did. Roy must be on his way through checkpoints and military zones, but how long it would take him in the aftermath of a disastrously lost war I couldn't guess. How I wished I hadn't waited so long to call him, when even now I hadn't the remotest idea how to take Lylia out. Yet I couldn't wait another instant in this trap. Police inquiries and the emergence of El Carnicero from behind his mask were dangers enough, now there was also my call to Marcos at his store. Telephone calls were logged and sooner or later that, too, would be traced to me; now I was calling Buenos Aires as well, and violation of a police ban would be taken as proof of spying.

'Hurry, hurry, please,' I whispered through stiff lips.

Lylia bounded down the stairs with her bear; something grubby had been used to scrub her face clear of tears and she had scrambled into a parka and padded pants. 'If I'm good as good promise forever, could I agoing too?'

I shook my head, throat too tight for words.

'But I'm *dressed* for out,' she said triumphantly.

'Yes?' The telephone hissed against my cheek. 'Sweetheart—'

'You are connected to your number, señorita.'

'Oh, thank you! Is Mr Huron there? It's Sally Martin.'

'Are we glad to hear from you, Sally. Sure, he's here.' I could have hugged that rich Louisiana drawl a thousand miles away in Buenos Aires.

'Sally?' Huron came on the line.

'Yes, it's Sally, just Sally,' I said quickly. 'Is there anything waiting for me at the embassy?'

'There was. But we guessed you'd be moving on soon so we didn't keep it.'

I could have shouted aloud; he must mean Roy had already left Buenos Aires for the south. 'That's just fine. Because you're right, I have to move.'

'You do?'

'Yes, I won't call again. Is it too late to redirect the mail?'

'I guess not, Sally.'

My confidence took off like a rocket. I'd been dreadfully afraid that once Roy left Buenos Aires he'd be out of touch. 'Send it to . . . You could try sending it to a place that's half a dozen times where he and I first met, okay? And nine hours after when.'

'I've got that. We'll do our best.' He sounded reassuringly calm. 'Good luck.'

I hung up carefully, torn between elation and a longing to call back just to hear American voices again.

Instead, I must get out of here, and fast. U.S. embassy calls above all would be monitored, someone already would be calling a duty officer about a transcript that needed following up.

'It's simply rushing rain.' Lylia's voice trembled on the edge of hopelessness. 'Too much rush for you to go.'

I hugged her, felt against me the racing patter of her heart; the butchery of emotions surely more terrible than more obvious kinds of violence. I am not sure what I said: promises, love, and anguish jumbled into incoherence I could not help. Which I had to help because next time I came, Lylia must still want to leave the only home she knew without an instant's hesitation. How to take her out of Argentina might remain beyond imagination, but my single most disastrous mistake now must be to leave her remembering only wretchedness instead of the joyful confidence we had built together. A three-year-old's memory is short, and Lylia's must work *for* me and not against. As it was working for me already, since she

303

could scarcely remember when Isabelita's malice may have been less barbed, and Josefina and General Valdez had more time to show her their affection. What she did know very clearly was that during these past weeks I had become her sole protection in an emotional minefield she could not understand. I must not become a part of that same menacing uncertainty: unstable, panicky, and deceiving.

So, breathing very fast, head bent so she would not clearly see my face, we laughed a little together through our tears. I promised again to return, and then I took her, still hiccoughing tears softly against my shoulder, to Josefina in the kitchen, who fortunately would have thought the oddest happening in the world unremarkable after drowning her own unhappiness in brandy. Then I changed into my thickest clothes and let myself out into the rushing rain.

20

Once I stayed on in Roballos after things began to go wrong, when Isabelita became hostile and the general suspicious, I realized I might have to run in a hurry. Even so, the precautions I was able to take had been pitifully few.

I bought boots, winterproofed pants, and a parka, packed a rucksack with supplies and kept it, together with a sleeping bag, under my bed. Passport, money, a map stolen from the general's office, made up the remainder of my kit. It wasn't much on which to survive the Patagonian winter. There was no question of taking the automobile; without the necessary authorization to move in a military zone and surrounded by empty country, it would simply advertise which way I went.

As soon as I left the house, rain and wind became my friends, hiding me from sight, sending guards scurrying for cover. I walked down the track that led from the governor's house to the coast road until the military post at its end loomed out of driving murk, then squeezed through a fence and cut across pasture until I reached the road north of Roballos, where it snaked between the shore and a marsh even the sheep avoided. Here I was beyond the Roballos checkpoints and my previous wanderings had established that it was nearly fifty miles until the next permanent post, at a cross-roads near Deseado.

By the time I reached the road I was pleasantly

warmed by exertion. Usually there were plenty of trucks traveling in both directions but today, probably because of the cataclysm of surrender in the Malvinas, there seemed no traffic at all. A single truck was what I wanted, not a convoy and definitely not one of the military police patrols. I hesitated, but decided to start walking; I should soon become chilled standing around. On the other hand, I didn't want to walk too far when every mile I traveled would have to be retraced.

Rain made my rucksack leaden, the road ahead vanished into mist. I kept imagining I heard a truck, or Lylia weeping brokenhearted into the storm; sometimes I knew for certain a truck was coming but it was the wind. I had never anticipated that the day I had to run would also see the end of a war and sweep the road so clear. Soon it would be too risky to continue walking, when the moment I was missed this would be the first direction everybody looked. At least General Valdez was out of the house for a while, Isabelita probably unapproachable until tomorrow and Josefina incapable of raising an alarm unprompted. But I needed to get under cover fast, after first laying a false trail north.

A truck came at last, traveling north, thank God. When I waved, the driver slowed, then stopped, understandably astonished by a solitary female walking through Patagonia in a downpour. '*A dónde va?*' he shouted.

'Not far, my brother has a farm a few kilometers up the road. Would you be in dreadful trouble if you gave me a lift?'

'Who cares?' he answered cheerfully. 'If God is good, then soon I shall finish my service. Jump up, señorita.'

I jumped, the snug cab enormously welcome after the road. I had to squeeze between the driver and a soldier called Diego, both jovial rogues who stank of fish.

'We are billeted in a factory where fish used to be turned into fertilizer,' explained Diego. 'I vomited every day until I became used to it.'

'So now there is vomit as well as fish to lie upon,' added the boy at the wheel. 'Most of our battalion are as sick as parrots, so Diego and me, we run errands for the officers and keep out of it.' He jerked his head at the back of the truck. 'Mutton for their mess at Comodoro Rivadavia, wine and brandy going back.'

No wonder Argentina lost a war, I thought. 'Would you drop me off at the next track to the left?'

'You're sure you wouldn't like us to run you all the way to your front door? It's godawful wet for walking, and I drive most places a truck shouldn't go.' He wiggled the wheel so we lurched crazily between ditches either side of the road. 'I like to deliver my freight in good condition.'

Hastily I invested my brother with a bad temper and erratic sense of honor, which made it safer for me not to arrive home sharing a truck with strangers.

'Oh, well,' said Diego philosophically, 'better wet than in trouble. Take a bottle of cognac to warm you up instead.'

I laughed. 'I thought you were delivering meat this way and the drink came south.'

'You couldn't expect us to unload everything each trip,' he exclaimed, shocked. 'Paunchy colonels don't deserve it all, is what I say.'

I stood, smiling, to watch them out of sight, a flat flask of brandy tucked inside my parka. Now for the long tramp back to Roballos, during which no one must see me.

I was very tired by the time I had covered the twelve miles or so back to the first Roballos checkpoint. Not many vehicles passed, but each time they did, I had to lie flat in soaking grass: taking cover in this barren land was extraordinarily difficult. I was glad to remember I'd never seen tracker dogs in Patagonia.

It was dark when the red lamps of the Roballos barrier came in sight at last. I had studied the road here with finicking care, and stepped aside at once. I needed to angle across tussocks, bearing right until I reached a stone-strewn wilderness below the governor's house. This I must cross as silently as I could in order to circle behind the town and reach a tumbledown shearer's hut, the only empty building I had discovered in an area packed with troops.

It sounded easy but I had no illusions. After the tensions of the day and a twelve-mile trudge through blowing rain, the degree of caution still required was likely to test my endurance to the uttermost. I will come back, I had promised Lylia, and that promise would be broken if I let myself get caught.

I dared not use the pocket flash I carried, even away from the road. On a slight rise to my right stood the governor's house, overlooking ground I had to cross and with a great hustle of movement on its gravel drive. One lit window upstairs: Lylia's room. I glanced at my watch. Bedtime, and no one to read her a story, hug her good night. Probably she would cry herself to sleep.

My eyes were adjusted to the dark, so I was able to pick my way across that slope without making too much noise: on scattered stones that rolled underfoot complete silence was impossible. Progress was also dishearteningly slow, and once, when my ankle turned on a rock, I felt my chances vanish. But after a rest the pain ebbed sufficiently to go on, even more slowly and carefully than before.

The rain stopped at last, the wind still cold and very strong. Now I could begin bypassing the town, a last lap

308

that helped me forget how long the day had been. Careful, very careful still; consciously reminding myself how a single mistake would finish Lylia's hope. Roy's, too, I thought, and smiled.

Once I reached my sheepshearer's hut, all I had to do was wait for him, and together we would take Lylia out.

How? Oh, God, somehow.

About half an hour after leaving the stones behind, I saw the coast road lights again, the last obstacle I had to cross. I stood quite a long time studying those lights; so far my luck had held miraculously, I must not take its strength for granted.

About a mile from where I stood, Roballos town was surprisingly well lit, the usual dim lamps overwhelmed by powerful arc lights switched on along the deep-water jetty. I could see soldiers spaced at intervals there, a couple of armored cars parked close by. Elsewhere the town was deathly still, as if under curfew. I just hoped Marcos had managed to panic everyone inside before El Carnicero moved those troops in.

I moved forward again at last, cautiously toward the road, where there was more activity than I liked. An armored car patrolled with a helmeted soldier in the turret; some trucks were drawn on to the verge, men brewing up beside them. I hunkered down quite close in to watch, beginning to shiver in the wind. I was too tired to add more miles to my journey in an attempt to outflank activity; besides, there seemed to be military movement as far as I could see.

This is how fugitives are caught, I realized. Once exhaustion takes over, you begin to skimp on caution, to choose the easiest rather than the safest way.

I was still wondering what to do, when I saw headlamps coming fast from the direction of the town. I dropped flat, expecting the beam to sweep over me, but

309

the driver braked hard enough to skid and General Valdez climbed out alongside the trucks. 'What the hell do you sons of goats think you're doing?' he blared at the troops huddled there.

The men froze to attention, while an n.c.o. stepped forward and said something I couldn't catch.

The general was not placated. 'Idiots! Cowards! Pigshit!'

'Excellency, the town is quiet,' the man answered respectfully.

'Then wake it up! My troops aren't sitting on their backsides like those whoresons in the Malvinas. *Jesumaria,* must I do everything myself?'

Immediately everyone was in such a panic to climb into the nearest truck, they fell over each other in the dark, chaos made worse when each driver set off the moment his engine started. Overtaking each other, thrusting into nonexistent gaps, forcing the general to leap for safety with a howl of rage. But after the trucks pulled past, he gestured the armored car to stop, stood talking earnestly with its commander as if rage were something he manufactured on demand, to throw at underlings. The commander climbed back into his turret, came down again with a map, which they huddled over in the light of headlamps. Eventually they came to an agreement, the commander saluted and climbed up again, his vehicle pulled away. I ducked as light spilled over me, but lifted my head to watch which road it took: not down to the town but north, toward Deseado and Rivadavia.

Almost certainly that car had been sent to join in the hunt for a female British spy: Diego and his friend most probably already picked up and questioned. At this very moment other units would be on the move elsewhere along the coast, extra checkpoints put in place on the road north. At dawn the helicopters would join in. Well, so long as they believed I had struck north . . .

Meanwhile, the general showed no impatience to drive off. I could feel icy wetness soaking my clothes and fairly willed him back into that automobile. Apart from him the road was clear, but still he waited, eyes fixed on Roballos.

I knew why a minute or two later, when the shooting began. Rippling sparks of automatic fire, single shots, whole magazines of tracer arcing into the dark. The sound of revving engines followed, and when I risked coming to my knees I could see trucks racing around otherwise deserted streets. Roballos was being taught, and not for the first time that day, that though their rulers had brought Argentina to defeat, at home they remained very much to be feared. The troops along the quayside joined in the fusillade, skipping bullets over the water, spraying volleys into the sky. So far as I could see, no one was firing directly at the houses.

As for the general . . . Mesmerised, I watched him observing this macabre scene. His head lifted, his feet stamping on the road, his hands beating together in self-absorbed celebration. An apparition, demoniacal, one of the rejoicing damned. This man had no connection with the attentive host I had known for nearly two months, who tomorrow in his home would most likely be courteously attentive again.

Gradually the shooting diminished until only the sound of soldiers shouting to each other could be heard. El Carnicero diminished, too, became calm. Eventually he stretched as though pleasantly tired and called for his driver to start up.

A moment later he was gone, and I crossed the road well ahead of a convoy of trucks coming up from the jetty.

Half an hour later I reached the shearer's hut.

As shelter it was pretty poor, the roof down in one corner and without any glass in the single window. But it was a great deal better than barren landscape, and the corner I'd selected as my hideout more or less wind- and water-tight. There was also an ancient bale of fleece, rancid-smelling and damp but very warm once I heaped the crumbling fragments over my sleeping bag. Although I was almost too tired to eat, I forced down biscuits, cheese, and chocolate before drinking some of the brandy Diego gave me. The mixture was a mistake. I lay feeling disagreeably sick until sleep struck like a triphammer, driving me into oblivion.

When I woke it was still dark and I was ravenously hungry. After a struggle I looked at my watch: eight o'clock. Corrugated iron flapped on the roof, but no glimmer of daylight to be seen, which meant it must be eight at night. Unbelievably, I had slept for over eighteen hours, the first time, undrugged, I had slept my untroubled fill since Roberto became a *desaparecido*. I lay savoring the luxury of long, oblivious rest, and its equally luxurious aftermath of renewal. Anyway, the longer I slept the better, if it gave time for the chase to draw away.

Eventually hunger brought me burrowing out from under wool. I grinned to myself: I no longer noticed its evil stench, so presumably others would notice mine. I washed perfunctorily in water blowing off the eaves, no point becoming chilled again just for the sake of pretending I was clean. I'd have to make sure Roy wallowed in rotten wool as well before he had time to decide he couldn't love a woman smelling like a sludgepit.

A meal was the next priority, and to take my mind off chewing cold hash on crackers, I tried imagining Roy in this place: an even more unnatural habitat than the last I'd inflicted on him. How very long it seemed since I lay with him in love at the Magnifico. How long a road traveled since I'd wanted him to leave, a longer one still since I rejected and fought him in Keg Bay. But Roy had been right even then about the kind of cure I had to find; the trouble was, he couldn't have imagined the malignant filth, not to mention inconvenience, this would stir into his life, too.

Anxieties such as these had been niggling a long time at the back of my mind, but only now was I sufficiently rested to allow them into the open. Immediately my mood changed, and in a way I believed I'd left behind. A vortex of panic opened at my feet, spinning hut walls around me and bringing with it the hatefully familiar urge to run, run blindly, so that before I realized what I was doing, I had blundered over to the door. Only the slap of wet wind brought me to my senses, the half-imagined speck of distant light that marked where my daughter lay. Surrounded as I was by empty land and sea, there was nowhere left to run.

All the same, the experience shocked me. My cure had survived living in El Carnicero's house, enabled me to hide the strength of my love for Lylia while I cast this way and that for a way of escape. It must not fail now that the stakes were doubled, to win or lose it all. I shivered and went back inside the hut, ashamed to find I had been sufficiently dazed not even to put on my boots. This time if I'd run I should have died, from exposure if not the police. Abstractedly, I was still worrying away at why my control should crumble now, when I'd woken feeling ten feet tall, and after a while I dragged the explanation free. I was afraid that when Roy came, I might detect some change in him.

I never doubted he would reach Roballos. More likely

313

by persistence than daring, but he'd said he would come when I wanted him, and he would.

But meanwhile, he'd had several weeks in which to reflect on the mess he'd strayed into, the ruin it could bring into his life. A jailbird and kidnapper wasn't the ideal wife for a partner in Blainey, Rosenthal, & McGeown. In fact I'd just realized how much of a liability I still was, with my poisoned past and frail emotions: haunted, insecure. A burden for a scrupulous man to carry, when he saw too late that if he walked away, I was finished. Now I was asking him to risk his life as well, and for Roberto's daughter, a man whose image I guessed he comprehensively detested.

Royston Leavis was a shrewd operator. He knew that no matter how persuasive desire or circumstance may be, some prices aren't worth paying. And, if time to think had brought him to this conclusion, then I should know within minutes of meeting him again.

At least I ought not to have too long a wait, I thought pessimistically.

After that I felt too much alone to wait patiently, fidgeted and prowled restlessly back and forth until my watch showed at last I could leave the hut, keeping to pasture tracks. Roballos glowed opaquely through mizzle blowing off the sea, a pattern of smears against darkness suggesting motorized patrols in the streets. It was by then about ten o'clock, which allowed plenty of time for me to reach the rendezvous if Roy should come tonight.

The town of Roballos normally contained about four thousand people, two schools, a monastery, a meat-packing plant, and several decaying warehouses used temporarily as barracks. Just then there were more military personnel than inhabitants, and with only army trucks apparently on the streets a curfew was probably still in force. The outer streets ended raggedly in a scatter of railings, dumped hardware, and barbed wire. Festoons of telephone wires dripped wetness between single-story houses and sheds. Nearby, a truck drove off in a flurry of gears, its lights sweeping the next corner I must pass.

I froze, straining my eyes to see if guards were lurking under cover, but nothing moved. Only mist, thickly curling between the outermost houses. There was nothing to do but to move forward as cautiously as I could.

I crept along, keeping close to the high boarded fences typical of the town, grateful for their shadow. Loose grit sucked noisily at my boots however carefully I moved, and I jumped when some twigs flicked my face, the silence so spooky I welcomed the faint drone of a radio sounding from behind a shutter. I was less than ten yards away from one of the wider midtown streets, when a patrol appeared, two soldiers cradling automatic rifles across their arms, who took a quick look around and then dodged out of the wind for a smoke.

I waited impatiently while they showed no sign of moving, shared a second cigarette. The annoying thing was, I could have met Roy more safely almost anywhere than in the middle of Roballos, but I'd been able to think of only one place whose identity he would guess from a message no one else could understand. The proprietor of a bar two streets away from here had decorated his boardwalk with six steel kegs: once Huron passed on my message, Roy would look for any link with Keg Bay, and nine hours after I sailed my dinghy into his racing yacht on a fine fall afternoon made eleven o'clock at night.

I glanced at my wrist. Ten-fifty. Those soldiers had to move soon. Goddamnit, why couldn't a sergeant happen along to kick their idle rumps?

In the end I had no choice but to retreat back to my hideout feeling painfully let down, because those soldiers were still skulking out of the wind a full hour later. I was tempted to climb a few fences to avoid them, but decided the risks were unjustifiable when probably Roy hadn't yet arrived. I would never climb in complete silence and I hadn't come so far to lose patience now, though waiting alone through another day was hard.

Very hard.

Interminable, if I'm truthful. I had slept too well the night before to do much more than doze, and nightmares lurked in ambush the moment dozing thickened. The weather stayed drearily cold. I longed for a fire and there was plenty of rubbish to burn, but this risk, too, remained too great. I tossed under my smelly fleeces, passing the time somehow by forcing myself to rethink all the many ways out of Patagonia I'd considered before; arranging them in order of preference, shuffling and discarding them. Nothing made escape with a child look possible. It irked me that when Roy came, I should have to confess failure to discover even a possible plan, hand over to male superiority a problem I had found insoluble. At least I eventually nailed down that particular conceit as simple injured pride; good luck, Roy, over finding any way out.

When darkness came I left for Roballos earlier than I needed to, because I was incapable of waiting any longer. This night was much finer than the previous one, a full moon flitting swiftly between ragged clouds, which would need careful watching. I reached the corner where I'd stuck the night before without too much difficulty, although at this earlier hour a few people were moving gingerly between the houses. The curfew must be lifted although no one looked as if they were trusting trigger-happy soldiers far.

Because there were people in the streets, I couldn't miss the atmosphere of discontent. You could hear it in surly voices, glimpse it in hunched figures exchanging monosyllables, feel the defensive edginess of soldiers patrolling in groups instead of pairs, as if numbers proved they hadn't lost a war. Argentine flags flapped everywhere still: patriotism rather than the lack of it fueled this discontent, when for as long as anyone could remember, the army had grabbed everything it wanted in the name of national strength.

I needed to nerve myself to cross that first main street, the moon revealing patrols moving to no particular pattern, its width too great for comfort. The fence stopped at a filling station, and away to my left stretched a row of the more substantial houses that marked the center of Roballos. A patrol was approaching between them, and as soon as it passed I must cross. I shrank back into shadow as the beat of boots came closer, that damned moon choosing the same moment to sail across open sky.

'. . . the accursed English,' one of the soldiers was saying morosely as, inevitably, or so it seemed, they paused at the corner. If they smoked for an hour again, perhaps I'd better try howling like a lovesick cat.

'My brother's in the Malvinas, but we haven't heard since he landed.'

'The English kill prisoners, so they say.'

'Who say?' grunted another skeptically. 'Better the English than our *commandante*.'

'How can you say that? Why, the English—'

'Well, I do say it. I know the *commandante*, and I don't know the English.'

There was a pause, as if this logic was accepted. 'As for your brother, you may see him sooner than you think,' the first voice observed. 'I heard the English are

317

sending a ship in here. Tomorrow we start clearing a space for them along the jetty.'

'A ship?'

'Bringing back our men they want out of the Malvinas.'

'Here? Why here?'

'And others to Santa Cruz and Deseado. You don't think we'd let the English sail bold as bulls into Buenos Aires, do you?'

'*Jesumaria,* no! Nor anywhere!'

'Then your brother would starve in prison camp. They say the English—'

The voices faded, leaving me flaming with excitement. The British were coming here. They were sending in a ship under flag of truce to repatriate prisoners. If Lylia and I could only get on board, we would be safe. Crouched beside my fence, I examined these simple propositions for error and decided they were sound.

The first item on their totem pole the British would definitely not be worrying about was whether I was justified in kidnapping a child from the Argentine military junta. They would want to believe the worst about a general nicknamed El Carnicero. Of all the nations in the world, at this moment the British must be safest.

God save the Queen, I thought happily. Now all we have to do is get Lylia on board that ship. At the very last moment I'd discovered a way out, without expecting Roy to work a miracle.

I crossed that street, walking openly but fast as soon as the soldiers were out of sight, since there wasn't any way to do it secretly. No one shouted or fired, and within seconds I was into shadow again. Down the next block and over a fence to avoid some sulkily drunken men; the bars must have reopened, too.

318

After that I stayed behind fences the rest of the way, in and out of yards, once through a passage between a house and some squawking hens. I crouched, alarmed, as they made enough racket for anyone to imagine a fox had come to Patagonia, but a woman only shrieked abuse from behind a shutter. Clearly, she thought a soldier was thieving for food and didn't dare come out to stop him.

I felt my way down that passage with the tips of my fingers, avoiding winter-dry tendrils of some climbing plant. This brought me to the next street, and diagonally on the far side stood the bar with six kegs in front. No reason to go any farther. The moon dipped into cloud and rain spattered on the wind; my feet and back chilled quickly once I had to stand and wait.

It soon became apparent that the military patrols called into that bar each time they passed; I couldn't have chosen a less convenient place for a rendezvous. Another patrol approached only minutes later, their pace picking up as the bar came into sight, and soon after they went inside, Roy moved out of the shadows to stand under dim boardwalk light.

I had been staring at that lamp until my eyes ached, willing him to come, and still the marvelous unexpectedness of him being there took me by surprise. He was moving into the shadows again before I found my voice. 'Roy,' I croaked.

His head snapped around, then back again while he studied the empty street. A moment later he had joined me and all we did was hold each other, whispering, Roy, Sally, Sally, Roy. We didn't kiss at all, not then, perhaps only partly because that infernal patrol came reeling out of the bar again and we had to crouch, still gripped tight together. In front of our eyes one of the soldiers leaned on his automatic weapon while he vomited, his grip slipped and a stream of bullets slashed past his nose.

His companions were quite as alarmed as we, the penalty for drinking on duty probably severe, and they all raced off in confusion. 'Christ,' Roy said softly, 'let's get out of here before they avoid trouble by pretending they saw something move.'

We dodged back past the chickens, the cursing woman, and a yard full of rusty iron, those shots enough to send everyone except soldiers diving into their homes.

'We have to cross here,' I said when we reached the corner of that wider street where I'd stuck on my way in.

'Best take it quick, then.'

Flip a coin, I thought. Quick or cautious, we wouldn't know until afterward which choice held our best chance. We ran together and reached the far side just as an armored car swept into the street a block away, and raked where we'd been only seconds before with its lights.

'Our lucky night,' I said.

21

By the time we reached the shearer's hut we hadn't breath or thought to spare for explanation, fell on the pile of fleeces in a tangle of arms and legs, trying to kiss and speak the words of love but having to take refuge in touch, gasped half phrases, and laughter.

That was how my fears ended. I'd thought I might not be able to face him, nor look into his eyes for terror of what I might see there, but in the end it didn't matter. I'm not even sure whether I looked or not. We made love instantly, impatiently, drowning in each other. Life itself blotting out the quite different anxieties we each had carried in the best and quickest way. Until at last we were forced to lie quiet and listen to the pound of the other's heart, savoring feel, caress, warmth, shape. Tears wet on my face and perhaps on Roy's as well.

'It's all right.' The first coherent words I had spoken.

'You thought it wouldn't be?'

'I wondered . . . Yes, I thought perhaps it wouldn't.'

'My God, you should have lived my life the past few weeks before you start imagining something worse.'

I chuckled, so tightly held I felt it vibrate through him as well. 'Yesterday I decided that if we were to be okay, I'd have to make sure you smelled of rotten fleeces, too.'

'You surely succeeded fast. Sally . . . if you only knew how it hurt to discover you still thought so little of me, that once I helped you reach where you wanted to be, you preferred to fight and beat your devil all alone.'

'That isn't true! It was myself I couldn't trust. I thought you understood I could face El Carnicero only if no one knew the hateful link between us. Anyway, you had to go; that federal case of yours, remember?'

'No,' he said more quietly. 'If you'd shown any sign of wanting me to stay, I would have thrown over every other obligation without a thought. But you were glad to be rid of me.'

'I couldn't help it.' This was something I had completely failed to grasp. Wrought up in my own affairs and fairly unbalanced, too, I had scarcely considered how he felt at all. 'I make mistakes all the time, and now with you as well. Somehow the best I seem to manage at the moment is to blunder from one thing to the next.'

'Me too. But how many times I cursed and detested you for causing me such pain. One night I got drunk and swore I was through.'

'But when I called, you came.'

'You called just in time. Don't ever push me so hard again.'

I sighed, content. 'No. Though we'll both have to settle for those mistakes.'

'Oh, sure, but why did you think we might not be all right?'

'Me,' I said simply.

He tensed, then held my face cupped in his hands. 'Of course, there's always you. My valiant love.'

I suppose we may have slept, but as I remember it, we loved and talked all night, gladly leaving tomorrow to care for itself.

But when tomorrow came, the intractable problem returned with it: how exactly were we to get out, taking Lylia with us?

'How did you come?' I asked.

'Through Chile. I thought it might be easier than

322

struggling across military zones all the way from Buenos Aires, and I guess it was. They're bastards at the frontier though.'

'Chile,' I said thoughtfully. 'That's a surprise. I never imagined you'd come that way.'

'I hoped no one else would either, if they happened to be looking. They weren't though, were they?'

'Not then. When I changed the message for Huron to send to you, I had only been told to stay inside the governor's house while they checked my story. Now that I've vanished, the police everywhere will be alerted, and if they happen to think about it, then they have your name from the telephone calls. Were you told at the frontier to check in with the police? This whole coast is run by the military now.'

'In a way, yes. But I've fixed a retainer from a New York firm who have oil litigation they hope to settle between drilling companies in Chile and Argentina. The authorities won't be eager to annoy me if they can help it.'

'You didn't waste the last six weeks, did you?' I paused, considering again the idea that had seemed so good last night, when I overheard the soldiers talk. 'Going north is impossible now that they're looking for me. West to Chile—'

'I slotted in some preliminaries as I came through in case we could use them, but that frontier is tough. A choice of mean-looking military or murderous terrain. It might help if I were a marine and you a mountaineer, but even then we'd be taking a hell of a chance in winter. As it is, we'd condemn a kid to death by trying to go that way.'

'I know. I drove east once or twice, but even from a distance it looked bad. Do you know anything about away down south: Tierra del Fuego?'

'I asked at the embassy in Valparaiso. They said no mountains, but awful weather and very jumpy troops. The British infiltrated men that way to watch the Argentine fleet.'

'Oh?' I couldn't help laughing. 'I'm glad that if I had to be a spy, I'd belong to a professional outfit.' I explained how I was suspected of being a British spy.

Roy wasn't amused, since keeping me safe looked difficult enough without the Argentine army also wanting me as a spy. 'Were they serious, or looking for a reason to be awkward?'

'You never know things like that in a military government; I just thought it was better they suspected me as a spy than the real reason I was there. They would watch Lylia then, and go on watching her.'

'You're sure no one did?'

'Suspect why I'd really come and put a watch on Lylia? Certain. Isabelita came nearest to guessing something because she hated me, but the connection is too . . . extraordinary for hate on its own to make it. And now that I've gone, she'll never think about me again.'

'That's something, I suppose,' he said wryly. 'If we can't go north, south, or west, that leaves the air. I flew out of Comodoro Rivadavia last time around, and military security at the airfield wasn't particularly tight. But I was flying with a general, if you remember.'

'We could go east.'

He stood up and went over to stare through the glassless window at an endless procession of Atlantic waves, white water blowing off their crests. 'I thought about that; I've done some ocean racing after all. It's my only useful skill in this situation. But I doubt if we'd be able to steal anything better than an inshore fishing boat, and when you think of the seas we'd be likely to meet – I'd be criminal to take you and a kid out there.'

'You wouldn't have to take us far. The British are sending in a ship.' I told him what I'd overheard. 'I don't know when, but one of those soldiers had already heard about orders to start clearing the jetty.'

He didn't turn, stood absently fidgeting with coins in his pocket and staring at that menacing horizon. I knew what he was thinking, the temptation he faced. He felt humiliated by the secondary role which, ever since we came to Argentina, had been forced on him by circumstance, was riled by his inability now to compensate by kicking down barriers to set me free. This chance to be a god in his machine was exactly what he needed.

He turned. 'No. The boats I've seen down here are too poor and the weather too unpredictable. You can't take chances with the South Atlantic in winter. If we're going to board that ship, then it will have to be in the harbor.'

'My love. I should hate to marry Superman.' I went over and kissed him.

He didn't pretend to misunderstand. 'I'm an arrogant son of a bitch at heart. This ship, then. We'll have to operate on some very slick timing if we're to hijack Lylia and get on board without being seen.'

'Timing is one problem,' I answered dryly.

'I'm going into Roballos,' he said abruptly. 'I can move around freely there, and if they've noticed my automobile, then it's better if I'm seen. Anyway, I'm meant to be conciliating drilling disputes, and there are some local *juristas* I ought to meet.'

I felt dismayingly solitary after he left, no question any longer of preferring to face my devils alone. I tried to pass the crawling hours by devising plans that might get us on board that ship; at least it was easier to think about a concrete situation than wonder about unseen but lethal possibilities. I felt reasonably confident I could bring Lylia safely out of the governor's house, nearly certain that when I went to fetch her she would still want to come away with me. Although it felt like an age, only two and a half days had passed since I left her alone, with my promise to return. Her memory ought still to be working for me. Two and a half days during which, after Chepito's death, Isabelita was only too likely to have revenged some of her grief on a bewildered child who had always been unwelcome in her house. Josefina, too, overworked as she was and sorrowing for Chepito, her own nursling, just at this most vital of moments, was more likely than usual to scold rather than comfort Lylia. As for the general, I knew he had spent at least part of that time high on violence . . . Yes, I was confident Lylia would come with me provided I reached her soon.

Nor was I bothered by conscience. Lylia was mine. She was also surely damned if she stayed in Argentina. How could anyone so instinctively generous survive when she grew up to learn the nature of a man she believed to be her father? Impossible to decide which would be worse once she discovered even part of the truth: for such a man to remain respected, or for him to be hounded and cursed as he deserved. Isabelita didn't care for her, and El Carnicero, who did, deserved to suffer a fraction of the pain he had inflicted. Afterward, if I safely could, for Josefina's sake I might send word that Lylia was well. I paused, considering. That might be a sound idea. I didn't fancy Argentine agents one day turning up in Boston, which, after all those phone calls, could be a place El Carnicero looked. Roy seemed to know some strings to pull; perhaps Huron could make my message seem to come from the Communists. General Valdez would willingly believe that they had enjoyed exacting a kind of justice by turning a torturer's child into a *desaparecido*, too.

Roy did not return until after dark. I heard a click of stone and he was there. 'Hot soup,' he said, and curled my fingers around a thermos bottle.

I don't think anything in my life tasted so good as that soup, the first hot food I'd eaten since I left the governor's house. I drank it all and licked the last drops from the rim of the bottle. 'You wouldn't believe how much better that makes me feel.'

'I hope it helped your optimism, too. The British ship is expected in at midday tomorrow.'

'Will it stay overnight?'

'No.'

My heart plummeted. 'That's awkward.'

'Very. It has clearance to tie up at the jetty and disembark four or five hundred prisoners including about fifty wounded. Given an efficient crew, say three hours alongside at most.'

'Optimsism doesn't come easy,' I said, bitterly disappointed. The possibility of simply sailing away from this nightmare within a matter of hours had become so enticing, I could scarcely bear to return to grimmer, more impossible alternatives.

'Not easy, no. I think it has to be worth the try. Come over here, will you?'

I joined him at the gaping window, where he had stood that morning. Wind shoved harshly at our bodies, the lights of Roballos smeared by squalls of rain.

'You see the jetty?'

I nodded. 'The line of lights over to the left.'

'It's about seventy yards long by twenty wide, and a fairly shaky structure. I doubt whether anything bigger than a coaster has tied up there for years. I don't know what the British are sending, but any ship carrying over four hundred people is likely to be a tight fit. Do you remember how the harbor arm curves at its outer end?'

327

I stared at those lights, thinking. 'Into a stone crosspiece with a light on the end? To help protect the quayside from currents, I suppose.'

'When a ship of any size is tied up, that outer end of the arm must be out of sight from the quay.'

'But not from the lightkeeper.'

Roy's arm tightened across my shoulders, a confident man wrung by the same uncertainties I had endured while trying to find ways out of Patagonia. 'This is what I think we have to do. The whole thing is as full of holes as a Cadillac's grille, but the best I've come up with so far. First of all, we get Lylia. You know the house and will have to decide the best way in, and while we're there I need to steal one of Valdez's uniforms. Afterward we'll come back to Roballos with Lylia and, before dawn, the two of you must hide out on that harbor arm. There's God knows how much junk piled up that they've cleared off the quay to give the British room to moor. You'll have to keep hidden for several hours until the ship comes; that could be the hardest part. It'll be goddamn cold and you won't be able to move. But sometime during the morning the harbor area is likely to be sealed off by troops, and you'll be inside the cordon. By then I shall have changed into General Valdez's uniform – you said he was quite tall?'

'Roy, you're crazy. You can't speak Spanish, for a start.'

'I learned a little these past weeks in Boston. You can use the next few hours before we have to go teaching me the rudest words you know. Then, when the British come, I go to the quay and shove my way on board. From what I hear, there's going to be a committee of military brass welcoming the prisoners home, help everyone forget those guys surrendered to inferior numbers. One more strange general shouldn't be

328

remarkable. I can wave one hell of a pack of official papers on oil disputes, which should look good to a guard.'

'But why take such a lunatic chance? Why not stay with us on the harbor arm? We take out the lightkeeper and . . . Is there a boat we could use?'

'Several, all small and in bad condition. Like I said, they've cleared all the clutter to the end of the jetty, boats as well. Okay, suppose I did stay with you and we tie up the lightkeeper, which oughtn't to be too difficult. Then we use a goddamn leaky crabpot skiff to pole up the far side of that British ship. Do you suppose they'd take us up just like that, in an enemy harbor? They're coming in under flag of truce while a state of war still exists; they'll be on guard against traps or provocation, will want to get in and out without trouble. But we can't climb a sheer hull without help, and quick slick help at that. The Argentines might easily put a gunboat out in the bay to watch. They've got two tied up farther along the jetty.'

'They haven't moved all through the war.'

'So they might like to show they can, when a British ship comes in.'

I bit my lip. 'We wouldn't have a hope of getting on board if they watch from out in the bay as well.'

'If it's impossible, then we don't go. But I have to talk to that British skipper before we decide. If he agreed to help, we just might get away with it.'

'So what could you tell him that might make violating a truce seem okay?'

'The truth,' he said gently. 'This one time it has to be the truth. I can't think of a more persuasive story to settle anyone's scruples. Violations of truce are politics, what I shall ask for is an act of personal mercy. The child is yours and stolen after torture. I'm a poor advocate if I can't make any civilized man see it the same way.'

I felt myself waver between hope and a terrible fear. 'If you spoke good Spanish, there might be a chance. Argentine officers are so distant from their men, I guess conscripts don't often question orders. But it must be suicide to try bluffing your way past guards you can't even order to get the hell out from underfoot.'

'That's why I need a general's uniform. A major or colonel couldn't pass on a snarl of rage alone.'

'Generals have chauffeurs, aides, staff captains. You wouldn't last five minutes among other officers on a cleared quay.'

He turned to face me. 'There isn't any other way. I have to get on board that British ship and talk to her captain, make sure he'll help. Remember, if they jump me, then you and the kid are still free, but I'm an American lawyer the Argentine government would prefer not to annoy.'

'Oh, sure, respectable lawyers often steal generals' uniforms,' I said sarcastically.

His hands tightened on my shoulders. 'What else do you suggest?'

And there, of course, he had me. Weeks of scheming had failed to suggest anything else at all. Nor could I simply give up, go home, and try again when the military were less active in Patagonia. I was trapped in Roballos even more than Lylia; that British ship the only hope of getting away before winter drove me out of this flimsy shelter and into the nearest jail.

'Okay, you win,' I said resignedly. 'It looks like we reached the Superman slot after all.'

We left the hut for the last time at three in the morning, the intervening hours spent arguing over details and searching my memory for words a bad-tempered Argentine general might yell at guards. Roy

330

possessed a quick ear and had applied his formidable intellect to tearing the guts out of Spanish since I saw him last; even so, a couple of sentences would find him out. We ate before leaving, and when we'd finished only some packets of chocolate and a mouthful of brandy remained of the stores I had brought. I bundled these into the rucksack together with jerseys, the map, and a flash, then we left down the track that led toward the town, our first objective Roy's Chilean automobile in a parking lot on the edge of town. So far as we knew, there weren't any checkpoints between Roballos and the governor's drive, and since Lylia was too young to walk to the quay before dawn, we had to risk driving. The wind had dropped and I thought how ironic it would be if tomorrow should turn into one of those rare Patagonian winter days when the sun pours molten light from a gleaming sky. Our chances then of boarding a guarded ship would be reduced close to zero.

We reached the parking lot without incident. Lights blazed from the only hotel, as if the military were holding an all-night party, otherwise the whole place seemed virtuously asleep.

The governor's house lay about four miles north of Roballos, and I sat on the edge of my seat every jouncing yard, watching huge shadows skim across the silver landscape, each seeming to spring its own ambush. Not many days had passed, but already I couldn't remember when last I drove anywhere legitimately, instinct insistently urging me to hide or take circuitous ways.

I was relieved when a red pinpoint of light at last came into view, marking the guardpost at the end of the drive. 'There,' I said, and pointed.

Roy swung off the road and backed until the wheels spun on spongy pasture. 'This goddamn country, you couldn't hide a bicycle.'

'You're far enough from the road to be out of headlamp range. If we don't make it back by daylight, then we won't be worried about someone spotting an abandoned automobile.'

He didn't answer, which made me feel better. When every nerve is on edge, attempts at optimism are infuriating. The next twelve hours would see our lives wrecked or set free, and it was impossible not to feel panicky about our chances. Too late to turn back now, nowhere to turn to if we did.

The governor's house lay over a slight rise from where we'd left the road, behind a rudimentary fence. I stopped as soon as it came into view, startled to see a single window glowing with light, its drapes undrawn. 'Someone's still awake.' Now that the war was over, I had been certain that as late as this everyone would be asleep.

'Can you tell who?' Roy asked softly.

'I think it's the general's dressing room,' I said reluctantly.

'You did say you weren't sure if he slept with his wife.'

'I thought she probably shut him out quite often, but does it make any difference? If he's awake, we haven't a chance of taking one of his uniforms.'

'Except perhaps an overcoat and cap.'

I shrugged in the darkness. Outdoor clothes were hung in a downstairs lobby, but Roy would never pass scrutiny on the quay wearing only a military cap and overcoat over civilian clothes.

Cautiously, we moved closer to the house. A thread of light showed downstairs as well, but that wasn't so worrying; during the war the general's office was often manned all night and a light could have been left on from habit. It was that upstairs window that signaled danger.

But time couldn't be allowed to waste, or we'd never

reach a hiding place out on the harbor arm before dawn. I touched Roy's arm and led the way around to the back of the house, where an old-fashioned conservatory provided an easy entry. 'What do you think?' I breathed.

'We go in.'

Still, I delayed. Our plan depended not only on fetching Lylia out, but on stealing a uniform, too. 'There are two other servants besides Josefina and Raul, the general's man. I don't know where he sleeps. A single shout could bring everyone running.'

'One thing at a time. First we get in.' He tried the door that led from the conservatory into the dining room. As I expected, it wasn't locked. Burglary isn't much of a problem in Patagonia, and this house had sentries on the gate. Roy turned the handle gently and we slipped inside; at once I recognized the tick of the mantelpiece clock, accompaniment to many strained and difficult meals.

'Which way to the lobby?' Roy's words as soft as ash.

'Careful, there isn't much room between the furnishings.' I edged past him again, eased open the door into the hall. Instantly, light knifed through the gap, thrown by a lamp on the stairs. Everywhere as still as you'd expect at three-thirty in the morning, the faintest of creaks underfoot only intensifying the silence. Heavy furniture, thick drapes, the familiar wallpaper with its livid yellow flowers, all looked menacing, and I knew the longer I waited, the harder it would become to cross that lighted space.

I pushed open the door and stepped out; after all, only at the height of the war had the household slept less than ten solid hours each night, from boredom, Isabelita said. Here everything nudged forward a memory. Over there General Valdez wept on the bottom stair, on that chair I had sat for hours, trying to telephone Roy or Huron. I tiptoed past the kitchen entry and opened the lobby door, my nostrils assailed by its characteristic odor of damp garments drying. Here the whole family hung their outdoor clothes, a radiator kept smoking hot to dry them. I stood aside while Roy chose an elaborately braided cap and coat from several hanging there.

We had just turned back into the hall when a vehicle crunched gravel outside. No warning of its coming, and crunch immediately followed by slammed doors and voices. That's why the light was on and the drapes undrawn, I realized. General Valdez must have been out, so naturally Raúl, his military servant, would wait up to help him undress. We just had time to bolt back into the dining room before the front door was flung open, the lobby door swinging, too, which we couldn't properly have latched.

I heard General Valdez swear at his driver, who was asking whether he wanted help. 'No,' he said too loudly, and added something blurred. In two months I had never seen him drink more than a few glasses of sherry or wine at mealtimes, but tonight he was certainly drunk. A consequence of shock, unnatural excitement, and sorrow perhaps, but the dignitaries who had come to welcome their returning prisoners off the British ship would have offered their own temptation. We had seen lights still on at the hotel; there wasn't often so good a chance for a governor in Patagonia to relax among his equals.

'. . . upstairs,' insisted the driver.

The general kicked the door shut in his face without answering, stood breathing heavily not five feet from where we stood, Roy watching through a crack in the door.

I'm not sure whether El Carnicero's animal senses warned him an enemy was close, but it felt like it. I discovered I was holding my breath, not deliberately but

334

as a kind of nervous spasm while his presence seemed to grope toward me. Then, thank God, he moved at last, dragging his feet and stumbling into a porcelain pot holder, sending it skidding across the floor. As soon as I was able to breathe again, my nostrils filled with the stench of spirits and cheap scent. For Patagonia, it must have been quite a party.

At that moment Roy moved. Swung open the door and stepped out into the hall. I thought he had run crazy. Nearly called out but snapped my mouth shut as I remembered a shout would bring calamity even faster. By then he was out of reach.

Mesmerized, I watched General Valdez begin to turn as he heard movement, saw Roy reach out for him, spin him close, hit him with his flashlamp on the jaw. Between the force of a blow that had all of Roy's strength behind it and the quantity of spirits he had drunk, General Valdez collapsed like a dropped sack, his fall broken by the grip of Roy's other hand. Then Roy struck him again, clinically hard between temple and cheekbone, before allowing him to slither nervelessly to the ground.

He turned, nostrils pinched white, eyes the glinting blue-green I had seen before. 'Quick. Help me off with his uniform.'

Christ, I thought numbly. Raul must be already on his way. A naked general on the carpet, whatever can Roy—

But by then I was frantically stripping pants, jerking free the tunic Roy unbuttoned. Belt; one shoe, heaven knew where the other vanished; I felt Roy drag something out of the rucksack I carried: the brandy flask. Roughly, he grasped El Carnicero's head, forced the bottle between drooling lips. Most of the spirit – there wasn't much – ran over his chin and into his hair,

335

the remainder practically throttled him. His face turned blue as his lungs seized up, his eyes rolled, the place where Roy had hit him on the cheekbone inflated.

I had known a long time ago that if Roy met El Carnicero, there was every chance he would kill him. That sharp glitter of an expression staying on his face as he picked up a retching carcass clad only in singlet and drawers, then stepped to the stair and threw it at the banisters with a force only vengeance could have given.

General Valdez hit the woodwork with an appalling crack and lay completely still, sprawled partway up the stairs with his head through splintered banisters. Coolly, Roy picked up the overcoat we had taken from the lobby and flung it any way over the body, tossed the cap beside it.

From first to last the assault couldn't have taken more than ninety seconds.

'General?' called a voice from upstairs. 'Excellency, are you all right?'

By then we were back in the dining room, the door closed, both our eyes to a crack by the hinge.

Raul came slowly into sight, stepping stiff-legged in astonishment, and staring at the shambles on the stair. He licked his lips. 'General?'

Not surprisingly, General Valdez didn't so much as moan.

Raul came down another step, sniffed as if he had just caught the reek of spirits, began to grin. 'Hey, you old slob!' He put his hands on his hips and began to laugh.

'What is it, Raul?' Josefina appeared next, bundled into a magenta flannel dressing jacket. '*Dios*, have mercy! Is he dead?'

'Not he. Just shit-drunk, the old bastard.' Raul heaved him unsympathetically out of the broken banisters. '*Jesucristo*, he's battered himself into pieces.'

Josefina squealed and crossed herself. 'Whoever dared to strip an excellency naked? We must call the police at once!'

'He won't thank you if you do. I heard his car drive up not five minutes ago, so don't think anyone except his pals did this. They had a party, didn't they? All cozy generals together. Perhaps the old sod passed out trying to screw a girl. Or a pansy lieutenant maybe. I bet those others enjoyed sending him back without his pants.'

'He's the governor,' said Josefina, scandalized.

'He's a bastard.' Raul heaved him on his shoulders, grunting. 'Serve him right. He'll never go anywhere again as long as he lives without wondering who's sniggering about the tale of him coming home in an overcoat and drawers.'

The general retched feebly, and Raul swore. 'Don't you dare puke over me, Excellency.'

Josefina giggled. 'He looks so silly.'

'I hope a few more torturing sods like him look worse before too long,' answered Raul sourly.

'What are you going to do?'

'What do you think? Put him to bed and keep my mouth shut. Can you see His Excellency asking in the morning whether he really did come home bareshanked from Roballos? If he asks about anything for a day or two, that is. He'll know I know and I'll know he knows all those officers are laughing up their sleeves. But the first to say anything gets himself shot. You go back to bed and forget you ever woke up.'

He trudged upstairs, El Carnicero's head thumping the wall unceremoniously as he turned. Josefina went to fetch a cloth, fussed perfunctorily over blood and vomit before vanishing upstairs as well, still chuckling to herself; how many undercurrents in this household I had been too preoccupied to grasp. In spite of appearances, evil did reap its own whirlwind of derision, hate, and callous unconcern.

'How near Lylia does she sleep?' Roy asked softly.

'Josefina? Quite near.'

'We'll have to wait until she settles, then.'

'Never mind, we got the uniform and I never thought we would. How could you guess so fast it would be safe to set him up like that?'

'If you serve a bastard like El Carnicero, you can't wait to jeer if ever he slips on shit.'

'I thought they couldn't know he was El Carnicero. Not once in all the weeks I lived here did anyone say a single word that suggested that they might.'

'Then they didn't want to admit they knew. Knowing shares the guilt, until there's some chance of revenge.'

Perhaps, I thought, as we waited in silence after that. Or does power overshadow every other consideration so long as it stays intact? Only defeat had begun to make Argentina's military rulers seem vulnerable, forced a fissure in their power through which disrespect and loathing could seep, and by doing so open other, wider cracks. In this case, the change had been symbolized by El Carnicero without his pants; elsewhere the variation would be infinite but, God willing, the reaction similar.

I hope a few more like him will look worse, Raul had said.

I couldn't see Roy in the darkness, but he fairly crackled satisfaction as if it were electric current. He had needed El Carnicero's blood quite as badly as I once needed to face my past. And as with me, success made some other things easier to face.

As Argentina, too, was beginning to need a victory over her own past, which then might help her to face the consequences of military defeat.

'We can't wait any longer,' Roy said as the clock struck half past four.

'I'll go up, then if Josefina should see me, she won't scream.'

'Okay. I'll wait by the stairs in case Raul shows up.'

But upstairs the house was still, Raul no doubt making sure he slept the sleep of innocence. Between the aftereffects of concussion and alcohol, and the confusion arising from the tale Josefina and Raul inevitably would whisper, I thought it would be a while before anyone believed General Valdez's version of events.

Josefina's door was ajar but I could hear her snoring, and pulled it gently shut. Lylia next. As I leaned over her bed, being back together was, briefly, the only thing that mattered.

22

The moon shone across her bed, lighting a curve of cheek and a soft fist clenched on Dodiebear. I woke her carefully, my hand stroking her hair. She opened an eye and was about to close it again when she focused on my face. 'Sallí!'

'Hush, sweetheart.' I kissed her. 'I promised to come back.'

'You not go 'gain?'

'Yes, I'm going again. Tonight, and this time for always. You can come, too, if you like.'

I chose offhand, almost casual words quite deliberately – God knows I had agonized over this moment long enough, trying coldly to estimate possibilities rather than my own heart's longing. Lylia had wanted to come with me before, but spontaneously, as a kind of unconsidered treat. Now was different, and young as she was, I thought she would sense it. I was asking her to tiptoe away in the middle of the night without farewells and forever; though, rationally, I had judged that solitary wretchedness since I left would have enormously increased her desire to come, the black uncertainty of within minutes leaving everything she knew must make her recoil. It almost made me recoil; taking a child away from the only home she knows is distasteful, no matter what the reason.

But it was even easier than I had hoped. Lylia gave a squeak and bounced up in bed. 'Really me come?'

'Quietly, *querida*. Yes, really you come if you want to.' Or even if you don't, I thought anxiously.

I need not have worried. Joy leapt across her face. 'Now I come? Sallí, please, is horridness after you gone and horrider every-every day.'

'That's why I thought we'd go while everyone's asleep, though we'll have to wait until later to catch a ship.'

'Yes,' she said simply, very terribly, too. A child ought not to step away from all she knows of life without so much as glancing over her shoulder. She pushed back the bedclothes and skipped to the floor. 'I takeit Dodiebear?'

'Of course.' I fetched her warmest clothes: jerseys, parka, padded pants. 'It's going to be cold outside, but a friend will drive us to the harbor.'

'Nice friend?' Her face appeared doubtfully through the neck of a jersey.

'Very nice. Keep as quiet as you can, little one. You know how we both hate shouting voices, and everyone will shout at once if they wake.'

'I hate squirmy ones more,' she said bleakly, which was a fair definition of Isabelita's destructive hurtfulness.

'No more squirmers, then,' I answered lightly. 'You can put on your boots outside. Let's go, sweetheart.'

She picked up her bear and reached for my hand, suddenly uncertain. 'Will I never be here?'

'Not for a long time, because I couldn't come back, not ever. We'd live in America instead.'

She hesitated a moment longer, then her hand tightened on mine. 'I'se come with you.'

It wasn't the moment for an emotional scene, but I guess I felt much as Roy had when he hit El Carnicero: wholly satisfied and satisfyingly whole.

I paused by the door; everything remained silent except for Josefina's snores.

'Say goodbye to Josefina?' asked Lilia pleadingly.

'Hush! Whisper, and then only if you have to. I know we ought to say goodbye, but Josefina would wake everyone if we did. I'll send a message later, so she won't worry.'

She hesitated as we reached Josefina's door, but perhaps all those scoldings took her past. Then the excitement of creeping through the dark house almost immediately switched her thoughts. She pressed close, tiptoeing with exaggerated care.

'What's that?' she hissed as we creaked past the broken banister.

'Papa and Mama quarreled after you were in bed.' I felt her flinch and was ashamed of my duplicity, but she flinched because she had already learned to dread the strange relationships in this house. Roy was waiting in the hall, where light might make an unknown man seem less frightening to a child. He smiled but did not speak; Lylia stayed silent, too, her eyes blank brown pools in a face abruptly drained of color.

I picked her up and held her against my shoulder; this the inevitable moment when escape ceased to be a game and became threateningly strange instead. Two minutes later we were outside the house.

Cold night air whisked my senses back to the perils of escape; we skirted the gravel and as soon as we reached the grass beyond, I set Lylia on her feet. 'You're too heavy for me to carry far, *querida*.'

'I better walking,' she said with dignity.

We followed behind Roy, hand in hand and concentrating on rough tussocks underfoot. Every step away from El Carnicero's house made me feel happier, as if we had escaped already when in reality we remained an infinite distance away from safety. The automobile was still where we left it; no sound, no suspicious signs during the short time which was all we could afford to spend watching in case there was an ambush. I looked all round, straining my eyes while Roy eased open a door, but only wind moaning through the grass disturbed the stillness.

'You steer while I set it rolling,' Roy whispered. 'We're too close to that guardpost to risk starting the engine.'

I shoved, too, one hand on the wheel, our combined strength needed before the automobile squelched reluctantly off grass and back on hard surface. A slight incline took us a farther fifty yards before we had to push again, up an imperceptible, seemingly endless slope. But at last the wheels began to roll with less effort, and we were far enough away to use the engine.

'We can't risk driving farther than the parking lot,' Roy said quietly.

'But—' I began, and thought better of it. He knew how dangerous it was to take Lylia through Roballos, when within hours everyone would be asked whether they had seen her. Also, time was racing past and very faintly above the sea, already the sky was changing from black to the palest of pale greens.

We cruised into a space in the parking lot, and Roy slewed to face Lylia and me. 'I go first. Tell the child she must follow exactly where I lead and what I do, without speaking, no matter how strange anything seems to her.'

Lylia nodded silently when I spoke to her in Spanish; impossible to know whether a child her age would obey in a crisis. The oddity of a stranger speaking a language she couldn't understand added yet another vast uncertainty to all the rest: I'm sure that given any chance at all, this was the moment she would have bolted back to her known warm bed.

The jetty lay a half-dozen blocks away from the parking lot, or most of the width of the town. Walking soft-footed, Lylia like a tiny chilly ghost beside me, we crossed four of the five intersections without mishap. People were beginning to stir, lights to come on in upper rooms; once among piles of waterfront clutter we should be safer, but also more liable to be shot on sight since the jetty was forbidden to civilians. In any case, if Lylia was so much as glimpsed near that quay before it was cordoned off to receive the British, then it would be the first place to be searched. Whereas if she wasn't, we would be desperately unlucky if anyone thought of looking for a runaway child along a windswept and guarded harbor arm.

Roy hissed a warning and I crouched, holding Lylia close. 'Keep absolutely quiet, *queridita*.'

She buried her face in my neck, too young to be able to sustain so many incomprehensible uncertainties for long. I could feel her swallowing wails, which wouldn't stay swallowed long.

Roy must have sensed something, too, because he turned, his words softer than a draft. 'Sally . . . there are some soldiers under that lamp over there. I'll talk to them and while they're trying to understand what I'm saying, you slip past. Go as near to the end of the harbor arm as you can without the lightkeeper seeing you and hide until I come.'

'No.' I grabbed at him.

'Try not to worry. I'll join you while the British ship is loading. If I should fail to come . . . If it prepares to sail and I haven't come, then take any worthwhile chance you see. I can always get out legally later. Take care, my love.' His lips brushed mine and he was gone.

I couldn't believe it. The parting I dreaded had come and gone while I stood stupid as a moose. I'd thought of a dozen fresh reasons why Roy would never get away with posing as an Argentine general, and now I'd bungled my chance to use them, had let him go without a single word of love. I might never see him again.

. . . *If I haven't come,* he'd said.

If he was caught, no way would he get out legally now or later. The Argentines would throw the whole penal code at an American they caught wearing General Valdez's uniform, easily unravel the evidence that led from assault to kidnapping to impersonation.

'Is you crying?' asked Lylia uneasily.

I held her so her face touched mine. 'Listen, *querida.* If I don't cry, then you won't either, will you? Instead, you're going to be brave and very obedient, so I'm proud of you.'

Hesitantly, she nodded.

'It's a deal. Brave, obedient, and very, very quiet. Hold on tight, run when I do, and soon we'll be able to rest for a while.'

We stood waiting for what seemed a long time, while daylight slowly strengthened. When one of the soldiers coughed, he made us jump, the silence was so complete. No wind or rain to cover movement, our only advantage a dawn mist rolling in off the sea. But more lights coming on in the houses behind our back, a motor starting up not too far away.

Roy must have been waiting for that mist, because as it curled like steam above the jetty I heard his footsteps somewhere to my right, changing note as he reached the timber waterfront. Confident, easy paces, an early waker with nothing to hide. I could just make out his shape as the soldiers called a challenge: a single slope of shoulder and spring of back instantly recognizable out of all others in the world.

The patrol gathered around him gesticulating.

I watched, nearly destroyed by fear for him, and indecision. There was so little he was able to say that might disarm hostility, although he had certainly learned some of the Spanish language's pithier phrases. Could I bear to leave him in such danger? And if I did, which moment should I choose to cross the remaining open space between us and the quay? Ought we to run or saunter that thirty yards or so that separated us from cover? Unanswerable questions quarreling like gulls inside my skull.

'Now,' I said softly as mist eddied, cleared, eddied again. 'We're going to walk quite slowly across to where you see that pile of nets.'

Slow movement might melt easier into mist, but walking slowly away from where Roy stood hedged about by soldiers was one of the most difficult things I've done in a life made up of difficult choices. Every nerve screaming at me to run, Lylia snatching at my hand as my fear infected her. We passed a streetlamp surrounded by an opalescent glow, where grit changed to timber underfoot. A shout from behind . . . instantly my muscles bunched to hurl me mindlessly away, but the shout was laughter; Lylia laughing, too, my lips drawn into a silent shout of relief as we ran the last short stretch to the heap I thought was nets and turned out to be rotting seaweed. Still grinning, Lylia held her nose, and in response I held mine, too, a mutual voiceless celebration. More laughter from behind us; Roy must have used one of his ruder words to deflect suspicion with an apparently innocent mistake.

Silently, step by step, we worked around the seaweed and found ourselves among piles of rusting metal:

obstruction rather than cover was the problem now. An ancient crane leaned over what looked like a heap of bones, beyond it a rowboat was rotting into pieces. Here the harbor arm began, curving out into the bay and ending some eighty yards away in a stone crosspiece topped by a flashing light.

Normally this whole length would be clear except for the scattered debris of past cargoes, but in order to make space for the British ship to tie up and disembark its prisoners, all kinds of gear, boxes, bales, and rubbish had been piled up there. A bulldozed heap of bagged cement marked the end of this haphazard cover, beyond it intermittent illumination from the harbor light swept shadows perilously aside.

'Stay where you are a moment,' I breathed.

Lylia held on with both hands instead of one. 'Me come, too.'

'Okay, but remember what I said.'

'Brave, 'bedient, quiet,' she agreed, and there was just enough light to see she was hugely enjoying herself again.

Together we crept to the end of the cement, where some twenty yards of open space separated us from a squat tower topped by red and green lamps. Twenty yards bare of cover but trapped with a slovenly tangle of hawsers, ancient bollards, crumbling asphalt. As we crouched, watching, a beam of light from the tower swept over us again, and though instinctively I ducked, for the moment mist was refracting most of a not very powerful glare. The tower itself seemed to be constructed of concrete blocks and I thought irrelevantly how bitterly cold it must usually be for the man on watch. I could see him moving around behind salt-encrusted windows and a little while later he came out, stretching, to stand on a tiny platform and admire the sunrise.

This was spectacular, throwing blades of bright pink light through lavender haze, although I would gladly have exchanged it for a steady downpour. Between the sunrise and that rotating light there was no chance of going farther until Roy came, and no point, either, until it was time to go together.

Carefully, Lylia and I retreated into the safety of some junked asbestos sheeting; by leaning a few chipped pieces together, I was able to construct a tiny burrow where we would be sheltered from a casual search. Once I had crawled into this minute space, Lylia was able to curl up on my knees, and I made a game of seeing how slowly we could suck squares of chocolate. One slab left in my rucksack when we finished; today we had our backs to the sea in more ways than one.

The truth was, we were both tired, thirsty after the chocolate, and wretchedly uncomfortable, sitting on hard asphalt through an endless winter morning in Patagonia.

After a while Lylia dozed in my arms, worn out by excitement, and then I had nothing to distract me from worrying about Roy. Because he made those soldiers laugh, probably they would accept him as *un norteamericano loco*, but next he must change into General Valdez's uniform – where? – then walk the streets of Roballos and bluff his way on board a British ship docked in an enemy port, when every word he spoke increased the likelihood of detection. If the British came. We were staking everything that they would, but a hundred chances could have delayed or altered their arrangements.

As soon as Lylia seemed soundly asleep I tucked her into a corner of our shelter and crawled out into daylight. The relief was enormous, my legs completely numb from her weight, each moment of idleness more insupportable than the last while racked by such anxiety. Roy could be under interrogation now. Be lying in a pool of blood, pulped by boots, burned with wires. No good telling me it didn't happen; and fast, when information was required.

Imagination bolting out of control because I knew, oh, God, I knew so well, how easily it could happen.

I crawled back to those cement shapes to see out again; the lamp keeper was energetically cleaning his windows, damn him. The sky less clear than before but visibility still far too good, a thin wind knifing out of the east which hadn't been there earlier. A ship hull-up over the horizon, steering directly for Roballos.

The British were coming, on time, ahead of time, would be alongside within the hour.

My stomach was already clenching nervily in tune with my fretting thoughts, and the moment I saw that ship it knotted so fiercely I had to clutch at myself to ease the pain. Relief, tension, delight, foreboding, terror; a nuclear cocktail of emotion reaching critical mass. Deliberately, I forced myself to look away and start deciding what I could do to help the next stage of our plan; unless I did something soon, by the time Roy came I would be useless.

The harbor arm was built of squared granite and protected on the outer side by rocks bulldozed into the water. On the deeper, or harbor side, a miscellaneous collection of boats was moored; swept there with all the other gear to clear a space for the British to tie up. Most of them looked waterlogged, and all lacked means of propulsion; I doubted whether there was much small craft fishing along this dangerous coast, or sailing for pleasure either. Of all those boats, only two looked possibly useful, I decided. One, a kind of punt, God knew what it was used for, light but clumsily difficult to

349

steer; the other a miniature ship's boat with a pointed stern. No sails, of course, or rowlocks, which was worse, and water slopping on the bottom boards, but at least it looked reasonably handy. I crept back to Lylia. She was still asleep, looking healthily rosy rather than chilled. Thumb in her mouth and Dodiebear under her chin, snuggling instinctively into her few scraps of familiarity.

I spent the next hour searching cautiously through piled rubbish while that ship came closer, entered the bay, came near enough to see large red British ensigns at jackstaff and foremast. I was looking for metal or wood that might fit into those rowlock holes, for wire and thin board. Eventually I found some steel reinforcing rods I thought might do, and strands of rusty hawser, but no timber. Instead, I chose some stiff plastic strips that might have come off cheap furniture.

As I took my loot back to our hideout, the ship gave a couple of yelps on its siren and Lylia woke up.

'Hello,' I said casually. As in her bedroom before, if I didn't make her situation seem remarkable, then she was less likely to think about it. 'Look what I've found.'

'What that noise, Sallí?'

'Our ship coming in, only we can't go on board yet.'

'Why not?'

'We have to wait for Roy, and there's a lot of soldiers to come off her first. You can come and look if you like, but keep your head well down.'

'Whoot-whoot.' She clapped her hands as the ship sounded her siren again and went astern in a froth of water. 'It lookit good, Sallí.'

I had to agree. You could tell the British had won a war just from looking at that swaggering little vessel. It must have been snatched away from civilian life without much warning because it didn't have a gun and was still painted its company colors of black hull, white upperworks, and bright red stack. But those jaunty flags, the way the crew showed how sweetly they could moor a ship, their understated air of smug exuberance, all added up to a slap in the face which the waiting crowd recognized with muttering resentment. Me, I was just overjoyed to see those British in Roballos. Miracles take on strange disguises, and the bluff little *Sussex Maid* of London happened to be mine.

She tied up stern-on to where we lay concealed, while the soldiers cordoning off the waterfront made a great fuss about shoving back people who until then had felt only an uncomplicated desire to welcome their young men home. This cordon, as we hoped, had some hours before it left Lylia and me inside, so out on the harbor arm I couldn't see exactly what was happening.

But I wasn't imagining the impression those British made. The more relaxed they appeared, the more aggressively the soldiers on the quay behaved, quickly provoking angry shouts from the crowd: uncanny how this reaction mirrored that of Raul and Josefina the previous night. In each case a tyranny so long accepted as to seem unremarkable ceased to be feared the moment it provoked contempt. When the soldiers struck out, this crowd jostled back; orders were greeted with derision, the strut of an officer mimicked. Pride alone probably prevented a fight from breaking out: while the British watched, no one wanted further to humiliate Argentina.

But if the junta had been there, and if they possessed the brains to recognize this mood of disrespectful fury, at last, at last, they should have felt afraid.

'It might help Roy,' I said aloud.

'What help?'

'I don't think Roballos likes this ship much, but they're disliking their own soldiers even more just at the moment.'

Lylia glanced over her shoulder. 'Soldiers coming.'

For an instant, relief fizzed like a rocket as I believed it must be Roy in his general's uniform, but of course it was too soon. Two soldiers patrolling the length of the harbor arm had caught me completely unawares.

23

They carried submachine guns with the usual light-fingered menace, but were arguing inattentively between themselves and passed without seeing us. The cement sacks offered very inadequate cover from any one coming so close, and I touched Lylia, finger to lips, before wriggling back with her to the pile of asbestos fragments.

'Why we hide? Soldiers nice 'cos of Papa,' she hissed as soon as we reached it.

'Yes, and Papa will have told them to look out for you.'

'Mama stop him. She be *pleased* I gone,' she said gruffly, after a pause.

'Shall I tell you a secret?'

She nodded.

'I'm really your mama.'

'Sallí?'

'If you like, but truly Mama just the same. That's why I came, to love you and take you home.'

She gave a little sigh and put her hand back in mine without speaking, that silence my reward. She believed what I said because she wanted to believe it. And I had told her now, on a quayside full of soldiers, when telling was very dangerous, because if things went wrong, I wanted her to keep at least a memory of love. We might easily fail to escape, and shadowy recollection be my last and only gift to her. It also seemed intolerable to divide her mind a single moment longer than was necessary, as guilt at leaving General Valdez's affection tangled inextricably with Isabelita's hostility toward her. A situation that should have been tidily reversed but wasn't, and either way the damage remained the same.

The soldiers had stopped at the end of the harbor arm and were gossiping to the lightkeeper. If they stayed there, any chance of getting on board the *Sussex Maid* was gone.

They did stay there, covertly drinking coffee and stamping their feet against the cold. We were beginning to freeze as well, unable to move, Lylia trembling against me, each of my muscles a stiff and separate pain. The wind was rising steadily, throwing spume sideways off gray water, while visibility remained depressingly good.

I could not keep both the soldiers and the way Roy must come in view, had to crawl back each time I wanted to check whether they were still talking to the light-keeper. Any movement dangerous while they stood idly scanning the whole length of harbor arm and quay, our best chance to avoid discovery staying squirreled out of sight.

The next time I looked, they were walking slowly back toward me.

I ducked down to hold Lylia. 'Stay quiet as a mouse now.'

'Is very too long going home. Please, Sallí, I want go your home now.'

'And me, but hush! You have to hush!' I rocked her in my arms. How could I have imagined it might be possible to escape from a sealed country with a child so young?

She hid her face inside my parka while the beat of boots came closer, as if they had indeed heard something. I'd already decided that if we were discovered, then I would give up right away, since a burst of automatic fire was the almost inevitable reaction to suspicion. Easy to decide, impossible tamely to surrender while a shred of hope remained. The footsteps clashed to a stop, voices . . . Roy's voice.

'It's Roy,' I breathed to Lylia. 'It's Roy, he's safe!'

I waited, never before so hard to wait, not knowing what was happening. At this last moment I must not risk a thing simply to satisfy curiosity.

Footsteps retreating quite soon after, a crisp military pace conscious of a general's eye at their back. 'Sally?' Roy said very low.

'Yes . . . we're here.'

'Stay where you are while I handle the lightkeeper.'

I knelt shakily to watch him walk on down the harbor arm, gold-leaf cap and decorated uniform gleaming. The purpose of uniforms is to militarize civilians, and from a distance Roy looked every inch a general. He stopped short of the light and called impatiently, words slurred by the wind. For a moment I thought the keeper either hadn't heard or refused to hear; he wasn't a soldier and had probably just been discussing with those two guards how Roballos now felt toward generals and their junta.

All that braid was too much for him, however, uneasy as he must have been over offering coffee to on-duty guards. He scuttled down the steps, torn between belligerence and fear. Roy stayed where he was, hands on his hips, until he was close; they seemed to pause, speak together, before the lightkeeper led the way back up the steps and inside. All of which looked unexceptional to a casual watcher. Only from where I knelt was it possible to realize that Roy's hand had not been on his hip, but on the holster of General Valdez's gun.

'Come on,' I said to Lylia. 'You bring those pieces of

plastic and I'll take the metal and wire.'

She lugged them trailing along the asphalt while I kept
looking to see if anyone was watching. Behind and
above, the bustle around the *Sussex Maid* continued, a
crane swinging casualties ashore on stretchers some
distance down the quay. Voices thin on the wind as
unwounded prisoners disembarked. The British would
be able to see us if they leaned over their stern rail, but
the curve of the harbor arm hid where we stood from
anyone watching from the quay. All the same, Roy
couldn't have managed more than gabbled expletives at
those soldiers; they might easily come back.

I met Roy on the steps leading up to the light, a swift
clash of a hug and stuttered, half-coherent words of
relief.

'. . . You're safe! . . .'
'. . . And you! . . .'
'. . . The lightkeeper? . . .'
'. . . Tied up safely while we have to wait.'
'Wait! Not more waiting now!'
'A torpedo boat is out in the bay.'
'Did you get on board the British . . .'
'Tell you later, we have to . . .'
'There's a boat I think we can use. Lylia . . .'
'. . . Good girl. These for rowlocks?'
'. . . I thought . . . these, look.'
'Yeah, that ought to work. I should have known . . .'
'I had to do something or go crazy.'

Gasped half phrases while we ran to the boat I thought
the best, choice approved with a quick nod. No good
looking around, if any Argentine should notice the odd
behavior of a general, a woman, and a child, then we
were finished. No bluff left that even an idiot would
accept. Yet there was something absurdly theatrical,
doubly terrifying about such antics in broad daylight; as

356

if we performed a petty diversion for an audience that would start shooting the moment we let them finish laughing.

The sharp-ended dinghy was moored fore and aft, awkward to reach from fourteen feet above the water when its bottom boards looked too rotten to risk a jump. 'The stonework is quite rough, use what footholds you can and hold on to me.' Roy lay flat and grasped a mooring ring with one hand while reaching for me with the other.

I lay, too, gingerly squirming until my legs hung over the edge, scrabbling one-handed for a grip on asphalt.

'Awful too wet down there,' said Lylia anxiously, squatting beside my face.

I blew her a kiss. 'I haven't come so far to fall in the Atlantic now.' Roy wasn't screaming on a blood-stained floor, but safe; measureless relief made everything else seem trivial.

Cracks had eroded between mortared stones, some large enough to accept a boot toe. I curled the fingers of my left hand over an edge of quayside and reached down, most of my weight hanging from Roy's arm. Move one leg, kick into a crack, move the other. 'How much farther?' My muscles beginning to quiver under the strain of fingertips only into minute holds, the other shoulder as tight as rope from his grip on my wrist.

'Two or three feet and then you must step back to reach the bow.' Roy was spreadeagled across the hard edge above, most of both our weights depending on his grip on a rusty mooring ring. Sweat on his face, a disagreeable crackle of sinew in my ear. He grinned. 'Daring trapeze act by the family Fabuloso.'

I could see a cranny by my nose but to reach it I should have to let go of the quay edge, allow Roy and one boot toe to take my whole weight for an instant. No other hold close enough, every second of delay making the strain worse. As I let go, inevitably my body swung, was snatched by the wind, swung farther. Frantically I scrabbled for the grip I knew was there, my nails ripping on rough stone. Confidence disintegrating in a nightmare of blurred sensation: panic, despair, heart thundering like a storm.

'It's there!' I said aloud, as if I didn't really believe in a handhold seen only seconds before. Then I fairly drove my left knee against stone to swing my body back, and with a final angry effort forced my fingers between mortared edges. 'Let go,' I croaked at Roy.

His hold had been so tight, it took time for feeling to seep back into my right hand, dangerous time, time for the rest of my body to begin locking into cramp. When I was ready at last to swing out and down into the boat, there was alarmingly little response left to call on.

Only a precise succession of movements would accomplish a maneuver that in itself was fairly simple. Using new footholds and with both hands now in reassuringly deep crevices, I must reach back to a bow snagging awkwardly in the swell, rest my weight on it, transfer my grip to the mooring rope, and snake the rest of my body inboard.

Slowly I groped left-footed, felt the bow smack painfully against my ankle, lost it, transferred enough weight to hold it steadier while a slow convulsion dragged the other foot beside the first. Then, while my body turned and lurched to the interplay of waves and my own movement on a small, moored boat, I slid backward and downward until I fell panting on wet bottom boards. Eyes closed and breath sobbing against my numb and aching arms, my only feeling astonishment that climbing into a boat could be so difficult.

After a moment I knelt stiffly and looked up.

'Stay as low as you can while I pass Lylia down to you.'
Roy was still lying flat, his face a whitish blob against
scudding gray clouds.

For the first time I glanced behind my back; from here
I could see down the far side of the *Sussex Maid* to where
an Argentine torpedo boat was moored in shallow water
off the town. It would be difficult, but not impossible for
them to see what we were doing; impossible to miss what
we were doing as soon as we cast off to reach that
outboard side of the *Sussex Maid*.

'No!' Lylia shied instinctively when Roy reached for
her.

'Lylia,' I called. 'You promised, remember? Brave
and obedient. If you won't come to me, then I can't
come back to you.'

She sidled unwillingly to the edge. 'I don't *enjoy* thisa
game.'

'I don't like it much either, so come on down and help
us finish it.'

Her lips trembled. 'Promise finish?'

'Yes, soon.'

Silently she let Roy grasp her by the front of her
parka, clutched like a kitten to his arm while he swung
her down and outward until, by hauling on the mooring
rope and reaching up on tiptoe, I could seize her ankles.
A few seconds later she was beside me in the boat, Roy
lowering strips of plastic, tossing down the scraps of
metal and wire out of which we must fashion rowlocks to
help us scull fifty yards. Fifty yards we couldn't cross,
rowlocks or no rowlocks, while that torpedo boat
watched. Then he climbed down that infernal wall
himself. He had twisted the longest strand of wire
around the mooring ring to give himself a grip, and his
longer reach helped; all the same, without any help from
above it was awkward to get himself far enough down to

reach for the boat. When he did, the roughening sea slapped at his legs, all of us nearly sinking when I went too far forward trying to help.

He made it at last, the three of us crouched together in icy water slopping across the bottom boards. 'Now we have to wait until the British leave,' he said.

'Until they *leave*?'

'They're going to warp out from the stern, which will mask that torpedo boat as they swing. If we can get out then, they'll take us up.'

'How about telling what happened? You say we have to wait.'

'Not long, I hope. Disembarkation seemed to be going well.' He tore a strip from his shirt and began winding it around one of the metal rods I'd found, to fit it tighter into the rowlock holes, twisted resistant wire strand into the roughest of rough holds for plastic sculls. 'They put guards on the gangways, of course, but the British didn't come ashore and no Argentine wanted to look like he was friendly with the enemy. Everything was fixed between London and Buenos Aires, I guess. So there wasn't much crush trying to walk on board. I waited until the crowd became restless—'

'From here it looked like against their own military, more than the British.'

'Sure. The usual kind of big-ass major started screaming orders and they took it badly. An admiral on the welcoming party bawled him out and calmed things down, but by then I'd pushed up the gangway while the guard was feeling jittery about a possible riot. He'd never felt less in the mood to question generals, especially one who shoved a fistful of papers under his nose.'

'What did the British say?'

'"Who-the-bloody-hell-do-you-think-you-are?"'

I laughed. 'So then you tried to tell them.'

'It took a while,' he admitted. 'Good captains are disbelieving bastards, and luckily this one seems pretty good. That ship is an English Channel ferry, and went straight to dodging missiles in the South Atlantic.'

Like us, I thought. We didn't know much about climbing down walls, impersonating generals, or kidnapping children when we started. But whatever happened now, we'd learned fast along the way. A lawyer's expressionless expression may have helped, but like a few others we'd done, Roy's quayside walk must represent the triumph of brass nerve over stacked odds.

'I think they're going.' I stared toward where I could just see the high tip of a crane lifting what might have been a gangway. A siren whooped.

'Okay. We wait until they're swinging on stern warps only before we paddle out. If we and the British both get it right, then there should be a moment when neither the people on the quay nor the torpedo boat can see past as that ship swings. The current should help sweep us down and the captain said he'd have men ready to hook us in. He can't wait, of course. The Argentines would drop on him at once if they see him picking anyone up, and quite right, too, by the terms of the truce. So we have to hurry the hell up once we start, because the moment he drops the warps, everyone and his brother will see us from the quay.' He stripped off his general's tunic and threw it overboard, pressing down until it disappeared; it would be washed up somewhere, and add another twist to the puzzle we left behind.

Unless we failed to leave it behind, and the Argentine police were able to ask all the questions they wanted.

'This is a very bouncing boat.' Lylia was trying unsuccessfully to look jaunty instead of green.

'Hold on tight, then. It's going to bounce a whole lot more in a minute.'

'I 'preciate a lot more,' she said stiffly.

Another whoop on the siren, sassy farewell from the British. Their stern beginning to lengthen into silhouette, bows swinging into the bay.

'There's two men on the quayside paying out the mooring hawser; they couldn't help seeing us if we go,' I said tensely.

'The captain said, leave him to screw the Argies.'

Wider and wider that ship swung, more than half her length visible now. Christ, we couldn't wait another moment, must chance the mooring crew. They couldn't stop us, after all. Yes, they could. The Argentines would enjoy any excuse to search a British ship that broke a truce, that torpedo boat could catch up easily inside territorial waters. The *Sussex Maid* lurched, appeared to swing too far, overcompensated by frothing dangerously full astern until it seemed she must crash into the quay. Everything except that towering black bulk blotted out from sight, the mooring crew scrambling for safety yelling with dismay.

'Now!' Roy slipped one mooring rope and I the other, both of us shoving off frantically from waterlogged craft bobbing on either side.

Grating and swaying we spun into the current before we could attempt paddling, spun again and began to drift sideways into the bay.

'Give me your scull,' Roy snapped. He dug in hard and the boat hesitated, straightened, shot forward, and then plunged into an eddy of churned-up water. Wash from the *Sussex Maid*'s propeller cascading over the side, deluging my legs with freezing water. I shrieked at Lylia to hold on, frantically grabbed another plastic strip, both Roy and I thrusting madly, blindly, at the black hull spinning past. The boat was uncontrollable, slipping and swinging in whirlpools of wash, spinning again in spite of all our efforts.

The din seemed tremendous; ship's engines, the hiss of water, the boom and thud of our frail little craft as it lurched into unseen troughs. We plunged, rolled, plunged again as that hull leaned out to smash us, heeled sharply while Lylia screamed with terror. Then, without any warning, the motion changed as the bow lifted, stern dropped and corkscrewed into a trough of foam, and all at once a sleek slope of water was racing smoothly past.

We were precariously hooked by a grapnel in the bows, and I looked up to see a couple of blue jerseyed seamen playing us like a fish. Noise faded, and, instead of racing through water, suddenly we were almost stopped and sinking.

''Op up,' called one of the seamen, throwing down a slatted wooden ladder.

The way taken off her, the *Sussex Maid* wallowed sluggishly to the accompaniment of Argentine jeers from the quayside, everyone there delighted by her sloppy British seamanship.

'Come on, sweetheart.' I snatched up Lylia while Roy strained to hold the end of that flimsy ladder, half jumped a distance I could never have managed if I'd thought about it. Clung like an ape while our weight slammed against steel plates; one step, two; damned treacherous steps with a child clinging to your neck. Marvelous steps, the last of my long journey out of the past. Then a seaman reached down to take Lylia and I followed him up the rest of the way.

The same instant I touched the deck I felt the engines bite again, turned in panic, imagining Roy sinking with the boat. But he was partway up the ladder, hauled over the rail as the quay came into view again and the *Sussex*

Maid set course for the open sea, plowing our water-logged dinghy under her keel as she went.

'The Old Man won't 'alf be wild 'aving to frig around like a prick in front of the Argies,' a sailor said with relish.

I gripped Roy with one hand and Lylia with the other. 'Did I ever say how I love you?'

'I know I did.' Roy kissed me.

The sailor who had carried Lylia up nudged his companion. 'Bleeding 'oneymoon trip, that's all it was.'

'I sicked all over the floor everywhere, and I feel a very lot better,' announced Lylia buoyantly.

THE END

I AM ENGLAND
by Patricia Wright

*'I am England now, let that be my life. The first Queen
Elizabeth said that, and was loved by her people for her
pride in Englishness. The rest of us, who made the look
and feel of England, should also be remembered, we are
England too.'*

In this remarkable epic, which spans fifteen centuries
from AD 70 to 1589, Furnace Green in the Weald of
Sussex is England. Set about with great trees, abundant
with deer and boar and wolves, the first people to come
to the Ridge were the shy forest people, then Brac the
ironsmith, who used a deer sign as his mark to express
his love for his wild strange wife.

Then came Edred, the Saxon, who left the Ridge to kill
the hated Danes, and returned with a Danish slave girl
with whom he could found a dynasty.

Their descendants, over many years, many calamitous
events, continued to love and fight and build and pray on
the Ridge. Robert the Falconer, doomed to die if he did
not carve out a Fief by the Ridge, and Benedict, the
priestly knight, fighting his last fight, and the Eliza-
bethan yeoman who forged the cannon to defeat the
Armada – these were the people of the Ridge – the
people of England.

0 552 13423 6

THAT NEAR AND DISTANT PLACE
by Patricia Wright

The story of the life, the drama, the passions of a great nation continues. 'By the end of the sixteenth century, Sussex had lived through invasions, plagues, a splendid flowering of abbeys and churches, and the feuds and passions of a mighty people.'

Here, the next four hundred years of Furnace Green begins, with a tale of secret bastardy and the violence of the Civil War – with the terror of the all-powerful smuggling gangs who held a county in craven fear.

It tells of Liddy, who worked and plotted and schemed her way out of nineteenth century poverty, and threw it all away to fulfil an old love.

The times change. The people remain the same, and are linked when John Smith, descendant of all who came before, flies above the village in 1940 to save the nation forged through nineteen centuries of epic history.

0 552 13379 5

THE COMING OF THE KING
by Nikolai Tolstoy

A WORLD OF MAGIC, MYSTICISM AND ENCHANTMENT

The first volume in Nikolai Tolstoy's epic *The Book of Merlin* trilogy is as rich and vivid an evocation of the world of Celtic Britain as one might expect from the pen of a direct descendant of the author of *War & Peace*.

The narrator and chief character, the poet and magician Merlin, takes us into an unfamiliar but utterly convincing world of warrior aristocrats, bards and druids, a world of cruelty and of exquisite beauty, mingling high adventure and mysticism, tragedy and laughter.

A *tour de force* of literary recreation, it will be recognised for years to come as the most convincing Arthurian saga written in modern times.

'*I was entranced . . . the book has so many strands, so many layers of meaning, that it defies summary . . . Here is a novel in which imagination and scholarship make a perfect marriage with craftmanship and narrative drive. Buy it, I beseech you*'.

Ted Willis, *Sunday Telegraph*

'*Grips the reader . . . I felt I could read this story for evermore*'.

Roy Kerridge, *Spectator*

'*I much preferred it to* The Lord Of The Rings'.
John Bayley, *Professor of English, Oxford University*

0 552 13221 7

A SELECTED LIST OF HISTORICAL NOVELS
AVAILABLE FROM CORGI BOOKS

THE PRICES SHOWN BELOW WERE CORRECT AT THE TIME OF GOING TO PRESS. HOWEVER TRANSWORLD PUBLISHERS RESERVE THE RIGHT TO SHOW NEW RETAIL PRICES ON COVERS WHICH MAY DIFFER FROM THOSE PREVIOUSLY ADVERTISED IN THE TEXT OR ELSEWHERE.